CHARLES DICKENS

COMPLETE
WORKS

CENTENNIAL EDITION

Charles Dickens

CHARLES DICKENS

DAVID COPPERFIELD II

Illustrations by Phiz

HERON BOOKS

CONTENTS

CONTENTS.

VIII

CONTENTS.

IX

CONTENTS.

LIST OF ILLUSTRATIONS

CHAPTER XXX.

I got down to Yarmouth in the evening, and went to the inn. I knew that Peggotty's spare room—my room—was likely to have occupation enough in a little while, if that great Visitor, before whose presence all the living must give place, were not already in the house; so I betook myself to the inn, and dined there, and engaged my bed.

It was ten o'clock when I went out. Many of the shops were shut, and the town was dull. When I came to Omer and Joram's, I found the shutters up, but the shop door standing open. As I could obtain a perspective view of Mr. Omer inside, smoking his pipe by the parlour-door, I entered, and asked him how he was.

"Why, bless my life and soul!" said Mr. Omer, "how do you find yourself? Take a seat.—Smoke not disagreeable, I hope?"

"By no means," said I. "I like it—in somebody else's pipe."

"What, not in your own, eh?" Mr. Omer returned,

1

laughing. "All the better, sir. Bad habit for a young man. Take a seat. I smoke, myself, for the asthma."

Mr. Omer had made room for me, and placed a chair. He now sat down again very much out of breath, gasping at his pipe as if it contained a supply of that necessary, without which he must perish.

"I am sorry to have heard bad news of Mr. Barkis," said I.

Mr. Omer looked at me, with a steady countenance, and shook his head.

"Do you know how he is to-night?" I asked.

"The very question I should have put to you, sir," returned Mr. Omer, "but on account of delicacy. It's one of the drawbacks of our line of business. When a party's ill, we *can't* ask how the party is."

The difficulty had not occurred to me; though I had had my apprehensions too, when I went in, of hearing the old tune. On its being mentioned, I recognised it, however, and said as much.

"Yes, yes, you understand," said Mr. Omer, nodding his head. "We dursn't do it. Bless you, it would be a shock that the generality of parties mightn't recover, to say 'Omer and Joram's compliments, and how do you find yourself this morning?'—or this afternoon—as it may be."

Mr. Omer and I nodded at each other, and Mr. Omer recruited his wind by the aid of his pipe.

"It's one of the things that cut the trade off from attentions they could often wish to show," said Mr. Omer. "Take myself. If I have known Barkis a year, to move to as he went by, I have known him forty year. But *I* can't go and say, 'how is he?'"

I felt it was rather hard on Mr. Omer, and I told him so.

"I'm not more self-interested, I hope, than another man," said Mr. Omer. "Look at me! My wind may fail me at any moment, and it ain't likely that, to my own knowledge, I'd be self-interested under such circumstances. I say it ain't likely, in a man who knows his wind will go, when it *does* go, as if a pair of bellows was cut open; and that man a grandfather," said Mr. Omer.

I said, "Not at all."

"It ain't that I complain of my line of business," said Mr. Omer. "It ain't that. Some good and some bad goes, no doubt, to all callings. What I wish is, that parties was brought up stronger-minded."

Mr. Omer, with a very complacent and amiable face, took several puffs in silence; and then said, resuming his first point:

"Accordingly we're obleeged, in ascertaining how Barkis goes on, to limit ourselves to Em'ly. She knows what our real objects are, and she don't have any more alarms or suspicions about us, than if we was so many lambs. Minnie and Joram have just stepped down to the house, in fact (she's there, after hours, helping her aunt a bit), to ask her how he is to-night; and if you was to please to wait till they come back, they'd give you full partic'lers. Will you take something? A glass of srub and water, now? I smoke on srub and water, myself," said Mr. Omer, taking up his glass, "because it's considered softening to the passages, by which this troublesome breath of mine gets into action. But, Lord bless you," said Mr. Omer, huskily, "it ain't the passages that's out of order! 'Give me breath enough,' says I to my daughter Minnie, 'and *I'll* find passages, my dear.'"

He really had no breath to spare, and it was very alarming to see him laugh. When he was again in a condition to be talked to, I thanked him for the proffered refreshment, which I declined, as I had just had dinner; and, observing that I would wait, since he was so good as to invite me, until his daughter and his son-in-law came back, I inquired how little Emily was?

"Well, sir," said Mr. Omer, removing his pipe, that he might rub his chin; "I tell you truly, I shall be glad when her marriage has taken place."

3

"Why so?" I inquired.

"Well, she's unsettled at present," said Mr. Omer. "It ain't that she's not as pretty as ever, for she's prettier—I do assure you, she is prettier. It ain't that she don't work as well as ever, for she does. She *was* worth any six, and she *is* worth any six. But somehow she wants heart. If you understand," said Mr. Omer, after rubbing his chin again, and smoking a little, "what I mean in a general way by the expression, 'A long pull, and a strong pull, and a pull altogether, my hearties, hurrah!' I should say to you, that *that* was—in a general way—what I miss in Em'ly."

Mr. Omer's face and manner went for so much, that I could conscientiously nod my head, as divining his meaning. My quickness of apprehension seemed to please him, and he went on:

"Now, I consider this is principally on account of her being in an unsettled state, you see. We have talked it over a good deal, her uncle and myself, and her sweetheart and myself, after business; and I consider it is principally on account of her being unsettled. You must always recollect of Em'ly," said Mr. Omer, shaking his head gently, "that she's a most extraordinary affectionate little thing. The proverb says, 'You can't make a silk purse out of a sow's ear.' Well, I don't know about that. I rather think you may, if you begin early in life. She has made a home out of that old boat, sir, that stone and marble couldn't beat."

"I am sure she has!" said I.

"To see the clinging of that pretty little thing to her uncle," said Mr. Omer; "to see the way she holds on to him, tighter and tighter, and closer and closer, every day, is to see a sight. Now, you know, there's a struggle going on when that's the case. Why should it be made a longer one than is needful?"

I listened attentively to the good old fellow, and acquiesced, with all my heart, in what he said.

4

THE LITTLE HOUSE FURNISHED.

"Therefore, I mentioned to them," said Mr. Omer, in a comfortable, easy-going tone, "this. I said, 'Now, don't consider Em'ly nailed down in point of time, at all. Make it your own time. Her services have been more valuable than was supposed; her learning has been quicker than was supposed; Omer and Joram can run their pen through what remains; and she's free when you wish. If she likes to make any little arrangement, afterwards, in the way of doing any little thing for us at home, very well. If she don't, very well still. We're no losers, anyhow.' For—don't you see," said Mr. Omer, touching me with his pipe, "it ain't likely that a man so short of breath as myself, and a grandfather too, would go and strain points with a little bit of a blue-eyed blossom, like *her*?"

"Not at all, I am certain," said I.

"Not at all! You're right!" said Mr. Omer. "Well, sir, her cousin—you know it's a cousin she's going to be married to?"

"Oh yes," I replied. "I know him well."

"Of course you do," said Mr. Omer. "Well, sir! Her cousin being, as it appears, in good work, and well to do, thanked me in a very manly sort of manner for this (conducting himself altogether, I must say, in a way that gives me a high opinion of him), and went and took as comfortable a little house as you or I could wish to clap eyes on. That little house is now furnished, right through, as neat and complete as a doll's parlour; and but for Barkis's illness having taken this bad turn, poor fellow, they would have been man and wife—I dare say, by this time. As it is, there's a postponement."

"And Emily, Mr. Omer?" I inquired. "Has she become more settled?"

"Why that, you know," he returned, rubbing his double chin again, "can't naturally be expected. The prospect of the change and separation, and all that, is, as one may say, close to her and far away from her, both at once. Barkis's

5

death needn't put it off much, but his lingering might. Anyway, it's an uncertain state of matters, you see."

"I see," said I.

"Consequently," pursued Mr. Omer, "Em'ly's still a little down and a little fluttered; perhaps, upon the whole, she's more so than she was. Every day she seems to get fonder and fonder of her uncle, and more loth to part from all of us. A kind word from me brings the tears into her eyes; and if you was to see her with my daughter Minnie's little girl, you'd never forget it. Bless my heart alive!" said Mr. Omer, pondering, "how she loves that child!"

Having so favourable an opportunity, it occurred to me to ask Mr. Omer, before our conversation should be interrupted by the return of his daughter and her husband, whether he knew anything of Martha.

"Ah!" he rejoined, shaking his head, and looking very much dejected. "No good. A sad story, sir, however you come to know it. I never thought there was harm in the girl. I wouldn't wish to mention it before my daughter Minnie—for she'd take me up directly—but I never did. None of us ever did."

Mr. Omer, hearing his daughter's footstep before I heard it, touched me with his pipe, and shut up one eye, as a caution. She and her husband came in immediately afterwards.

Their report was, that Mr. Barkis was "as bad as bad could be;" that he was quite unconscious; and that Mr. Chillip had mournfully said in the kitchen, on going away just now, that the College of Physicians, the College of Surgeons, and Apothecaries' Hall, if they were all called in together, couldn't help him. He was past both Colleges, Mr. Chillip said, and the Hall could only poison him.

Hearing this, and learning that Mr. Peggotty was there, I determined to go to the house at once. I bade good-night to Mr. Omer, and to Mr. and Mrs. Joram; and directed my steps thither, with a solemn feeling, which made Mr. Barkis quite a new and different creature.

LITTLE EMILY HERSELF.

My low tap at the door was answered by Mr. Peggotty. He was not so much surprised to see me as I had expected. I remarked this in Peggotty, too, when she came down; and I have seen it since; and I think, in the expectation of that dread surprise, all other changes and surprises dwindle into nothing.

I shook hands with Mr. Peggotty, and passed into the kitchen, while he softly closed the door. Little Emily was sitting by the fire, with her hands before her face. Ham was standing near her.

We spoke in whispers; listening, between whiles, for any sound in the room above. I had not thought of it on the occasion of my last visit, but how strange it was to me now, to miss Mr. Barkis out of the kitchen!

"This is very kind of you, Mas'r Davy," said Mr. Peggotty.

"It's oncommon kind," said Ham.

"Em'ly, my dear," cried Mr. Peggotty. "See here! Here's Mas'r Davy come! What, cheer up, pretty! Not a wured to Mas'r Davy?"

There was a trembling upon her, that I can see now. The coldness of her hand when I touched it, I can feel yet. Its only sign of animation was to shrink from mine; and then she glided from the chair, and, creeping to the other side of her uncle, bowed herself, silently and trembling still, upon his breast.

"It's such a loving art," said Mr. Peggotty, smoothing her rich hair with his great hard hand, "that it can't abear the sorrer of this. It's nat'ral in young folk, Mas'r Davy, when they're new to these here trials, and timid, like my little bird,—it's nat'ral."

She clung the closer to him, but neither lifted up her face, nor spoke a word.

"It's getting late, my dear," said Mr. Peggotty, "and here's Ham come fur to take you home. Theer! Go along with t' other loving art! What, Em'ly? Eh, my pretty?"

7

The sound of her voice had not reached me, but he bent his head as if he listened to her, and then said:

"Let you stay with your uncle? Why, you doesn't mean to ask me that! Stay with your uncle, Moppet? When your husband that'll be so soon, is here fur to take you home? Now a person wouldn't think it, fur to see this little thing alongside a rough-weather chap like me," said Mr. Peggotty, looking round at both of us, with infinite pride; "but the sea ain't more salt in it than she has fondness in her for her uncle—a foolish little Em'ly!"

"Em'ly's in the right in that, Mas'r Davy!" said Ham. "Lookee here! As Em'ly wishes of it, and as she's hurried and frightened, like, besides, I'll leave her till morning. Let me stay too!"

"No, no," said Mr. Peggotty. "You doesn't ought—a married man like you—or what's as good—to take and hull away a day's work. And you doesn't ought to watch and work both. That won't do. You go home and turn in. You ain't afeerd of Em'ly not being took good care on, *I* know.'

Ham yielded to this persuasion, and took his hat to go. Even when he kissed her,—and I never saw him approach her, but I felt that nature had given him the soul of a gentleman,—she seemed to cling closer to her uncle, even to the avoidance of her chosen husband. I shut the door after him, that it might cause no disturbance of the quiet that prevailed; and when I turned back, I found Mr. Peggotty still talking to her.

"Now, I'm a going up-stairs to tell your aunt as Mas'r Davy's here, and that'll cheer her up a bit," he said. "Sit ye down by the fire, the while, my dear, and warm these mortal cold hands. You doesn't need to be so fearsome, and take on so much. What? You'll go along with me?— Well! come along with me—come! If her uncle was turned out of house and home, and forced to lay down in a dyke, Mas'r Davy," said Mr. Peggotty, with no less pride than before, "it's my belief she'd go along with him, now! But there'll be some one else, soon,—some one else, soon, Em'ly!"

Afterwards, when I went up-stairs, as I passed the door of my little chamber, which was dark, I had an indistinct impression of her being within it, cast down upon the floor. But, whether it was really she, or whether it was a confusion of the shadows in the room, I don't know now.

I had leisure to think, before the kitchen-fire, of pretty little Em'ly's dread of death—which, added to what Mr. Omer had told me, I took to be the cause of her being so unlike herself—and I had leisure, before Peggotty came down, even to think more leniently of the weakness of it: as I sat counting the ticking of the clock, and deepening my sense of the solemn hush around me. Peggotty took me in her arms, and blessed and thanked me over and over again for being such a comfort to her (that was what she said) in her distress. She then entreated me to come up-stairs, sobbing that Mr. Barkis had always liked me and admired me; that he had often talked of me, before he fell into a stupor; and that she believed, in case of his coming to himself again, he would brighten up at sight of me, if he could brighten up at any earthly thing.

The probability of his ever doing so, appeared to me, when I saw him, to be very small. He was lying with his head and shoulders out of bed, in an uncomfortable attitude, half resting on the box which had cost him so much pain and trouble. I learned, that, when he was past creeping out of bed to open it, and past assuring himself of its safety by means of the divining rod I had seen him use, he had required to have it placed on the chair at the bedside, where he had ever since embraced it, night and day. His arm lay on it now. Time and the world were slipping from beneath him, but the box was there; and the last words he had uttered were (in an explanatory tone) "Old clothes!"

"Barkis, my dear!" said Peggotty, almost cheerfully: bending over him, while her brother and I stood at the bed's foot. "Here's my dear boy—my dear boy, Master Davy, who brought us together, Barkis! That you sent messages by, you know! Won't you speak to Master Davy?"

He was as mute and senseless as the box, from which his form derived the only expression it had.

"He's a going out with the tide," said Mr. Peggotty to me, behind his hand.

My eyes were dim, and so were Mr. Peggotty's; but I repeated in a whisper, "With the tide?"

"People can't die, along the coast," said Mr. Peggotty, "except when the tide's pretty nigh out. They can't be born, unless it's pretty nigh in—not properly born, till flood. He's a going out with the tide. It's ebb at half-arter three, slack water half-an-hour. If he lives 'till it turns, he'll hold his own till past the flood, and go out with the next tide."

We remained there, watching him, a long time—hours. What mysterious influence my presence had upon him in that state of his senses, I shall not pretend to say; but when he at last began to wander feebly, it is certain he was muttering about driving me to school.

"He's coming to himself," said Peggotty.

Mr. Peggotty touched me, and whispered with much awe and reverence, "They are both a going out fast."

"Barkis, my dear!" said Peggotty.

"C. P. Barkis," he cried faintly. "No better woman anywhere!"

"Look! Here's Master Davy!" said Peggotty. For he now opened his eyes.

I was on the point of asking him if he knew me, when he tried to stretch out his arm, and said to me, distinctly, with a pleasant smile:

"Barkis is willin'!"

And, it being low water, he went out with the tide.

I find Mr. Barkis going out with the Tide

CHAPTER XXXI.

A GREATER LOSS.

It was not difficult for me, on Peggotty's solicitation, to resolve to stay where I was, until after the remains of the poor carrier should have made their last journey to Blunderstone. She had long ago bought, out of her own savings, a little piece of ground in our old churchyard near the grave "of her sweet girl," as she always called my mother; and there they were to rest.

In keeping Peggotty company, and doing all I could for her (little enough at the utmost), I was as grateful, I rejoice to think, as even now I could wish myself to have been. But I am afraid I had a supreme satisfaction, of a personal and professional nature, in taking charge of Mr. Barkis's will, and expounding its contents.

I may claim the merit of having originated the suggestion that the will should be looked for in the box. After some search, it was found in the box, at the bottom of a horse's nose-bag; wherein (besides hay) there was discovered an old gold watch, with chain and seals, which Mr. Barkis had worn on his wedding-day, and which had never been seen before or since; a silver tobacco-stopper, in the form of a leg; an imitation lemon, full of minute cups and saucers, which I have some idea Mr. Barkis must have purchased to present to me when I was a child, and afterwards found himself unable to part with; eighty-seven guineas and a half, in guineas and

11

half-guineas; two hundred and ten pounds, in perfectly clean Bank notes; certain receipts for Bank of England stock; an old horse-shoe, a bad shilling, a piece of camphor, and an oyster-shell. From the circumstance of the latter article having been much polished, and displaying prismatic colours on the inside, I conclude that Mr. Barkis had some general ideas about pearls, which never resolved themselves into anything definite.

For years and years, Mr. Barkis had carried this box, on all his journeys, every day. That it might the better escape notice, he had invented a fiction that it belonged to "Mr. Blackboy," and was "to be left with Barkis till called for;" a fable he had elaborately written on the lid, in characters now scarcely legible.

He had hoarded, all these years, I found, to good purpose. His property in money amounted to nearly three thousand pounds. Of this he bequeathed the interest of one thousand to Mr. Peggotty for his life; on his decease, the principal to be equally divided between Peggotty, little Emily, and me, or the survivor or survivors of us, share and share alike. All the rest he died possessed of, he bequeathed to Peggotty; whom he left residuary legatee, and sole executrix of that his last will and testament.

I felt myself quite a proctor when I read this document aloud with all possible ceremony, and set forth its provisions, any number of times, to those whom they concerned. I began to think there was more in the Commons than I had supposed. I examined the will with the deepest attention, pronounced it perfectly formal in all respects, made a pencil-mark or so in the margin, and thought it rather extra-ordinary that I knew so much.

In this abstruse pursuit; in making an account for Peggotty, of all the property into which she had come; in arranging all the affairs in an orderly manner; and in being her referee and adviser on every point, to our joint delight; I passed the week before the funeral. I did not see little Emily in that interval, but they told me she was to be quietly married in a fortnight.

I did not attend the funeral in character, if I may venture to say so. I mean I was not dressed up in a black cloak and a streamer, to frighten the birds; but I walked over to Blunderstone early in the morning, and was in the churchyard when it came, attended only by Peggotty and her brother. The mad gentleman looked on, out of my little window; Mr. Chillip's baby wagged its heavy head, and rolled its goggle eyes, at the clergyman, over its nurse's shoulder; Mr. Omer breathed short in the background; no one else was there; and it was very quiet. We walked about the churchyard for an hour, after all was over; and pulled some young leaves from the tree above my mother's grave.

A dread falls on me here. A cloud is lowering on the distant town, towards which I retraced my solitary steps. I fear to approach it. I cannot bear to think of what did come, upon that memorable night; of what must come again, if I go on.

It is no worse, because I write of it. It would be no better, if I stopped my most unwilling hand. It is done. Nothing can undo it; nothing can make it otherwise than as it was.

My old nurse was to go to London with me next day, on the business of the will. Little Emily was passing that day at Mr. Omer's. We were all to meet in the old boathouse that night. Ham would bring Emily at the usual hour. I would walk back at my leisure. The brother and sister would return as they had come, and be expecting us, when the day closed in, at the fireside.

I parted from them at the wicket-gate, where visionary Straps had rested with Roderick Random's knapsack in the days of yore; and, instead of going straight back, walked a little distance on the road to Lowestoft. Then I turned, and walked back towards Yarmouth. I stayed to dine at a decent alehouse, some mile or two from the Ferry I have mentioned before; and thus the day wore away, and it was evening when I reached it. Rain was falling heavily by that time, and it was a wild night; but there was a moon behind the clouds, and it was not dark.

I was soon within sight of Mr. Peggotty's house, and of the light within it shining through the window. A little floundering across the sand, which was heavy, brought me to the door, and I went in.

It looked very comfortable indeed. Mr. Peggotty had smoked his evening pipe, and there were preparations for some supper by-and-by. The fire was bright, the ashes were thrown up, the locker was ready for little Emily in her old place. In her own old place sat Peggotty, once more, looking (but for her dress) as if she had never left it. She had fallen back, already, on the society of the work-box with Saint Paul's upon the lid, the yard-measure in the cottage, and the bit of wax candle: and there they all were, just as if they had never been disturbed. Mrs. Gummidge appeared to be fretting a little, in her old corner; and consequently looked quite natural, too.

"You're first of the lot, Mas'r Davy!" said Mr. Peggotty, with a happy face. "Doen't keep in that coat, sir, if it's wet."

"Thank you, Mr. Peggotty," said I, giving him my outer coat to hang up. "It's quite dry."

"So 'tis!" said Mr. Peggotty, feeling my shoulders. "As a chip! Sit ye down, sir. It ain't o' no use saying welcome to you, but you're welcome, kind and hearty."

"Thank you, Mr. Peggotty, I am sure of that. Well, Peggotty!" said I, giving her a kiss. "And how are you, old woman?"

"Ha, ha!" laughed Mr. Peggotty, sitting down beside us, and rubbing his hands in his sense of relief from recent trouble, and in the genuine heartiness of his nature; "there's not a woman in the wureld, sir—as I tell her—that need to feel more easy in her mind than her! She done her dooty by the departed, and the departed know'd it; and the departed done what was right by her, as she done what was right by the departed;—and—and—and it's *all* right!"

Mrs. Gummidge groaned.

"Cheer up, my pretty mawther!" said Mr. Peggotty. (But he shook his head aside at us, evidently sensible of the tendency of the late occurrences to recall the memory of the old one.) "Doen't be down! Cheer up, for your own self, on'y a little bit, and see if a good deal more doen't come nat'ral!"

"Not to me, Dan'l," returned Mrs. Gummidge. "Nothink's nat'ral to me but to be lone and lorn."

"No, no," said Mr. Peggotty, soothing her sorrows.

"Yes, yes, Dan'l!" said Mrs. Gummidge. "I ain't a person to live with them as has had money left. Thinks go too contrairy with me. I had better be a riddance."

"Why, how should I ever spend it without you?" said Mr. Peggotty, with an air of serious remonstrance. "What are you a talking on? Doen't I want you more now, than ever I did?"

"I know'd I was never wanted before!" cried Mrs. Gummidge, with a pitiable whimper, "and now I'm told so! How could I expect to be wanted, being so lone and lorn, and so contrairy!"

Mr. Peggotty seemed very much shocked at himself for having made a speech capable of this unfeeling construction, but was prevented from replying, by Peggotty's pulling his sleeve, and shaking her head. After looking at Mrs. Gummidge for some moments, in sore distress of mind, he glanced at the Dutch clock, rose, snuffed the candle, and put it in the window.

"Theer!" said Mr. Peggotty, cheerily. "Theer we are, Missis Gummidge!" Mrs. Gummidge slightly groaned. "Lighted up, accordin' to custom! You're a wonderin' what that's fur, sir! Well, it's fur our little Em'ly. You see, the path ain't over light or cheerful arter dark; and

15

when I'm here at the hour as she's a comin' home, I puts the light in the winder. That, you see," said Mr. Peggotty, bending over me with great glee, "meets two objects. She says, says Em'ly, 'Theer's home!' she says. And likewise, says Em'ly, 'My uncle's theer!' Fur if I ain't theer, I never have no light showed."

"You're a baby!" said Peggotty; very fond of him for it, if she thought so.

"Well," returned Mr. Peggotty, standing with his legs pretty wide apart, and rubbing his hands up and down them in his comfortable satisfaction, as he looked alternately at us and at the fire, "I doen't know but I am. Not, you see, to look at."

"Not azackly," observed Peggotty.

"No," laughed Mr. Peggotty, "not to look at, but to—to consider on, you know. *I* doen't care, bless you! Now I tell you. When I go a looking and looking about that theer pritty house of our Em'ly's, I'm—I'm Gormed," said Mr. Peggotty, with sudden emphasis—"theer! I can't say more —if I doen't feel as if the littlest things was her, a'most. I takes 'em up and I puts 'em down, and I touches of 'em as delicate as if they was our Em'ly. So 'tis with her little bonnets and that. I couldn't see one on 'em rough used a purpose—not fur the whole wureld. There's a babby for you, in the form of a great Sea Porkypine!" said Mr. Peggotty, relieving his earnestness with a roar of laughter.

Peggotty and I both laughed, but not so loud.

"It's my opinion, you see," said Mr. Peggotty, with a delighted face, after some further rubbing of his legs, "as this is along of my havin' played with her so much, and made believe as we was Turks, and French, and sharks, and every wariety of forinners—bless you, yes; and lions and whales, and I doen't know what all!—when she warn't no higher than my knee. I've got into the way on it, you know. Why, this here candle, now!" said Mr. Peggotty, glcefully holding out his hand towards it, "*I* know wery well that arter she's married and gone, I shall put that candle theer, just that same as now. I know wery well that when I'm here o' nights (and where else should *I* live, bless your arts, whatever fortun I come into!) and she ain't here, or I ain't theer, I shall put the candle in the winder, and sit afore the fire, pretending I'm expecting of her, like I'm a doing now. *There's* a babby for you," said Mr. Peggotty, with another roar, "in the form of a Sea Porkypine! Why, at the present minute, when I see the candle sparkle up, I says to myself, 'She's a looking at it! Em'ly's a coming!' *There's* a babby for you, in the form of a Sea Porkypine! Right for all that," said Mr. Peggotty, stopping in his roar, and smiting his hands together; "fur here she is!"

It was only Ham. The night should have turned more wet since I came in, for he had a large sou'wester hat on, slouched over his face.

"Wheer's Em'ly?" said Mr. Peggotty.

Ham made a motion with his head, as if she were outside. Mr. Peggotty took the light from the window, trimmed it, put it on the table, and was busily stirring the fire, when Ham, who had not moved, said:

"Mas'r Davy, will you come out a minute, and see what Em'ly and me has got to show you?"

We went out. As I passed him at the door, I saw, to my astonishment and fright, that he was deadly pale. He pushed me hastily into the open air, and closed the door upon us. Only upon us two.

"Ham! what's the matter?"

"Mas'r Davy!—" Oh, for his broken heart, how dreadfully he wept!

I was paralyzed by the sight of such grief. I don't know what I thought, or what I dreaded. I could only look at him.

"Ham! Poor good fellow! For Heaven's sake, tell me what's the matter!"

17

"My love, Mas'r Davy—the pride and hope of my art—her that I'd have died for, and would die for now—she's gone!"

"Gone!"

"Em'ly's run away! Oh, Mas'r Davy, think *how* she's run away, when I pray my good and gracious God to kill her (her that is so dear above all things) sooner than let her come to ruin and disgrace!"

The face he turned up to the troubled sky, the quivering of his clasped hands, the agony of his figure, remain associated with that lonely waste, in my remembrance, to this hour. It is always night there, and he is the only object in the scene.

"You're a scholar," he said, hurriedly, "and know what's right and best. What am I to say, indoors? How am I ever to break it to him, Mas'r Davy?"

I saw the door move, and instinctively tried to hold the latch on the outside, to gain a moment's time. It was too late. Mr. Peggotty thrust forth his face; and never could I forget the change that came upon it when he saw us, if I were to live five hundred years.

I remember a great wail and cry, and the women hanging about him, and we all standing in the room; I with a paper in my hand, which Ham had given me; Mr. Peggotty, with his vest torn open, his hair wild, his face and lips quite white, and blood trickling down his bosom (it had sprung from his mouth, I think), looking fixedly at me.

"Read it, sir," he said, in a low shivering voice. "Slow, please. I doen't know as I can understand."

In the midst of the silence of death, I read thus, from a blotted letter:

"'When you, who love me so much better than I ever have deserved, even when my mind was innocent, see this, I shall be far away.'"

"I shall be fur away," he repeated slowly. "Stop! Em'ly fur away. Well!"

EMILY LOST AND GONE.

"'When I leave my dear home—my dear home—oh, my dear home!—in the morning—'"

the letter bore date on the previous night:

"'—it will be never to come back, unless he brings me back a lady. This will be found at night, many hours after, instead of me. Oh, if you knew how my heart is torn. If even you, that I have wronged so much, that never can forgive me, could only know what I suffer! I am too wicked to write about myself. Oh, take comfort in thinking that I am so bad. Oh, for mercy's sake, tell uncle that I never loved him half so dear as now. Oh, don't remember how affectionate and kind you have all been to me—don't remember we were ever to be married—but try to think as if I died when I was little, and was buried somewhere. Pray Heaven that I am going away from, have compassion on my uncle! Tell him that I never loved him half so dear. Be his comfort. Love some good girl, that will be what I was once to uncle, and be true to you, and worthy of you, and know no shame but me. God bless all! I'll pray for all, often, on my knees. If he don't bring me back a lady, and I don't pray for my own self, I'll pray for all. My parting love to uncle. My last tears, and my last thanks, for uncle!'"

That was all.

He stood, long after I had ceased to read, still looking at me. At length I ventured to take his hand, and to entreat him, as well as I could, to endeavour to get some command of himself. He replied, "I thankee, sir, I thankee!" without moving.

Ham spoke to him. Mr. Peggotty was so far sensible of *his* affliction, that he wrung his hand; but, otherwise, he remained in the same state, and no one dared to disturb him.

Slowly, at last he moved his eyes from my face, as if he were waking from a vision, and cast them round the room. Then he said, in a low voice:

"Who's the man? I want to know his name."

Ham glanced at me, and suddenly I felt a shock that struck me back.

"There's a man suspected," said Mr. Peggotty. "Who is it?"

"Mas'r Davy!" implored Ham. "Go out a bit, and let me tell him what I must. You doen't ought to hear it, sir."

I felt the shock again. I sank down in a chair, and tried to utter some reply; but my tongue was fettered, and my sight was weak.

"I want to know his name!" I heard said, once more.

"For some time past," Ham faltered, "there's been a servant about here, at odd times. There's been a gen'lm'n too. Both of 'em belonged to one another."

Mr. Peggotty stood fixed as before, but now looking at him.

"The servant," pursued Ham, "was seen along with—our poor girl—last night. He's been in hiding about here, this week or over. He was thought to have gone, but he was hiding. Doen't stay, Mas'r Davy, doen't!"

I felt Peggotty's arm round my neck, but I could not have moved if the house had been about to fall upon me.

"A strange chay and hosses was outside town, this morning, on the Norwich road, a'most afore the day broke," Ham went on. "The servant went to it, and come from it, and went to it again. When he went to it again, Em'ly was nigh him. The t'other was inside. He's the man."

"For the Lord's love," said Mr. Peggotty, falling back, and putting out his hand, as if to keep off what he dreaded. "Doen't tell me his name's Steerforth!"

"Mas'r Davy," exclaimed Ham, in a broken voice, "it ain't no fault of yourn—and I am far from laying of it to you—but his name is Steerforth, and he's a damned villain!"

Mr. Peggotty uttered no cry, and shed no tear, and moved no more, until he seemed to wake again, all at once, and pulled down his rough coat from its peg in a corner.

"Bear a hand with this! I'm struck of a heap, and can't do it," he said, impatiently. "Bear a hand and help me. Well!" when somebody had done so. "Now give me that theer hat!"

Ham asked him whither he was going.

"I'm a going to seek my niece. I'm a going to seek my Em'ly. I'm a going, first, to stave in that theer boat, and sink it where I would have drownded *him*, as I'm a livin' soul, if I had had one thought of what was in him! As he sat afore me," he said, wildly, holding out his clenched right hand, "as he sat afore me, face to face, strike me down dead, but I'd have drownded him, and thought it right!—I'm a going to seek my niece."

"Where?" cried Ham, interposing himself before the door.

"Anywhere! I'm a going to seek my niece through the wureld. I'm a going to find my poor niece in her shame, and bring her back. No one stop me! I tell you I'm a going to seek my niece!"

"No, no!" cried Mrs. Gummidge, coming between them, in a fit of crying. "No, no, Dan'l, not as you are now. Seek her in a little while, my lone lorn Dan'l, and that'll be but right! but not as you are now. Sit ye down, and give me your forgiveness for having ever been a worrit to you, Dan'l—what have *my* contrairies ever been to this!— and let us speak a word about them times when she was first an orphan, and when Ham was too, and when I was a poor widder woman, and you took me in. It'll soften your poor heart, Dan'l," laying her head upon his shoulder, "and you'll bear your sorrow better; for you know the promise, Dan'l, 'As you have done it unto one of the least of these, you have done it unto me'; and that can never fail under this roof, that's been our shelter for so many, many year!"

He was quite passive now; and when I heard him crying, the impulse that had been upon me to go down upon my knees, and ask their pardon for the desolation I had caused, and curse Steerforth, yielded to a better feeling. My over-charged heart found the same relief, and I cried too.

CHAPTER XXXII.

THE BEGINNING OF A LONG JOURNEY.

WHAT is natural in me, is natural in many other men, I infer, and so I am not afraid to write that I never had loved Steerforth better than when the ties that bound me to him were broken. In the keen distress of the discovery of his unworthiness, I thought more of all that was brilliant in him, I softened more towards all that was good in him, I did more justice to the qualities that might have made him a man of a noble nature and a great name, than ever I had done in the height of my devotion to him. Deeply as I felt my own unconscious part in his pollution of an honest home, I believed that if I had been brought face to face with him, I could not have uttered one reproach. I should have loved him so well still—though he fascinated me no longer—I should have held in so much tenderness the memory of my affection for him, that I think I should have been as weak as a spirit-wounded child, in all but the entertainment of a thought that we could ever be re-united. That thought I never had. I felt, as he had felt, that all was at an end between us. What his remembrances of me were, I have never known—they were light enough, perhaps, and easily dismissed—but mine of him were as the remembrances of a cherished friend, who was dead.

Yes, Steerforth, long removed from the scenes of this poor history! My sorrow may bear involuntary witness against you at the Judgment Throne; but my angry thoughts or my reproaches never will, I know!

The news of what had happened soon spread through the town; insomuch that as I passed along the streets next morning, I overheard the people speaking of it at their doors. Many were hard upon her, some few were hard upon him, but towards her second father and her lover there was but one sentiment. Among all kinds of people a respect for them in their distress prevailed, which was full of gentleness and delicacy. The seafaring men kept apart, when those two were seen early, walking with slow steps on the beach; and stood in knots, talking compassionately among themselves.

It was on the beach, close down by the sea, that I found them. It would have been easy to perceive that they had not slept all last night, even if Peggotty had failed to tell me of their still sitting just as I left them, when it was broad day. They looked worn; and I thought Mr. Peggotty's head was bowed in one night more than in all the years I had known him. But they were both as grave and steady as the sea itself: then lying beneath a dark sky, waveless—yet with a heavy roll upon it, as if it breathed in its rest—and touched, on the horizon, with a strip of silvery light from the unseen sun.

"We have had a mort of talk, sir," said Mr. Peggotty to me, when we had all three walked a little while in silence, "of what we ought and doen't ought to do. But we see our course now."

I happened to glance at Ham, then looking out to sea upon the distant light, and a frightful thought came into my mind—not that his face was angry, for it was not; I recall nothing but an expression of stern determination in it —that if ever he encountered Steerforth, he would kill him.

"My dooty here, sir," said Mr. Peggotty, "is done. I'm a going to seek my—" he stopped, and went on in a firmer voice: "I'm a going to seek her. That's my dooty ever-more,"

He shook his head when I asked him where he would seek her, and inquired if I were going to London to-morrow? I told him I had not gone to-day, fearing to lose the chance of being of any service to him; but that I was ready to go when he would.

"I'll go along with you, sir," he rejoined, "if you're agreeable, to-morrow."

We walked again, for a while, in silence.

"Ham," he presently resumed, "he'll hold to his present work, and go and live along with my sister. The old boat yonder—"

"Will you desert the old boat, Mr. Peggotty?" I gently interposed.

"My station, Mas'r Davy," he returned, "ain't there no longer; and if ever a boat foundered, since there was darkness on the face of the deep, that one's gone down. But no, sir, no; I doen't mean as it should be deserted. Fur from that."

We walked again for a while, as before, until he explained:

"My wishes is, sir, as it shall look, day and night, winter and summer, as it has always looked, since she fust know'd it. If ever she should come a wandering back, I wouldn't have the old place seem to cast her off, you understand, but seem to tempt her to draw nigher to 't, and to peep in, maybe, like a ghost, out of the wind and rain, through the old winder, at the old seat by the fire. Then, maybe, Mas'r Davy, seein' none but Missis Gummidge there, she might take heart to creep in, trembling; and might come to be laid down in her old bed, and rest her weary head where it was once so gay."

I could not speak to him in reply, though I tried.

"Every night," said Mr. Peggotty, "as reg'lar as the night comes, the candle must be stood in its old pane of glass, that if ever she should see it, it may seem to say 'Come back, my child, come back!' If ever there's a knock, Ham (partic'ler a soft knock), arter dark, at your aunt's door, doen't you go nigh it. Let it be her—not you—that sees my fallen child!"

He walked a little in front of us, and kept before us for some minutes. During this interval, I glanced at Ham again, and observing the same expression on his face, and his eye, still directed to the distant light, I touched his arm.

Twice I called him by his name, in the tone in which I might have tried to rouse a sleeper, before he heeded me. When I at last inquired on what his thoughts were so bent, he replied:

"On what's afore me, Mas'r Davy; and over yon."

"On the life before you, do you mean?" He had pointed confusedly out to sea.

"Ay, Mas'r Davy. I doen't rightly know how 'tis, but from over yon there seemed to me to come—the end of it like;" looking at me as if he were waking, but with the same determined face.

"What end?" I asked, possessed by my former fear.

"I doen't know," he said, thoughtfully; "I was calling to mind that the beginning of it all did take place here—and then the end come. But it's gone! Mas'r Davy," he added; answering, as I think, my look; "you han't no call to be afeerd of me: but I'm kiender muddled; I don't fare to feel no matters,"—which was as much as to say that he was not himself, and quite confounded.

Mr. Peggotty stopping for us to join him: we did so, and said no more. The remembrance of this, in connexion with my former thought, however, haunted me at intervals, even until the inexorable end came at its appointed time.

We insensibly approached the old boat, and entered. Mrs. Gummidge, no longer moping in her especial corner, was busy preparing breakfast. She took Mr. Peggotty's hat, and placed his seat for him, and spoke so comfortably and softly, that I hardly knew her.

"Dan'l, my good man," said she, "you must eat and drink, and keep up your strength, for without it you'll do nowt.

Try, that's a dear soul! And if I disturb you with my clicketten," she meant her chattering, "tell me so, Dan'l, and I won't."

When she had served us all, she withdrew to the window, where she sedulously employed herself in repairing some shirts and other clothes belonging to Mr. Peggotty, and neatly folding and packing them in an old oilskin bag, such as sailors carry. Meanwhile, she continued talking, in the same quiet manner:

"All times and seasons, you know, Dan'l," said Mrs. Gummidge, "I shall be allus here, and everythink will look accordin' to your wishes. I'm a poor scholar, but I shall write to you, odd times, when you're away, and send my letters to Mas'r Davy. Maybe you'll write to me too, Dan'l, odd times, and tell me how you fare to feel upon your lone lorn journies."

"You'll be a solitary woman here, I'm afeerd!" said Mr. Peggotty.

"No, no, Dan'l," she returned, "I shan't be that. Doen't you mind me. I shall have enough to do to keep a Beein for you" (Mrs. Gummidge meant a home), "again you come back—to keep a Beein here for any that may hap to come back, Dan'l. In the fine time, I shall set outside the door as I used to do. If any *should* come nigh, they shall see the old widder woman true to 'em, a long way off."

What a change in Mrs. Gummidge in a little time! She was another woman. She was so devoted, she had such a quick perception of what it would be well to say, and what it would be well to leave unsaid; she was so forgetful of herself, and so regardful of the sorrow about her, that I held her in a sort of veneration. The work she did that day! There were many things to be brought up from the beach and stored in the outhouse—as oars, nets, sails, cordage, spars, lobster-pots, bags of ballast, and the like; and though there was abundance of assistance rendered, there being not a pair of working hands on all that shore but would have laboured

26

hard for Mr. Peggotty, and been well paid in being asked
to do it, yet she persisted, all day long, in toiling under
weights that she was quite unequal to, and fagging to and
fro on all sorts of unnecessary errands. As to deploring her
misfortunes, she appeared to have entirely lost the recollection
of ever having had any. She preserved an equable cheerfulness in the midst of her sympathy, which was not the
least astonishing part of the change that had come over her.
Querulousness was out of the question. I did not even observe
her voice to falter, or a tear to escape from her eyes, the
whole day through, until twilight; when she and I and Mr.
Peggotty being alone together, and he having fallen asleep
in perfect exhaustion, she broke into a half-suppressed fit of
sobbing and crying, and taking me to the door, said, "Ever
bless you, Mas'r Davy, be a friend to him, poor dear!"
Then, she immediately ran out of the house to wash her
face, in order that she might sit quietly beside him, and be
found at work there, when he should awake. In short, I left
her, when I went away at night, the prop and staff of Mr.
Peggotty's affliction: and I could not meditate enough upon
the lesson that I read in Mrs. Gummidge, and the new
experience she unfolded to me.

It was between nine and ten o'clock when, strolling in a
melancholy manner through the town, I stopped at Mr.
Omer's door. Mr. Omer had taken it so much to heart, his
daughter told me, that he had been very low and poorly all
day, and had gone to bed without his pipe.

"A deceitful, bad-hearted girl," said Mrs. Joram. "There
was no good in her, ever!"

"Don't say so," I returned. "You don't think so."

"Yes, I do!" cried Mrs. Joram, angrily.

"No, no," said I.

Mrs. Joram tossed her head, endeavouring to be very stern
and cross; but she could not command her softer self, and
began to cry. I was young, to be sure; but I thought
much the better of her for this sympathy, and fancied it

became her, as a virtuous wife and mother, very well indeed.

"What will she ever do!" sobbed Minnie. "Where will she go! What will become of her! Oh, how could she be so cruel, to herself and him!"

I remembered the time when Minnie was a young and pretty girl; and I was glad that she remembered it too, so feelingly.

"My little Minnie," said Mrs. Joram, "has only just now been got to sleep. Even in her sleep she is sobbing for Em'ly. All day long, little Minnie has cried for her, and asked me, over and over again, whether Em'ly was wicked? What can I say to her, when Em'ly tied a ribbon off her own neck round little Minnie's the last night she was here, and laid her head down on the pillow beside her till she was fast asleep! The ribbon's round my little Minnie's neck now. It ought not to be, perhaps, but what can I do? Em'ly is very bad, but they were fond of one another. And the child knows nothing!"

Mrs. Joram was so unhappy, that her husband came out to take care of her. Leaving them together, I went home to Peggotty's; more melancholy myself, if possible, than I had been yet.

That good creature—I mean Peggotty—all untired by her late anxieties and sleepless nights, was at her brother's, where she meant to stay till morning. An old woman, who had been employed about the house for some weeks past, while Peggotty had been unable to attend to it, was the house's only other occupant besides myself. As I had no occasion for her services, I sent her to bed, by no means against her will; and sat down before the kitchen fire a little while, to think about all this.

I was blending it with the deathbed of the late Mr. Barkis, and was driving out with the tide towards the distance at which Ham had looked so singularly in the morning, when I was recalled from my wanderings by a knock at the door.

AN UNEXPECTED VISITOR.

There was a knocker upon the door, but it was not that which made the sound. The tap was from a hand, and low down upon the door, as if it were given by a child.

It made me start as much as if it had been the knock of a footman to a person of distinction. I opened the door; and at first looked down, to my amazement, on nothing but a great umbrella that appeared to be walking about of itself. But presently I discovered underneath it, Miss Mowcher.

I might not have been prepared to give the little creature a very kind reception, if, on her removing the umbrella, which her utmost efforts were unable to shut up, she had shown me the " volatile " expression of face which had made so great an impression on me at our first and last meeting. But her face, as she turned it up to mine, was so earnest; and when I relieved her of the umbrella (which would have been an inconvenient one for the Irish giant), she wrung her little hands in such an afflicted manner; that I rather inclined towards her.

" Miss Mowcher ! " said I, after glancing up and down the empty street, without distinctly knowing what I expected to see besides; " how do you come here ? What is the matter ? "

She motioned to me with her short right arm, to shut the umbrella for her; and passing me hurriedly, went into the kitchen. When I had closed the door, and followed, with the umbrella in my hand, I found her sitting on the corner of the fender—it was a low iron one, with two flat bars at top to stand plates upon—in the shadow of the boiler, swaying herself backwards and forwards, and chafing her hands upon her knees like a person in pain.

Quite alarmed at being the only recipient of this untimely visit, and the only spectator of this portentous behaviour, I exclaimed again, " Pray tell me, Miss Mowcher, what is the matter ! are you ill ? "

" My dear young soul," returned Miss Mowcher, squeezing her hands upon her heart one over the other. " I am ill here, I am very ill. To think that it should come to this, when I might have known it and perhaps prevented it, if I hadn't been a thoughtless fool!"

Again her large bonnet (very disproportionate to her figure) went backwards and forwards, in her swaying of her little body to and fro; while a most gigantic bonnet rocked, in unison with it, upon the wall.

"I ám surprised," I began, "to see you so distressed and serious"—when she interrupted me.

"Yes, it's always so!" she said. "They are all surprised, these inconsiderate young people, fairly and full grown, to see any natural feeling in a little thing like me! They make a plaything of me, use me for their amusement, throw me away when they are tired, and wonder that I feel more than a toy horse or a wooden soldier! Yes, yes, that's the way. The old way!"

"It may be, with others," I returned, "but I do assure you it is not with me. Perhaps I ought not to be at all surprised to see you as you are now: I know so little of you. I said, without consideration, what I thought."

"What can I do?" returned the little woman, standing up, and holding out her arms to show herself. "See! What I am, my father was; and my sister is; and my brother is. I have worked for sister and brother these many years—hard, Mr. Copperfield—all day. I must live. I do no harm. If there are people so unreflecting or so cruel, as to make a jest of me, what is left for me to do but to make a jest of myself, them, and everything? If I do so, for the time, whose fault is that? Mine?"

No. Not Miss Mowcher's, I perceived.

"If I had shown myself a sensitive dwarf to your false friend," pursued the little woman, shaking her head at me, with reproachful earnestness, "how much of his help or good-will do you think *I* should ever have had? If little Mowcher (who had no hand, young gentleman, in the making of her-self) addressed herself to him, or the like of him, because of her misfortunes, when do you suppose her small voice would have been heard? Little Mowcher would have as much need to live, if she was the bitterest and dullest of pigmies; but she couldn't do it. No. She might whistle for her bread and butter till she died of Air."

Miss Mowcher sat down on the fender again, and took out her handkerchief, and wiped her eyes.

"Be thankful for me, if you have a kind heart, as I think you have," she said, "that while I know well what I am, I can be cheerful and endure it all. I am thankful for myself, at any rate, that I can find my tiny way through the world, without being beholden to any one; and that in return for all that is thrown at me, in folly or vanity, as I go along, I can throw bubbles back. If I don't brood over all I want, it is the better for me, and not the worse for any one. If I am a plaything for you giants, be gentle with me."

Miss Mowcher replaced her handkerchief in her pocket, looking at me with very intent expression all the while, and pursued:

"I saw you in the street just now. You may suppose I am not able to walk as fast as you, with my short legs and short breath, and I couldn't overtake you; but I guessed where you came, and came after you. I have been here before, to-day, but the good woman wasn't at home."

"Do you know her?" I demanded.

"I know *of* her, and about her," she replied, "from Omer and Joram. I was there at seven o'clock this morning. Do you remember what Steerforth said to me about this unfortunate girl, that time when I saw you both at the inn?"

The great bonnet on Miss Mowcher's head, and the greater bonnet on the wall, began to go backwards and forwards again when she asked this question.

I remembered very well what she referred to, having had it in my thoughts many times that day. I told her so.

"May the Father of all Evil confound him," said the little woman, holding up her forefinger between me and her sparkling eyes; "and ten times more confound that wicked servant; but I believed it was *you* who had a boyish passion for her!"

"I?" I repeated.

"Child, child! In the name of blind ill-fortune," cried Miss Mowcher, wringing her hands impatiently, as she went to and fro again upon the fender, "why did you praise her so, and blush, and look disturbed?"

I could not conceal from myself that I had done this, though for a reason very different from her supposition.

"What did I know?" said Miss Mowcher, taking out her handkerchief again, and giving one little stamp on the ground whenever, at short intervals, she applied it to her eyes with both hands at once. "He was crossing you and wheedling you, I saw; and you were soft wax in his hands, I saw. Had I left the room a minute, when his man told me that 'Young Innocence' (so he called you, and you may call him 'Old Guilt' all the days of your life) had set his heart upon her, and she was giddy and liked him, but his master was resolved that no harm should come of it—more for your sake than for hers—and that that was their business here? How could I *but* believe him? I saw Steerforth soothe and please you by his praise of her! You were the first to mention her name. You owned to an old admiration of her. You were hot and cold, and red and white, all at once when I spoke to you of her. What could I think— what *did* I think—but that you were a young libertine in everything but experience, and had fallen into hands that had experience enough, and could manage you (having the fancy) for your own good? Oh! oh! oh! They were afraid of my finding out the truth," exclaimed Miss Mowcher, getting off the fender, and trotting up and down the kitchen with her two short arms distressfully lifted up, "because I am a sharp little thing—I need be, to get through the world at all!—and they deceived me altogether, and I gave the poor unfortunate girl a letter, which I fully believe was the beginning of her ever speaking to Littimer, who was left behind on purpose!"

I stood amazed at the revelation of all this perfidy, looking at Miss Mowcher as she walked up and down the kitchen until she was out of breath: when she sat upon the fender again, and, drying her face with her handkerchief, shook her head for a long time, without otherwise moving, and without breaking silence.

"My country rounds," she added at length, "brought me to Norwich, Mr. Copperfield, the night before last. What I happened to find out there, about their secret way of coming and going, without you—which was strange—led to my suspecting something wrong. I got into the coach from London last night, as it came through Norwich, and was here this morning. Oh, oh, oh! too late!"

Poor little Mowcher turned so chilly after all her crying and fretting, that she turned round on the fender, putting her poor little wet feet in among the ashes to warm them, and sat looking at the fire, like a large doll. I sat in a chair on the other side of the hearth, lost in unhappy reflections, and looking at the fire too, and sometimes at her.

"I must go," she said at last, rising as she spoke. "It's late. You don't mistrust me?"

Meeting her sharp glance, which was as sharp as ever when she asked me, I could not on that short challenge answer no, quite frankly.

"Come!" said she, accepting the offer of my hand to help her over the fender, and looking wistfully up into my face, "you know you wouldn't mistrust me, if I was a full-sized woman!"

I felt that there was much truth in this; and I felt rather ashamed of myself.

"You are a young man," she said, nodding. "Take a word of advice, even from three foot nothing. Try not to associate bodily defects with mental, my good friend, except for a solid reason."

She had got over the fender now, and I had got over my suspicion. I told her that I believed she had given me a faithful account of herself, and that we had both been hapless instruments in designing hands. She thanked me, and said I was a good fellow.

"Now, mind!" she exclaimed, turning back on her way to the door, and looking shrewdly at me, with her forefinger up again. "I have some reason to suspect, from what I have heard—my ears are always open; I can't afford to spare what powers I have—that they are gone abroad. But if ever they return, if ever any one of them returns, while I am alive, I am more likely than another, going about as I do, to find it out soon. Whatever I know, you shall know. If ever I can do anything to serve the poor betrayed girl, I will do it faithfully, please Heaven! And Littimer had better have a bloodhound at his back, than little Mowcher!"

I placed implicit faith in this last statement, when I marked the look with which it was accompanied.

"Trust me no more, but trust me no less, than you would trust a full-sized woman," said the little creature, touching me appealingly on the wrist. "If ever you see me again, unlike what I am now, and like what I was when you first saw me, observe what company I am in. Call to mind that I am a very helpless and defenceless little thing. Think of me at home with my brother like myself and sister like myself, when my day's work is done. Perhaps you won't, then, be very hard upon me, or surprised if I can be distressed and serious. Good-night!"

I gave Miss Mowcher my hand, with a very different opinion of her from that which I had hitherto entertained, and opened the door to let her out. It was not a trifling business to get the great umbrella up, and properly balanced in her grasp; but at last I successfully accomplished this, and saw it go bobbing down the street through the rain, without the least appearance of having anybody underneath it, except when a heavier fall than usual from some overcharged

waterspout sent it toppling over, on one side, and discovered
Miss Mowcher struggling violently to get it right. After
making one or two sallies to her relief, which were rendered
futile by the umbrella's hopping on again, like an immense
bird, before I could reach it, I came in, went to bed, and
slept till morning.

In the morning I was joined by Mr. Peggotty and by my
old nurse, and we went at an early hour to the coach-office,
where Mrs. Gummidge and Ham were waiting to take leave
of us.

"Mas'r Davy," Ham whispered, drawing me aside, while
Mr. Peggotty was stowing his bag among the luggage, "his
life is quite broke up. He doen't know wheer he's going;
he doen't know what's afore him; he's bound upon a voyage
that'll last, on and off, all the rest of his days, take my wured
for 't, unless he finds what he's a seeking of. I am sure you'll
be a friend to him, Mas'r Davy?"

"Trust me, I will indeed," said I, shaking hands with Ham
earnestly.

"Thankee. Thankee, very kind, sir. One thing furder.
I'm in good employ, you know, Mas'r Davy, and I han't no
way now of spending what I gets. Money's of no use to me
no more, except to live. If you can lay it out for him, I
shall do my work with a better art. Though as to that,
sir," and he spoke very steadily and mildly, "you're not to
think but I shall work at all times, like a man, and act the
best that lays in my power!"

I told him I was well convinced of it; and I hinted that I
hoped the time might even come, when he would cease to
lead the lonely life he naturally contemplated now.

"No, sir," he said, shaking his head, "all that's past and
over with me, sir. No one can never fill the place that's
empty. But you'll bear in mind about the money, as theer's
at all times some laying by for him?"

Reminding him of the fact, that Mr. Peggotty derived a
steady, though certainly a very moderate income from the

bequest of his late brother-in-law, I promised to do so. We then took leave of each other. I cannot leave him even now, without remembering with a pang, at once his modest fortitude and his great sorrow.

As to Mrs. Gummidge, if I were to endeavour to describe how she ran down the street by the side of the coach, seeing nothing but Mr. Peggotty on the roof, through the tears she tried to repress, and dashing herself against the people who were coming in the opposite direction, I should enter on a task of some difficulty. Therefore I had better leave her sitting on a baker's door-step, out of breath, with no shape at all remaining in her bonnet, and one of her shoes off, lying on the pavement at a considerable distance.

When we got to our journey's end, our first pursuit was to look about for a little lodging for Peggotty, where her brother could have a bed. We were so fortunate as to find one, of a very clean and cheap description, over a chandler's shop, only two streets removed from me. When we had engaged this domicile, I bought some cold meat at an eating-house, and took my fellow-travellers home to tea; a proceeding, I regret to state, which did not meet with Mrs. Crupp's approval, but quite the contrary. I ought to observe, however, in explanation of that lady's state of mind, that she was much offended by Peggotty's tucking up her widow's gown before she had been ten minutes in the place, and setting to work to dust my bedroom. This Mrs. Crupp regarded in the light of a liberty, and a liberty, she said, was a thing she never allowed.

Mr. Peggotty had made a communication to me on the way to London for which I was not unprepared. It was, that he purposed first seeing Mrs. Steerforth. As I felt bound to assist him in this, and also to mediate between them; with the view of sparing the mother's feelings as much as possible, I wrote to her that night. I told her as mildly as I could what his wrong was, and what my own share in his injury. I said he was a man in very common life, but of a most gentle and upright character; and that I ventured to express a hope that she would not refuse to see him in his heavy trouble. I mentioned two o'clock in the afternoon as the hour of our coming, and I sent the letter myself by the first coach in the morning.

At the appointed time, we stood at the door—the door of that house where I had been, a few days since, so happy: where my youthful confidence and warmth of heart had been yielded up so freely: which was closed against me henceforth: which was now a waste, a ruin.

No Littimer appeared. The pleasanter face which had replaced his, on the occasion of my last visit, answered to our summons, and went before us to the drawing-room. Mrs. Steerforth was sitting there. Rosa Dartle glided, as we went in, from another part of the room, and stood behind her chair.

I saw, directly, in his mother's face, that she knew from himself what he had done. It was very pale, and bore the traces of deeper emotion than my letter alone, weakened by the doubts her fondness would have raised upon it, would have been likely to create. I thought her more like him than ever I had thought her; and I felt, rather than saw, that the resemblance was not lost on my companion.

She sat upright in her arm-chair, with a stately, immove-able, passionless air, that it seemed as if nothing could disturb. She looked very stedfastly at Mr. Peggotty when he stood before her; and he looked quite as stedfastly at her. Rosa Dartle's keen glance comprehended all of us. For some moments not a word was spoken. She motioned to Mr. Peggotty to be seated. He said, in a low voice, "I shouldn't feel it nat'ral, ma'am, to sit down in this house. I'd sooner stand." And this was succeeded by another silence, which she broke thus:

"I know, with deep regret, what has brought you here. What do you want of me? What do you ask me to do?"

He put his hat under his arm, and feeling in his breast

for Emily's letter, took it out, unfolded it, and gave it to her.

"Please to read that, ma'am. That's my niece's hand!"

She read it, in the same stately and impassive way,— untouched by its contents, as far as I could see,—and returned it to him.

"'Unless he brings me back a lady,'" said Mr. Peggotty, tracing out that part with his finger. "I come to know, ma'am, whether he will keep his wured?"

"No," she returned.

"Why not?" said Mr. Peggotty.

"It is impossible. He would disgrace himself. You cannot fail to know that she is far below him."

"Raise her up!" said Mr. Peggotty.

"She is uneducated and ignorant."

"Maybe she's not; maybe she is," said Mr. Peggotty. "*I* think not, ma'am; but I'm no judge of them things. Teach her better!"

"Since you oblige me to speak more plainly, which I am very unwilling to do, her humble connexions would render such a thing impossible, if nothing else did."

"Hark to this, ma'am," he returned, slowly and quietly. "You know what it is to love your child. So do I. If she was a hundred times my child, I couldn't love her more. You doen't know what it is to lose your child. I do. All the heaps of riches in the wureld would be nowt to me (if they was mine) to buy her back! But save her from this disgrace, and she shall never be disgraced by us. Not one of us that she's growed up among, not one of us that's lived along with her, and had her for their all in all these many year, will ever look upon her pritty face again. We'll be content to let her be; we'll be content to think of her, far off, as if she was underneath another sun and sky; we'll be content to trust her to her husband,—to her little children, p'raps,—and bide the time when all of us shall be alike in quality afore our God!"

Mr. Peggotty and Mrs. Steerforth

The rugged eloquence with which he spoke, was not devoid of all effect. She still preserved her proud manner, but there was a touch of softness in her voice, as she answered:

"I justify nothing. I make no counter-accusations. But I am sorry to repeat, it is impossible. Such a marriage would irretrievably blight my son's career, and ruin his prospects. Nothing is more certain than that it never can take place, and never will. If there is any other compensation——"

"I am looking at the likeness of the face," interrupted Mr. Peggotty, with a steady but a kindling eye, "that has looked at me, in my home, at my fireside, in my boat—wheer not?—smiling and friendly, when it was so treacherous, that I go half wild when I think of it. If the likeness of that face don't turn to burning fire, at the thought of offering money to me for my child's blight and ruin, it's as bad. I doen't know, being a lady's, but what it's worse."

She changed now, in a moment. An angry flush overspread her features; and she said, in an intolerant manner, grasping the arm-chair tightly with her hands:

"What compensation can you make to *me* for opening such a pit between me and my son? What is your love to mine? What is your separation to ours?"

Miss Dartle softly touched her, and bent down her head to whisper, but she would not hear a word.

"No, Rosa, not a word! Let the man listen to what I say! My son, who has been the object of my life, to whom its every thought has been devoted, whom I have gratified from a child in every wish, from whom I have had no separate existence since his birth,—to take up in a moment with a miserable girl, and avoid me! To repay my confidence with systematic deception, for her sake, and quit me for her! To set this wretched fancy, against his mother's claims upon his duty, love, respect, gratitude—claims that every day and hour of his life should have strengthened into ties that nothing could be proof against! Is this no injury?"

Again Rosa Dartle tried to soothe her; again ineffectually. "I say, Rosa, not a word! If he can stake his all upon the lightest object, I can stake my all upon a greater purpose. Let him go where he will, with the means that my love has secured to him! Does he think to reduce me by long absence? He knows his mother very little if he does. Let him put away his whim now, and he is welcome back. Let him not put her away now, and he never shall come near me, living or dying, while I can raise my hand to make a sign against it, unless, being rid of her for ever, he comes humbly to me and begs for my forgiveness. This is my right. This is the acknowledgment I *will have*. This is the separation that there is between us! And is this," she added, looking at her visitor with the proud intolerant air with which she had begun, "no injury?"

While I heard and saw the mother as she said these words, I seemed to hear and see the son, defying them. All that I had ever seen in him of an unyielding, wilful spirit, I saw in her. All the understanding that I had now of his misdirected energy, became an understanding of her character too, and a perception that it was, in its strongest springs, the same.

She now observed to me, aloud, resuming her former restraint, that it was useless to hear more, or to say more, and that she begged to put an end to the interview. She rose with an air of dignity to leave the room, when Mr. Peggotty signified that it was needless.

"Doen't fear me being any hindrance to you, I have no more to say, ma'am," he remarked as he moved towards the door. "I come heer with no hope, and I take away no hope. I have done what I thowt should be done, but I never looked fur any good to come of my stan'ning where I do. This has been too evil a house fur me and mine, fur me to be in my right senses and expect it."

With this, we departed; leaving her standing by her elbow-chair, a picture of a noble presence and a handsome face.

We had, on our way out, to cross a paved hall, with glass sides and roof, over which a vine was trained. Its leaves and shoots were green then, and the day being sunny, a pair of glass doors leading to the garden were thrown open. Rosa Dartle, entering this way with a noiseless step, when we were close to them, addressed herself to me :

"You do well," she said, " indeed, to bring this fellow here !"

Such a concentration of rage and scorn as darkened her face, and flashed in her jet-black eyes, I could not have thought compressible even into that face. The scar made by the hammer was, as usual in this excited state of her features, strongly marked. When the throbbing I had seen before, came into it as I looked at her, she absolutely lifted up her hand and struck it.

"This is a fellow," she said, " to champion and bring here, is he not? You are a true man !"

"Miss Dartle," I returned, "you are surely not so unjust as to condemn *me!*"

"Why do you bring division between these two mad creatures?" she returned. " Don't you know that they are both mad with their own self-will and pride ? "

" Is it my doing?" I returned.

" Is it your doing!" she retorted. " Why do you bring this man here ? "

" He is a deeply injured man, Miss Dartle," I replied. " You may not know it."

" I know that James Steerforth," she said, with her hand on her bosom, as if to prevent the storm that was raging there from being loud, " has a false, corrupt heart, and is a traitor. But what need I know or care about this fellow, and his common niece ? "

" Miss Dartle," I returned, " you deepen the injury. It is sufficient already. I will only say, at parting, that you do him a great wrong."

" I do him no wrong," she returned. " They are a depraved, worthless set. I would have her whipped ! "

41

Mr. Peggotty passed on, without a word, and went out at the door.

"Oh, shame, Miss Dartle! shame!" I said indignantly. "How can you bear to trample on his undeserved affliction!"

"I would trample on them all," she answered. "I would have his house pulled down. I would have her branded on the face, drest in rags, and cast out in the streets to starve. If I had the power to sit in judgment on her, I would see it done. See it done? I would do it! I detest her. If I ever could reproach her with her infamous condition, I would go anywhere to do so. If I could hunt her to her grave, I would. If there was any word of comfort that would be a solace to her in her dying hour, and only I possessed it, I wouldn't part with it for Life itself."

The mere vehemence of her words can convey, I am sensible, but a weak impression of the passion by which she was possessed, and which made itself articulate in her whole figure, though her voice, instead of being raised, was lower than usual. No description I could give of her would do justice to my recollection of her, or to her entire deliverance of herself to her anger. I have seen passion in many forms, but I have never seen it in such a form as that.

When I joined Mr. Peggotty, he was walking slowly and thoughtfully down the hill. He told me, as soon as I came up with him, that having now discharged his mind of what he had purposed doing in London, he meant "to set out on his travels," that night. I asked him where he meant to go? He only answered, "I'm a going, sir, to seek my niece."

We went back to the little lodging over the chandler's shop, and there I found an opportunity of repeating to Peggotty what he had said to me. She informed me, in return, that he had said the same to her that morning. She knew no more than I did, where he was going, but she thought he had some project shaped out in his mind.

I did not like to leave him, under such circumstances,

and we all three dined together off a beefsteak pie—which was one of the many good things for which Peggotty was famous—and which was curiously flavoured on this occasion, I recollect well, by a miscellaneous taste of tea, coffee, butter, bacon, cheese, new loaves, firewood, candles, and walnut ketchup, continually ascending from the shop. After dinner we sat for an hour or so near the window, without talking much; and then Mr. Peggotty got up, and brought his oilskin bag and his stout stick, and laid them on the table.

He accepted, from his sister's stock of ready money, a small sum on account of his legacy; barely enough, I should have thought, to keep him for a month. He promised to communicate with me, when anything befell him; and he slung his bag about him, took his hat and stick, and bade us both "Good-bye!"

"All good attend you, dear old woman," he said, embracing Peggotty, "and you too, Mas'r Davy!" shaking hands with me. "I'm a going to seek her, fur and wide. If she should come home while I'm away,—but ah, that ain't like to be!—or if I should bring her back, my meaning is, that she and me shall live and die where no one can't reproach her. If any hurt should come to me, remember that the last words I left for her was, 'My unchanged love is with my darling child, and I forgive her!'"

He said this solemnly, bare-headed; then, putting on his hat, he went down the stairs, and away. We followed to the door. It was a warm, dusty evening, just the time when, in the great main thoroughfare out of which that bye-way turned, there was a temporary lull in the eternal tread of feet upon the pavement, and a strong red sunshine. He turned, alone, at the corner of our shady street, into a glow of light, in which we lost him.

Rarely did that hour of the evening come, rarely did I wake at night, rarely did I look up at the moon, or stars, or watch the falling rain, or hear the wind, but I thought of his solitary figure toiling on, poor pilgrim, and recalled the words :

"I'm a going to seek her, fur and wide. If any hurt should come to me, remember that the last words I left for her was, 'My unchanged love is with my darling child, and I forgive her!'"

CHAPTER XXXIII.

ALL this time, I had gone on loving Dora, harder than ever. Her idea was my refuge in disappointment and distress, and made some amends to me, even for the loss of my friend. The more I pitied myself, or pitied others, the more I sought for consolation in the image of Dora. The greater the accumulation of deceit and trouble in the world, the brighter and the purer shone the star of Dora high above the world. I don't think I had any definite idea where Dora came from, or in what degree she was related to a higher order of beings; but I am quite sure I should have scouted the notion of her being simply human, like any other young lady, with indignation and contempt.

If I may so express it, I was steeped in Dora. I was not merely over head and ears in love with her, but I was saturated through and through. Enough love might have been wrung out of me, metaphorically speaking, to drown anybody in; and yet there would have remained enough within me, and all over me, to pervade my entire existence.

The first thing I did, on my own account, when I came back, was to take a night-walk to Norwood, and, like the subject of a venerable riddle of my childhood, to go "round and round the house, without ever touching the house," thinking about Dora. I believe the theme of this incomprehensible conundrum was the moon. No matter what it was, I, the

45

moon-struck slave of Dora, perambulated round and round
the house and garden for two hours, looking through crevices
in the palings, getting my chin by dint of violent exertion
above the rusty nails on the top, blowing kisses at the lights
in the windows, and romantically calling on the night, at
intervals, to shield my Dora—I don't exactly know what
from, I suppose from fire. Perhaps from mice, to which she
had a great objection.

My love was so much on my mind, and it was so natural
to me to confide in Peggotty, when I found her again by
my side of an evening with the old set of industrial implements, busily making the tour of my wardrobe, that I imparted to her, in a sufficiently roundabout way, my great
secret. Peggotty was strongly interested, but I could not
get her into my view of the case at all. She was audaciously
prejudiced in my favour, and quite unable to understand why
I should have any misgivings, or be low-spirited about it.
"The young lady might think herself well off," she observed,
"to have such a beau. And as to her Pa," she said, "what
did the gentleman expect, for gracious sake!"

I observed, however, that Mr. Spenlow's Proctorial gown
and stiff cravat took Peggotty down a little, and inspired
her with a greater reverence for the man who was gradually
becoming more and more etherealized in my eyes every day,
and about whom a reflected radiance seemed to me to beam
when he sat erect in Court among his papers, like a little
lighthouse in a sea of stationery. And by-the-bye, it used
to be uncommonly strange to me to consider, I remember,
as I sat in Court too, how those dim old judges and doctors
wouldn't have cared for Dora, if they had known her; how
they wouldn't have gone out of their senses with rapture, if
marriage with Dora had been proposed to them; how Dora
might have sung and played upon that glorified guitar, until
she led *me* to the verge of madness, yet not have tempted
one of those slow-goers an inch out of his road!

I despised them, to a man. Frozen-out old gardeners in

the flower-beds of the heart, I took a personal offence against
them all. The Bench was nothing to me but an insensible
blunderer. The Bar had no more tenderness or poetry in it,
than the Bar of a public-house.

Taking the management of Peggotty's affairs into my own
hands, with no little pride, I proved the will, and came to
a settlement with the Legacy Duty-office, and took her to
the Bank, and soon got everything into an orderly train.
We varied the legal character of these proceedings by going
to see some perspiring Wax-work, in Fleet Street (melted, I
should hope, these twenty years); and by visiting Miss
Linwood's Exhibition, which I remember as a Mausoleum of
needlework, favourable to self-examination and repentance;
and by inspecting the Tower of London; and going to the
top of St. Paul's. All these wonders afforded Peggotty as
much pleasure as she was able to enjoy, under existing circumstances: except, I think, St. Paul's, which, from her long
attachment to her work-box, became a rival of the picture
on the lid, and was, in some particulars, vanquished, she
considered, by that work of art.

Peggotty's business, which was what we used to call
"common-form business" in the Commons (and very light
and lucrative the common-form business was), being settled,
I took her down to the office one morning to pay her bill.
Mr. Spenlow had stepped out, old Tiffey said, to get a gentleman sworn for a marriage licence; but as I knew he would be
back directly, our place lying close to the Surrogate's, and
to the Vicar-General's office too, I told Peggotty to wait.

We were a little like undertakers, in the Commons, as
regarded Probate transactions; generally making it a rule to
look more or less cut up, when we had to deal with clients
in mourning. In a similar feeling of delicacy, we were always
blithe and light-hearted with the licence clients. Therefore
I hinted to Peggotty that she would find Mr. Spenlow much
recovered from the shock of Mr. Barkis's decease; and indeed
he came in like a bridegroom.

But neither Peggotty nor I had eyes for him, when we saw, in company with him, Mr. Murdstone. He was very little changed. His hair looked as thick, and was certainly as black, as ever; and his glance was as little to be trusted as of old.

"Ah, Copperfield?" said Mr. Spenlow. "You know this gentleman, I believe?"

I made my gentleman a distant bow, and Peggotty barely recognised him. He was, at first, somewhat disconcerted to meet us two together; but quickly decided what to do, and came up to me.

"I hope," he said, "that you are doing well?"

"It can hardly be interesting to you," said I. "Yes, if you wish to know."

We looked at each other, and he addressed himself to Peggotty.

"And you," said he. "I am sorry to observe that you have lost your husband."

"It's not the first loss I have had in my life, Mr. Murdstone," replied Peggotty, trembling from head to foot. "I am glad to hope that there is nobody to blame for this one, —nobody to answer for it."

"Ha!" said he; "that's a comfortable reflection. You have done your duty?"

"I have not worn anybody's life away," said Peggotty, "I am thankful to think! No, Mr. Murdstone, I have not worried and frightened any sweet creetur to an early grave!"

He eyed her gloomily—remorsefully I thought—for an instant; and said, turning his head towards me, but looking at my feet instead of my face:

"We are not likely to encounter soon again; a source of satisfaction to us both, no doubt, for such meetings as this can never be agreeable. I do not expect that you, who always rebelled against my just authority, exerted for your benefit and reformation, should owe me any good-will now. There is an antipathy between us——"

48

"An old one, I believe?" said I, interrupting him.

He smiled, and shot as evil a glance at me as could come from his dark eyes.

"It rankled in your baby breast," he said. "It embittered the life of your poor mother. You are right. I hope you may do better, yet; I hope you may correct yourself."

Here he ended the dialogue, which had been carried on in a low voice, in a corner of the outer office, by passing into Mr. Spenlow's room, and saying aloud, in his smoothest manner:

"Gentlemen of Mr. Spenlow's profession are accustomed to family differences, and know how complicated and difficult they always are!" With that, he paid the money for his licence; and, receiving it neatly folded from Mr. Spenlow, together with a shake of the hand, and a polite wish for his happiness and the lady's, went out of the office.

I might have had more difficulty in constraining myself to be silent under his words, if I had had less difficulty in impressing upon Peggotty (who was only angry on my account, good creature!) that we were not in a place for recrimination, and that I besought her to hold her peace. She was so unusually roused, that I was glad to compound for an affectionate hug, elicited by this revival in her mind of our old injuries, and to make the best I could of it, before Mr. Spenlow and the clerks.

Mr. Spenlow did not appear to know what the connexion between Mr. Murdstone and myself was; which I was glad of, for I could not bear to acknowledge him, even in my own breast, remembering what I did of the history of my poor mother. Mr. Spenlow seemed to think, if he thought anything about the matter, that my aunt was the leader of the state party in our family, and that there was a rebel party commanded by somebody else—so I gathered at least from what he said, while we were waiting for Mr. Tiffey to make out Peggotty's bill of costs.

"Miss Trotwood," he remarked, "is very firm, no doubt, and

not likely to give way to opposition. I have an admiration for her character, and I may congratulate you, Copperfield, on being on the right side. Differences between relations are much to be deplored—but they are extremely general—and the great thing is, to be on the right side:" meaning, I take it, on the side of the moneyed interest.

"Rather a good marriage this, I believe?" said Mr. Spenlow.

I explained that I knew nothing about it.

"Indeed!" he said. "Speaking from the few words Mr. Murdstone dropped—as a man frequently does on these occasions—and from what Miss Murdstone let fall, I should say it was rather a good marriage."

"Do you mean that there is money, sir?" I asked.

"Yes," said Mr. Spenlow, "I understand there's money. Beauty too, I am told."

"Indeed! Is his new wife young?"

"Just of age," said Mr. Spenlow. "So lately, that I should think they had been waiting for that."

"Lord deliver her!" said Peggotty. So very emphatically and unexpectedly, that we were all three discomposed; until Tiffey came in with the bill.

Old Tiffey soon appeared, however, and handed it to Mr. Spenlow, to look over. Mr. Spenlow, settling his chin in his cravat and rubbing it softly, went over the items with a deprecatory air—as if it were all Jorkins's doing—and handed it back to Tiffey with a bland sigh.

"Yes," he said. "That's right. Quite right. I should have been extremely happy, Copperfield, to have limited these charges to the actual expenditure out of pocket, but it is an irksome incident in my professional life, that I am not at liberty to consult my own wishes. I have a partner— Mr. Jorkins."

As he said this with a gentle melancholy, which was the next thing to making no charge at all, I expressed my acknowledgments on Peggotty's behalf, and paid Tiffey in bank-notes. Peggotty then retired to her lodging, and Mr. Spenlow and I went into Court, where we had a divorce-suit coming on, under an ingenious little statute (repealed now, I believe, but in virtue of which I have seen several marriages annulled), of which the merits were these. The husband, whose name was Thomas Benjamin, had taken out his marriage licence as Thomas only; suppressing the Benjamin, in case he should not find himself as comfortable as he expected. *Not* finding himself as comfortable as he expected, or being a little fatigued with his wife, poor fellow, he now came forward, by a friend, after being married a year or two, and declared that his name was Thomas Benjamin, and therefore he was not married at all. Which the Court confirmed, to his great satisfaction.

I must say that I had my doubts about the strict justice of this, and was not even frightened out of them by the bushel of wheat which reconciles all anomalies.

But Mr. Spenlow argued the matter with me. He said, Look at the world, there was good and evil in that; look at the ecclesiastical law, there was good and evil in *that*. It was all part of a system. Very good. There you were!

I had not the hardihood to suggest to Dora's father that possibly we might even improve the world a little, if we got up early in the morning, and took off our coats to the work; but I confessed that I thought we might improve the Commons. Mr. Spenlow replied that he would particularly advise me to dismiss that idea from my mind, as not being worthy of my gentlemanly character; but that he would be glad to hear from me of what improvement I thought the Commons susceptible?

Taking that part of the Commons which happened to be nearest to us—for our man was unmarried by this time, and we were out of Court, and strolling past the Prerogative Office—I submitted that I thought the Prerogative Office rather a queerly managed institution. Mr. Spenlow inquired in what respect? I replied, with all due deference to his experience (but with more deference, I am afraid, to his being Dora's father), that perhaps it was a little nonsensical that the Registry of that Court, containing the original wills of all persons leaving effects within the immense province of Canterbury, for three whole centuries, should be an accidental building, never designed for the purpose, leased by the registrars for their own private emolument, unsafe, not even ascertained to be fire-proof, choked with the important documents it held, and positively, from the roof to the basement, a mercenary speculation of the registrars, who took great fees from the public, and crammed the public's wills away anyhow and anywhere, having no other object than to get rid of them cheaply. That, perhaps, it was a little unreasonable that these registrars in the receipt of profits amounting to eight or nine thousand pounds a year (to say nothing of the profits of the deputy registrars, and clerks of seats), should not be obliged to spend a little of that money, in finding a reasonably safe place for the important documents which all classes of people were compelled to hand over to them, whether they would or no. That, perhaps, it was a little unjust, that all the great offices in this great office, should be magnificent sinecures, while the unfortunate working-clerks in the cold dark room up-stairs were the worst rewarded, and the least considered men, doing important services, in London. That perhaps it was a little indecent that the principal registrar of all, whose duty it was to find the public, constantly resorting to this place, all needful accommodation, should be an enormous sinecurist in virtue of that post (and might be, besides, a clergyman, a pluralist, the holder of a stall in a cathedral, and what not), while the public was put to the inconvenience of which we had a specimen every afternoon when the office was busy, and which we knew to be quite monstrous. That, perhaps, in short, this Prerogative Office of the diocese of Canterbury was altogether such a pestilent job, and such a pernicious absurdity, that but for its being squeezed away in a corner of Saint Paul's Churchyard, which few people knew, it must have been turned completely inside out, and upside down, long ago.

Mr. Spenlow smiled as I became modestly warm on the subject, and then argued this question with me as he had argued the other. He said, what was it after all? It was a question of feeling. If the public felt that their wills were in safe keeping, and took it for granted that the office was not to be made better, who was the worse for it? Nobody. Who was the better for it? All the sinecurists. Very well. Then the good predominated. It might not be a perfect system; nothing *was* perfect; but what he objected to, was, the insertion of the wedge. Under the Prerogative Office, the country had been glorious. Insert the wedge into the Prerogative Office, and the country would cease to be glorious. He considered it the principle of a gentleman to take things as he found them; and he had no doubt the Prerogative Office would last our time. I deferred to his opinion, though I had great doubts of it myself. I find he was right, however; for it has not only lasted to the present moment, but has done so in the teeth of a great parliamentary report made (not too willingly) eighteen years ago, when all these objections of mine were set forth in detail, and when the existing stowage for wills was described as equal to the accumulation of only two years and a half more. What they have done with them since; whether they have lost many, or whether they sell any, now and then, to the butter shops; I don't know. I am glad mine is not there, and I hope it may not go there, yet awhile.

I have set all this down, in my present blissful chapter, because here it comes into its natural place. Mr. Spenlow and I falling into this conversation, prolonged it and our saunter to and fro until we diverged into general topics. And so it came about, in the end, that Mr. Spenlow told me this day week was Dora's birthday, and he would be glad if I would come down and join a little pic-nic on the occasion. I went out of my senses immediately; became a mere driveller next day, on receipt of a little lace-edged sheet of note-paper, "Favoured by papa. To remind;" and passed the intervening period in a state of dotage.

I think I committed every possible absurdity in the way of preparation for this blessed event. I turn hot when I remember the cravat I bought. My boots might be placed in any collection of instruments of torture. I provided, and sent down by the Norwood coach the night before, a delicate little hamper, amounting in itself, I thought, almost to a declaration. There were crackers in it with the tenderest mottoes that could be got for money. At six in the morning, I was in Covent Garden Market, buying a bouquet for Dora. At ten I was on horseback (I hired a gallant grey, for the occasion), with the bouquet in my hat, to keep it fresh, trotting down to Norwood.

I suppose that when I saw Dora in the garden and pretended not to see her, and rode past the house pretending to be anxiously looking for it, I committed two small fooleries which other young gentlemen in my circumstances might have committed—because they came so very natural to me. But oh! when I *did* find the house, and *did* dismount at the garden gate, and drag those stony-hearted boots across the lawn to Dora sitting on a garden seat under a lilac tree, what a spectacle she was, upon that beautiful morning, among the butterflies, in a white chip bonnet and a dress of celestial blue!

There was a young lady with her—comparatively stricken in years—almost twenty, I should say. Her name was Miss Mills, and Dora called her Julia. She was the bosom friend of Dora. Happy Miss Mills!

Jip was there, and Jip *would* bark at me again. When I presented my bouquet, he gnashed his teeth with jealousy. Well he might. If he had the least idea how I adored his mistress, well he might!

"Oh, thank you, Mr. Copperfield! What dear flowers!" said Dora.

I PRESENT MY BOUQUET.

I had had an intention of saying (and had been studying the best form of words for three miles) that I thought them beautiful before I saw them so near *her*. But I couldn't manage it. She was too bewildering. To see her lay the flowers against her little dimpled chin, was to lose all presence of mind and power of language in a feeble ecstasy. I wonder I didn't say, "Kill me, if you have a heart, Miss Mills. Let me die here!"

Then Dora held my flowers to Jip to smell. Then Jip growled, and wouldn't smell them. Then Dora laughed, and held them a little closer to Jip, to make him. Then Jip laid hold of a bit of geranium with his teeth, and worried imaginary cats in it. Then Dora beat him, and pouted, and said, "My poor beautiful flowers!" as compassionately, I thought, as if Jip had laid hold of me. I wished he had!

"You'll be so glad to hear, Mr. Copperfield," said Dora, "that that cross Miss Murdstone is not here. She has gone to her brother's marriage, and will be away at least three weeks. Isn't that delightful?"

I said I was sure it must be delightful to her, and all that was delightful to her was delightful to me. Miss Mills, with an air of superior wisdom and benevolence, smiled upon us.

"She is the most disagreeable thing I ever saw," said Dora. "You can't believe how ill-tempered and shocking she is, Julia."

"Yes, I can, my dear!" said Julia.

"*You* can, perhaps, love," returned Dora, with her hand on Julia's. "Forgive my not excepting you, my dear, at first."

I learnt, from this, that Miss Mills had had her trials in the course of a chequered existence; and that to these, perhaps, I might refer that wise benignity of manner which I had already noticed. I found, in the course of the day, that this was the case: Miss Mills having been unhappy in a misplaced affection, and being understood to have retired from the world on her awful stock of experience, but still to take a calm interest in the unblighted hopes and loves of youth.

But now Mr. Spenlow came out of the house, and Dora went to him, saying, "Look, papa, what beautiful flowers!" And Miss Mills smiled thoughtfully, as who should say, "Ye May-flies, enjoy your brief existence in the bright morning of life!" And we all walked from the lawn towards the carriage, which was getting ready.

I shall never have such a ride again. I have never had such another. There were only those three, their hamper, my hamper, and the guitar-case, in the phaeton; and, of course, the phaeton was open; and I rode behind it, and Dora sat with her back to the horses, looking towards me. She kept the bouquet close to her on the cushion, and wouldn't allow Jip to sit on that side of her at all, for fear he should crush it. She often carried it in her hand, often refreshed herself with its fragrance. Our eyes at those times often met; and my great astonishment is that I didn't go over the head of my gallant grey into the carriage.

There was dust, I believe. There was a good deal of dust, I believe. I have a faint impression that Mr. Spenlow remonstrated with me for riding in it; but I knew of none. I was sensible of a mist of love and beauty about Dora, but of nothing else. He stood up sometimes, and asked me what I thought of the prospect. I said it was delightful, and I dare say it was; but it was all Dora to me. The sun shone Dora, and the birds sang Dora. The south wind blew Dora, and the wild flowers in the hedges were all Doras, to a bud. My comfort is, Miss Mills understood me. Miss Mills alone could enter into my feelings thoroughly.

I don't know how long we were going, and to this hour I know as little where we went. Perhaps it was near Guildford. Perhaps some Arabian-night magician opened up the place for the day, and shut it up for ever when we came away. It was a green spot, on a hill, carpeted with soft turf. There were shady trees, and heather, and, as far as the eye could see, a rich landscape.

It was a trying thing to find people here, waiting for us;

and my jealousy, even of the ladies, knew no bounds. But all of my own sex—especially one impostor, three or four years my elder, with a red whisker, on which he established an amount of presumption not to be endured—were my mortal foes.

We all unpacked our baskets, and employed ourselves in getting dinner ready. Red Whisker pretended he could make a salad (which I don't believe), and obtruded himself on public notice. Some of the young ladies washed the lettuces for him, and sliced them under his directions. Dora was among these. I felt that fate had pitted me against this man, and one of us must fall.

Red Whisker made his salad (I wondered how they could eat it. Nothing should have induced *me* to touch it!) and voted himself into the charge of the wine-cellar, which he constructed, being an ingenious beast, in the hollow trunk of a tree. By-and-bye, I saw him, with the majority of a lobster on his plate, eating his dinner at the feet of Dora!

I have but an indistinct idea of what happened for some time after this baleful object presented itself to my view. I was very merry, I know; but it was hollow merriment. I attached myself to a young creature in pink, with little eyes, and flirted with her desperately. She received my attentions with favour; but whether on my account solely, or because she had any designs on Red Whisker, I can't say. Dora's health was drunk. When I drank it, I affected to interrupt my conversation for that purpose, and to resume it immediately afterwards. I caught Dora's eye as I bowed to her, and I thought it looked appealing. But it looked at me over the head of Red Whisker, and I was adamant.

The young creature in pink had a mother in green; and I rather think the latter separated us from motives of policy. Howbeit, there was a general breaking up of the party, while the remnants of the dinner were being put away; and I strolled off by myself among the trees, in a raging and remorseful state. I was debating whether I should pretend that I was not well, and fly—I don't know where—upon my gallant grey, when Dora and Miss Mills met me.

"Mr. Copperfield," said Miss Mills, "you are dull."

I begged her pardon. Not at all.

"And Dora," said Miss Mills, "*you* are dull."

Oh dear no! Not in the least.

"Mr. Copperfield and Dora," said Miss Mills, with an almost venerable air. "Enough of this. Do not allow a trivial misunderstanding to wither the blossoms of spring, which, once put forth and blighted, cannot be renewed. I speak," said Miss Mills, "from experience of the past—the remote irrevocable past. The gushing fountains which sparkle in the sun, must not be stopped in mere caprice; the oasis in the desert of Sahara, must not be plucked up idly."

I hardly knew what I did, I was burning all over to that extraordinary extent; but I took Dora's little hand and kissed it—and she let me! I kissed Miss Mills's hand; and we all seemed, to my thinking, to go straight up to the seventh heaven.

We did not come down again. We stayed up there all the evening. At first we strayed to and fro among the trees: I with Dora's shy arm drawn through mine: and Heaven knows, folly as it all was, it would have been a happy fate to have been struck immortal with those foolish feelings, and have strayed among the trees for ever!

But, much too soon, we heard the others laughing and talking, and calling "where's Dora?" So we went back, and they wanted Dora to sing. Red Whisker would have got the guitar-case out of the carriage, but Dora told him nobody knew where it was, but I. So Red Whisker was done for in a moment; and *I* got it, and *I* unlocked it, and *I* took the guitar out, and *I* sat by her, and *I* held her handkerchief and gloves, and *I* drank in every note of her dear voice, and she sang to *me* who loved her, and all the others might applaud as much as they liked, but they had nothing to do with it!

I HAVE A GLORIFIED RIDE.

I was intoxicated with joy. I was afraid it was too happy to be real, and that I should wake in Buckingham Street presently, and hear Mrs. Crupp clinking the teacups in getting breakfast ready. But Dora sang, and others sang, and Miss Mills sang—about the slumbering echoes in the caverns of Memory; as if she were a hundred years old—and the evening came on; and we had tea, with the kettle boiling gipsy-fashion; and I was still as happy as ever.

I was happier than ever when the party broke up, and the other people, defeated Red Whisker and all, went their several ways, and we went ours through the still evening and the dying light, with sweet scents rising up around us. Mr. Spenlow being a little drowsy after the champagne—honour to the soil that grew the grape, to the grape that made the wine, to the sun that ripened it, and to the merchant who adulterated it!—and being fast asleep in a corner of the carriage, I rode by the side and talked to Dora. She admired my horse and patted him—oh, what a dear little hand it looked upon a horse!—and her shawl would not keep right, and now and then I drew it round her with my arm; and I even fancied that Jip began to see how it was, and to understand that he must make up his mind to be ·friends with me.

That sagacious Miss Mills, too; that amiable, though quite used-up, recluse; that little patriarch of something less than twenty, who had done with the world, and mustn't on any account have the slumbering echoes in the caverns of Memory awakened; what a kind thing *she* did!

"Mr. Copperfield," said Miss Mills, "come to this side of the carriage a moment—if you can spare a moment. I want to speak to you."

Behold me, on my gallant grey, bending at the side of Miss Mills, with my hand upon the carriage door!

"Dora is coming to stay with me. She is coming home with me the day after to-morrow. If you would like to call. I am sure papa would be happy to see you."

What could I do but invoke a silent blessing on Miss Mills's head, and store Miss Mills's address in the securest corner of my memory! What could I do but tell Miss Mills, with grateful looks and fervent words, how much I appreciated her good offices, and what an inestimable value I set upon her friendship!

Then Miss Mills benignantly dismissed me, saying, "Go back to Dora!" and I went; and Dora leaned out of the carriage to talk to me, and we talked all the rest of the way; and I rode my gallant grey so close to the wheel that I grazed his near fore leg against it, and "took the bark off," as his owner told me, "to the tune of three pun' sivin" —which I paid, and thought extremely cheap for so much joy. What time Miss Mills sat looking at the moon, murmuring verses and recalling, I suppose, the ancient days when she and earth had anything in common.

Norwood was many miles too near, and we reached it many hours too soon; but Mr. Spenlow came to himself a little short of it, and said, "You must come in, Copperfield, and rest!" and I consenting, we had sandwiches and wine-and-water. In the light room, Dora blushing looked so lovely, that I could not tear myself away, but sat there staring, in a dream, until the snoring of Mr. Spenlow inspired me with sufficient consciousness to take my leave. So we parted; I riding all the way to London with the farewell touch of Dora's hand still light on mine, recalling every incident and word ten thousand times; lying down in my own bed at last, as enraptured a young noodle as ever was carried out of his five wits by love.

When I awoke next morning, I was resolute to declare my passion to Dora, and know my fate. Happiness or misery was now the question. There was no other question that I knew of in the world, and only Dora could give the answer to it. I passed three days in a luxury of wretchedness, torturing myself by putting every conceivable variety of discouraging construction on all that ever had taken place between Dora and me. At last, arrayed for the purpose at a vast expense, I went to Miss Mills's, fraught with a declaration.

How many times I went up and down the street, and round the square—painfully aware of being a much better answer to the old riddle than the original one—before I could persuade myself to go up the steps and knock, is no matter now. Even when, at last, I had knocked, and was waiting at the door, I had some flurried thought of asking if that were Mr. Blackboy's (in imitation of poor Barkis), begging pardon, and retreating. But I kept my ground.

Mr. Mills was not at home. I did not expect he would be. Nobody wanted *him*. Miss Mills was at home. Miss Mills would do.

I was shown into a room up-stairs, where Miss Mills and Dora were. Jip was there. Miss Mills was copying music (I recollect, it was a new song, called Affection's Dirge), and Dora was painting flowers. What were my feelings, when I recognised my own flowers; the identical Covent Garden Market purchase! I cannot say that they were very like, or that they particularly resembled any flowers that have ever come under my observation; but I knew from the paper round them, which was accurately copied, what the composition was.

Miss Mills was very glad to see me, and very sorry her papa was not at home: though I thought we all bore that with fortitude. Miss Mills was conversational for a few minutes, and then, laying down her pen upon Affection's Dirge, got up, and left the room.

I began to think I would put it off till to-morrow.

"I hope your poor horse was not tired, when he got home at night," said Dora, lifting up her beautiful eyes. "It was a long way for him."

I began to think I would do it to-day.

"It was a long way for *him*," said I, "for *he* had nothing to uphold him on the journey."

"Wasn't he fed, poor thing?" asked Dora.

I began to think I would put it off till to-morrow.

"Ye—yes," I said, "he was well taken care of. I mean he had not the unutterable happiness that I had in being so near you."

Dora bent her head over her drawing, and said, after a little while—I had sat, in the interval, in a burning fever, and with my legs in a very rigid state—

"You didn't seem to be sensible of that happiness yourself, at one time of the day."

I saw now that I was in for it, and it must be done on the spot.

"You didn't care for that happiness in the least," said Dora, slightly raising her eyebrows, and shaking her head, "when you were sitting by Miss Kitt."

Kitt, I should observe, was the name of the creature in pink, with the little eyes.

"Though certainly I don't know why you should," said Dora, "or why you should call it a happiness at all. But of course you don't mean what you say. And I am sure no one doubts your being at liberty to do whatever you like. Jip, you naughty boy, come here!"

I don't know how I did it. I did it in a moment. I intercepted Jip. I had Dora in my arms. I was full of eloquence. I never stopped for a word. I told her how I loved her. I told her I should die without her. I told her that I idolised and worshipped her. Jip barked madly all the time.

When Dora hung her head and cried, and trembled, my eloquence increased so much the more. If she would like me to die for her, she had but to say the word, and I was ready. Life without Dora's love was not a thing to have on any terms. I couldn't bear it, and I wouldn't. I had loved her every minute, day and night, since I first saw her. I loved her at that minute to distraction. I should always love her, every minute, to distraction. Lovers had loved before, and lovers would love again; but no lover had ever loved, might, could, would, or should ever love, as I loved Dora. The more I raved, the more Jip barked. Each of us, in his own way, got more mad every moment.

Well, well! Dora and I were sitting on the sofa by-and-by, quiet enough, and Jip was lying in her lap, winking peacefully at me. It was off my mind. I was in a state of perfect rapture. Dora and I were engaged.

I suppose we had some notion that this was to end in marriage. We must have had some, because Dora stipulated that we were never to be married without her papa's consent. But, in our youthful ecstasy, I don't think that we really looked before us or behind us; or had any aspiration beyond the ignorant present. We were to keep our secret from Mr. Spenlow; but I am sure the idea never entered my head, then, that there was anything dishonourable in that.

Miss Mills was more than usually pensive when Dora, going to find her, brought her back;—I apprehend, because there was a tendency in what had passed to awaken the slumbering echoes in the caverns of Memory. But she gave us her blessing, and the assurance of her lasting friendship, and spoke to us, generally, as became a Voice from the Cloister.

What an idle time it was! What an unsubstantial, happy, foolish time it was!

When I measured Dora's finger for a ring that was to be made of Forget-me-nots, and when the jeweller, to whom I took the measure, found me out, and laughed over his order-book, and charged me anything he liked for the pretty little toy, with its blue stones—so associated in my remembrance with Dora's hand, that yesterday, when I saw such another, by chance, on the finger of my own daughter, there was a momentary stirring in my heart, like pain!

When I walked about, exalted with my secret, and full of my own interest, and felt the dignity of loving Dora, and of being beloved, so much, that if I had walked the air, I could

DAVID COPPERFIELD.

not have been more above the people not so situated, who were creeping on the earth!

When we had those meetings in the garden of the square, and sat within the dingy summer-house, so happy, that I love the London sparrows to this hour, for nothing else, and see the plumage of the tropics in their smoky feathers!

When we had our first great quarrel (within a week of our betrothal), and when Dora sent me back the ring, enclosed in a despairing cocked-hat note, wherein she used the terrible expression that "our love had begun in folly, and ended in madness!" which dreadful words occasioned me to tear my hair, and cry that all was over!

When, under cover of the night, I flew to Miss Mills, whom I saw by stealth in a back kitchen where there was a mangle, and implored Miss Mills to interpose between us and avert insanity. When Miss Mills undertook the office and returned with Dora, exhorting us, from the pulpit of her own bitter youth, to mutual concession, and the avoidance of the desert of Sahara!

When we cried, and made it up, and were so blest again, that the back kitchen, mangle and all, changed to Love's own temple, where we arranged a plan of correspondence through Miss Mills, always to comprehend at least one letter on each side every day!

What an idle time! What an unsubstantial, happy, foolish time! Of all the times of mine that Time has in his grip, there is none that in one retrospect I can smile at half so much, and think of half so tenderly.

CHAPTER XXXIV.

I WROTE to Agnes as soon as Dora and I were engaged. I wrote her a long letter, in which I tried to make her comprehend how blest I was, and what a darling Dora was. I entreated Agnes not to regard this as a thoughtless passion which could ever yield to any other, or had the least resemblance to the boyish fancies that we used to joke about. I assured her that its profundity was quite unfathomable, and expressed my belief that nothing like it had ever been known.

Somehow, as I wrote to Agnes on a fine evening by my open window, and the remembrance of her clear calm eyes and gentle face came stealing over me, it shed such a peaceful influence upon the hurry and agitation in which I had been living lately, and of which my very happiness partook in some degree, that it soothed me into tears. I remember that I sat resting my head upon my hand, when the letter was half done, cherishing a general fancy as if Agnes were one of the elements of my natural home. As if, in the retirement of the house made almost sacred to me by her presence, Dora and I must be happier than anywhere. As if, in love, joy, sorrow, hope, or disappointment; in all emotions; my heart turned naturally there, and found its refuge and best friend.

Of Steerforth, I said nothing. I only told her there had been sad grief at Yarmouth, on account of Emily's flight;

65

and that on me it made a double wound, by reason of the circumstances attending it. I knew how quick she always was to divine the truth, and that she would never be the first to breathe his name.

To this letter, I received an answer by return of post. As I read it, I seemed to hear Agnes speaking to me. It was like her cordial voice in my ears. What can I say more!

While I had been away from home lately, Traddles had called twice or thrice. Finding Peggotty within, and being informed by Peggotty (who always volunteered that information to whomsoever would receive it), that she was my old nurse, he had established a good-humoured acquaintance with her, and had stayed to have a little chat with her about me. So Peggotty said; but I am afraid the chat was all on her own side, and of immoderate length, as she was very difficult indeed to stop, God bless her! when she had me for her theme.

This reminds me, not only that I expected Traddles on a certain afternoon of his own appointing, which was now come, but that Mrs. Crupp had resigned everything appertaining to her office (the salary excepted) until Peggotty should cease to present herself. Mrs. Crupp, after holding divers conversations respecting Peggotty, in a very high-pitched voice, on the staircase—with some invisible Familiar it would appear, for corporeally speaking she was quite alone at those times—addressed a letter to me, developing her views. Beginning it with that statement of universal application, which fitted every occurrence of her life, namely, that she was a mother herself, she went on to inform me that she had once seen very different days, but that at all periods of her existence she had had a constitutional objection to spies, intruders, and informers. She named no names, she said; let them the cap fitted, wear it; but spies, intruders, and informers, especially in widders' weeds (this clause was underlined), she had ever accustomed herself to look down upon. If a gentleman was the victim of spies, intruders, and informers (but still naming no names), that was his own pleasure. He had a right to please himself; so let him do. All that she, Mrs. Crupp, stipulated for, was, that she should not be "brought in contract" with such persons. Therefore she begged to be excused from any further attendance on the top set, until things were as they formerly was, and as they could be wished to be; and further mentioned that her little book would be found upon the breakfast-table every Saturday morning, when she requested an immediate settlement of the same, with the benevolent view of saving trouble, "and an ill-con-wenience" to all parties.

After this, Mrs. Crupp confined herself to making pitfalls on the stairs, principally with pitchers, and endeavouring to delude Peggotty into breaking her legs. I found it rather harassing to live in this state of siege, but was too much afraid of Mrs. Crupp to see any way out of it.

"My dear Copperfield," cried Traddles, punctually appearing at my door, in spite of all these obstacles, "how do you do?"

"My dear Traddles," said I, "I am delighted to see you at last, and very sorry I have not been at home before. But I have been so much engaged—"

"Yes, yes, I know," said Traddles, "of course. Yours lives in London, I think."

"What did you say?"

"She—excuse me—Miss D., you know," said Traddles, colouring in his great delicacy, "lives in London, I believe?"

"Oh yes. Near London."

"Mine, perhaps you recollect," said Traddles, with a serious look, "lives down in Devonshire—one of ten. Consequently, I am not so much engaged as you—in that sense."

"I wonder you can bear," I returned, "to see her so seldom."

"Hah!" said Traddles, thoughtfully. "It does seem a wonder. I suppose it is, Copperfield, because there's no help for it?"

"I suppose so," I replied with a smile, and not without a blush. "And because you have so much constancy and patience, Traddles."

"Dear me!" said Traddles, considering about it, "do I strike you in that way, Copperfield? Really I didn't know that I had. But she is such an extraordinarily dear girl herself, that it's possible she may have imparted something of those virtues to me. Now you mention it, Copperfield, I shouldn't wonder at all. I assure you she is always forgetting herself, and taking care of the other nine."

"Is she the eldest?" I inquired.

"Oh dear, no," said Traddles. "The eldest is a Beauty."

He saw, I suppose, that I could not help smiling at the simplicity of this reply; and added, with a smile upon his own ingenuous face:

"Not, of course, but that my Sophy—pretty name, Copperfield, I always think?"

"Very pretty!" said I.

"Not, of course, but that Sophy is beautiful too in my eyes, and would be one of the dearest girls that ever was, in anybody's eyes (I should think). But when I say the eldest is a Beauty, I mean she really is a—" he seemed to be describing clouds about himself, with both hands: "Splendid, you know," said Traddles, energetically.

"Indeed!" said I.

"Oh, I assure you," said Traddles, "something very uncommon, indeed! Then, you know, being formed for society and admiration, and not being able to enjoy much of it in consequence of their limited means, she naturally gets a little irritable and exacting, sometimes. Sophy puts her in good humour!"

"Is Sophy the youngest?" I hazarded.

"Oh dear, no!" said Traddles, stroking his chin. "The two youngest are only nine and ten. Sophy educates 'em."

"The second daughter, perhaps?" I hazarded.

"No," said Traddles. "Sarah's the second. Sarah has

something the matter with her spine, poor girl. The malady will wear out by-and-bye, the doctors say, but in the meantime she has to lie down for a twelvemonth. Sophy nurses her. Sophy's the fourth."

"Is the mother living?" I inquired.

"Oh yes," said Traddles, "she is alive. She is a very superior woman indeed, but the damp country is not adapted to her constitution, and—in fact, she has lost the use of her limbs."

"Dear me!" said I.

"Very sad, is it not?" returned Traddles. "But in a merely domestic view it is not so bad as it might be, because Sophy takes her place. She is quite as much a mother *to* her mother, as she is to the other nine."

I felt the greatest admiration for the virtues of this young lady; and, honestly with the view of doing my best to prevent the good-nature of Traddles from being imposed upon, to the detriment of their joint prospects in life, inquired how Mr. Micawber was?

"He is quite well, Copperfield, thank you," said Traddles. "I am not living with him at present."

"No?"

"No. You see the truth is," said Traddles, in a whisper, "he has changed his name to Mortimer, in consequence of his temporary embarrassments; and he don't come out till after dark—and then in spectacles. There was an execution put into our house, for rent. Mrs. Micawber was in such a dreadful state that I really couldn't resist giving my name to that second bill we spoke of here. You may imagine how delightful it was to my feelings, Copperfield, to see the matter settled with it, and Mrs. Micawber recover her spirits."

"Hum!" said I.

"Not that her happiness was of long duration," pursued Traddles, "for, unfortunately, within a week another execution came in. It broke up the establishment. I have been living in a furnished apartment since then, and the Mortimers have been very private indeed. I hope you won't think it selfish, Copperfield, if I mention that the broker carried off my little round table with the marble top, and Sophy's flower-pot and stand ?"

"What a hard thing!" I exclaimed indignantly.

"It was a——it was a pull," said Traddles, with his usual wince at that expression. "I don't mention it reproachfully, however, but with a motive. The fact is, Copperfield, I was unable to repurchase them at the time of their seizure; in the first place, because the broker, having an idea that I wanted them, ran the price up to an extravagant extent; and, in the second place, because I—hadn't any money. Now, I have kept my eye since, upon the broker's shop," said Traddles, with a great enjoyment of his mystery, "which is up at the top of Tottenham Court Road, and, at last, to-day I find them put out for sale. I have only noticed them from over the way, because if the broker saw *me*, bless you, he'd ask any price for them! What has occurred to me, having now the money, is, that perhaps you wouldn't object to ask that good nurse of yours to come with me to the shop—I can show it her from round the corner of the next street—and make the best bargain for them, as if they were for herself, that she can!"

The delight with which Traddles propounded this plan to me, and the sense he had of its uncommon artfulness, are among the freshest things in my remembrance.

I told him that my old nurse would be delighted to assist him, and that we would all three take the field together, but on one condition. That condition was, that he should make a solemn resolution to grant no more loans of his name, or anything else, to Mr. Micawber.

"My dear Copperfield," said Traddles, "I have already done so, because I begin to feel that I have not only been inconsiderate, but that I have been positively unjust to Sophy. My word being passed to myself, there is no longer any apprehension; but I pledge it to you, too, with the greatest readiness. That first unlucky obligation, I have paid. I have no doubt Mr. Micawber would have paid it if he could, but he could not. One thing I ought to mention, which I like very much in Mr. Micawber, Copperfield. It refers to the second obligation, which is not yet due. He don't tell me that it *is* provided for, but he says it *will be*. Now, I think there is something very fair and honest about that!"

I was unwilling to damp my good friend's confidence, and therefore assented. After a little further conversation, we went round to the chandler's shop, to enlist Peggotty; Traddles declining to pass the evening with me, both because he endured the liveliest apprehensions that his property would be bought by somebody else before he could repurchase it, and because it was the evening he always devoted to writing to the dearest girl in the world.

I never shall forget him peeping round the corner of the street in Tottenham Court Road, while Peggotty was bargaining for the precious articles; or his agitation when she came slowly towards us after vainly offering a price, and was hailed by the relenting broker, and went back again. The end of the negotiation was, that she bought the property on tolerably easy terms, and Traddles was transported with pleasure.

"I am very much obliged to you, indeed," said Traddles, on hearing it was to be sent to where he lived, that night. "If I might ask one other favour, I hope you would not think it absurd, Copperfield?"

I said beforehand, certainly not.

"Then if you *would* be good enough," said Traddles to Peggotty, "to get the flower-pot now, I think I should like (it being Sophy's, Copperfield) to carry it home myself!"

Peggotty was glad to get it for him, and he overwhelmed her with thanks, and went his way up Tottenham Court

Road, carrying the flower-pot affectionately in his arms, with one of the most delighted expressions of countenance I ever saw.

We then turned back towards my chambers. As the shops had charms for Peggotty which I never knew them possess in the same degree for anybody else, I sauntered easily along, amused by her staring in at the windows, and waiting for her as often as she chose. We were thus a good while in getting to the Adelphi.

On our way up-stairs, I called her attention to the sudden disappearance of Mrs. Crupp's pitfalls, and also to the prints of recent footsteps. We were both very much surprised, coming higher up, to find my outer door standing open (which I had shut), and to hear voices inside.

We looked at one another, without knowing what to make of this, and went into the sitting-room. What was my amazement to find, of all people upon earth, my aunt there, and Mr. Dick! My aunt sitting on a quantity of luggage, with her two birds before her, and her cat on her knee, like a female Robinson Crusoe, drinking tea. Mr. Dick leaning thoughtfully on a great kite, such as we had often been out together to fly, with more luggage piled about him!

"My dear aunt!" cried I. "Why, what an unexpected pleasure!"

We cordially embraced; and Mr. Dick and I cordially shook hands; and Mrs. Crupp, who was busy making tea, and could not be too attentive, cordially said she had knowed well as Mr. Copperfull would have his heart in his mouth, when he see his dear relations.

"Holloa!" said my aunt to Peggotty, who quailed before her awful presence. "How are *you?*"

"You remember my aunt, Peggotty?" said I.

"For the love of goodness, child," exclaimed my aunt, "don't call the woman by that South Sea Island name! If she married and got rid of it, which was the best thing she could do, why don't you give her the benefit of the change?

My Aunt astonishes me

What's your name now,—P?" said my aunt, as a compromise for the obnoxious appellation.

"Barkis, ma'am," said Peggotty, with a curtsey.

"Well! That's human," said my aunt. "It sounds less as if you wanted a Missionary. How d'ye do, Barkis? I hope you're well?"

Encouraged by these gracious words, and by my aunt's extending her hand, Barkis came forward, and took the hand, and curtseyed her acknowledgments.

"We are older than we were, I see," said my aunt. "We have only met each other once before, you know. A nice business we made of it then! Trot, my dear, another cup."

I handed it dutifully to my aunt, who was in her usual inflexible state of figure; and ventured a remonstrance with her on the subject of her sitting on a box.

"Let me draw the sofa here, or the easy chair, aunt," said I. "Why should you be so uncomfortable?"

"Thank you, Trot," replied my aunt, "I prefer to sit upon my property." Here my aunt looked hard at Mrs. Crupp, and observed, "We needn't trouble you to wait, ma'am."

"Shall I put a little more tea in the pot afore I go, ma'am?" said Mrs. Crupp.

"No, I thank you, ma'am," replied my aunt.

"Would you let me fetch another pat of butter, ma'am?" said Mrs. Crupp. "Or would you be persuaded to try a new-laid hegg? or should I brile a rasher? Ain't there nothing I could do for your dear aunt, Mr. Copperfull?"

"Nothing, ma'am," returned my aunt. "I shall do very well, I thank you."

Mrs. Crupp, who had been incessantly smiling to express sweet temper, and incessantly holding her head on one side, to express a general feebleness of constitution, and incessantly rubbing her hands, to express a desire to be of service to all deserving objects, gradually smiled herself, one-sided herself, and rubbed herself, out of the room.

"Dick!" said my aunt. "You know what I told you about time-servers and wealth-worshippers?'

Mr. Dick—with rather a scared look, as if he had forgotten it—returned a hasty answer in the affirmative.

"Mrs. Crupp is one of them," said my aunt. "Barkis, I'll trouble you to look after the tea, and let me have another cup, for I don't fancy that woman's pouring-out!"

I knew my aunt sufficiently well to know that she had something of importance on her mind, and that there was far more matter in this arrival than a stranger might have supposed. I noticed how her eye lighted on me, when she thought my attention otherwise occupied; and what a curious process of hesitation appeared to be going on within her, while she preserved her outward stiffness and composure. I began to reflect whether I had done anything to offend her; and my conscience whispered me that I had not yet told her about Dora. Could it by any means be that, I wondered!

As I knew she would only speak in her own good time, I sat down near her, and spoke to the birds, and played with the cat, and was as easy as I could be. But I was very far from being really easy; and I should still have been so, even if Mr. Dick, leaning over the great kite behind my aunt, had not taken every secret opportunity of shaking his head darkly at me, and pointing at her.

"Trot," said my aunt at last, when she had finished her tea, and carefully smoothed down her dress, and wiped her lips—"you needn't go, Barkis!—Trot, have you got to be firm, and self-reliant?"

"I hope so, aunt."

"What do you think?" inquired Miss Betsey.

"I think so, aunt."

"Then why, my love," said my aunt, looking earnestly at me, "why do you think I prefer to sit upon this property of mine to-night?"

I shook my head, unable to guess.

I RECEIVE A GREAT SHOCK.

"Because," said my aunt, "it's all I have. Because I'm ruined, my dear!"

If the house, and every one of us, had tumbled out into the river together, I could hardly have received a greater shock.

"Dick knows it," said my aunt, laying her hand calmly on my shoulder. "I am ruined, my dear Trot! All I have in the world is in this room, except the cottage; and that I have left Janet to let. Barkis, I want to get a bed for this gentleman to-night. To save expense, perhaps you can make up something here for myself. Anything will do. It's only for to-night. We'll talk about this, more, to-morrow."

I was roused from my amazement, and concern for her—I am sure, for her—by her falling on my neck for a moment, and crying that she only grieved for me. In another moment she suppressed this emotion; and said with an aspect more triumphant than dejected:

"We must meet reverses boldly, and not suffer them to frighten us, my dear. We must learn to act the play out. We must live misfortune down, Trot!"

CHAPTER XXXV.

DEPRESSION.

As soon as I could recover my presence of mind, which quite deserted me in the first overpowering shock of my aunt's intelligence, I proposed to Mr. Dick to come round to the chandler's shop, and take possession of the bed which Mr. Peggotty had lately vacated. The chandler's shop being in Hungerford Market, and Hungerford Market being a very different place in those days, there was a low wooden colonnade before the door (not very unlike that before the house where the little man and woman used to live, in the old weather-glass), which pleased Mr. Dick mightily. The glory of lodging over this structure would have compensated him, I dare say, for many inconveniences; but, as there were really few to bear, beyond the compound of flavours I have already mentioned, and perhaps the want of a little more elbow-room, he was perfectly charmed with his accommodation. Mrs. Crupp had indignantly assured him that there wasn't room to swing a cat there; but, as Mr. Dick justly observed to me, sitting down on the foot of the bed, nursing his leg, "You know, Trotwood, I don't want to swing a cat. I never do swing a cat. Therefore, what does that signify to *me!*"

I tried to ascertain whether Mr. Dick had any understanding of the causes of this sudden and great change in my aunt's affairs. As I might have expected, he had none at

76

all. The only account he could give of it, was, that my aunt had said to him, the day before yesterday, "Now, Dick, are you really and truly the philosopher I take you for?" That then he had said, Yes, he hoped so. That then my aunt had said, "Dick, I am ruined." That then he had said, "Oh, indeed!" That then my aunt had praised him highly, which he was very glad of. And that then they had come to me, and had had bottled porter and sandwiches on the road.

Mr. Dick was so very complacent, sitting on the foot of the bed, nursing his leg, and telling me this, with his eyes wide open and a surprised smile, that I am sorry to say I was provoked into explaining to him that ruin meant distress, want, and starvation; but, I was soon bitterly reproved for this harshness, by seeing his face turn pale, and tears course down his lengthened cheeks, while he fixed upon me a look of such unutterable woe, that it might have softened a far harder heart than mine. I took infinitely greater pains to cheer him up again than I had taken to depress him; and I soon understood (as I ought to have known at first) that he had been so confident, merely because of his faith in the wisest and most wonderful of women, and his unbounded reliance on my intellectual resources. The latter, I believe, he considered a match for any kind of disaster not absolutely mortal.

"What can we do, Trotwood?" said Mr. Dick. "There's the Memorial—"

"To be sure there is," said I. "But all we can do just now, Mr. Dick, is to keep a cheerful countenance, and not let my aunt see that we are thinking about it."

He assented to this in the most earnest manner; and implored me, if I should see him wandering an inch out of the right course, to recall him by some of those superior methods which were always at my command. But I regret to state that the fright I had given him proved too much for his best attempts at concealment. All the evening his eyes wandered to my aunt's face, with an expression of the most dismal apprehension, as if he saw her growing thin on the spot. He was conscious of this, and put a constraint upon his head; but his keeping that immovable, and sitting rolling his eyes like a piece of machinery, did not mend the matter at all. I saw him look at the loaf at supper (which happened to be a small one), as if nothing else stood between us and famine; and when my aunt insisted on his making his customary repast, I detected him in the act of pocketing fragments of his bread and cheese; I have no doubt for the purpose of reviving us with those savings, when we should have reached an advanced stage of attenuation.

My aunt, on the other hand, was in a composed frame of mind, which was a lesson to all of us—to me, I am sure. She was extremely gracious to Peggotty, except when I inadvertently called her by that name; and, strange as I knew she felt in London, appeared quite at home. She was to have my bed, and I was to lie in the sitting-room, to keep guard over her. She made a great point of being so near the river, in case of a conflagration; and I suppose really did find some satisfaction in that circumstance.

"Trot, my dear," said my aunt, when she saw me making preparations for compounding her usual night-draught, "No!"

"Nothing, aunt?"

"Not wine, my dear. Ale."

"But there is wine here, aunt. And you always have it made of wine."

"Keep that, in case of sickness," said my aunt. "We mustn't use it carelessly, Trot. Ale for me. Half a pint."

I thought Mr. Dick would have fallen, insensible. My aunt being resolute, I went out and got the ale myself. As it was growing late, Peggotty and Mr. Dick took that opportunity of repairing to the chandler's shop together. I parted from him, poor fellow, at the corner of the street, with his great kite at his back, a very monument of human misery.

ALONE WITH MY AUNT.

My aunt was walking up and down the room when I returned, crimping the borders of her nightcap with her fingers. I warmed the ale and made the toast on the usual infallible principles. When it was ready for her, she was ready for it, with her nightcap on, and the skirt of her gown turned back on her knees.

"My dear," said my aunt, after taking a spoonful of it; "it's a great deal better than wine. Not half so bilious."

I suppose I looked doubtful, for she added:

"Tut, tut, child. If nothing worse than Ale happens to us, we are well off."

"I should think so myself, aunt, I am sure," said I.

"Well, then, why *don't* you think so?" said my aunt.

"Because you and I are very different people," I returned.

"Stuff and nonsense, Trot!" replied my aunt.

My aunt went on with a quiet enjoyment, in which there was very little affectation, if any; drinking the warm ale with a tea-spoon, and soaking her strips of toast in it.

"Trot," said she, "I don't care for strange faces in general, but I rather like that Barkis of yours, do you know!"

"It's better than a hundred pounds to hear you say so!" said I.

"It's a most extraordinary world," observed my aunt, rubbing her nose; "how that woman ever got into it with that name, is unaccountable to me. It would be much more easy to be born a Jackson, or something of that sort, one would think."

"Perhaps she thinks so, too; it's not her fault," said I.

"I suppose not," returned my aunt, rather grudging the admission; "but it's very aggravating. However, she's Barkis *now*. That's some comfort. Barkis is uncommonly fond of you, Trot."

"There is nothing she would leave undone to prove it," said I.

"Nothing, I believe," returned my aunt. "Here, the poor fool has been begging and praying about handing over some of her money—because she has got too much of it. A simpleton!"

My aunt's tears of pleasure were positively trickling down into the warm ale.

"She's the most ridiculous creature that ever was born," said my aunt. "I knew, from the first moment when I saw her with that poor dear blessed baby of a mother of yours, that she was the most ridiculous of mortals. But there are good points in Barkis!"

Affecting to laugh, she got an opportunity of putting her hand to her eyes. Having availed herself of it, she resumed her toast and her discourse together.

"Ah! Mercy upon us!" sighed my aunt. "I know all about it, Trot! Barkis and myself had quite a gossip while you were out with Dick. I know all about it. I don't know where these wretched girls expect to go to, for my part. I wonder they don't knock out their brains against —against mantelpieces," said my aunt; an idea which was probably suggested to her by her contemplation of mine.

"Poor Emily!" said I.

"Oh, don't talk to me about poor," returned my aunt. "She should have thought of that, before she caused so much misery! Give me a kiss, Trot. I am sorry for your early experience."

As I bent forward, she put her tumbler on my knee to detain me, and said:

"Oh, Trot, Trot! And so you fancy yourself in love! Do you?"

"Fancy, aunt!" I exclaimed, as red as I could be. "I adore her with my whole soul!"

"Dora, indeed!" returned my aunt. "And you mean to say the little thing is very fascinating, I suppose?"

"My dear aunt," I replied, "no one can form the least idea what she is!"

"Ah! And not silly?" said my aunt.

"Silly, aunt!"

MY AUNT'S GENTLENESS.

I seriously believe it had never once entered my head for a single moment, to consider whether she was or not. I resented the idea, of course; but I was in a manner struck by it, as a new one altogether.

"Not light-headed?" said my aunt.

"Light-headed, aunt!" I could only repeat this daring speculation with the same kind of feeling with which I had repeated the preceding question.

"Well, well!" said my aunt. "I only ask. I don't depreciate her. Poor little couple! And so you think you were formed for one another, and are to go through a party-supper-table kind of life, like two pretty pieces of confectionery, do you, Trot?"

She asked me this so kindly, and with such a gentle air, half playful and half sorrowful, that I was quite touched.

"We are young and inexperienced, aunt, I know," I replied; "and I dare say we say and think a good deal that is rather foolish. But we love one another truly, I am sure. If I thought Dora could ever love anybody else, or cease to love me; or that I could ever love anybody else, or cease to love her; I don't know what I should do—go out of my mind, I think!"

"Ah, Trot!" said my aunt, shaking her head, and smiling gravely, "blind, blind, blind!"

"Some one that I know, Trot," my aunt pursued, after a pause, "though of a very pliant disposition, has an earnestness of affection in him that reminds me of poor Baby. Earnestness is what that Somebody must look for, to sustain him and improve him, Trot. Deep, downright, faithful earnestness."

"If you only knew the earnestness of Dora, aunt!" I cried.

"Oh, Trot!" she said again; "blind, blind!" and without knowing why, I felt a vague unhappy loss or want of something overshadow me like a cloud.

"However," said my aunt, "I don't want to put two young

81

creatures out of conceit with themselves, or to make them unhappy; so, though it is a girl and boy attachment, and girl and boy attachments very often—mind! I don't say always!—come to nothing, still we'll be serious about it, and hope for a prosperous issue one of these days. There's time enough for it to come to anything!"

This was not upon the whole very comforting to a rapturous lover; but I was glad to have my aunt in my confidence, and I was mindful of her being fatigued. So I thanked her ardently for this mark of her affection, and for all her other kindnesses towards me; and after a tender good-night, she took her nightcap into my bedroom.

How miserable I was, when I lay down! How I thought and thought about my being poor, in Mr. Spenlow's eyes; about my not being what I thought I was, when I proposed to Dora; about the chivalrous necessity of telling Dora what my worldly condition was, and releasing her from her engagement if she thought fit; about how I should contrive to live, during the long term of my articles, when I was earning nothing; about doing something to assist my aunt, and seeing no way of doing anything; about coming down to have no money in my pocket, and to wear a shabby coat, and to be able to carry Dora no little presents, and to ride no gallant greys, and to show myself in no agreeable light! Sordid and selfish as I knew it was, and as I tortured myself by knowing that it was, to let my mind run on my own distress so much, I was so devoted to Dora that I could not help it. I knew that it was base in me not to think more of my aunt, and less of myself; but, so far, selfishness was inseparable from Dora, and I could not put Dora on one side for any mortal creature. How exceedingly miserable I was, that night!

As to sleep, I had dreams of poverty in all sorts of shapes, but I seemed to dream without the previous ceremony of going to sleep. Now I was ragged, wanting to sell Dora matches, six bundles for a halfpenny; now I was at the office in a nightgown and boots, remonstrated with by Mr. Spenlow on appearing before the clients in that airy attire; now I was hungrily picking up the crumbs that fell from old Tiffey's daily biscuit, regularly eaten when St. Paul's struck one; now I was hopelessly endeavouring to get a licence to marry Dora, having nothing but one of Uriah Heep's gloves to offer in exchange, which the whole Commons rejected; and still, more or less conscious of my own room, I was always tossing about like a distressed ship in a sea of bed-clothes.

My aunt was restless, too, for I frequently heard her walking to and fro. Two or three times in the course of the night, attired in a long flannel wrapper in which she looked seven feet high, she appeared, like a disturbed ghost, in my room, and came to the side of the sofa on which I lay. On the first occasion I started up in alarm, to learn that she inferred from a particular light in the sky, that Westminster Abbey was on fire; and to be consulted in reference to the probability of its igniting Buckingham Street, in case the wind changed. Lying still, after that, I found that she sat down near me, whispering to herself "Poor boy!" And then it made me twenty times more wretched, to know how unselfishly mindful she was of me, and how selfishly mindful I was of myself.

It was difficult to believe that a night so long to me, could be short to anybody else. This consideration set me thinking and thinking of an imaginary party where people were dancing the hours away, until that became a dream too, and I heard the music incessantly playing one tune, and saw Dora incessantly dancing one dance, without taking the least notice of me. The man who had been playing the harp all night, was trying in vain to cover it with an ordinary-sized nightcap, when I awoke; or I should rather say, when I left off trying to go to sleep, and saw the sun shining in through the window at last.

There was an old Roman bath in those days at the bottom of one of the streets out of the Strand—it may be there still

—in which I have had many a cold plunge. Dressing myself as quietly as I could, and leaving Peggotty to look after my aunt, I tumbled head foremost into it, and then went for a walk to Hampstead. I had a hope that this brisk treatment might freshen my wits a little; and I think it did them good, for I soon came to the conclusion that the first step I ought to take was to try if my articles could be cancelled and the premium recovered. I got some breakfast on the Heath, and walked back to Doctors' Commons, along the watered roads and through a pleasant smell of summer flowers, growing in gardens and carried into town on hucksters' heads, intent on this first effort to meet our altered circumstances.

I arrived at the office so soon, after all, that I had half an hour's loitering about the Commons, before old Tiffey, who was always first, appeared with his key. Then I sat down in my shady corner, looking up at the sunlight on the opposite chimney-pots, and thinking about Dora; until Mr. Spenlow came in, crisp and curly.

"How are you, Copperfield?" said he. "Fine morning!"

"Beautiful morning, sir," said I. "Could I say a word to you before you go into Court?"

"By all means," said he. "Come into my room."

I followed him into his room, and he began putting on his gown, and touching himself up before a little glass he had, hanging inside a closet door.

"I am sorry to say," said I, "that I have some rather disheartening intelligence from my aunt."

"No!" said he. "Dear me! Not paralysis, I hope?"

"It has no reference to her health, sir," I replied. "She has met with some large losses. In fact, she has very little left, indeed."

"You as-tound me, Copperfield!" cried Mr. Spenlow.

I shook my head. "Indeed, sir," said I, "her affairs are so changed, that I wished to ask you whether it would be possible—at a sacrifice on our part of some portion of the premium, of course," I put in this, on the spur of the moment, warned by the blank expression of his face—"to cancel my articles?"

What it cost me to make this proposal, nobody knows. It was like asking, as a favour, to be sentenced to transportation from Dora.

"To cancel your articles, Copperfield? Cancel?"

I explained with tolerable firmness, that I really did not know where my means of subsistence were to come from, unless I could earn them for myself. I had no fear for the future, I said—and I laid great emphasis on that, as if to imply that I should still be decidedly eligible for a son-in-law one of these days—but, for the present, I was thrown upon my own resources.

"I am extremely sorry to hear this, Copperfield," said Mr. Spenlow. "Extremely sorry. It is not usual to cancel articles for any such reason. It is not a professional course of proceeding. It is not a convenient precedent at all. Far from it. At the same time—"

"You are very good, sir," I murmured, anticipating a concession.

"Not at all. Don't mention it," said Mr. Spenlow. "At the same time, I was going to say, if it had been my lot to have my hands unfettered—if I had not a partner—Mr. Jorkins—"

My hopes were dashed in a moment, but I made another effort.

"Do you think, sir," said I, "if I were to mention it to Mr. Jorkins—"

Mr. Spenlow shook his head discouragingly. "Heaven forbid, Copperfield," he replied, "that I should do any man an injustice : still less, Mr. Jorkins. But I know my partner, Copperfield. Mr. Jorkins is *not* a man to respond to a proposition of this peculiar nature. Mr. Jorkins is very difficult to move from the beaten track. You know what he is!"

I am sure I knew nothing about him, except that he had

originally been alone in the business, and now lived by himself in a house near Montagu Square, which was fearfully in want of painting; that he came very late of a day, and went away very early; that he never appeared to be consulted about anything; and that he had a dingy little black-hole of his own up-stairs, where no business was ever done, and where there was a yellow old cartridge-paper pad upon his desk, unsoiled by ink, and reported to be twenty years of age.

"Would you object to my mentioning it to him, sir?" I asked.

"By no means," said Mr. Spenlow. "But I have some experience of Mr. Jorkins, Copperfield. I wish it were otherwise, for I should be happy to meet your views in any respect. I cannot have the least objection to your mentioning it to Mr. Jorkins, Copperfield, if you think it worth while."

Availing myself of this permission, which was given with a warm shake of the hand, I sat thinking about Dora, and looking at the sunlight stealing from the chimney-pots down the wall of the opposite house, until Mr. Jorkins came. I then went up to Mr. Jorkins's room, and evidently astonished Mr. Jorkins very much by making my appearance there.

"Come in, Mr. Copperfield," said Mr. Jorkins. "Come in!"

I went in, and sat down; and stated my case to Mr. Jorkins pretty much as I had stated it to Mr. Spenlow. Mr. Jorkins was not by any means the awful creature one might have expected, but a large, mild, smooth-faced man of sixty, who took so much snuff that there was a tradition in the Commons that he lived principally on that stimulant, having little room in his system for any other article of diet.

"You have mentioned this to Mr. Spenlow, I suppose?" said Mr. Jorkins; when he had heard me, very restlessly, to an end.

I answered Yes, and told him that Mr. Spenlow had introduced his name.

"He said I should object?" asked Mr. Jorkins.

I was obliged to admit that Mr. Spenlow had considered it probable.

"I am sorry to say, Mr. Copperfield, I can't advance your object," said Mr. Jorkins, nervously. "The fact is—but I have an appointment at the Bank, if you'll have the goodness to excuse me."

With that he rose in a great hurry, and was going out of the room, when I made bold to say that I feared, then, there was no way of arranging the matter?

"No!" said Mr. Jorkins, stopping at the door to shake his head. "Oh, no! I object, you know," which he said very rapidly, and went out. "You must be aware, Mr. Copperfield," he added, looking restlessly in at the door again, "if Mr. Spenlow objects—"

"Personally, he does not object, sir," said I.

"Oh! Personally!" repeated Mr. Jorkins, in an impatient manner. "I assure you there's an objection, Mr. Copperfield. Hopeless! What you wish to be done, can't be done. I—I really have got an appointment at the Bank." With that he fairly ran away; and to the best of my knowledge, it was three days before he showed himself in the Commons again.

Being very anxious to leave no stone unturned, I waited until Mr. Spenlow came in, and then described what had passed; giving him to understand that I was not hopeless of his being able to soften the adamantine Jorkins, if he would undertake the task.

"Copperfield," returned Mr. Spenlow, with a gracious smile, "you have not known my partner, Mr. Jorkins, as long as I have. Nothing is farther from my thoughts than to attribute any degree of artifice to Mr. Jorkins. But Mr. Jorkins has a way of stating his objections which often deceives people. No, Copperfield!" shaking his head. "Mr. Jorkins is not to be moved, believe me!"

I was completely bewildered between Mr. Spenlow and Mr. Jorkins, as to which of them really was the objecting partner; but I saw with sufficient clearness that there was obduracy somewhere in the firm, and that the recovery of my aunt's thousand pounds was out of the question. In a state of despondency, which I remember with anything but satisfaction, for I know it still had too much reference to myself (though always in connexion with Dora), I left the office, and went homeward.

I was trying to familiarise my mind with the worst, and to present to myself the arrangements we should have to make for the future in their sternest aspect, when a hackney chariot coming after me, and stopping at my very feet, occasioned me to look up. A fair hand was stretched forth to me from the window; and the face I had never seen without a feeling of serenity and happiness, from the moment when it first turned back on the old oak staircase with the great broad balustrade, and when I associated its softened beauty with the stained glass window in the church, was smiling on me.

"Agnes!" I joyfully exclaimed. "Oh, my dear Agnes, of all people in the world, what a pleasure to see you!"

"Is it, indeed?" she said, in her cordial voice.

"I want to talk to you so much!" said I. "It's such a lightening of my heart, only to look at you! If I had had a conjurer's cap, there is no one I should have wished for but you!"

"What?" returned Agnes.

"Well! perhaps Dora first," I admitted, with a blush.

"Certainly, Dora first, I hope," said Agnes, laughing.

"But you next!" said I. "Where are you going?"

She was going to my rooms to see my aunt. The day being very fine, she was glad to come out of the chariot, which smelt (I had my head in it all this time) like a stable put under a cucumber-frame. I dismissed the coachman, and she took my arm, and we walked on together. She was like Hope embodied, to me. How different I felt in one short minute, having Agnes at my side!

My aunt had written her one of the odd, abrupt notes—

very little longer than a Bank note—to which her epistolary efforts were usually limited. She had stated therein that she had fallen into adversity, and was leaving Dover for good, but had quite made up her mind to it, and was so well that nobody need be uncomfortable about her. Agnes had come to London to see my aunt, between whom and herself there had been a mutual liking these many years; indeed, it dated from the time of my taking up my residence in Mr. Wickfield's house. She was not alone, she said. Her papa was with her—and Uriah Heep.

"And now they are partners," said I. "Confound him!"

"Yes," said Agnes. "They have some business here; and I took advantage of their coming, to come too. You must not think my visit all friendly and disinterested, Trotwood, for—I am afraid I may be cruelly prejudiced—I do not like to let papa go away alone, with him."

"Does he exercise the same influence over Mr. Wickfield still, Agnes?"

Agnes shook her head. "There is such a change at home," said she, "that you would scarcely know the dear old house. They live with us now."

"They?" said I.

"Mr. Heep and his mother. He sleeps in your old room," said Agnes, looking up into my face.

"I wish I had the ordering of his dreams," said I. "He wouldn't sleep there long."

"I keep my own little room," said Agnes, "where I used to learn my lessons. How the time goes! You remember? The little panelled room that opens from the drawing-room?"

"Remember, Agnes? When I saw you, for the first time, coming out at the door, with your quaint little basket of keys hanging at your side?"

"It is just the same," said Agnes, smiling. "I am glad you think of it so pleasantly. We were very happy."

"We were, indeed," said I.

"I keep that room to myself still; but I cannot always

desert Mrs. Heep, you know. And so," said Agnes, quietly, "I feel obliged to bear her company, when I might prefer to be alone. But I have no other reason to complain of her. If she tires me, sometimes, by her praises of her son, it is only natural in a mother. He is a very good son to her."

I looked at Agnes when she said these words, without detecting in her any consciousness of Uriah's design. Her mild but earnest eyes met mine with their own beautiful frankness, and there was no change in her gentle face.

"The chief evil of their presence in the house," said Agnes, "is that I cannot be as near papa as I could wish—Uriah Heep being so much between us—and cannot watch over him, if that is not too bold a thing to say, as closely as I would. But, if any fraud or treachery is practising against him, I hope that simple love and truth will be stronger, in the end. I hope that real love and truth are stronger in the end than any evil or misfortune in the world."

A certain bright smile, which I never saw on any other face, died away, even while I thought how good it was, and how familiar it had once been to me; and she asked me, with a quick change of expression (we were drawing very near my street), if I knew how the reverse in my aunt's circumstances had been brought about. On my replying no, she had not told me yet, Agnes became thoughtful, and I fancied I felt her arm tremble in mine.

We found my aunt alone, in a state of some excitement. A difference of opinion had arisen between herself and Mrs. Crupp, on an abstract question (the propriety of chambers being inhabited by the gentler sex); and my aunt, utterly indifferent to spasms on the part of Mrs. Crupp, had cut the dispute short, by informing that lady that she smelt of my brandy, and that she would trouble her to walk out. Both of these expressions Mrs. Crupp considered actionable, and had expressed her intention of bringing before a "British Judy"—meaning, it was supposed, the bulwark of our national liberties.

My aunt, however, having had time to cool, while Peggotty was out showing Mr. Dick the soldiers at the Horse Guards —and being, besides, greatly pleased to see Agnes—rather plumed herself on the affair than otherwise, and received us with unimpaired good humour. When Agnes laid her bonnet on the table, and sat down beside her, I could not but think, looking on her mild eyes and her radiant forehead, how natural it seemed to have her there: how trustfully, although she was so young and inexperienced, my aunt confided in her; how strong she was, indeed, in simple love and truth.

We began to talk about my aunt's losses, and I told them what I had tried to do that morning.

"Which was injudicious, Trot," said my aunt, "but well meant. You are a generous boy—I suppose I must say, young man, now—and I am proud of you, my dear. So far so good. Now, Trot and Agnes, let us look the case of Betsey Trotwood in the face, and see how it stands."

I observed Agnes turn pale, as she looked very attentively at my aunt. My aunt, patting her cat, looked very attentively at Agnes.

"Betsey Trotwood," said my aunt, who had always kept her money matters to herself: "—I don't mean your sister, Trot, my dear, but myself—had a certain property. It don't matter how much; enough to live on. More; for she had saved a little, and added to it. Betsey funded her property for some time, and then, by the advice of her man of business, laid it out on landed security. That did very well, and returned very good interest, till Betsey was paid off. I am talking of Betsey as if she was a man-of-war. Well! Then, Betsey had to look about her, for a new investment. She thought she was wiser, now, than her man of business, who was not such a good man of business by this time, as he used to be—I am alluding to your father, Agnes—and she took it into her head to lay it out for herself. So she took her pigs," said my aunt, "to a foreign market; and a very bad market it turned out to be. First, she lost in the mining way, and then she lost in the diving way—fishing up treasure, or some such Tom Tidler nonsense," explained my aunt, rubbing her nose; "and then she lost in the mining way again, and, last of all, to set the thing entirely to rights, she lost in the banking way. I don't know what the Bank shares were worth for a little while," said my aunt; "cent per cent was the lowest of it, I believe; but the Bank was at the other end of the world, and tumbled into space, for what I know; anyhow, it fell to pieces, and never will and never can pay sixpence; and Betsey's sixpences were all there, and there's an end of them. Least said, soonest mended!"

My aunt concluded this philosophical summary, by fixing her eyes with a kind of triumph on Agnes, whose colour was gradually returning.

"Dear Miss Trotwood, is that all the history?" said Agnes.

"I hope it's enough, child," said my aunt. "If there had been more money to lose, it wouldn't have been all, I dare say. Betsey would have contrived to throw that after the rest, and make another chapter, I have little doubt. But, there was no more money, and there's no more story."

Agnes had listened at first with suspended breath. Her colour still came and went, but she breathed more freely. I thought I knew why. I thought she had had some fear that her unhappy father might be in some way to blame for what had happened. My aunt took her hand in hers, and laughed.

"Is that all?" repeated my aunt. "Why, yes, that's all, except, 'And she lived happy ever afterwards.' Perhaps I may add that of Betsey yet, one of these days. Now, Agnes, you have a wise head. So have you, Trot, in some things, though I can't compliment you always;" and here my aunt shook her own at me, with an energy peculiar to herself. "What's to be done? Here's the cottage, taking one time with another, will produce, say seventy pounds a-year. I think we may safely put it down at that. Well!—That's all we've got," said my aunt; with whom it was an idiosyncrasy, as it is with some horses, to stop very short when she appeared to be in a fair way of going on for a long while.

"Then," said my aunt, after a rest, "there's Dick. He's good for a hundred a-year, but of course that must be expended on himself. I would sooner send him away, though I know I am the only person who appreciates him, than have him, and not spend his money on himself. How can Trot and I do best, upon our means? What do you say, Agnes?"

"*I* say, aunt," I interposed, "that I must do something!"

"Go for a soldier, do you mean?" returned my aunt, alarmed; "or go to sea? I won't hear of it. You are to be a proctor. We're not going to have any knockings on the head in *this* family, if you please, sir."

I was about to explain that I was not desirous of introducing that mode of provision into the family, when Agnes inquired if my rooms were held for any long term?

"You come to the point, my dear," said my aunt. "They are not to be got rid of, for six months at least, unless they could be underlet, and that I don't believe. The last man died here. Five people out of six *would* die—of course—of that woman in nankeen with the flannel petticoat. I have a little ready money; and I agree with you, the best thing we can do, is, to live the term out here, and get Dick a bedroom hard by."

I thought it my duty to hint at the discomfort my aunt would sustain, from living in a continual state of guerilla warfare with Mrs. Crupp; but she disposed of that objection summarily by declaring, that, on the first demonstration of hostilities, she was prepared to astonish Mrs. Crupp for the whole remainder of her natural life.

"I have been thinking, Trotwood," said Agnes, diffidently, "that if you had time—"

"I have a good deal of time, Agnes. I am always disengaged after four or five o'clock, and I have time early in the morning. In one way and another," said I, conscious of reddening a little as I thought of the hours and hours I had devoted to fagging about town, and to and fro upon the Norwood Road, "I have abundance of time."

"I know you would not mind," said Agnes, coming to me, and speaking in a low voice, so full of sweet and hopeful consideration that I hear it now, "the duties of a secretary."

"Mind, my dear Agnes?"

"Because," continued Agnes, "Doctor Strong has acted on his intention of retiring, and has come to live in London; and he asked papa, I know, if he could recommend him one. Don't you think he would rather have his favourite old pupil near him, than anybody else?"

"Dear Agnes!" said I. "What should I do without you! You are always my good angel. I told you so. I never think of you in any other light."

Agnes answered with her pleasant laugh, that one good Angel (meaning Dora) was enough; and went on to remind me that the Doctor had been used to occupy himself in his study, early in the morning, and in the evening—and that probably my leisure would suit his requirements very well. I was scarcely more delighted with the prospect of earning my own bread, than with the hope of earning it under my old master; in short, acting on the advice of Agnes, I sat down and wrote a letter to the Doctor, stating my object, and appointing to call on him next day at ten in the forenoon. This I addressed to Highgate—for in that place, so memorable to me, he lived—and went and posted, myself, without losing a minute.

Wherever Agnes was, some agreeable token of her noiseless presence seemed inseparable from the place. When I came back, I found my aunt's birds hanging, just as they had hung so long in the parlour window of the cottage; and my easy chair imitating my aunt's much easier chair in its position at the open window; and even the round green fan, which my aunt had brought away with her, screwed on to the window-sill. I knew who had done all this, by its seeming to have quietly done itself; and I should have known in a moment who had arranged my neglected books in the old order of my school days, even if I had supposed Agnes to be miles away, instead of seeing her busy with them, and smiling at the disorder into which they had fallen.

My aunt was quite gracious on the subject of the Thames (it really did look very well with the sun upon it, though not like the sea before the cottage), but she could not relent towards the London smoke, which, she said, "peppered everything." A complete revolution, in which Peggotty bore a prominent part, was being effected in every corner of my rooms, in regard of this pepper; and I was looking on, thinking how little even Peggotty seemed to do with a good deal of bustle, and how much Agnes did without any bustle at all, when a knock came at the door.

"I think," said Agnes, turning pale, "it's papa. He promised me that he would come."

I opened the door, and admitted, not only Mr. Wickfield, but Uriah Heep. I had not seen Mr. Wickfield for some time. I was prepared for a great change in him, after what I had heard from Agnes, but his appearance shocked me.

It was not that he looked many years older, though still dressed with the old scrupulous cleanliness; or that there was an unwholesome ruddiness upon his face; or that his eyes were full and bloodshot; or that there was a nervous trembling in his hand, the cause of which I knew, and had for some years seen at work. It was not that he had lost his good looks, or his old bearing of a gentleman—for that he had not—but the thing that struck me most was, that with the evidences of his native superiority still upon him, he should submit himself to that crawling impersonation of meanness, Uriah Heep. The reversal of the two natures, in their relative positions, Uriah's of power and Mr. Wickfield's of dependence, was a sight more painful to me than I can express. If I had seen an Ape taking command of a Man, I should hardly have thought it a more degrading spectacle.

He appeared to be only too conscious of it himself. When he came in, he stood still; and with his head bowed, as if he felt it. This was only for a moment; for Agnes softly said to him, "Papa! Here is Miss Trotwood—and Trotwood, whom you have not seen for a long while!" and then he approached, and constrainedly gave my aunt his hand, and shook hands more cordially with me. In the moment's pause I speak of, I saw Uriah's countenance form itself into a most ill-favoured smile. Agnes saw it too, I think, for she shrank from him.

What my aunt saw, or did not see, I defy the science of physiognomy to have made out, without her own consent. I believe there never was anybody with such an imperturbable countenance when she chose. Her face might have been a dead wall on the occasion in question, for any light it threw upon her thoughts; until she broke silence with her usual abruptness.

"Well, Wickfield!" said my aunt; and he looked up at her for the first time. "I have been telling your daughter how well I have been disposing of my money for myself, because I couldn't trust it to you, as you were growing rusty in business matters. We have been taking counsel together, and getting on very well, all things considered. Agnes is worth the whole firm, in my opinion."

"If I may umbly make the remark," said Uriah Heep, with a writhe, "I fully agree with Miss Betsey Trotwood, and should be only too appy if Miss Agnes was a partner."

"You're a partner yourself, you know," returned my aunt, "and that's about enough for you, I expect. How do you find yourself, sir?"

In acknowledgment of this question, addressed to him with extraordinary curtness, Mr. Heep, uncomfortably clutching the blue bag he carried, replied that he was pretty well, he thanked my aunt, and hoped she was the same.

"And you, Master—I should say, Mister Copperfield," pursued Uriah. "I hope I see you well! I am rejoiced to see you, Mister Copperfield, even under present circumstances." I believed that; for he seemed to relish them very much. "Present circumstances is not what your friends would wish for you, Mister Copperfield, but it isn't money makes the man: it's—I am really unequal with my umble powers to express what it is," said Uriah, with a fawning jerk, "but it isn't money!"

Here he shook hands with me: not in the common way, but standing at a good distance from me, and lifting my hand up and down like a pump handle, that he was a little afraid of.

"And how do you think we are looking, Master Copperfield,—I should say, Mister?" fawned Uriah. "Don't you find Mr. Wickfield blooming, sir? Years don't tell much in our firm, Master Copperfield, except in raising up the umble, namely, mother and self—and in developing," he added, as an after-thought, "the beautiful, namely, Miss Agnes."

He jerked himself about, after this compliment, in such an intolerable manner, that my aunt, who had sat looking straight at him, lost all patience.

"Deuce take the man!" said my aunt, sternly, "what's he about? Don't be galvanic, sir!"

"I ask your pardon, Miss Trotwood," returned Uriah; "I'm aware you're nervous."

"Go along with you, sir!" said my aunt, anything but appeased. "Don't presume to say so! I am nothing of the sort. If you're an eel, sir, conduct yourself like one. If you're a man, control your limbs, sir! Good God!" said my aunt, with great indignation, "I am not going to be serpentined and corkscrewed out of my senses!"

Mr. Heep was rather abashed, as most people might have been, by this explosion; which derived great additional force from the indignant manner in which my aunt afterwards moved in her chair, and shook her head as if she were making snaps or bounces at him. But, he said to me aside in a meek voice :

"I am well aware, Master Copperfield, that Miss Trotwood, though an excellent lady, has a quick temper (indeed I think I had the pleasure of knowing her, when I was an umble clerk, before you did, Master Copperfield), and it's only natural, I am sure, that it should be made quicker by present circumstances. The wonder is, that it isn't much worse! I only called to say that if there was anything we could do, in present circumstances, mother or self, or Wickfield and Heep, we should be really glad. I may go so far?" said Uriah, with a sickly smile at his partner.

"Uriah Heep," said Mr. Wickfield, in a monotonous forced way, "is active in the business, Trotwood. What he says, I quite concur in. You know I had an old interest in you. Apart from that, what Uriah says I quite concur in!"

"Oh, what a reward it is," said Uriah, drawing up one leg, at the risk of bringing down upon himself another visitation from my aunt, "to be so trusted in! But I hope I am able to do something to relieve him from the fatigues of business, Master Copperfield!"

"Uriah Heep is a great relief to me," said Mr. Wickfield, in the same dull voice. "It's a load off my mind, Trotwood, to have such a partner."

The red fox made him say all this, I knew, to exhibit him to me in the light he had indicated on the night when he poisoned my rest. I saw the same ill-favoured smile upon his face again, and saw how he watched me.

"You are not going, papa?" said Agnes, anxiously. "Will you not walk back with Trotwood and me?"

He would have looked to Uriah, I believe, before replying, if that worthy had not anticipated him.

"I am bespoke myself," said Uriah, "on business; otherwise I should have been appy to have kept with my friends. But I leave my partner to represent the firm. Miss Agnes, ever yours! I wish you good-day, Master Copperfield, and leave my umble respects for Miss Betsey Trotwood."

With those words, he retired, kissing his great hand, and leering at us like a mask.

We sat there, talking about our pleasant old Canterbury days, an hour or two. Mr. Wickfield, left to Agnes, soon became more like his former self; though there was a settled depression upon him, which he never shook off. For all that, he brightened; and had an evident pleasure in hearing us recall the little incidents of our old life, many of which he remembered very well. He said it was like those times, to be alone with Agnes and me again; and he wished to Heaven they had never changed. I am sure there was an influence in the placid face of Agnes, and in the very touch of her hand upon his arm, that did wonders for him.

My aunt (who was busy nearly all this while with Peggotty, in the inner room) would not accompany us to the place where they were staying, but insisted on my going; and I went. We dined together. After dinner, Agnes sat beside him, as of old, and poured out his wine. He took what she gave him, and no more—like a child—and we all three sat together at a window as the evening gathered in. When it was almost dark, he lay down on a sofa, Agnes pillowing his head and bending over him a little while; and when she came back to the window, it was not so dark but I could see tears glittering in her eyes.

I pray Heaven that I never may forget the dear girl in her love and truth, at that time of my life; for if I should, I must be drawing near the end, and then I would desire to remember her best! She filled my heart with such good resolutions, strengthened my weakness so, by her example, so directed—I know not how, she was too modest and gentle to advise me in many words—the wandering ardour and un-settled purpose within me, that all the little good I have done, and all the harm I have forborne, I solemnly believe I may refer to her.

And how she spoke to me of Dora, sitting at the window in the dark; listened to my praises of her; praised again; and round the little fairy-figure shed some glimpses of her own pure light, that made it yet more precious and more innocent to me! Oh, Agnes, sister of my boyhood, if I had known then, what I knew long afterwards!—

There was a beggar in the street, when I went down; and as I turned my head towards the window, thinking of her calm seraphic eyes, he made me start by muttering, as if he were an echo of the morning:

"Blind! Blind! Blind!"

CHAPTER XXXVI.

ENTHUSIASM.

I began the next day with another dive into the Roman bath, and then started for Highgate. I was not dispirited now. I was not afraid of the shabby coat, and had no yearnings after gallant greys. My whole manner of thinking of our late misfortune was changed. What I had to do, was, to show my aunt that her past goodness to me had not been thrown away on an insensible, ungrateful object. What I had to do, was, to turn the painful discipline of my younger days to account, by going to work with a resolute and steady heart. What I had to do, was, to take my woodman's axe in my hand, and clear my own way through the forest of difficulty, by cutting down the trees until I came to Dora. And I went on at a mighty rate, as if it could be done by walking.

When I found myself on the familiar Highgate road, pursuing such a different errand from that old one of pleasure, with which it was associated, it seemed as if a complete change had come on my whole life. But that did not discourage me. With the new life, came new purpose, new intention. Great was the labour; priceless the reward. Dora was the reward, and Dora must be won.

I got into such a transport, that I felt quite sorry my coat was not a little shabby already. I wanted to be cutting at those trees in the forest of difficulty, under circumstances that should prove my strength. I had a good mind to ask

101

an old man, in wire spectacles, who was breaking stones upon the road, to lend me his hammer for a little while, and let me begin to beat a path to Dora out of granite. I stimulated myself into such a heat, and got so out of breath, that I felt as if I had been earning I don't know how much. In this state, I went into a cottage that I saw was to let, and examined it narrowly,—for I felt it necessary to be practical. It would do for me and Dora admirably: with a little front garden for Jip to run about in, and bark at the tradespeople through the railings, and a capital room up-stairs for my aunt. I came out again, hotter and faster than ever, and dashed up to Highgate, at such a rate that I was there an hour too early; and, though I had not been, should have been obliged to stroll about to cool myself, before I was at all presentable.

My first care, after putting myself under this necessary course of preparation, was to find the Doctor's house. It was not in that part of Highgate where Mrs. Steerforth lived, but quite on the opposite side of the little town. When I had made this discovery, I went back, in an attraction I could not resist, to a lane by Mrs. Steerforth's, and looked over the corner of the garden wall. His room was shut up close. The conservatory doors were standing open, and Rosa Dartle was walking, bareheaded, with a quick impetuous step, up and down a gravel walk on one side of the lawn. She gave me the idea of some fierce thing, that was dragging the length of its chain to and fro upon a beaten track, and wearing its heart out.

I came softly away from my place of observation, and avoiding that part of the neighbourhood, and wishing I had not gone near it, strolled about until it was ten o'clock. The church with the slender spire, that stands on the top of the hill now, was not there then to tell me the time. An old red-brick mansion, used as a school, was in its place; and a fine old house it must have been to go to school at, as I recollect it.

I CALL ON DOCTOR STRONG.

When I approached the Doctor's cottage—a pretty old place, on which he seemed to have expended some money, if I might judge from the embellishments and repairs that had the look of being just completed—I saw him walking in the garden at the side, gaiters and all, as if he had never left off walking since the days of my pupilage. He had his old companions about him, too; for there were plenty of high trees in the neighbourhood, and two or three rooks were on the grass, looking after him, as if they had been written to about him by the Canterbury rooks, and were observing him closely in consequence.

Knowing the utter hopelessness of attracting his attention from that distance, I made bold to open the gate, and walk after him, so as to meet him when he should turn round. When he did, and came towards me, he looked at me thoughtfully for a few moments, evidently without thinking about me at all; and then his benevolent face expressed extraordinary pleasure, and he took me by both hands.

"Why, my dear Copperfield," said the Doctor; "you are a man! How do you do? I am delighted to see you. My dear Copperfield, how very much you have improved! You are quite—yes—dear me!"

I hoped he was well, and Mrs. Strong too.

"Oh dear, yes!" said the Doctor; "Annie's quite well, and she'll be delighted to see you. You were always her favourite. She said so, last night, when I showed her your letter. And—yes, to be sure—you recollect Mr. Jack Maldon, Copperfield?"

"Perfectly, sir."

"Of course," said the Doctor. "To be sure. *He's* pretty well, too."

"Has he come home, sir?" I inquired.

"From India?" said the Doctor. "Yes. Mr. Jack Maldon couldn't bear the climate, my dear. Mrs. Markleham—you have not forgotten Mrs. Markleham?"

Forgotten the Old Soldier! And in that short time!

"Mrs. Markleham," said the Doctor, "was quite vexed about him, poor thing; so we have got him at home again; and we have bought him a little Patent place, which agrees with him much better."

I knew enough of Mr. Jack Maldon to suspect from this account that it was a place where there was not much to do, and which was pretty well paid. The Doctor, walking up and down with his hand on my shoulder, and his kind face turned encouragingly to mine, went on:

"Now, my dear Copperfield, in reference to this proposal of yours. It's very gratifying and agreeable to me, I am sure; but don't you think you could do better? You achieved distinction, you know, when you were with us. You are qualified for many good things. You have laid a foundation that any edifice may be raised upon; and is it not a pity that you should devote the spring-time of your life to such a poor pursuit as I can offer?"

I became very glowing again, and, expressing myself in a rhapsodical style, I am afraid, urged my request strongly: reminding the Doctor that I had already a profession.

"Well, well," said the Doctor, "that's true. Certainly, your having a profession, and being actually engaged in studying it, makes a difference. But, my good young friend, what's seventy pounds a-year?"

"It doubles our income, Doctor Strong," said I.

"Dear me!" replied the Doctor. "To think of that! Not that I mean to say it's rigidly limited to seventy pounds a-year, because I have always contemplated making any young friend I might thus employ, a present too. Undoubtedly," said the Doctor, still walking me up and down with his hand on my shoulder. "I have always taken an annual present into account."

"My dear tutor," said I (now, really, without any nonsense), "to whom I owe more obligations already than I ever can acknowledge—"

"No, no," interposed the Doctor. "Pardon me!"

"If you will take such time as I have, and that is my mornings and evenings, and can think it worth seventy pounds a-year, you will do me such a service as I cannot express."

"Dear me!" said the Doctor, innocently. "To think that so little should go for so much! Dear, dear! And when you can do better, you will? On your word, now?" said the Doctor,—which he had always made a very grave appeal to the honour of us boys.

"On my word, sir!" I returned, answering in our old school manner.

"Then be it so," said the Doctor, clapping me on the shoulder, and still keeping his hand there, as we still walked up and down.

"And I shall be twenty times happier, sir," said I, with a little—I hope innocent—flattery, "if my employment is to be on the Dictionary."

The Doctor stopped, smilingly clapped me on the shoulder again, and exclaimed, with a triumph most delightful to behold, as if I had penetrated to the profoundest depths of mortal sagacity, "My dear young friend, you have hit it. It is the Dictionary!"

How could it be anything else! His pockets were as full of it as his head. It was sticking out of him in all directions. He told me that since his retirement from scholastic life, he had been advancing with it wonderfully; and that nothing could suit him better than the proposed arrangements for morning and evening work, as it was his custom to walk about in the day-time with his considering cap on. His papers were in a little confusion, in consequence of Mr. Jack Maldon having lately proffered his occasional services as an amanuensis, and not being accustomed to that occupation; but we should soon put right what was amiss, and go on swimmingly. Afterwards, when we were fairly at our work, I found Mr. Jack Maldon's efforts more troublesome to me than I had expected, as he had not confined himself to making numerous mistakes, but had sketched so many soldiers, and ladies' heads, over the Doctor's manuscript, that I often became involved in labyrinths of obscurity.

The Doctor was quite happy in the prospect of our going to work together on that wonderful performance, and we settled to begin next morning at seven o'clock. We were to work two hours every morning, and two or three hours every night, except on Saturdays, when I was to rest. On Sundays, of course, I was to rest also, and I considered these very easy terms.

Our plans being thus arranged to our mutual satisfaction, the Doctor took me into the house to present me to Mrs. Strong, whom we found in the Doctor's new study, dusting his books,—a freedom which he never permitted anybody else to take with those sacred favourites.

They had postponed their breakfast on my account, and we sat down to table together. We had not been seated long, when I saw an approaching arrival in Mrs. Strong's face, before I heard any sound of it. A gentleman on horseback came to the gate, and leading his horse into the little court, with the bridle over his arm, as if he were quite at home, tied him to a ring in the empty coach-house wall, and came into the breakfast parlour, whip in hand. It was Mr. Jack Maldon; and Mr. Jack Maldon was not at all improved by India, I thought. I was in a state of ferocious virtue, however, as to young men who were not cutting down the trees in the forest of difficulty; and my impression must be received with due allowance.

" Mr. Jack ! " said the Doctor. " Copperfield ! "

Mr. Jack Maldon shook hands with me; but not very warmly, I believed; and with an air of languid patronage, at which I secretly took great umbrage. But his languor altogether was quite a wonderful sight; except when he addressed himself to his cousin Annie.

" Have you breakfasted this morning, Mr. Jack ? " said the Doctor.

"I hardly ever take breakfast, sir," he replied, with his head thrown back in an easy chair. "I find it bores me."

"Is there any news to-day?" inquired the Doctor.

"Nothing at all, sir," replied Mr. Maldon. "There's an account about the people being hungry and discontented down in the North, but they are always being hungry and discontented somewhere."

The Doctor looked grave, and said, as though he wished to change the subject, "Then there's no news at all; and no news, they say, is good news."

"There's a long statement in the papers, sir, about a murder," observed Mr. Maldon. "But somebody is always being murdered, and I didn't read it."

A display of indifference to all the actions and passions of mankind was not supposed to be such a distinguished quality at that time, I think, as I have observed it to be considered since. I have known it very fashionable indeed. I have seen it displayed with such success, that I have encountered some fine ladies and gentlemen who might as well have been born caterpillars. Perhaps it impressed me the more then, because it was new to me, but it certainly did not tend to exalt my opinion of, or to strengthen my confidence in, Mr. Jack Maldon.

"I came out to inquire whether Annie would like to go to the opera to-night," said Mr. Maldon, turning to her. "It's the last good night there will be, this season; and there's a singer there, whom she really ought to hear. She is perfectly exquisite. Besides which, she is so charmingly ugly," relapsing into languor.

The Doctor, ever pleased with what was likely to please his young wife, turned to her and said:

"You must go, Annie. You must go."

"I would rather not," she said to the Doctor. "I prefer to remain at home. I would much rather remain at home."

Without looking at her cousin, she then addressed me, and asked me about Agnes, and whether she should see her, and

107

whether she was not likely to come that day; and was so much disturbed, that I wondered how even the Doctor, buttering his toast, could be blind to what was so obvious.

But he saw nothing. He told her, good-naturedly, that she was young and ought to be amused and entertained, and must not allow herself to be made dull by a dull old fellow. Moreover, he said, he wanted to hear her sing all the new singer's songs to him; and how could she do that well, unless she went? So the Doctor persisted in making the engagement for her, and Mr. Jack Maldon was to come back to dinner. This concluded, he went to his Patent place, I suppose; but at all events went away on his horse, looking very idle.

I was curious to find out next morning, whether she had been. She had not, but had sent into London to put her cousin off; and had gone out in the afternoon to see Agnes, and had prevailed upon the Doctor to go with her; and they had walked home by the fields, the Doctor told me, the evening being delightful. I wondered then, whether she would have gone if Agnes had not been in town, and whether Agnes had some good influence over her too!

She did not look very happy, I thought, but it was a good face, or a very false one. I often glanced at it, for she sat in the window all the time we were at work; and made our breakfast, which we took by snatches as we were employed. When I left, at nine o'clock, she was kneeling on the ground at the Doctor's feet, putting on his shoes and gaiters for him. There was a softened shade upon her face, thrown from some green leaves overhanging the open window of the low room; and I thought all the way to Doctors' Commons, of the night when I had seen it looking at him as he read.

I was pretty busy now; up at five in the morning, and home at nine or ten at night. But I had infinite satisfaction in being so closely engaged, and never walked slowly on any account, and felt enthusiastically that the more I tired myself, the more I was doing to deserve Dora. I had not revealed myself in my altered character to Dora yet, because she was coming to see Miss Mills in a few days, and I deferred all I had to tell her until then; merely informing her in my letters (all our communications were secretly forwarded through Miss Mills), that I had much to tell her. In the meantime, I put myself on a short allowance of bear's grease, wholly abandoned scented soap and lavender water, and sold off three waistcoats at a prodigious sacrifice, as being too luxurious for my stern career.

Not satisfied with all these proceedings, but burning with impatience to do something more, I went to see Traddles, now lodging up behind the parapet of a house in Castle Street, Holborn. Mr. Dick, who had been with me to Highgate twice already, and had resumed his companionship with the Doctor, I took with me.

I took Mr. Dick with me, because, acutely sensitive to my aunt's reverses, and sincerely believing that no galley-slave or convict worked as I did, he had begun to fret and worry himself out of spirits and appetite, as having nothing useful to do. In this condition, he felt more incapable of finishing the Memorial than ever; and the harder he worked at it, the oftener that unlucky head of King Charles the First got into it. Seriously apprehending that his malady would increase, unless we put some innocent deception upon him and caused him to believe that he was useful, or unless we could put him in the way of being really useful (which would be better), I made up my mind to try if Traddles could help us. Before we went, I wrote Traddles a full statement of all that had happened, and Traddles wrote me back a capital answer, expressive of his sympathy and friendship.

We found him hard at work with his inkstand and papers, refreshed by the sight of the flower-pot stand and the little round table in a corner of the small apartment. He received us cordially, and made friends with Mr. Dick in a moment. Mr. Dick professed an absolute certainty of having seen him before, and we both said, "Very likely."

The first subject on which I had to consult Traddles was

109

this.—I had heard that many men distinguished in various pursuits had begun life by reporting the debates in Parliament. Traddles having mentioned newspapers to me, as one of his hopes, I had put the two things together, and told Traddles in my letter that I wished to know how I could qualify myself for this pursuit. Traddles now informed me, as the result of his inquiries, that the mere mechanical acquisition necessary, except in rare cases, for thorough excellence in it, that is to say, a perfect and entire command of the mystery of short-hand writing and reading, was about equal in difficulty to the mastery of six languages; and that it might perhaps be attained, by dint of perseverance, in the course of a few years. Traddles reasonably supposed that this would settle the business; but I, only feeling that here indeed were a few tall trees to be hewn down, immediately resolved to work my way on to Dora through this thicket, axe in hand.

"I am very much obliged to you, my dear Traddles!" said I. "I'll begin to-morrow."

Traddles looked astonished, as he well might; but he had no notion as yet of my rapturous condition.

"I'll buy a book," said I, "with a good scheme of this art in it; I'll work at it at the Commons, where I haven't half enough to do; I'll take down the speeches in our court for practice—Traddles, my dear fellow, I'll master it!"

"Dear me," said Traddles, opening his eyes, "I had no idea you were such a determined character, Copperfield!"

I don't know how he should have had, for it was new enough to me. I passed that off, and brought Mr. Dick on the carpet.

"You see," said Mr. Dick, wistfully, "if I could exert myself, Mr. Traddles—if I could beat a drum—or blow anything!"

Poor fellow! I have little doubt he would have preferred such an employment in his heart to all others. Traddles, who would not have smiled for the world, replied composedly:

MR. DICK IS SET TO WORK.

"But you are a very good penman, sir. You told me so, Copperfield?"

"Excellent!" said I. And indeed he was. He wrote with extraordinary neatness.

"Don't you think," said Traddles, "you could copy writings, sir, if I got them for you?"

Mr. Dick looked doubtfully at me. "Eh, Trotwood?"

I shook my head. Mr. Dick shook his, and sighed. "Tell him about the Memorial," said Mr. Dick.

I explained to Traddles that there was a difficulty in keeping King Charles the First out of Mr. Dick's manuscripts; Mr. Dick in the meanwhile looking very deferentially and seriously at Traddles, and sucking his thumb.

"But these writings, you know, that I speak of, are already drawn up and finished," said Traddles after a little consideration. "Mr. Dick has nothing to do with them. Wouldn't that make a difference, Copperfield? At all events, wouldn't it be well to try?"

This gave us new hope. Traddles and I laying our heads together apart, while Mr. Dick anxiously watched us from his chair, we concocted a scheme in virtue of which we got him to work next day, with triumphant success.

On a table by the window in Buckingham Street, we set out the work Traddles procured for him—which was to make, I forget how many copies of a legal document about some right of way—and on another table we spread the last unfinished original of the great Memorial. Our instructions to Mr. Dick were that he should copy exactly what he had before him, without the least departure from the original; and that when he felt it necessary to make the slightest allusion to King Charles the First, he should fly to the Memorial. We exhorted him to be resolute in this, and left my aunt to observe him. My aunt reported to us, afterwards, that, at first, he was like a man playing the kettle-drums, and constantly divided his attentions between the two; but that, finding this confuse and fatigue him, and having his copy there, plainly before his eyes, he soon sat at it in an orderly business-like manner, and postponed the Memorial to a more convenient time. In a word, although we took great care that he should have no more to do than was good for him, and although he did not begin with the beginning of a week, he earned by the following Saturday night ten shillings and nine pence; and never, while I live, shall I forget his going about to all the shops in the neighbourhood to change this treasure into sixpences, or his bringing them to my aunt arranged in the form of a heart upon a waiter, with tears of joy and pride in his eyes. He was like one under the propitious influence of a charm, from the moment of his being usefully employed; and if there were a happy man in the world, that Saturday night, it was the grateful creature who thought my aunt the most wonderful woman in existence, and me the most wonderful young man.

"No starving now, Trotwood," said Mr. Dick, shaking hands with me in a corner. "I'll provide for her, sir!" and he flourished his ten fingers in the air, as if they were ten banks.

I hardly know which was the better pleased, Traddles or I. "It really," said Traddles, suddenly, taking a letter out of his pocket, and giving it to me, "put Mr. Micawber quite out of my head!"

The letter (Mr. Micawber never missed any possible opportunity of writing a letter) was addressed to me, "By the kindness of T. Traddles, Esquire, of the Inner Temple." It ran thus:

"MY DEAR COPPERFIELD,

"You may possibly not be unprepared to receive the intimation that something has turned up. I may have mentioned to you on a former occasion that I was in expectation of such an event.

"I am about to establish myself in one of the provincial towns of our favoured island (where the society may be described as a happy admixture of the agricultural and the clerical), in immediate connexion with one of the learned professions. Mrs. Micawber and our offspring will accompany me. Our ashes, at a future period, will probably be found commingled in the cemetery attached to a venerable pile, for which the spot to which I refer, has acquired a reputation, shall I say from China to Peru?

"In bidding adieu to the modern Babylon, where we have undergone many vicissitudes, I trust not ignobly, Mrs. Micawber and myself cannot disguise from our minds that we part, it may be for years and it may be for ever, with an individual linked by strong associations to the altar of our domestic life. If, on the eve of such a departure, you will accompany our mutual friend, Mr. Thomas Traddles, to our present abode, and there reciprocate the wishes natural to the occasion, you will confer a Boon

"On

"One

"Who

"Is

"Ever yours,

"WILKINS MICAWBER."

I was glad to find that Mr. Micawber had got rid of his dust and ashes, and that something really had turned up at last. Learning from Traddles that the invitation referred to the evening then wearing away, I expressed my readiness to do honour to it; and we went off together to the lodging which Mr. Micawber occupied as Mr. Mortimer, and which was situated near the top of the Gray's Inn Road.

The resources of this lodging were so limited, that we found the twins, now some eight or nine years old, reposing in a turn-up bedstead in the family sitting-room, where Mr. Micawber had prepared, in a wash-hand-stand jug, what he called a "Brew" of the agreeable beverage for which he was famous. I had the pleasure, on this occasion, of renewing the acquaintance of Master Micawber, whom I found a promising boy of about twelve or thirteen, very subject to that restlessness of limb which is not an unfrequent phenomenon in youths of his age. I also became once more known to his sister, Miss Micawber, in whom, as Mr. Micawber told us, "her mother renewed her youth, like the Phœnix."

"My dear Copperfield," said Mr. Micawber, "yourself and Mr. Traddles find us on the brink of migration, and will excuse any little discomforts incidental to that position."

Glancing round as I made a suitable reply, I observed that the family effects were already packed, and that the amount of luggage was by no means overwhelming. I congratulated Mrs. Micawber on the approaching change.

"My dear Mr. Copperfield," said Mrs. Micawber, "of your friendly interest in all our affairs, I am well assured. My family may consider it banishment, if they please; but I am a wife and mother, and I never will desert Mr. Micawber."

Traddles, appealed to, by Mrs. Micawber's eye, feelingly acquiesced.

"That," said Mrs. Micawber, "that, at least, is my view, my dear Mr. Copperfield and Mr. Traddles, of the obligation which I took upon myself when I repeated the irrevocable words, 'I, Emma, take thee, Wilkins.' I read the service over with a flat-candle on the previous night, and the conclusion I derived from it was, that I never could desert Mr. Micawber. And," said Mrs. Micawber, "though it is possible I may be mistaken in my view of the ceremony, I never will!"

"My dear," said Mr. Micawber, a little impatiently, "I am not conscious that you are expected to do anything of the sort."

"I am aware, my dear Mr. Copperfield," pursued Mrs. Micawber, "that I am now about to cast my lot among strangers; and I am also aware that the various members of my family, to whom Mr. Micawber has written in the most gentlemanly terms, announcing that fact, have not taken the least notice of Mr. Micawber's communication. Indeed I may be superstitious," said Mrs. Micawber, "but it appears to me that Mr. Micawber is destined never to receive any answers whatever to the great majority of the communications he writes. I may augur from the silence of my family, that they object to the resolution I have taken; but I should not allow myself to be swerved from the path of duty, Mr. Copperfield, even by my papa and mama, were they still living."

I expressed my opinion that this was going in the right direction.

"It may be a sacrifice," said Mrs. Micawber, "to immure one's-self in a Cathedral town; but surely, Mr. Copperfield, if it is a sacrifice in me, it is much more a sacrifice in a man of Mr. Micawber's abilities."

"Oh! You are going to a Cathedral town?" said I.

Mr. Micawber, who had been helping us all, out of the wash-hand-stand jug, replied:

"To Canterbury. In fact, my dear Copperfield, I have entered into arrangements, by virtue of which I stand pledged and contracted to our friend Heep, to assist and serve him in the capacity of—and to be—his confidential clerk."

I stared at Mr. Micawber, who greatly enjoyed my surprise.

"I am bound to state to you," he said, with an official air, "that the business habits, and the prudent suggestions, of Mrs. Micawber, have in a great measure conduced to this result. The gauntlet, to which Mrs. Micawber referred upon a former occasion, being thrown down in the form of an advertisement, was taken up by my friend Heep, and led to a mutual recognition. Of my friend Heep," said Mr. Micawber, "who is a man of remarkable shrewdness, I desire to speak with all possible respect. My friend Heep has not fixed the positive remuneration at too high a figure, but he has made a great deal, in the way of extrication from the pressure of pecuniary difficulties, contingent on the value of my services; and on the value of those services, I pin my faith. Such address and intelligence as I chance to possess," said Mr. Micawber, boastfully disparaging himself, with the old genteel air, "will be devoted to my friend Heep's service. I have already some acquaintance with the law— as a defendant on civil process—and I shall immediately apply myself to the Commentaries of one of the most eminent and remarkable of our English Jurists. I believe it is unnecessary to add that I allude to Mr. Justice Blackstone."

These observations, and indeed the greater part of the observations made that evening, were interrupted by Mrs. Micawber's discovering that Master Micawber was sitting on his boots, or holding his head on with both arms as if he felt it loose, or accidentally kicking Traddles under the table, or shuffling his feet over one another, or producing them at distances from himself apparently outrageous to nature, or lying sideways with his hair among the wine-glasses, or developing his restlessness of limb in some other form incompatible with the general interests of society; and by Master Micawber's receiving those discoveries in a resentful spirit. I sat all the while, amazed by Mr. Micawber's disclosure, and wondering what it meant; until Mrs. Micawber resumed the thread of the discourse, and claimed my attention.

"What I particularly request Mr. Micawber to be careful of, is," said Mrs. Micawber, "that he does not, my dear Mr. Copperfield, in applying himself to this subordinate branch of the law, place it out of his power to rise, ultimately, to the top of the tree. I am convinced that Mr. Micawber, giving his mind to a profession so adapted to his fertile resources, and his flow of language, *must* distinguish himself. Now, for example, Mr. Traddles," said Mrs. Micawber, assuming a profound air, "a Judge, or even say a Chancellor. Does an individual place himself beyond the pale of those preferments by entering on such an office as Mr. Micawber has accepted?"

"My dear," observed Mr. Micawber—but glancing inquisitively at Traddles, too; "we have time enough before us, for the consideration of those questions."

"Micawber," she returned, "no! Your mistake in life is, that you do not look forward far enough. You are bound, in justice to your family, if not to yourself, to take in at a comprehensive glance the extremest point in the horizon to which your abilities may lead you."

Mr. Micawber coughed, and drank his punch with an air of exceeding satisfaction—still glancing at Traddles, as if he desired to have his opinion.

"Why, the plain state of the case, Mrs. Micawber," said Traddles, mildly breaking the truth to her, "I mean the real prosaic fact, you know—"

"Just so," said Mrs. Micawber, "my dear Mr. Traddles, I wish to be as prosaic and literal as possible on a subject of so much importance."

"—Is," said Traddles, "that this branch of the law, even if Mr. Micawber were a regular solicitor—"

"Exactly so," returned Mrs. Micawber. ("Wilkins, you are squinting, and will not be able to get your eyes back.")

"—Has nothing," pursued Traddles, "to do with that. Only a barrister is eligible for such preferments; and Mr. Micawber could not be a barrister, without being entered at an inn of court as a student, for five years."

"Do I follow you?" said Mrs. Micawber, with her most affable air of business. "Do I understand, my dear Mr. Traddles, that, at the expiration of that period, Mr. Micawber would be eligible as a Judge or Chancellor?"

"He would be *eligible*," returned Traddles, with a strong emphasis on that word.

"Thank you," said Mrs. Micawber. "That is quite sufficient. If such is the case, and Mr. Micawber forfeits no privilege by entering on these duties, my anxiety is set at rest. I speak," said Mrs. Micawber, "as a female, necessarily; but I have always been of opinion that Mr. Micawber possesses

117

what I have heard my papa call, when I lived at home, the judicial mind; and I hope Mr. Micawber is now entering on a field where that mind will develop itself, and take a commanding station."

I quite believe that Mr. Micawber saw himself, in his judicial mind's eye, on the woolsack. He passed his hand complacently over his bald head, and said with ostentatious resignation:

"My dear, we will not anticipate the decrees of fortune. If I am reserved to wear a wig, I am at least prepared, externally," in allusion to his baldness, "for that distinction. I do not," said Mr. Micawber, "regret my hair, and I may have been deprived of it for a specific purpose. I cannot say. It is my intention, my dear Copperfield, to educate my son for the Church; I will not deny that I should be happy, on his account, to attain to eminence."

"For the Church?" said I, still pondering, between whiles, on Uriah Heep.

"Yes," said Mr. Micawber. "He has a remarkable head-voice, and will commence as a chorister. Our residence at Canterbury, and our local connexion, will, no doubt, enable him to take advantage of any vacancy that may arise in the Cathedral corps."

On looking at Master Micawber again, I saw that he had a certain expression of face, as if his voice were behind his eyebrows; where it presently appeared to be, on his singing us (as an alternative between that and bed), "The Wood-Pecker tapping." After many compliments on this performance, we fell into some general conversation; and as I was too full of my desperate intentions to keep my altered circumstances to myself, I made them known to Mr. and Mrs. Micawber. I cannot express how extremely delighted they both were, by the idea of my aunt's being in difficulties; and how comfortable and friendly it made them.

When we were nearly come to the last round of the punch, I addressed myself to Traddles, and reminded him that we must not separate, without wishing our friends health, happiness, and success in their new career. I begged Mr. Micawber to fill us bumpers, and proposed the toast in due form: shaking hands with him across the table, and kissing Mrs. Micawber, to commemorate that eventful occasion. Traddles imitated me in the first particular, but did not consider himself a sufficiently old friend to venture on the second.

"My dear Copperfield," said Mr. Micawber, rising with one of his thumbs in each of his waistcoat pockets, "the companion of my youth: if I may be allowed the expression —and my esteemed friend Traddles: if I may be permitted to call him so—will allow me, on the part of Mrs. Micawber, myself, and our offspring, to thank them in the warmest and most uncompromising terms for their good wishes. It may be expected that on the eve of a migration which will consign us to a perfectly new existence," Mr. Micawber spoke as if they were going five hundred thousand miles, "I should offer a few valedictory remarks to two such friends as I see before me. But all that I have to say in this way, I have said. Whatever station in society I may attain, through the medium of the learned profession of which I am about to become an unworthy member, I shall endeavour not to disgrace, and Mrs. Micawber will be safe to adorn. Under the temporary pressure of pecuniary liabilities, contracted with a view to their immediate liquidation, but remaining unliquidated through a combination of circumstances, I have been under the necessity of assuming a garb from which my natural instincts recoil—I allude to spectacles— and possessing myself of a cognomen, to which I can establish no legitimate pretensions. All I have to say on that score is, that the cloud has passed from the dreary scene, and the God of Day is once more high upon the mountain tops. On Monday next, on the arrival of the four o'clock afternoon coach at Canterbury, my foot will be on my native heath—my name, Micawber!"

Mr. Micawber resumed his seat on the close of these

remarks, and drank two glasses of punch in grave succession. He then said with much solemnity:

"One thing more I have to do, before this separation is complete, and that is to perform an act of justice. My friend Mr. Thomas Traddles has, on two several occasions, 'put his name,' if I may use a common expression, to bills of exchange for my accommodation. On the first occasion Mr. Thomas Traddles was left—let me say, in short, in the lurch. The fulfilment of the second has not yet arrived. The amount of the first obligation," here Mr. Micawber carefully referred to papers, "was, I believe, twenty-three, four, nine and a half; of the second, according to my entry of that transaction, eighteen, six, two. These sums, united, make a total, if my calculation is correct, amounting to forty-one, ten, eleven and a half. My friend Copperfield will perhaps do me the favour to check that total?"

I did so and found it correct.

"To leave this metropolis," said Mr. Micawber, "and my friend Mr. Thomas Traddles, without acquitting myself of the pecuniary part of this obligation, would weigh upon my mind to an insupportable extent. I have, therefore, prepared for my friend Mr. Thomas Traddles, and I now hold in my hand, a document, which accomplishes the desired object. I beg to hand to my friend Mr. Thomas Traddles my I. O. U. for forty-one, ten, eleven and a half, and I am happy to recover my moral dignity, and to know that I can once more walk erect befo e my fellow man!"

With this .ntroduction (which greatly affected him), Mr. Micawber placed his I. O. U. in the hands of Traddles, and said he wished him well in every relation of life. I am persuaded, not only that this was quite the same to Mr. Micawber as paying the money, but that Traddles himself hardly knew the difference until he had had time to think about it.

Mr. Micawber walked so erect before his fellow man, on the strength of this virtuous action, that his chest looked

Mr. Micawber delivers some Valedictory Remarks

half as broad again when he lighted us down-stairs. We parted with great heartiness on both sides; and when I had seen Traddles to his own door, and was going home alone, I thought, among the other odd and contradictory things I mused upon, that, slippery as Mr. Micawber was, I was probably indebted to some compassionate recollection he retained of me as his boy-lodger, for never having been asked by him for money. I certainly should not have had the moral courage to refuse it; and I have no doubt he knew that (to his credit be it written), quite as well as I did.

CHAPTER XXXVII.

A LITTLE COLD WATER.

My new life had lasted for more than a week, and I was stronger than ever in those tremendous practical resolutions that I felt the crisis required. I continued to walk extremely fast, and to have a general idea that I was getting on. I made it a rule to take as much out of myself as I possibly could, in my way of doing everything to which I applied my energies. I made a perfect victim of myself. I even entertained some idea of putting myself on a vegetable diet, vaguely conceiving that, in becoming a graminivorous animal, I should sacrifice to Dora.

As yet, little Dora was quite unconscious of my desperate firmness, otherwise than as my letters darkly shadowed it forth. But, another Saturday came, and on that Saturday evening she was to be at Miss Mills's ; and when Mr. Mills had gone to his whist-club (telegraphed to me in the street, by a bird-cage in the drawing-room middle window), I was to go there to tea.

By this time, we were quite settled down in Buckingham Street, where Mr. Dick continued his copying in a state of absolute felicity. My aunt had obtained a signal victory over Mrs. Crupp, by paying her off, throwing the first pitcher she planted on the stairs out of window, and protecting in person, up and down the staircase, a supernumerary whom she engaged from the outer world. These vigorous measures

struck such terror to the breast of Mrs. Crupp, that she subsided into her own kitchen, under the impression that my
aunt was mad. My aunt being supremely indifferent to Mrs.
Crupp's opinion and everybody else's, and rather favouring
than discouraging the idea, Mrs. Crupp, of late the bold,
became within a few days so faint-hearted, that rather than
encounter my aunt upon the staircase, she would endeavour
to hide her portly form behind doors—leaving visible, however, a wide margin of flannel petticoat—or would shrink
into dark corners. This gave my aunt such unspeakable
satisfaction, that I believe she took a delight in prowling up
and down, with her bonnet insanely perched on the top of
her head, at times when Mrs. Crupp was likely to be in
the way.

My aunt, being uncommonly neat and ingenious, made so
many little improvements in our domestic arrangements, that
I seemed to be richer instead of poorer. Among the rest,
she converted the pantry into a dressing-room for me; and
purchased and embellished a bedstead for my occupation,
which looked as like a bookcase in the daytime as a bedstead
could. I was the object of her constant solicitude; and my
poor mother herself could not have loved me better, or
studied more how to make me happy.

Peggotty had considered herself highly privileged in being
allowed to participate in these labours; and, although she still
retained something of her old sentiment of awe in reference
to my aunt, had received so many marks of encouragement
and confidence, that they were the best friends possible. But
the time had now come (I am speaking of the Saturday when
I was to take tea at Miss Mills's) when it was necessary for
her to return home, and enter on the discharge of the duties
she had undertaken in behalf of Ham. "So good-bye,
Barkis," said my aunt, "and take care of yourself! I am sure
I never thought I could be sorry to lose you!"

I took Peggotty to the coach-office and saw her off. She
cried at parting, and confided her brother to my friendship

as Ham had done. We had heard nothing of him since he went away, that sunny afternoon.

"And now, my own dear Davy," said Peggotty, "if, while you're a prentice, you should want any money to spend; or if, when you're out of your time, my dear, you should want any to set you up (and you must do one or other, or both, my darling); who has such a good right to ask leave to lend it you, as my sweet girl's own old stupid me!"

I was not so savagely independent as to say anything in reply, but that if ever I borrowed money of any one, I would borrow it of her. Next to accepting a large sum on the spot, I believe this gave Peggotty more comfort than anything I could have done.

"And, my dear!" whispered Peggotty, "tell the pretty little angel that I should so have liked to see her, only for a minute! And tell her that before she marries my boy, I'll come and make your house so beautiful for you, if you'll let me!"

I declared that nobody else should touch it; and this gave Peggotty such delight, that she went away in good spirits.

I fatigued myself as much as I possibly could in the Commons all day, by a variety of devices, and at the appointed time in the evening repaired to Mr. Mills's street. Mr. Mills, who was a terrible fellow to fall asleep after dinner, had not yet gone out, and there was no bird-cage in the middle window.

He kept me waiting so long, that I fervently hoped the club would fine him for being late. At last he came out; and then I saw my own Dora hang up the bird-cage, and peep into the balcony to look for me, and run in again when she saw I was there, while Jip remained behind, to bark injuriously at an immense butcher's dog in the street, who could have taken him like a pill.

Dora came to the drawing-room door to meet me; and Jip came scrambling out, tumbling over his own growls, under the impression that I was a Bandit; and we all three went in, as happy and loving as could be. I soon carried desolation into the bosom of our joys—not that I meant to do it, but that I was so full of the subject—by asking Dora, without the smallest preparation, if she could love a beggar?

My pretty, little, startled Dora! Her only association with the word was a yellow face and a nightcap, or a pair of crutches, or a wooden leg, or a dog with a decanter-stand in his mouth, or something of that kind; and she stared at me with the most delightful wonder.

"How can you ask me anything so foolish?" pouted Dora. "Love a beggar!"

"Dora, my own dearest!" said I. "*I* am a beggar!"

"How can you be such a silly thing," replied Dora, slapping my hand, "as to sit there, telling such stories? I'll make Jip bite you!"

Her childish way was the most delicious way in the world to me, but it was necessary to be explicit, and I solemnly repeated:

"Dora, my own life, I am your ruined David!"

"I declare I'll make Jip bite you!" said Dora, shaking her curls, "if you are so ridiculous."

But I looked so serious, that Dora left off shaking her curls, and laid her trembling little hand upon my shoulder, and first looked scared and anxious, then began to cry. That was dreadful. I fell upon my knees before the sofa, caressing her, and imploring her not to rend my heart; but, for some time, poor little Dora did nothing but exclaim Oh dear! Oh dear! And oh, she was so frightened! And where was Julia Mills! And oh, take her to Julia Mills, and go away, please! until I was almost beside myself.

At last, after an agony of supplication and protestation, I got Dora to look at me, with a horrified expression of face, which I gradually soothed until it was only loving, and her soft, pretty cheek was lying against mine. Then I told her, with my arms clasped round her, how I loved her, so dearly, and so dearly; how I felt it right to offer to release her from her engagement, because now I was poor; how I never could bear it, or recover it, if I lost her; how I had no fears of poverty, if she had none, my arm being nerved and my heart inspired by her; how I was already working with a courage such as none but lovers knew; how I had begun to be practical, and look into the future ; how a crust well-earned was sweeter far than a feast inherited ; and much more to the same purpose, which I delivered in a burst of passionate eloquence quite surprising to myself, though I had been thinking about it, day and night, ever since my aunt had astonished me.

"Is your heart mine still, dear Dora?" said I, rapturously, for I knew by her clinging to me that it was.

"Oh, yes!" cried Dora. "Oh, yes, it's all yours. Oh, don't be dreadful!"

I dreadful! To Dora!

"Don't talk about being poor, and working hard!" said Dora, nestling closer to me. "Oh, don't, don't!"

"My dearest love," said I, "the crust well-earned—"

"Oh, yes; but I don't want to hear any more about crusts!" said Dora. "And Jip must have a mutton-chop every day at twelve, or he'll die!"

I was charmed with her childish, winning way. I fondly explained to Dora that Jip should have his mutton-chop with his accustomed regularity. I drew a picture of our frugal home, made independent by my labour—sketching in the little house I had seen at Highgate, and my aunt in her room up-stairs.

"I am not dreadful now, Dora?" said I, tenderly.

"Oh, no, no!" cried Dora. "But I hope your aunt will keep in her own room a good deal. And I hope she's not a scolding old thing!"

If it were possible for me to love Dora more than ever, I am sure I did. But I felt she was a little impracticable. It damped my new-born ardour, to find that ardour so difficult of communication to her. I made another trial. When she was quite herself again, and was curling Jip's ears, as he lay upon her lap, I became grave, and said

"My own! May I mention something?"

"Oh, please don't be practical!" said Dora coaxingly. "Because it frightens me so!"

"Sweet heart!" I returned; "there is nothing to alarm you in all this. I want you to think of it quite differently. I want to make it nerve you, and inspire you, Dora!"

"Oh, but that's so shocking!" cried Dora.

"My love, no. Perseverance and strength of character will enable us to bear much worse things."

"But I haven't got any strength at all," said Dora, shaking her curls. "Have I, Jip? Oh, do kiss Jip, and be agreeable!"

It was impossible to resist kissing Jip, when she held him up to me for that purpose, putting her own bright, rosy little mouth into kissing form, as she directed the operation, which she insisted should be performed symmetrically, on the centre of his nose. I did as she bade me—rewarding myself afterwards for my obedience—and she charmed me out of my graver character for I don't know how long.

"But, Dora, my beloved!" said I, at last resuming it; "I was going to mention something."

The Judge of the Prerogative Court might have fallen in love with her, to see her fold her little hands and hold them up, begging and praying me not to be dreadful any more.

"Indeed I am not going to be, my darling!" I assured her. "But, Dora, my love, if you will sometimes think—not despondingly, you know; far from that!—but if you will sometimes think—just to encourage yourself—that you are engaged to a poor man—"

"Don't, don't! Pray don't!" cried Dora. "It's so very dreadful!"

"My soul, not at all!" said I cheerfully. "If you will sometimes think of that, and look about now and then at your papa's housekeeping, and endeavour to acquire a little habit—of accounts, for instance—"

Poor little Dora received this suggestion with something that was half a sob and half a scream.

"—It would be so useful to us afterwards," I went on. "And if you would promise me to read a little—a little Cookery Book that I would send you, it would be so excellent for both of us. For our path in life, my Dora," said I, warming with the subject, "is stony and rugged now, and it rests with us to smooth it. We must fight our way onward. We must be brave. There are obstacles to be met, and we must meet, and crush them!"

I was going on at a great rate, with a clenched hand, and a most enthusiastic countenance; but it was quite unnecessary to proceed. I had said enough. I had done it again. Oh, she was so frightened! Oh, where was Julia Mills! Oh, take her to Julia Mills, and go away, please! So that, in short, I was quite distracted, and raved about the drawing-room.

I thought I had killed her, this time. I sprinkled water on her face. I went down on my knees. I plucked at my hair. I denounced myself as a remorseless brute and a ruthless beast. I implored her forgiveness. I besought her to look up. I ravaged Miss Mills's work-box for a smelling-bottle, and in my agony of mind applied an ivory needle-case instead, and dropped all the needles over Dora. I shook my fists at Jip, who was as frantic as myself. I did every wild extravagance that could be done, and was a long way beyond the end of my wits when Miss Mills came into the room.

"Who has done this!" exclaimed Miss Mills, succouring her friend.

I replied, "I, Miss Mills! I have done it! Behold the destroyer!"—or words to that effect—and hid my face from the light, in the sofa cushion.

At first Miss Mills thought it was a quarrel, and that we

were verging on the Desert of Sahara; but she soon found out how matters stood, for my dear affectionate little Dora, embracing her, began exclaiming that I was " a poor labourer; " and then cried for me, and embraced me, and asked me would I let her give me all her money to keep, and then fell on Miss Mills's neck, sobbing as if her tender heart were broken.

Miss Mills must have been born to be a blessing to us. She ascertained from me in a few words what it was all about, comforted Dora, and gradually convinced her that I was not a labourer—from my manner of stating the case I believe Dora concluded that I was a navigator, and went balancing myself up and down a plank all day with a wheelbarrow—and so brought us together in peace. When we were quite composed, and Dora had gone up-stairs to put some rose-water to her eyes, Miss Mills rang for tea. In the ensuing interval, I told Miss Mills that she was evermore my friend, and that my heart must cease to vibrate ere I could forget her sympathy.

I then expounded to Miss Mills what I had endeavoured, so very unsuccessfully, to expound to Dora. Miss Mills replied, on general principles, that the Cottage of content was better than the Palace of cold splendour, and that where love was, all was.

I said to Miss Mills that this was very true, and who should know it better than I, who loved Dora with a love that never mortal had experienced yet? But on Miss Mills observing, with despondency, that it were well indeed for some hearts if this were so, I explained that I begged leave to restrict the observation to mortals of the masculine gender.

I then put it to Miss Mills, to say whether she considered that there was or was not any practical merit in the suggestion I had been anxious to make, concerning the accounts, the housekeeping, and the Cookery Book?

Miss Mills, after some consideration, thus replied:

"Mr. Copperfield, I will be plain with you. Mental suffering and trial supply, in some natures, the place of years, and

I will be as plain with you as if I were a Lady Abbess. No. The suggestion is not appropriate to our Dora. Our dearest Dora is a favourite child of nature. She is a thing of light, and airiness, and joy. I am free to confess that if it could be done, it might be well, but—" And Miss Mills shook her head.

I was encouraged by this closing admission on the part of Miss Mills to ask her, whether, for Dora's sake, if she had any opportunity of luring her attention to such preparations for an earnest life, she would avail herself of it? Miss Mills replied in the affirmative so readily, that I further asked her if she would take charge of the Cookery Book; and, if she ever could insinuate it upon Dora's acceptance, without frightening her, undertake to do me that crowning service. Miss Mills accepted this trust, too; but was not sanguine.

And Dora returned, looking such a lovely little creature, that I really doubted whether she ought to be troubled with anything so ordinary. And she loved me so much, and was so captivating (particularly when she made Jip stand on his hind legs for toast, and when she pretended to hold that nose of his against the hot tea-pot for punishment because he wouldn't), that I felt like a sort of Monster who had got into a Fairy's bower, when I thought of having frightened her, and made her cry.

After tea we had the guitar; and Dora sang those same dear old French songs about the impossibility of ever on any account leaving off dancing, La ra la, La ra la, until I felt a much greater Monster than before.

We had only one check to our pleasure, and that happened a little while before I took my leave, when, Miss Mills chancing to make some allusion to to-morrow morning, I unluckily let out that, being obliged to exert myself now, I got up at five o'clock. Whether Dora had any idea that I was a Private Watchman, I am unable to say; but it made a great impression on her, and she neither played nor sang any more.

I KEEP ALL MY IRONS IN THE FIRE.

It was still on her mind when I bade her adieu; and she said to me, in her pretty coaxing way—as if I were a doll, I used to think—

"Now don't get up at five o'clock, you naughty boy. It's so nonsensical!"

"My love," said I, "I have work to do."

"But don't do it!" returned Dora. "Why should you?"

It was impossible to say to that sweet little surprised face, otherwise than lightly and playfully, that we must work, to live.

"Oh! How ridiculous!" cried Dora.

"How shall we live without, Dora?" said I.

"How? Any how!" said Dora.

She seemed to think she had quite settled the question, and gave me such a triumphant little kiss, direct from her innocent heart, that I would hardly have put her out of conceit with her answer, for a fortune.

Well! I loved her, and I went on loving her, most absorbingly, entirely, and completely. But going on, too, working pretty hard, and busily keeping red-hot all the irons I now had in the fire, I would sit sometimes of a night, opposite my aunt, thinking how I had frightened Dora that time, and how I could best make my way with a guitar-case through the forest of difficulty, until I used to fancy that my head was turning quite grey.

131

CHAPTER XXXVIII

A DISSOLUTION OF PARTNERSHIP.

I DID not allow my resolution, with respect to the Parliamentary Debates, to cool. It was one of the irons I began to heat immediately, and one of the irons I kept hot, and hammered at, with a perseverance I may honestly admire. I bought an approved scheme of the noble art and mystery of stenography (which cost me ten and sixpence), and plunged into a sea of perplexity that brought me, in a few weeks, to the confines of distraction. The changes that were rung upon dots, which in such a position meant such a thing, and in such another position something else, entirely different; the wonderful vagaries that were played by circles; the unaccountable consequences that resulted from marks like flies' legs; the tremendous effects of a curve in a wrong place; not only troubled my waking hours, but reappeared before me in my sleep. When I had groped my way, blindly, through these difficulties, and had mastered the alphabet, which was an Egyptian Temple in itself, there then appeared a procession of new horrors, called arbitrary characters; the most despotic characters I have ever known; who insisted, for instance, that a thing like the beginning of a cobweb, meant expectation, and that a pen-and-ink sky-rocket stood for disadvantageous. When I had fixed these wretches in my mind, I found that they had driven everything else out of it; then, beginning again, I forgot them; while I was picking hem up, I dropped the other fragments of the system; in short, it was almost heart-breaking.

It might have been quite heart-breaking, but for Dora, who was the stay and anchor of my tempest-driven bark. Every scratch in the scheme was a gnarled oak in the forest of difficulty, and I went on cutting them down, one after another, with such vigour, that in three or four months I was in a condition to make an experiment on one of our crack speakers in the Commons. Shall I ever forget how the crack speaker walked off from me before I began, and left my imbecile pencil staggering about the paper as if it were in a fit!

This would not do, it was quite clear. I was flying too high, and should never get on, so. I resorted to Traddles for advice; who suggested that he should dictate speeches to me, at a pace, and with occasional stoppages, adapted to my weakness. Very grateful for this friendly aid, I accepted the proposal; and night after night, almost every night, for a long time, we had a sort of Private Parliament in Buckingham Street, after I came home from the Doctor's.

I should like to see such a Parliament anywhere else! My aunt and Mr. Dick represented the Government or the Opposition (as the case might be), and Traddles, with the assistance of Enfield's Speaker or a volume of parliamentary orations, thundered astonishing invectives against them. Standing by the table, with his finger in the page to keep the place, and his right arm flourishing above his head, Traddles, as Mr. Pitt, Mr. Fox, Mr. Sheridan, Mr. Burke, Lord Castlereagh, Viscount Sidmouth, or Mr. Canning, would work himself into the most violent heats, and deliver the most withering denunciations of the profligacy and corruption of my aunt and Mr. Dick; while I used to sit, at a little distance, with my note-book on my knee, fagging after him with all my might and main. The inconsistency and reck-lessness of Traddles were not to be exceeded by any real politician. He was for any description of policy, in the compass of a week; and nailed all sorts of colours to every denomination of mast. My aunt, looking very like an immoveable Chancellor of the Exchequer, would occasionally throw in an interruption or two, as "Hear!" or "No!" or "Oh!" when the text seemed to require it: which was always a signal to Mr. Dick (a perfect country gentleman) to follow lustily with the same cry. But Mr. Dick got taxed with such things in the course of his Parliamentary career, and was made responsible for such awful consequences, that he became uncomfortable in his mind sometimes. I believe he actually began to be afraid he really had been doing something, tending to the annihilation of the British constitution, and the ruin of the country.

Often and often we pursued these debates until the clock pointed to midnight, and the candles were burning down. The result of so much good practice was, that by-and-by I began to keep pace with Traddles pretty well, and should have been quite triumphant if I had had the least idea what my notes were about. But, as to reading them after I had got them, I might as well have copied the Chinese inscriptions on an immense collection of tea-chests, or the golden characters on all the great red and green bottles in the chemists' shops!

There was nothing for it, but to turn back and begin all over again. It was very hard, but I turned back, though with a heavy heart, and began laboriously and methodically to plod over the same tedious ground at a snail's pace; stopping to examine minutely every speck in the way, on all sides, and making the most desperate efforts to know these elusive characters by sight wherever I met them. I was always punctual at the office; at the Doctor's too; and I really did work, as the common expression is, like a carthorse.

One day, when I went to the Commons as usual, I found Mr. Spenlow in the doorway looking extremely grave, and talking to himself. As he was in the habit of complaining

Traddles makes a Figure in Parliament, and I report him

of pains in his head—he had naturally a short throat, and I do seriously believe he overstarched himself—I was at first alarmed by the idea that he was not quite right in that direction; but he soon relieved my uneasiness.

Instead of returning my "Good morning" with his usual affability, he looked at me in a distant, ceremonious manner, and coldly requested me to accompany him to a certain coffee-house, which, in those days, had a door opening into the Commons, just within the little archway in St. Paul's Churchyard. I complied, in a very uncomfortable state, and with a warm shooting all over me, as if my apprehensions were breaking out into buds. When I allowed him to go on a little before, on account of the narrowness of the way, I observed that he carried his head with a lofty air that was particularly unpromising; and my mind misgave me that he had found out about my darling Dora.

If I had not guessed this, on the way to the coffee-house, I could hardly have failed to know what was the matter when I followed him into an up-stairs room, and found Miss Murdstone there, supported by a background of sideboard, on which were several inverted tumblers sustaining lemons, and two of those extraordinary boxes, all corners and flutings, for sticking knives and forks in, which, happily for mankind, are now obsolete.

Miss Murdstone gave me her chilly finger-nails, and sat severely rigid. Mr. Spenlow shut the door, motioned me to a chair, and stood on the hearth-rug in front of the fire-place.

"Have the goodness to show Mr. Copperfield," said Mr. Spenlow, "what you have in your reticule, Miss Murdstone."

I believe it was the old identical steel-clasped reticule of my childhood, that shut up like a bite. Compressing her lips, in sympathy with the snap, Miss Murdstone opened it —opening her mouth a little at the same time—and produced my last letter to Dora, teeming with expressions of devoted affection.

"I believe that is your writing, Mr. Copperfield?" said Mr. Spenlow.

I was very hot, and the voice I heard was very unlike mine, when I said, "It is, sir!"

"If I am not mistaken," said Mr. Spenlow, as Miss Murdstone brought a parcel of letters out of her reticule, tied round with the dearest bit of blue ribbon, "those are also from your pen, Mr. Copperfield?"

I took them from her with a most desolate sensation; and, glancing at such phrases at the top, as "My ever dearest and own Dora," "My best beloved angel," "My blessed one for ever," and the like, blushed deeply, and inclined my head.

"No, thank you!" said Mr. Spenlow, coldly, as I mechanically offered them back to him. "I will not deprive you of them. Miss Murdstone, be so good as to proceed!"

That gentle creature, after a moment's thoughtful survey of the carpet, delivered herself with much dry unction as follows:

"I must confess to having entertained my suspicions of Miss Spenlow, in reference to David Copperfield, for some time. I observed Miss Spenlow and David Copperfield, when they first met; and the impression made upon me then was not agreeable. The depravity of the human heart is such—"

"You will oblige me, ma'am," interrupted Mr. Spenlow, "by confining yourself to facts."

Miss Murdstone cast down her eyes, shook her head as if protesting against this unseemly interruption, and with frowning dignity resumed:

"Since I am to confine myself to facts, I will state them as dryly as I can. Perhaps that will be considered an acceptable course of proceeding. I have already said, sir, that I have had my suspicions of Miss Spenlow, in reference to David Copperfield, for some time. I have frequently endeavoured to find decisive corroboration of those suspicions, but without effect. I have therefore forborne to mention them to Miss Spenlow's father;" looking severely at him; "knowing how little disposition there usually is in such cases, to acknowledge the conscientious discharge of duty."

Mr. Spenlow seemed quite cowed by the gentlemanly sternness of Miss Murdstone's manner, and deprecated her severity with a conciliatory little wave of his hand.

"On my return to Norwood, after the period of absence occasioned by my brother's marriage," pursued Miss Murdstone in a disdainful voice, "and on the return of Miss Spenlow from her visit to her friend Miss Mills, I imagined that the manner of Miss Spenlow gave me greater occasion for suspicion than before. Therefore I watched Miss Spenlow closely."

Dear, tender little Dora, so unconscious of this Dragon's eye.

"Still," resumed Miss Murdstone, "I found no proof until last night. It appeared to me that Miss Spenlow received too many letters from her friend Miss Mills; but Miss Mills being her friend with her father's full concurrence," another telling blow at Mr. Spenlow, "it was not for me to interfere. If I may not be permitted to allude to the natural depravity of the human heart, at least I may—I must—be permitted, so far to refer to misplaced confidence."

Mr. Spenlow apologetically murmured his assent.

"Last evening after tea," pursued Miss Murdstone, "I observed the little dog starting, rolling, and growling about the drawing-room, worrying something. I said to Miss Spenlow, 'Dora, what is that the dog has in his mouth? It's paper.' Miss Spenlow immediately put her hand to her frock, gave a sudden cry, and ran to the dog. I interposed, and said, 'Dora my love, you must permit me.'"

Oh Jip, miserable Spaniel, this wretchedness, then, was your work!

"Miss Spenlow endeavoured," said Miss Murdstone, "to bribe me with kisses, work-boxes, and small articles of jewellery—that, of course, I pass over. The little dog retreated under the sofa on my approaching him, and was with great difficulty dislodged by the fire-irons. Even when dislodged, he still kept the letter in his mouth; and on my endeavouring to take it from him, at the imminent risk of being bitten, he kept it between his teeth so pertinaciously as to suffer himself to be held suspended in the air by means of the document. At length I obtained possession of it. After perusing it, I taxed Miss Spenlow with having many such letters in her possession; and ultimately obtained from her the packet which is now in David Copperfield's hand."

Here she ceased; and snapping her reticule again, and shutting her mouth, looked as if she might be broken, but could never be bent.

"You have heard Miss Murdstone," said Mr. Spenlow, turning to me. "I beg to ask, Mr. Copperfield, if you have anything to say in reply?"

The picture I had before me, of the beautiful little treasure of my heart, sobbing and crying all night—of her being alone, frightened, and wretched, then—of her having so piteously begged and prayed that stony-hearted woman to forgive her—of her having vainly offered her those kisses, work-boxes, and trinkets—of her being in such grievous distress, and all for me—very much impaired the little dignity I had been able to muster. I am afraid I was in a tremulous state for a minute or so, though I did my best to disguise it.

"There is nothing I can say, sir," I returned, "except that all the blame is mine. Dora—"

"Miss Spenlow, if you please," said her father, majestically.

"—was induced and persuaded by me," I went on, swallowing that colder designation, "to consent to this concealment, and I bitterly regret it."

"You are very much to blame, sir," said Mr. Spenlow, walking to and fro upon the hearth-rug, and emphasizing what he said with his whole body instead of his head, on account of the stiffness of his cravat and spine. "You have done a stealthy and unbecoming action, Mr. Copperfield. When I take a gentleman to my house, no matter whether he is nineteen, twenty-nine, or ninety, I take him there in a spirit of confidence. If he abuses my confidence, he commits a dishonourable action, Mr. Copperfield."

"I feel it, sir, I assure you," I returned. "But I never thought so, before. Sincerely, honestly, indeed, Mr. Spenlow, I never thought so, before. I love Miss Spenlow to that extent—"

"Pooh! nonsense!" said Mr. Spenlow, reddening. "Pray don't tell me to my face that you love my daughter, Mr. Copperfield!"

"Could I defend my conduct if I did not, sir?" I returned, with all humility.

"Can you defend your conduct if you do, sir?" said Mr. Spenlow, stopping short upon the hearth-rug. "Have you considered your years, and my daughter's years, Mr. Copperfield? Have you considered what it is to undermine the confidence that should subsist between my daughter and myself? Have you considered my daughter's station in life, the projects I may contemplate for her advancement, the testamentary intentions I may have with reference to her? Have you considered anything, Mr. Copperfield?"

"Very little, sir, I am afraid;" I answered, speaking to him as respectfully and sorrowfully as I felt; "but pray believe me, I have considered my own worldly position. When I explained it to you, we were already engaged—"

"I BEG," said Mr. Spenlow, more like Punch than I had ever seen him, as he energetically struck one hand upon the other—I could not help noticing that even in my despair; "that you will NOT talk to me of engagements, Mr. Copperfield!"

The otherwise immoveable Miss Murdstone laughed contemptuously in one short syllable.

"When I explained my altered position to you, sir," I began again, substituting a new form of expression for what was so unpalatable to him, "this concealment, into which I am so unhappy as to have led Miss Spenlow, had begun. Since I have been in that altered position, I have strained every nerve, I have exerted every energy, to improve it. I am sure I shall improve it in time. Will you grant me time —any length of time? We are both so young, sir,—"

"You are right," interrupted Mr. Spenlow, nodding his head a great many times, and frowning very much, "you are both very young. It's all nonsense. Let there be an end of the nonsense. Take away those letters, and throw them in the fire. Give me Miss Spenlow's letters to throw in the fire; and although our future intercourse must, you are aware, be restricted to the Commons here, we will agree to make no further mention of the past. Come, Mr. Copperfield, you don't want sense; and this is the sensible course."

No. I couldn't think of agreeing to it. I was very sorry, but there was a higher consideration than sense. Love was above all earthly considerations, and I loved Dora to idolatry, and Dora loved me. I didn't exactly say so; I softened it down as much as I could; but I implied it, and I was resolute upon it. I don't think I made myself very ridiculous, but I know I was resolute.

"Very well, Mr. Copperfield," said Mr. Spenlow, "I must try my influence with my daughter."

Miss Murdstone, by an expressive sound, a long-drawn respiration, which was neither a sigh nor a moan, but was like both, gave it as her opinion that he should have done this at first.

"I must try," said Mr. Spenlow, confirmed by this support, "my influence with my daughter. Do you decline to take those letters, Mr. Copperfield?" For I had laid them on the table.

Yes. I told him I hoped he would not think it wrong, but I couldn't possibly take them from Miss Murdstone.

"Nor from me?" said Mr. Spenlow.

No, I replied with the profoundest respect; nor from him. "Very well!" said Mr. Spenlow.

A silence succeeding, I was undecided whether to go or stay. At length I was moving quietly towards the door, with the intention of saying that perhaps I should consult his feelings best by withdrawing: when he said, with his hands in his coat pockets, into which it was as much as he could do to get them; and with what I should call, upon the whole, a decidedly pious air:

"You are probably aware, Mr. Copperfield, that I am not altogether destitute of worldly possessions, and that my daughter is my nearest and dearest relative?"

I hurriedly made him a reply to the effect, that I hoped the error into which I had been betrayed by the desperate nature of my love, did not induce him to think me mercenary too?

"I don't allude to the matter in that light," said Mr. Spenlow. "It would be better for yourself, and all of us, if you *were* mercenary, Mr. Copperfield—I mean, if you were more discreet, and less influenced by all this youthful nonsense. No. I merely say, with quite another view, you are probably aware I have some property to bequeath to my child!"

I certainly supposed so.

"And you can hardly think," said Mr. Spenlow, "having experience of what we see, in the Commons here, every day, of the various unaccountable and negligent proceedings of men, in respect of their testamentary arrangements—of all subjects, the one on which perhaps the strangest revelations of human inconsistency are to be met with—but that mine are made?"

I inclined my head in acquiescence.

"I should not allow," said Mr. Spenlow, with an evident increase of pious sentiment, and slowly shaking his head as he poised himself upon his toes and heels alternately, "my suitable provision for my child to be influenced by a piece of youthful folly like the present. It is mere folly. Mere nonsense. In a little while, it will weigh lighter than any feather. But I might—I might—if this silly business were not completely relinquished altogether, be induced in some anxious moment to guard her from, and surround her with protections against, the consequences of any foolish step in the way of marriage. Now, Mr. Copperfield, I hope that you will not render it necessary for me to open, even for a quarter of an hour, that closed page in the book of life, and unsettle, even for a quarter of an hour, grave affairs long since composed."

There was a serenity, a tranquillity, a calm-sunset air about him, which quite affected me. He was so peaceful and resigned—clearly had his affairs in such perfect train, and so systematically wound up—that he was a man to feel touched in the contemplation of. I really think I saw tears rise to his eyes, from the depth of his own feeling of all this.

But what could I do? I could not deny Dora, and my own heart. When he told me I had better take a week to consider of what he had said, how could I say I wouldn't take a week, yet how could I fail to know that no amount of weeks could influence such love as mine?

"In the meantime, confer with Miss Trotwood, or with any person with any knowledge of life," said Mr. Spenlow, adjusting his cravat with both hands. "Take a week, Mr. Copperfield."

I submitted; and, with a countenance as expressive as I was able to make it of dejected and despairing constancy, came out of the room. Miss Murdstone's heavy eyebrows followed me to the door—I say her eyebrows rather than her eyes, because they were much more important in her face—and she looked so exactly as she used to look, at about that hour of the morning, in our parlour at Blunderstone, that I could have fancied I had been breaking down in my lessons again, and that the dead weight on my mind was that horrible old spelling-book with oval woodcuts, shaped to my youthful fancy, like the glasses out of spectacles.

ONLY TO FORGET DORA!

When I got to the office, and, shutting out old Tiffey and the rest of them with my hands, sat at my desk, in my own particular nook, thinking of this earthquake that had taken place so unexpectedly, and in the bitterness of my spirit cursing Jip, I fell into such a state of torment about Dora, that I wonder I did not take up my hat and rush insanely to Norwood. The idea of their frightening her, and making her cry, and of my not being there to comfort her, was so excruciating, that it impelled me to write a wild letter to Mr. Spenlow, beseeching him not to visit upon her the consequences of my awful destiny. I implored him to spare her gentle nature—not to crush a fragile flower—and addressed him generally, to the best of my remembrance, as if, instead of being her father, he had been an Ogre, or the Dragon of Wantley. This letter I sealed and laid upon his desk before he returned; and when he came in, I saw him, through the half-opened door of his room, take it up and read it.

He said nothing about it all the morning; but before he went away in the afternoon he called me in, and told me that I need not make myself at all uneasy about his daughter's happiness. He had assured her, he said, that it was all nonsense; and he had nothing more to say to her. He believed he was an indulgent father (as indeed he was), and I might spare myself any solicitude on her account.

"You may make it necessary, if you are foolish or obstinate, Mr. Copperfield," he observed, "for me to send my daughter abroad again, for a term; but I have a better opinion of you. I hope you will be wiser than that, in a few days. As to Miss Murdstone," for I had alluded to her in the letter, "I respect that lady's vigilance, and feel obliged to her; but she has strict charge to avoid the subject. All I desire, Mr. Copperfield, is, that it should be forgotten. All you have got to do, Mr. Copperfield, is to forget it."

All! In the note I wrote to Miss Mills, I bitterly quoted this sentiment. All I had to do, I said, with gloomy sarcasm, was to forget Dora. That was all, and what was that? I entreated Miss Mills to see me, that evening. If it could not be done with Mr. Mills's sanction and concurrence, I besought a clandestine interview in the back kitchen where the Mangle was. I informed her that my reason was tottering on its throne, and only she, Miss Mills, could prevent its being deposed. I signed myself, hers distractedly; and I couldn't help feeling, while I read this composition over, before sending it by a porter, that it was something in the style of Mr. Micawber.

However, I sent it. At night I repaired to Miss Mills's street, and walked up and down, until I was stealthily fetched in by Miss Mills's maid, and taken the area way to the back kitchen. I have since seen reason to believe that there was nothing on earth to prevent my going in at the front door, and being shown up into the drawing-room, except Miss Mills's love of the romantic and mysterious.

In the back kitchen I raved as became me. I went there, I suppose, to make a fool of myself, and I am quite sure I did it. Miss Mills had received a hasty note from Dora, telling her that all was discovered, and saying, "Oh pray come to me, Julia, do, do!" But Miss Mills, mistrusting the acceptability of her presence to the higher powers, had not yet gone; and we were all benighted in the Desert of Sahara.

Miss Mills had a wonderful flow of words, and liked to pour them out. I could not help feeling, though she mingled her tears with mine, that she had a dreadful luxury in our afflictions. She petted them, as I may say, and made the most of them. A deep gulf, she observed, had opened between Dora and me, and Love could only span it with its rainbow. Love must suffer in this stern world; it ever had been so, it ever would be so. No matter, Miss Mills remarked. Hearts confined by cobwebs would burst at last, and then Love was avenged.

This was small consolation, but Miss Mills wouldn't encourage fallacious hopes. She made me much more wretched than I was before, and I felt (and told her with the deepest gratitude) that she was indeed a friend. We resolved that she should go to Dora the first thing in the morning, and find some means of assuring her, either by looks or words, of my devotion and misery. We parted, overwhelmed with grief; and I think Miss Mills enjoyed herself completely.

I confided all to my aunt when I got home; and in spite of all she could say to me, went to bed despairing. I got up despairing, and went out despairing. It was Saturday morning, and I went straight to the Commons.

I was surprised, when I came within sight of our office-door, to see the ticket-porters standing outside talking together, and some half-dozen stragglers gazing at the windows which were shut up. I quickened my pace, and, passing among them, wondering at their looks, went hurriedly in.

The clerks were there, but nobody was doing anything. Old Tiffey, for the first time in his life I should think, was sitting on somebody else's stool, and had not hung up his hat.

"This is a dreadful calamity, Mr. Copperfield," said he, as I entered.

"What is?" I exclaimed. "What's the matter?"

"Don't you know?" cried Tiffey, and all the rest of them, coming round me.

"No!" said I, looking from face to face.

"Mr. Spenlow," said Tiffey.

"What about him?"

"Dead!"

I thought it was the office reeling, and not I, as one of the clerks caught hold of me. They sat me down in a chair, untied my neckcloth, and brought me some water. I have no idea whether this took any time.

"Dead?" said I.

"He dined in town yesterday, and drove down in the phaeton by himself," said Tiffey, "having sent his own groom home by the coach, as he sometimes did, you know—"

"Well?"

"The phaeton went home without him. The horses stopped at the stable gate. The man went out with a lantern. Nobody in the carriage."

"Had they run away?"

"They were not hot," said Tiffey, putting on his glasses; "no hotter, I understand, than they would have been, going down at the usual pace. The reins were broken, but they had been dragging on the ground. The house was roused up directly, and three of them went out along the road. They found him a mile off."

"More than a mile off, Mr. Tiffey," interposed a junior.

"Was it? I believe you are right," said Tiffey,—"more than a mile off—not far from the church—lying partly on the road-side, and partly on the path, upon his face. Whether he fell out in a fit, or got out, feeling ill before the fit came on—or even whether he was quite dead then, though there is no doubt he was quite insensible—no one appears to know. If he breathed, certainly he never spoke. Medical assistance was got as soon as possible, but it was quite useless."

I cannot describe the state of mind into which I was thrown by this intelligence. The shock of such an event happening so suddenly, and happening to one with whom I had been in any respect at variance—the appalling vacancy in the room he had occupied so lately, where his chair and table seemed to wait for him, and his handwriting of yesterday was like a ghost—the indefinable impossibility of separating him from the place, and feeling, when the door opened, as if he might come in—the lazy hush and rest there was in the office, and the insatiable relish with which our people talked about it, and other people came in and out all day, and gorged themselves with the subject—this is easily intelligible to any one. What I cannot describe is, how, in the inner-most recesses of my own heart, I had a lurking jealousy even of Death. How I felt as if its might would push me from my ground in Dora's thoughts. How I was, in a grudging way I have no words for, envious of her grief. How it made me restless to think of her weeping to others, or being consoled by others. How I had a grasping, avaricious wish to shut out everybody from her but myself, and to be all in all to her, at that unseasonable time of all times.

In the trouble of this state of mind—not exclusively my own, I hope, but known to others—I went down to Norwood that night; and finding from one of the servants, when I made my inquiries at the door, that Miss Mills was there, got my aunt to direct a letter to her, which I wrote. I deplored the untimely death of Mr. Spenlow most sincerely, and shed tears in doing so. I entreated her to tell Dora, if Dora were in a state to hear it, that he had spoken to me with the utmost kindness and consideration; and had coupled nothing but tenderness, not a single or reproachful word, with her name. I know I did this selfishly, to have my name brought before her; but I tried to believe it was an act of justice to his memory. Perhaps I did believe it.

My aunt received a few lines next day in reply; addressed, outside, to her; within, to me. Dora was overcome by grief; and when her friend had asked her should she send her love to me, had only cried, as she was always crying, "Oh, dear papa! oh, poor papa!" But she had not said No, and that I made the most of.

Mr. Jorkins, who had been at Norwood since the occurrence, came to the office a few days afterwards. He and Tiffey were closeted together for some few moments, and then Tiffey looked out at the door and beckoned me in.

"Oh!" said Mr. Jorkins. "Mr. Tiffey and myself, Mr. Copperfield, are about to examine the desks, the drawers, and other such repositories of the deceased, with the view of sealing up his private papers, and searching for a Will. There is no trace of any, elsewhere. It may be as well for you to assist us, if you please."

I had been in agony to obtain some knowledge of the circumstances in which my Dora would be placed—as, in whose guardianship, and so forth—and this was something towards it. We began the search at once; Mr. Jorkins unlocking the drawers and desks, and we all taking out the papers. The office-papers we placed on one side, and the private papers (which were not numerous) on the other. We were very grave; and when we came to a stray seal, or pencil-case, or ring, or any little article of that kind which we associated personally with him, we spoke very low.

We had sealed up several packets; and were still going on dustily and quietly, when Mr. Jorkins said to us, applying exactly the same words to his late partner as his late partner had applied to him:

" Mr. Spenlow was very difficult to move from the beaten track. You know what he was ! I am disposed to think he had made no will."

" Oh, I know he had ! " said I.

They both stopped and looked at me.

" On the very day when I last saw him," said I, " he told me that he had, and that his affairs were long since settled."

Mr. Jorkins and old Tiffey shook their heads with one accord.

" That looks unpromising," said Tiffey.

" Very unpromising," said Mr. Jorkins.

" Surely you don't doubt— " I began.

" My good Mr. Copperfield ! " said Tiffey, laying his hand upon my arm, and shutting up both his eyes as he shook his head : " if you had been in the Commons as long as I have, you would know that there is no subject on which men are so inconsistent, and so little to be trusted."

" Why, bless my soul, he made that very remark ! " I replied persistently.

" I should call that almost final," observed Tiffey. " My opinion is—no will."

It appeared a wonderful thing to me, but it turned out that there *was* no will. He had never so much as thought of making one, so far as his papers afforded any evidence :

for there was no kind of hint, sketch, or memorandum, of any testamentary intention whatever. What was scarcely less astonishing to me was, that his affairs were in a most disordered state. It was extremely difficult, I heard, to make out what he owed, or what he had paid, or of what he died possessed. It was considered likely that for years he could have had no clear opinion on these subjects himself. By little and little it came out, that, in the competition on all points of appearance and gentility then running high in the Commons, he had spent more than his professional income, which was not a very large one, and had reduced his private means, if they ever had been great (which was exceedingly doubtful), to a very low ebb indeed. There was a sale of the furniture and lease, at Norwood; and Tiffey told me, little thinking how interested I was in the story, that, paying all the just debts of the deceased, and deducting his share of outstanding bad and doubtful debts due to the firm, he wouldn't give a thousand pounds for all the assets remaining.

This was at the expiration of about six weeks. I had suffered tortures all the time, and thought I really must have laid violent hands upon myself, when Miss Mills still reported to me, that my broken-hearted little Dora would say nothing, when I was mentioned, but "Oh, poor papa! Oh, dear papa!" Also, that she had no other relations than two aunts, maiden sisters of Mr. Spenlow, who lived at Putney, and who had not held any other than chance communication with their brother for many years. Not that they had ever quarrelled (Miss Mills informed me); but that having been, on the occasion of Dora's christening, invited to tea, when they considered themselves privileged to be invited to dinner, they had expressed their opinion in writing, that it was "better for the happiness of all parties" that they should stay away. Since which they had gone their road, and their brother had gone his.

These two ladies now emerged from their retirement, and proposed to take Dora to live at Putney. Dora, clinging to them both, and weeping, exclaimed, " O yes, aunts! Please take Julia Mills and me and Jip to Putney!" So they went, very soon after the funeral.

How I found time to haunt Putney, I am sure I don't know; but I contrived, by some means or other, to prowl about the neighbourhood pretty often. Miss Mills, for the more exact discharge of the duties of friendship, kept a journal; and she used to meet me sometimes, on the Common, and read it, or (if she had not time to do that) lend it to me. How I treasured up the entries, of which I subjoin a sample!—

" Monday. My sweet D. still much depressed. Headache. Called attention to J. as being beautifully sleek. D. fondled J. Associations thus awakened, opened floodgates of sorrow. Rush of grief admitted. (Are tears the dewdrops of the heart? J. M.)

" Tuesday. D. weak and nervous. Beautiful in pallor. (Do we not remark this in moon likewise? J. M.) D. J. M. and J. took airing in carriage. J. looking out of window, and barking violently at dustman, occasioned smile to overspread features of D. (Of such slight links is chain of life composed! J. M.)

" Wednesday. D. comparatively cheerful. Sang to her, as congenial melody, Evening Bells. Effect not soothing, but reverse. D. inexpressibly affected. Found sobbing afterwards, in own room. Quoted verses respecting self and young Gazelle. Ineffectually. Also referred to Patience on Monument. (Qy. Why on monument? J. M.)

" Thursday. D. certainly improved. Better night. Slight tinge of damask revisiting cheek. Resolved to mention name of D. C. Introduced same, cautiously, in course of airing. D. immediately overcome. 'Oh, dear, dear Julia! Oh, I have been a naughty and undutiful child!' Soothed and caressed. Drew ideal picture of D. C. on verge of tomb. D. again overcome. 'Oh, what shall I do, what shall I do? Oh, take me somewhere!' Much alarmed. Fainting of D. and glass of water from public-house. (Poetical affinity. Chequered sign on door-post: chequered human life. Alas! J. M.)

"Friday. Day of incident. Man appears in kitchen, with blue bag, 'for lady's boots left out to heel.' Cook replies, 'No such orders.' Man argues point. Cook withdraws to inquire, leaving man alone with J. On Cook's return, man still argues point, but ultimately goes. J. missing. D. distracted. Information sent to police. Man to be identified by broad nose, and legs like balustrades of bridge. Search made in every direction. No J. D. weeping bitterly, and inconsolable. Renewed reference to young Gazelle. Appropriate, but unavailing. Towards evening, strange boy calls. Brought into parlour. Broad nose, but no balustrades. Says he wants a pound, and knows a dog. Declines to explain further, though much pressed. Pound being produced by D. takes Cook to little house, where J. alone tied up to leg of table. Joy of D. who dances round J. while he eats his supper. Emboldened by this happy change, mention D. C. up-stairs. D. weeps afresh, cries piteously, 'Oh, don't, don't, don't! It is so wicked to think of anything but poor papa!' —embraces J. and sobs herself to sleep. (Must not D. C. confine himself to the broad pinions of Time? J. M.)"

Miss Mills and her journal were my sole consolation at this period. To see her, who had seen Dora but a little while before—to trace the initial letter of Dora's name through her sympathetic pages—to be made more and more miserable by her—were my only comforts. I felt as if I had been living in a palace of cards, which had tumbled down, leaving only Miss Mills and me among the ruins; I felt as if some grim enchanter had drawn a magic circle round the innocent goddess of my heart, which nothing indeed but those same strong pinions, capable of carrying so many people over so much, would enable me to enter!

CHAPTER XXXIX.

My aunt, beginning, I imagine, to be made seriously uncomfortable by my prolonged dejection, made a pretence of being anxious that I should go to Dover to see that all was working well at the cottage, which was let; and to conclude an agreement, with the same tenant, for a longer term of occupation. Janet was drafted into the service of Mrs. Strong, where I saw her every day. She had been undecided, on leaving Dover, whether or no to give the finishing touch to that renunciation of mankind in which she had been educated, by m   rying a pilot; but she decided against that venture. Not so much for the sake of principle, I believe, as because she happened not to like him.

Although it required an effort to leave Miss Mills, I fell rather willingly into my aunt's pretence, as a means of enabling me to pass a few tranquil hours with Agnes. I consulted the good Doctor relative to an absence of three days ; and the Doctor wishing me to take that relaxation,— he wished me to take more; but my energy could not bear that,—I made up my mind to go.

As to the Commons, I had no great occasion to be particular about my duties in that quarter. To say the truth, we were getting in no very good odour among the tip-top proctors, and were rapidly sliding down to but a doubtful position. The business had been indifferent under Mr.

Jorkins, before Mr. Spenlow's time; and although it had been quickened by the infusion of new blood, and by the display which Mr. Spenlow made, still it was not established on a sufficiently strong basis to bear, without being shaken, such a blow as the sudden loss of its active manager. It fell off very much. Mr. Jorkins, notwithstanding his reputation in the firm, was an easy-going, incapable sort of man, whose reputation out of doors was not calculated to back it up. I was turned over to him now, and when I saw him take his snuff and let the business go, I regretted my aunt's thousand pounds more than ever.

But this was not the worst of it. There were a number of hangers-on and outsiders about the Commons, who, without being proctors themselves, dabbled in common-form business, and got it done by real proctors, who lent their names in consideration of a share in the spoil;—and there were a good many of these too. As our house now wanted business on any terms, we joined this noble band; and threw out lures to the hangers-on and outsiders, to bring their business to us. Marriage licences and small probates were what we all looked for, and what paid us best; and the competition for these ran very high indeed. Kidnappers and inveiglers were planted in all the avenues of entrance to the Commons, with instructions to do their utmost to cut off all persons in mourning, and all gentlemen with anything bashful in their appearance, and entice them to the offices in which their respective employers were interested; which instructions were so well observed, that I myself, before I was known by sight, was twice hustled into the premises of our principal opponent. The conflicting interests of these touting gentlemen being of a nature to irritate their feelings, personal collisions took place; and the Commons was even scandalised by our principal inveigler (who had formerly been in the wine trade, and afterwards in the sworn brokery line) walking about for some days with a black eye. Any one of these scouts used to think nothing of politely assisting an old lady

153

in black out of a vehicle, killing any proctor whom she inquired for, representing his employer as the lawful successor and representative of that proctor, and bearing the old lady off (sometimes greatly affected) to his employer's office. Many captives were brought to me in this way. As to marriage licences, the competition rose to such a pitch, that a shy gentleman in want of one, had nothing to do but submit himself to the first inveigler, or be fought for, and become the prey of the strongest. One of our clerks, who was an outsider, used, in the height of this contest, to sit with his hat on, that he might be ready to rush out and swear before a surrogate any victim who was brought in. The system of inveigling continues, I believe, to this day. The last time I was in the Commons, a civil able-bodied person in a white apron pounced out upon me from a doorway, and whispering the word "Marriage-licence" in my ear, was with great difficulty prevented from taking me up in his arms and lifting me into a proctor's.

From this digression, let me proceed to Dover.

I found everything in a satisfactory state at the cottage; and was enabled to gratify my aunt exceedingly by reporting that the tenant inherited her feud, and waged incessant war against donkeys. Having settled the little business I had to transact there, and slept there one night, I walked on to Canterbury early in the morning. It was now winter again; and the fresh, cold windy day, and the sweeping downland, brightened up my hopes a little.

Coming into Canterbury, I loitered through the old streets with a sober pleasure that calmed my spirits, and eased my heart. There were the old signs, the old names over the shops, the old people serving in them. It appeared so long, since I had been a schoolboy there, that I wondered the place was so little changed, until I reflected how little I was changed myself. Strange to say, that quiet influence which was inseparable in my mind from Agnes, seemed to pervade even the city where she dwelt. The venerable cathedral towers, and the old jackdaws and rooks whose airy voices made them more retired than perfect silence would have done; the battered gateways, once stuck full with statues, long thrown down, and crumbled away, like the reverential pilgrims who had gazed upon them ; the still nooks, where the ivied growth of centuries crept over gabled ends and ruined walls ; the ancient houses, the pastoral landscape of field, orchard, and garden ; everywhere—on everything—I felt the same serener air, the same calm, thoughtful, softening spirit.

Arrived at Mr. Wickfield's house, I found, in the little lower room on the ground floor, where Uriah Heep had been of old accustomed to sit, Mr. Micawber plying his pen with great assiduity. He was dressed in a legal-looking suit of black, and loomed, burly and large, in that small office.

Mr. Micawber was extremely glad to see me, but a little confused too. He would have conducted me immediately into the presence of Uriah, but I declined.

"I know the house of old, you recollect," said I, "and will find my way up-stairs. How do you like the law, Mr. Micawber?"

"My dear Copperfield," he replied. "To a man possessed of the higher imaginative powers, the objection to legal studies is the amount of detail which they involve. Even in our professional correspondence," said Mr. Micawber, glancing at some letters he was writing, "the mind is not at liberty to soar to any exalted form of expression. Still, it is a great pursuit. A great pursuit!"

He then told me that he had become the tenant of Uriah Heep's old house ; and that Mrs. Micawber would be delighted to receive me, once more, under her own roof.

"It is humble," said Mr. Micawber, "to quote a favourite expression of my friend Heep ; but it may prove the stepping-stone to more ambitious domiciliary accommodation."

I asked him whether he had reason, so far, to be satisfied with his friend Heep's treatment of him? He got up to ascertain if the door were close shut, before he replied, in a lower voice:

"My dear Copperfield, a man who labours under the pressure of pecuniary embarrassments, is, with the generality of people, at a disadvantage. That disadvantage is not diminished, when that pressure necessitates the drawing of stipendiary emoluments, before those emoluments are strictly due and payable. All I can say is, that my friend Heep has responded to appeals to which I need not more particularly refer, in a manner calculated to redound equally to the honour of his head, and of his heart."

"I should not have supposed him to be very free with his money either," I observed.

"Pardon me!" said Mr. Micawber, with an air of constraint, "I speak of my friend Heep as I have experience."

"I am glad your experience is so favourable," I returned.

"You are very obliging, my dear Copperfield," said Mr. Micawber; and hummed a tune.

"Do you see much of Mr. Wickfield?" I asked, to change the subject.

"Not much," said Mr. Micawber, slightingly. "Mr. Wickfield is, I dare say, a man of very excellent intentions; but he is—in short, he is obsolete."

"I am afraid his partner seeks to make him so," said I.

"My dear Copperfield!" returned Mr. Micawber, after some uneasy evolutions on his stool, "allow me to offer a remark! I am here, in a capacity of confidence. I am here, in a position of trust. The discussion of some topics, even with Mrs. Micawber herself (so long the partner of my various vicissitudes, and a woman of a remarkable lucidity of intellect), is, I am led to consider, incompatible with the functions now devolving on me. I would therefore take the liberty of suggesting that in our friendly intercourse—which I trust will never be disturbed!—we draw a line. On one side of this line," said Mr. Micawber, representing it on the desk with the office ruler, "is the whole range of the human intellect, with a trifling exception; on the other, *is* that exception; that is to say, the affairs of Messrs. Wickfield and Heep, with all belonging and appertaining thereunto. I trust I give no offence to the companion of my youth, in submitting this proposition to his cooler judgment?"

Though I saw an uneasy change in Mr. Micawber, which sat tightly on him, as if his new duties were a misfit, I felt I had no right to be offended. My telling him so, appeared to relieve him; and he shook hands with me.

"I am charmed, Copperfield," said Mr. Micawber, "let me assure you, with Miss Wickfield. She is a very superior young lady, of very remarkable attractions, graces, and virtues. Upon my honour," said Mr. Micawber, indefinitely kissing his hand and bowing with his genteelest air, "I do Homage to Miss Wickfield! Hem!"

"I am glad of that, at least," said I.

"If you had not assured us, my dear Copperfield, on the occasion of that agreeable afternoon we had the happiness of passing with you, that D. was your favourite letter," said Mr. Micawber, "I should unquestionably have supposed that A. had been so."

We have all some experience of a feeling, that comes over us occasionally, of what we are saying and doing having been said and done before, in a remote time—of our having been surrounded, dim ages ago, by the same faces, objects, and circumstances—of our knowing perfectly what will be said next, as if we suddenly remembered it! I never had this mysterious impression more strongly in my life, than before he uttered those words.

I took my leave of Mr. Micawber, for the time, charging him with my best remembrances to all at home. As I left him, resuming his stool and his pen, and rolling his head in his stock, to get it into easier writing order, I clearly perceived that there was something interposed between him and me, since he had come into his new functions, which prevented our getting at each other as we used to do, and quite altered the character of our intercourse.

There was no one in the quaint old drawing-room, though it presented tokens of Mrs. Heep's whereabout. I looked into the room still belonging to Agnes, and saw her sitting by the fire, at a pretty old-fashioned desk she had, writing.

My darkening the light made her look up. What a pleasure to be the cause of that bright change in her attentive face, and the object of that sweet regard and welcome!

"Ah, Agnes!" said I, when we were sitting together, side by side; "I have missed you so much, lately!"

"Indeed?" she replied. "Again! And so soon?"

I shook my head.

"I don't know how it is, Agnes; I seem to want some faculty of mind that I ought to have. You were so much in the habit of thinking for me, in the happy old days here, and I came so naturally to you for counsel and support, that I really think I have missed acquiring it?"

"And what is it?" said Agnes, cheerfully.

"I don't know what to call it," I replied. "I think I am earnest and persevering?"

"I am sure of it," said Agnes.

"And patient, Agnes?" I inquired, with a little hesitation.

"Yes," returned Agnes, laughing. "Pretty well."

"And yet," said I, "I get so miserable and worried, and am so unsteady and irresolute in my power of assuring myself, that I know I must want—shall I call it—reliance, of some kind?"

"Call it so, if you will," said Agnes.

"Well!" I returned. "See here! You come to London, I rely on you, and I have an object and a course at once. I am driven out of it, I come here, and in a moment I feel an altered person. The circumstances that distressed me are not changed, since I came into this room; but an influence comes over me in that short interval that alters me, oh, how much for the better! What is it? What is your secret, Agnes?"

Her head was bent down, looking at the fire.

"It's the old story," said I. "Don't laugh, when I say it was always the same in little things as it is in greater ones. My old troubles were nonsense, and now they are serious; but whenever I have gone away from my adopted sister—"

Agnes looked up—with such a Heavenly face!—and gave me her hand, which I kissed.

"Whenever I have not had you, Agnes, to advise and approve in the beginning, I have seemed to go wild, and to get into all sorts of difficulty. When I have come to you, at last (as I have always done), I have come to peace and happiness. I come home, now, like a tired traveller, and find such a blessed sense of rest!"

I felt so deeply what I said, it affected me so sincerely, that my voice failed, and I covered my face with my hand, and broke into tears. I write the truth. Whatever contradictions and inconsistencies there were within me, as there are within so many of us; whatever might have been so different, and so much better; whatever I had done, in which I had perversely wandered away from the voice of my own heart; I knew nothing of. I only knew that I was fervently in earnest, when I felt the rest and peace of having Agnes near me.

In her placid sisterly manner; with her beaming eyes; with her tender voice; and with that sweet composure, which had long ago made the house that held her quite a sacred place to me; she soon won me from this weakness, and led me on to tell all that had happened since our last meeting.

"And there is not another word to tell, Agnes," said I, when I had made an end of my confidence. "Now, my reliance is on you."

"But it must not be on me, Trotwood," returned Agnes with a pleasant smile. "It must be on some one else."

" On Dora ? " said I.

" Assuredly."

" Why, I have not mentioned, Agnes," said I, a little embarrassed, " that Dora is rather difficult to—I would not, for the world, say, to rely upon, because she is the soul of purity and truth—but rather difficult to—I hardly know how to express it, really, Agnes. She is a timid little thing, and easily disturbed and frightened. Some time ago, before her father's death, when I thought it right to mention to her—but I'll tell you, if you will bear with me, how it was."

Accordingly, I told Agnes about my declaration of poverty, about the cookery-book, the housekeeping accounts, and all the rest of it.

" Oh, Trotwood ! " she remonstrated, with a smile. " Just your old headlong way ! You might have been in earnest in striving to get on in the world, without being so very sudden with a timid, loving, inexperienced girl. Poor Dora ! "

I never heard such sweet forbearing kindness expressed in a voice, as she expressed in making this reply. It was as if I had seen her admiringly and tenderly embracing Dora, and tacitly reproving me, by her considerate protection, for my hot haste in fluttering that little heart. It was as if I had seen Dora, in all her fascinating artlessness, caressing Agnes, and thanking her, and coaxingly appealing against me, and loving me with all her childish innocence.

I felt so grateful to Agnes, and admired her so ! I saw those two together, in a bright perspective, such well-associated friends, each adorning the other so much !

" What ought I to do then, Agnes ? " I inquired, after looking at the fire a little while. " What would it be right to do ? "

" I think," said Agnes, " that the honourable course to take, would be to write to those two ladies. Don't you think that any secret course is an unworthy one ? "

" Yes. If *you* think so," said I.

" I am poorly qualified to judge of such matters," replied

Agnes, with a modest hesitation, " but I certainly feel—in short, I feel that your being secret and clandestine, is not being like yourself."

"Like myself, in the too high opinion you have of me, Agnes, I am afraid," said I.

"Like yourself, in the candour of your nature," she returned; "and therefore I would write to those two ladies. I would relate, as plainly and as openly as possible, all that has taken place; and I would ask their permission to visit sometimes at their house. Considering that you are young, and striving for a place in life, I think it would be well to say that you would readily abide by any conditions they might impose upon you. I would entreat them not to dismiss your request, without a reference to Dora; and to discuss it with her when they should think the time suitable. I would not be too vehement," said Agnes, gently, " or propose too much. I would trust to my fidelity and perseverance—and to Dora."

"But if they were to frighten Dora again, Agnes, by speaking to her," said I. "And if Dora were to cry, and say nothing about me!"

"Is that likely?" inquired Agnes, with the same sweet consideration in her face.

"God bless her, she is as easily scared as a bird," said I. "It might be! Or if the two Miss Spenlows (elderly ladies of that sort are odd characters sometimes) should not be likely persons to address in that way!"

"I don't think, Trotwood," returned Agnes, raising her soft eyes to mine, " I would consider that. Perhaps it would be better only to consider whether it is right to do this; and, if it is, to do it."

I had no longer any doubt on the subject. With a lightened heart, though with a profound sense of the weighty importance of my task, I devoted the whole afternoon to the composition of the draft of this letter; for which great purpose, Agnes relinquished her desk to me. But first I went down-stairs to see Mr. Wickfield and Uriah Heep.

I found Uriah in possession of a new, plaster-smelling office, built out in the garden; looking extraordinarily mean, in the midst of a quantity of books and papers. He received me in his usual fawning way, and pretended not to have heard of my arrival from Mr. Micawber; a pretence I took the liberty of disbelieving. He accompanied me into Mr. Wickfield's room, which was the shadow of its former self—having been divested of a variety of conveniences, for the accommodation of the new partner—and stood before the fire, warming his back, and shaving his chin with his bony hand, while Mr. Wickfield and I exchanged greetings.

"You stay with us, Trotwood, while you remain in Canterbury?" said Mr. Wickfield, not without a glance at Uriah for his approval.

"Is there room for me?" said I.

"I am sure, Master Copperfield—I should say Mister, but the other comes so natural," said Uriah,—"I would turn out of your old room with pleasure, if it would be agreeable."

"No, no," said Mr. Wickfield. "Why should *you* be inconvenienced? There's another room. There's another room."

"Oh, but you know," returned Uriah, with a grin, "I should really be delighted!"

To cut the matter short, I said I would have the other room or none at all; so it was settled that I should have the other room; and, taking my leave of the firm until dinner, I went up-stairs again.

I had hoped to have no other companion than Agnes. But Mrs. Heep had asked permission to bring herself and her knitting near the fire, in that room; on pretence of its having an aspect more favourable for her rheumatics, as the wind then was, than the drawing-room or dining-parlour. Though I could almost have consigned her to the mercies of the wind on the topmost pinnacle of the Cathedral, without remorse, I made a virtue of necessity, and gave her a friendly salutation.

AN EVIL EYE.

"I'm umbly thankful to you, sir," said Mrs. Heep, in acknowledgment of my inquiries concerning her health, "but I'm only pretty well. I haven't much to boast of. If I could see my Uriah well settled in life, I couldn't expect much more, I think. How do you think my Ury looking, sir?"

I thought him looking as villanous as ever, and I replied that I saw no change in him.

"Oh, don't you think he's changed?" said Mrs. Heep. "There I must umbly beg leave to differ from you. Don't you see a thinness in him?"

"Not more than usual," I replied.

"*Don't* you though!" said Mrs. Heep. "But you don't take notice of him with a mother's eye!"

His mother's eye was an evil eye to the rest of the world, I thought as it met mine, howsoever affectionate to him; and I believe she and her son were devoted to one another. It passed me, and went on to Agnes.

"Don't *you* see a wasting and a wearing in him, Miss Wickfield?" inquired Mrs. Heep.

"No," said Agnes, quietly pursuing the work on which she was engaged. "You are too solicitous about him. He is very well."

Mrs. Heep, with a prodigious sniff, resumed her knitting.

She never left off, or left us for a moment. I had arrived early in the day, and we had still three or four hours before dinner; but she sat there, plying her knitting-needles as monotonously as an hour-glass might have poured out its sands. She sat on one side of the fire; I sat at the desk in front of it; a little beyond me, on the other side, sat Agnes. Whensoever, slowly pondering over my letter, I lifted up my eyes, and meeting the thoughtful face of Agnes, saw it clear, and beam encouragement upon me, with its own angelic expression, I was conscious presently of the evil eye passing me, and going on to her, and coming back to me again, and dropping furtively upon the knitting. What the knitting was, I don't know, not being learned in that art;

but it looked like a net; and as she worked away with those Chinese chopsticks of knitting-needles, she showed in the fire-light like an ill-looking enchantress, baulked as yet by the radiant goodness opposite, but getting ready for a cast of her net by-and-by.

At dinner she maintained her watch, with the same un-winking eyes. After dinner, her son took his turn; and when Mr. Wickfield, himself, and I were left alone together, leered at me, and writhed until I could hardly bear it. In the drawing-room, there was the mother knitting and watch-ing again. All the time that Agnes sang and played, the mother sat at the piano. Once she asked for a particular ballad, which she said her Ury (who was yawning in a great chair) doted on; and at intervals she looked round at him, and reported to Agnes that he was in raptures with the music. But she hardly ever spoke—I question if she ever did—without making some mention of him. It was evident to me that this was the duty assigned to her.

This lasted until bedtime. To have seen the mother and son, like two great bats hanging over the whole house, and darkening it with their ugly forms, made me so uncom-fortable, that I would rather have remained down-stairs, knitting and all, than gone to bed. I hardly got any sleep. Next day the knitting and watching began again, and lasted all day.

I had not an opportunity of speaking to Agnes, for ten minutes. I could barely show her my letter. I proposed to her to walk out with me; but Mrs. Heep repeatedly com-plaining that she was worse, Agnes charitably remained within, to bear her company. Towards the twilight I went out by myself, musing on what I ought to do, and whether I was justified in withholding from Agnes, any longer, what Uriah Heep had told me in London: for that began to trouble me again, very much.

I had not walked out far enough to be quite clear of the town, upon the Ramsgate road, where there was a good path, when I was hailed, through the dust, by somebody behind me. The shambling figure, and the scanty great coat, were not to be mistaken. I stopped, and Uriah Heep came up.

"Well?" said I.

"How fast you walk!" said he. "My legs are pretty long, but you've given 'em quite a job."

"Where are you going?" said I.

"I am coming with you, Master Copperfield, if you'll allow me the pleasure of a walk with an old acquaintance." Saying this, with a jerk of his body, which might have been either propitiatory or derisive, he fell into step beside me.

"Uriah!" said I, as civilly as I could, after a silence.

"Master Copperfield!" said Uriah.

"To tell you the truth (at which you will not be offended), I came out to walk alone, because I have had so much company."

He looked at me sideways, and said with his hardest grin,—"You mean mother."

"Why yes, I do," said I.

"Ah! But you know we're so very umble," he returned. "And having such a knowledge of our own umbleness, we must really take care that we're not pushed to the wall by them as isn't umble. All stratagems are fair in love, sir."

Raising his great hands until they touched his chin, he rubbed them softly, and softly chuckled; looking as like a malevolent baboon, I thought, as anything human could look.

"You see," he said, still hugging himself in that unpleasant way, and shaking his head at me, "you're quite a dangerous rival, Master Copperfield. You always was, you know."

"Do you set a watch upon Miss Wickfield, and make her home no home, because of me?" said I.

"Oh! Master Copperfield! Those are very arsh words," he replied.

"Put my meaning into any words you like," said I. "You know what it is, Uriah, as well as I do."

"Oh no! You must put it into words," he said. "Oh, really! I couldn't myself."

"Do you suppose," said I, constraining myself to be very temperate and quiet with him, on account of Agnes, "that I regard Miss Wickfield otherwise than as a very dear sister?"

"Well, Master Copperfield," he replied, "you perceive I am not bound to answer that question. You may not, you know. But then, you see, you may!"

Anything to equal the low cunning of his visage, and of his shadowless eyes without the ghost of an eyelash, I never saw.

"Come then!" said I. "For the sake of Miss Wickfield—"

"My Agnes!" he exclaimed, with a sickly, angular contortion of himself. "Would you be so good as call her Agnes, Master Copperfield!"

"For the sake of Agnes Wickfield—Heaven bless her!"

"Thank you for that blessing, Master Copperfield!" he interposed.

"I will tell you what I should, under any other circumstances, as soon have thought of telling to—Jack Ketch."

"To who, sir?" said Uriah, stretching out his neck, and shading his ear with his hand.

"To the hangman," I returned. "The most unlikely person I could think of,"—though his own face had suggested the allusion quite as a natural sequence. "I am engaged to another young lady. I hope that contents you."

"Upon your soul?" said Uriah.

I was about indignantly to give my assertion the confirmation he required, when he caught hold of my hand, and gave it a squeeze.

"Oh, Master Copperfield," he said. "If you had only had the condescension to return my confidence when I poured out the fulness of my art, the night I put you so much out of the way by sleeping before your sitting-room fire, I never should have doubted you. As it is, I'm sure I'll take off mother directly, and only too appy. I know you'll excuse the precautions of affection, won't you? What a pity, Master Copperfield, that you didn't condescend to return my confidence! I'm sure I gave you every opportunity. But you never have condescended to me, as much as I could have wished. I know you have never liked me, as I have liked you!"

All this time he was squeezing my hand with his damp fishy fingers, while I made every effort I decently could to get it away. But I was quite unsuccessful. He drew it under the sleeve of his mulberry-coloured great coat, and I walked on, almost upon compulsion, arm in arm with him.

"Shall we turn?" said Uriah, by-and-by wheeling me face about towards the town, on which the early moon was now shining, silvering the distant windows.

"Before we leave the subject, you ought to understand," said I, breaking a pretty long silence, "that I believe Agnes Wickfield to be as far above *you*, and as far removed from all *your* aspirations, as that moon herself!"

"Peaceful! Ain't she!" said Uriah. "Very! Now confess, Master Copperfield, that you haven't liked me quite as I have liked you. All along you've thought me too umble now, I shouldn't wonder?"

"I am not fond of professions of humility," I returned, "or professions of anything else."

"There now!" said Uriah, looking flabby and lead-coloured in the moonlight. "Didn't I know it! But how little you think of the rightful umbleness of a person in my station, Master Copperfield! Father and me was both brought up at a foundation school for boys; and mother, she was likewise brought up at a public, sort of charitable, establishment. They taught us all a deal of umbleness—not much else that I know of, from morning to night. We was to be umble to this person, and umble to that; and to pull off our caps here, and to make bows there; and always to know our place, and abase ourselves before our betters. And we had such a lot of betters! Father got the monitor-medal by being umble. So did I. Father got made a sexton by being umble. He had the character, among the gentlefolks, of being such a well-behaved man, that they were determined to bring him in. 'Be umble, Uriah,' says father to me, 'and you'll get on. It was what was always being dinned into you and me at school; it's what goes down best. Be umble,' says father, 'and you'll do!' And really it ain't done bad!"

It was the first time it had ever occurred to me, that this detestable cant of false humility might have originated out of the Heep family. I had seen the harvest, but had never thought of the seed.

"When I was quite a young boy," said Uriah, "I got to know what umbleness did, and I took to it. I ate umble pie with an appetite. I stopped at the umble point of my learning, and says I, 'Hold hard!' When you offered to teach me Latin, I knew better. 'People like to be above you,' says father, 'keep yourself down.' I am very umble to the present moment, Master Copperfield, but I've got a little power!"

And he said all this—I knew, as I saw his face in the moonlight—that I might understand he was resolved to recompense himself by using his power. I had never doubted his meanness, his craft and malice; but I fully comprehended now, for the first time, what a base, unrelenting, and revengeful spirit, must have been engendered by this early, and this long, suppression.

His account of himself was so far attended with an agreeable result, that it led to his withdrawing his hand in order that he might have another hug of himself under the chin. Once apart from him, I was determined to keep apart; and we walked back, side by side, saying very little more by the way.

Whether his spirits were elevated by the communication I had made to him, or by his having indulged in this retrospect, I don't know; but they were raised by some influence.

He talked more at dinner than was usual with him; asked his mother (off duty from the moment of our re-entering the house) whether he was not growing too old for a bachelor; and once looked at Agnes so, that I would have given all I had, for leave to knock him down.

When we three males were left alone after dinner, he got into a more adventurous state. He had taken little or no wine; and I presume it was the mere insolence of triumph that was upon him, flushed perhaps by the temptation my presence furnished to its exhibition.

I had observed yesterday, that he tried to entice Mr. Wickfield to drink; and interpreting the look which Agnes had given me as she went out, had limited myself to one glass, and then proposed that we should follow her. I would have done so again to-day; but Uriah was too quick for me.

"We seldom see our present visitor, sir," he said, addressing Mr. Wickfield, sitting, such a contrast to him, at the end of the table, "and I should propose to give him welcome in another glass or two of wine, if you have no objections. Mr. Copperfield, your elth and appiness!"

I was obliged to make a show of taking the hand he stretched across to me; and then, with very different emotions, I took the hand of the broken gentleman, his partner.

"Come, fellow-partner," said Uriah, "if I may take the liberty,—now, suppose you give us something or another appropriate to Copperfield!"

I pass over Mr. Wickfield's proposing my aunt, his proposing Mr. Dick, his proposing Doctors' Commons, his proposing Uriah, his drinking everything twice; his consciousness of his own weakness, the ineffectual effort that he made against it; the struggle between his shame in Uriah's deportment, and his desire to conciliate him; the manifest exultation with which Uriah twisted and turned, and held him up before me. It made me sick at heart to see, and my hand recoils from writing it.

"Come, fellow-partner!" said Uriah, at last, "*I*'ll give you another one, and I umbly ask for bumpers, seeing I intend to make it the divinest of her sex."

Her father had his empty glass in his hand. I saw him set it down, look at the picture she was so like, put his hand to his forehead, and shrink back in his elbow-chair.

"I'm an umble individual to give you her elth," proceeded Uriah, "but I admire—adore her."

No physical pain that her father's grey head could have borne, I think could have been more terrible to me, than the mental endurance I saw compressed now within both his hands.

"Agnes," said Uriah, either not regarding him, or not knowing what the nature of his action was, "Agnes Wickfield is, I am safe to say, the divinest of her sex. May I speak out, among friends? To be her father is a proud distinction, but to be her usband—"

Spare me from ever again hearing such a cry, as that with which her father rose up from the table!

"What's the matter?" said Uriah, turning of a deadly colour. "You are not gone mad, after all, Mr. Wickfield, I hope? If I say I've an ambition to make your Agnes my Agnes, I have as good a right to it as another man. I have a better right to it than any other man!"

I had my arms round Mr. Wickfield, imploring him by everything that I could think of, oftenest of all by his love for Agnes, to calm himself a little. He was mad for the moment; tearing out his hair, beating his head, trying to force me from him, and to force himself from me, not answering a word, not looking at or seeing any one; blindly striving for he knew not what, his face all staring and distorted—a frightful spectacle.

I conjured him, incoherently, but in the most impassioned manner, not to abandon himself to this wildness, but to hear me. I besought him to think of Agnes, to connect me with Agnes, to recollect how Agnes and I had grown up together, how I honoured her and loved her, how she was his pride and joy. I tried to bring her idea before him in any form ; I even reproached him with not having firmness to spare her the knowledge of such a scene as this. I may have effected something, or his wildness may have spent itself ; but by degrees he struggled less, and began to look at me—strangely at first, then with recognition in his eyes. At length he said, "I know, Trotwood ! My darling child and you—I know ! But look at him ! "

He pointed to Uriah, pale and glowering in a corner, evidently very much out in his calculations, and taken by surprise.

"Look at my torturer," he replied. "Before him I have step by step abandoned name and reputation, peace and quiet, house and home."

"I have kept your name and reputation for you, and your peace and quiet, and your house and home too," said Uriah, with a sulky, hurried, defeated air of compromise. "Don't be foolish, Mr. Wickfield. If I have gone a little beyond what you were prepared for, I can go back, I suppose ? There's no harm done."

"I looked for single motives in every one," said Mr. Wickfield, "and I was satisfied I had bound him to me by motives of interest. But see what he is—oh, see what he is ! "

"You had better stop him, Copperfield, if you can," cried Uriah, with his long forefinger pointing towards me. "He'll say something presently—mind you !—he'll be sorry to have said afterwards, and you'll be sorry to have heard ! "

"I'll say anything ! " cried Mr. Wickfield, with a desperate air. "Why should I not be in all the world's power if I am in yours ? "

"Mind ! I tell you ! " said Uriah, continuing to warn me. "If you don't stop his mouth, you're not his friend ! Why shouldn't you be in all the world's power, Mr. Wickfield ? Because you have got a daughter. You and me know what we know, don't we ? Let sleeping dogs lie—who wants to rouse 'em ? I don't. Can't you see I am as umble as I can be? I tell you, if I've gone too far, I'm sorry. What would you have, sir?"

"Oh, Trotwood, Trotwood!" exclaimed Mr. Wickfield, wringing his hands. "What I have come down to be, since I first saw you in this house! I was on my downward way then, but the dreary, dreary, road I have traversed since! Weak indulgence has ruined me. Indulgence in remembrance, and indulgence in forgetfulness. My natural grief for my child's mother turned to disease; my natural love for my child turned to disease. I have infected everything I touched. I have brought misery on what I dearly love, I know—*You* know! I thought it possible that I could truly love one creature in the world, and not love the rest; I thought it possible that I could truly mourn for one creature gone out of the world, and not have some part in the grief of all who mourned. Thus the lessons of my life have been perverted! I have preyed on my own morbid coward heart, and it has preyed on me. Sordid in my grief, sordid in my love, sordid in my miserable escape from the darker side of both, oh see the ruin I am, and hate me, shun me!"

He dropped into a chair, and weakly sobbed. The excitement into which he had been roused was leaving him. Uriah came out of his corner.

"I don't know all I have done, in my fatuity," said Mr. Wickfield, putting out his hands, as if to deprecate my condemnation. "*He* knows best," meaning Uriah Heep, "for he has always been at my elbow, whispering me. You see the millstone that he is about my neck. You find him in my house, you find him in my business. You heard him, but a little time ago. What need have I to say more!"

"You haven't need to say so much, nor half so much, nor anything at all," observed Uriah, half defiant, and half fawning. "You wouldn't have took it up so, if it hadn't been for the wine. You'll think better of it to-morrow, sir. If I have said too much, or more than I meant, what of it? I haven't stood by it!"

ANOTHER PARTING FROM AGNES.

The door opened, and Agnes, gliding in, without a vestige of colour in her face, put her arm round his neck, and steadily said, "Papa, you are not well. Come with me!" He laid his head upon her shoulder, as if he were oppressed with heavy shame, and went out with her. Her eyes met mine for but an instant, yet I saw how much she knew of what had passed.

"I didn't expect he'd cut up so rough, Master Copperfield," said Uriah. "But it's nothing. I'll be friends with him to-morrow. It's for his good. I'm umbly anxious for his good."

I gave him no answer, and went up-stairs into the quiet room where Agnes had so often sat beside me at my books. Nobody came near me until late at night. I took up a book and tried to read. I heard the clocks strike twelve, and was still reading, without knowing what I read, when Agnes touched me.

"You will be going early in the morning, Trotwood! Let us say good-bye, now!"

She had been weeping, but her face then was so calm and beautiful!

"Heaven bless you!" she said, giving me her hand.

"Dearest Agnes!" I returned, "I see you ask me not to speak of to-night—but is there nothing to be done?"

"There is God to trust in!" she replied.

"Can *I* do nothing—*I*, who come to you with *my* poor sorrows?"

"And make mine so much lighter," she replied. "Dear Trotwood, no!"

"Dear Agnes," I said, "it is presumptuous for me, who am so poor in all in which you are so rich—goodness, resolution, all noble qualities—to doubt or direct you; but you know how much I love you, and how much I owe you. You will never sacrifice yourself to a mistaken sense of duty, Agnes?"

More agitated for a moment than I had ever seen her, she took her hand from me, and moved a step back.

"Say you have no such thought, dear Agnes! Much more than sister! Think of the priceless gift of such a heart a yours, of such a love as yours!"

Oh! long, long afterwards, I saw that face rise up befor me, with its momentary look, not wondering, not accusing not regretting. Oh, long, long afterwards, I saw that lool subside, as it did now, into the lovely smile, with which sh told me she had no fear for herself—I need have none for he —and parted from me by the name of Brother, and was gone

It was dark in the morning when I got upon the coach a the inn door. The day was just breaking when we wer about to start, and then, as I sat thinking of her, cam struggling up the coach side, through the mingled day an night, Uriah's head.

"Copperfield!" said he, in a croaking whisper, as he hung by the iron on the roof, "I thought you'd be glad to hear before you went off, that there are no squares broke betweer us. I've been into his room already, and we've made it all smooth. Why, though I'm umble, I'm useful to him, you know; and he understands his interest when he isn't in liquor What an agreeable man he is, after all, Master Copperfield!"

I obliged myself to say that I was glad he had made hi apology.

"Oh, to be sure!" said Uriah. "When a person's umble you know, what's an apology? So easy! I say! I suppose," with a jerk, "you have sometimes plucked a pear before i was ripe, Master Copperfield?"

"I suppose I have," I replied.

"*I* did that last night," said Uriah; "but it'll ripen yet It only wants attending to. I can wait!"

Profuse in his farewells, he got down again as the coachmar got up. For anything I know, he was eating something t keep the raw morning air out; but he made motions witl his mouth as if the pear were ripe already, and he wer smacking his lips over it.

CHAPTER XL.

THE WANDERER.

We had a very serious conversation in Buckingham Street that night, about the domestic occurrences I have detailed in the last chapter. My aunt was deeply interested in them, and walked up and down the room with her arms folded, for more than two hours afterwards. Whenever she was particularly discomposed, she always performed one of these pedestrian feats; and the amount of her discomposure might always be estimated by the duration of her walk. On this occasion she was so much disturbed in mind as to find it necessary to open the bedroom door, and make a course for herself, comprising the full extent of the bedrooms from wall to wall; and while Mr. Dick and I sat quietly by the fire, she kept passing in and out, along this measured track, at an unchanging pace, with the regularity of a clock-pendulum.

When my aunt and I were left to ourselves by Mr. Dick's going out to bed, I sat down to write my letter to the two old ladies. By that time she was tired of walking, and sat by the fire with her dress tucked up as usual. But instead of sitting in her usual manner, holding her glass upon her knee, she suffered it to stand neglected on the chimney-piece; and, resting her left elbow on her right arm, and her chin on her left hand, looked thoughtfully at me. As often as I raised my eyes from what I was about, I met hers. "I am in the lovingest of tempers, my dear," she would assure me with a nod, " but I am fidgeted and sorry ! "

I had been too busy to observe, until after she was gone to bed, that she had left her night-mixture, as she always called it, untasted on the chimney-piece. She came to her door, with even more than her usual affection of manner, when I knocked to acquaint her with this discovery; but only said, "I have not the heart to take it, Trot, to-night," and shook her head, and went in again.

She read my letter to the two old ladies, in the morning, and approved of it. I posted it, and had nothing to do then, but wait, as patiently as I could, for the reply. I was still in this state of expectation, and had been, for nearly a week; when I left the Doctor's one snowy night, to walk home.

It had been a bitter day, and a cutting north-east wind had blown for some time. The wind had gone down with the light, and so the snow had come on. It was a heavy, settled fall, I recollect, in great flakes; and it lay thick. The noise of wheels and tread of people were as hushed, as if the streets had been strewn that depth with feathers.

My shortest way home,—and I naturally took the shortest way on such a night—was through Saint Martin's Lane. Now, the church which gives its name to the lane, stood in a less free situation at that time; there being no open space before it, and the lane winding down to the Strand. As I passed the steps of the portico, I encountered, at the corner, a woman's face. It looked in mine, passed across the narrow lane, and disappeared. I knew it. I had seen it somewhere. But I could not remember where. I had some association with it, that struck upon my heart directly; but I was thinking of anything else when it came upon me, and was confused.

On the steps of the church, there was the stooping figure of a man, who had put down some burden on the smooth snow, to adjust it; my seeing the face, and my seeing him, were simultaneous. I don't think I had stopped in my surprise; but, in any case, as I went on, he rose, turned, and came down towards me. I stood face to face with Mr. Peggotty!

Then I remembered the woman. It was Martha, to whom Emily had given the money that night in the kitchen. Martha Endell—side by side with whom, he would not have seen his dear niece, Ham had told me, for all the treasures wrecked in the sea.

We shook hands heartily. At first, neither of us could speak a word.

"Mas'r Davy!" he said, griping me tight, "it do my art good to see you, sir. Well met, well met!"

"Well met, my dear old friend!" said I.

"I had my thowts o' coming to make inquiration for you, sir, to-night," he said, "but knowing as your aunt was living along wi' you—for I've been down yonder—Yarmouth way— I was afeerd it was too late. I should have come early in the morning, sir, afore going away."

"Again?" said I.

"Yes, sir," he replied, patiently shaking his head, "I'm away to-morrow."

"Where were you going now?" I asked.

"Well!" he replied, shaking the snow out of his long hair, "I was a going to turn in somewheers."

In those days there was a side-entrance to the stable-yard of the Golden Cross, the inn so memorable to me in connexion with his misfortune, nearly opposite to where we stood. I pointed out the gateway, put my arm through his, and we went across. Two or three public-rooms opened out of the stable-yard; and looking into one of them, and finding it empty, and a good fire burning, I took him in there.

When I saw him in the light, I observed, not only that his hair was long and ragged, but that his face was burnt dark by the sun. He was greyer, the lines in his face and forehead were deeper, and he had every appearance of having toiled and wandered through all varieties of weather; but he looked very strong, and like a man upheld by stedfastness of purpose, whom nothing could tire out. He shook the snow from his hat and clothes, and brushed it away from his face while I was inwardly making these remarks. As he sate down opposite to me at a table, with his back to the door by which we had entered, he put out his rough hand again and grasped mine warmly.

"I'll tell you, Mas'r Davy," he said,—"wheer all I've been and what-all we've heerd. I've been fur, and we've heerd little; but I'll tell you!"

I rang the bell for something hot to drink. He would have nothing stronger than ale; and while it was being brought, and being warmed at the fire, he sat thinking. There was a fine massive gravity in his face, I did not venture to disturb.

"When she was a child," he said, lifting up his head soon after we were left alone, "she used to talk to me a deal about the sea, and about them coasts where the sea got to be dark blue, and to lay a-shining and a-shining in the sun. I thowt, odd times, as her father being drownded made her think on it so much. I doen't know, you see, but maybe she believed—or hoped—he had drifted out to them parts, where the flowers is always a blowing, and the country bright."

"It is likely to have been a childish fancy," I replied.

"When she was—lost," said Mr. Peggotty, "I know'd in my mind, as he would take her to them countries. I know'd in my mind, as he'd have told her wonders of 'em, and how she was to be a lady theer, and how he got her listen to him fust, along o' sech like. When we see his mother, I know'd quite well as I was right. I went across-channel to France, and landed theer, as if I'd fell down from the sky."

I saw the door move, and the snow drift in. I saw it move a little more, and a hand softly interpose to keep it open.

"I found out an English gen'leman as was in authority," said Mr. Peggotty, "and told him I was a going to seek my

The Wanderer

niece. He got me them papers as I wanted fur to carry me through—I doen't rightly know how they're called—and he would have give me money, but that I was thankful to have no need on. I thank him kind, for all he done, I'm sure! 'I've wrote afore you,' he says to me, 'and I shall speak to many as will come that way, and many will know you, fur distant from here, when you're a travelling alone.' I told him, best as I was able, what my gratitoode was, and went away through France."

"Alone, and on foot?" said I.

"Mostly a-foot," he rejoined; "sometimes in carts along with people going to market; sometimes in empty coaches. Many mile a day a-foot, and often with some poor soldier or another, travelling to see his friends. I couldn't talk to him," said Mr. Peggotty, "nor he to me; but we was company for one another, too, along the dusty roads."

I should have known that by his friendly tone.

"When I come to any town," he pursued, "I found the inn, and waited about the yard till some one turned up (some one mostly did) as know'd English. Then I told how that I was on my way to seek my niece, and they told me what manner of gentlefolks was in the house, and I waited to see any as seemed like her, going in or out. When it warn't Em'ly, I went on agen. By little and little, when I come to a new village or that, among the poor people, I found they know'd about me. They would set me down at their cottage doors, and give me what-not fur to eat and drink, and show me where to sleep; and many a woman, Mas'r Davy, as has had a daughter of about Em'ly's age, I've found a-waiting for me, at Our Saviour's Cross outside the village, fur to do me sim'lar kindnesses. Some has had daughters as was dead. And God only knows how good them mothers was to me!"

It was Martha at the door. I saw her haggard, listening face distinctly. My dread was lest he should turn his head, and see her too.

"They would often put their children—partic'lar their little girls," said Mr. Peggotty, "upon my knee; and many a time you might have seen me sitting at their doors, when night was coming on, a'most as if they'd been my Darling's children. Oh, my Darling!"

Overpowered by sudden grief, he sobbed aloud. I laid my trembling hand upon the hand he put before his face. "Thankee, sir," he said, "doen't take no notice."

In a very little while he took his hand away and put it on his breast, and went on with his story.

"They often walked with me," he said, "in the morning, maybe a mile or two upon my road; and when we parted, and I said, 'I'm very thankful to you! God bless you!' they always seemed to understand, and answered pleasant. At last I come to the sea. It warn't hard, you may suppose, for a seafaring man like me to work his way over to Italy. When I got theer, I wandered on as I had done afore. The people was just as good to me, and I should have gone from town to town, maybe the country through, but that I got news of her being seen among them Swiss mountains yonder. One as know'd his sarvant see 'em there, all three, and told me how they travelled, and where they was. I made for them mountains, Mas'r Davy, day and night. Ever so fur as I went, ever so fur the mountains seemed to shift away from me. But I come up with 'em, and I crossed 'em. When I got nigh the place as I had been told of, I began to think within my own self, 'What shall I do when I see her?'"

The listening face, insensible to the inclement night, still drooped at the door, and the hands begged me—prayed me —not to cast it forth.

"I never doubted her," said Mr. Peggotty. "No! Not a bit! On'y let her see my face—on'y let her heer my voice— on'y let my stanning still afore her bring to her thoughts the home she had fled away from, and the child she had been— and if she had growed to be a royal lady, she'd have fell down at my feet! I know'd it well! Many a time in my sleep had I heerd her cry out, 'Uncle!' and seen her fall like death afore me. Many a time in my sleep had I raised her up, and whispered to her, 'Em'ly, my dear, I am come fur to bring forgiveness, and to take you home!'"

He stopped and shook his head, and went on with a sigh.

"*He* was nowt to me now. Em'ly was all. I bought a country dress to put upon her; and I know'd that, once found, she would walk beside me over them stony roads, go where I would, and never, never, leave me more. To put that dress upon her, and to cast off what she wore—to take her on my arm again, and wander towards home—to stop sometimes upon the road, and heal her bruised feet and her worse-bruised heart—was all that I thowt of now. I doen't believe I should have done so much as look at him. But, Mas'r Davy, it warn't to be—not yet! I was too late, and they was gone. Wheer, I couldn't learn. Some said heer, some said theer. I travelled heer, and I travelled theer, but I found no Em'ly, and I travelled home."

"How long ago?" I asked.

"A matter o' fower days," said Mr. Peggotty. "I sighted the old boat arter dark, and the light a shining in the winder. When I come nigh and looked in through the glass, I see the faithful creetur Missis Gummidge sittin' by the fire, as we had fixed upon, alone. I called out, 'Doen't be afeerd! It's Dan'l!' and I went in. I never could have thowt the old boat would have been so strange!"

From some pocket in his breast he took out, with a very careful hand, a small paper bundle containing two or three letters or little packets, which he laid upon the table.

"This fust one come," he said, selecting it from the rest, "afore I had been gone a week. A fifty pound Bank note, in a sheet of paper, directed to me, and put underneath the door in the night. She tried to hide her writing, but she couldn't hide it from Me!"

He folded up the note again, with great patience and care, in exactly the same form, and laid it on one side.

"This come to Missis Gummidge," he said, opening another, "two or three months ago." After looking at it for some moments, he gave it to me, and added in a low voice, "Be so good as read it, sir."

I read as follows:

"Oh what will you feel when you see this writing, and know it comes from my wicked hand! But try, try—not for my sake, but for uncle's goodness, try to let your heart soften to me, only for a little little time! Try, pray do to relent towards a miserable girl, and write down on a bit of paper whether he is well, and what he said about me before you left off ever naming me among yourselves—and whether, of a night, when it is my old time of coming home, you ever see him look as if he thought of one he used to love so dear. Oh, my heart is breaking when I think about it! I am kneeling down to you, begging and praying you not to be as hard with me as I deserve—as I well well know I deserve—but to be so gentle and so good, as to write down something of him, and to send it to me. You need not call me Little, you need not call me by the name I have disgraced; but oh, listen to my agony, and have mercy on me so far as to write me some word of uncle, never, never to be seen in this world by my eyes again!

"Dear, if your heart is hard towards me—justly hard, I know—but, Listen, if it is hard, dear, ask him I have wronged the most—him whose wife I was to have been—before you quite decide against my poor poor prayer! If he should be so compassionate as to say that you might write something for me to read—I think he would, oh, I think he would, if you would only ask him, for he always was so brave and so forgiving—tell him then (but not else), that when I hear the wind blowing at night, I feel as if it was passing angrily from seeing him and uncle, and was going up to God against me. Tell him that if I was to die to-morrow (and oh, if I was fit, I would be so glad to die!) I would bless him and uncle with my last words, and pray for his happy home with my last breath!"

Some money was enclosed in this letter also. Five pounds. It was untouched like the previous sum, and he refolded it in the same way. Detailed instructions were added relative to the address of a reply, which, although they betrayed the intervention of several hands, and made it difficult to arrive at any very probable conclusion in reference to her place of concealment, made it at least not unlikely that she had written from that spot where she was stated to have been seen.

"What answer was sent?" I inquired of Mr. Peggotty.

"Missis Gummidge," he returned, "not being a good

scholar, sir, Ham kindly drawed it out, and she made a copy on it. They told her I was gone to seek her, and what my parting words was."

"Is that another letter in your hand?" said I.

"It's money, sir," said Mr. Peggotty, unfolding it a little way. "Ten pound, you see. And wrote inside, 'From a true friend,' like the fust. But the fust was put underneath the door, and this come by the post, day afore yesterday. I'm a going to seek her at the post-mark."

He showed it to me. It was a town on the Upper Rhine. He had found out, at Yarmouth, some foreign dealers who knew that country, and they had drawn him a rude map on paper, which he could very well understand. He laid it between us on the table; and, with his chin resting on one hand, tracked his course upon it with the other.

I asked him how Ham was? He shook his head.

"He works," he said, "as bold as a man can. His name's as good, in all that part, as any man's is, anywheres in the wureld. Any one's hand is ready to help him, you understand, and his is ready to help them. He's never been heerd fur to complain. But my sister's belief is ('twixt ourselves) as it has cut him deep."

"Poor fellow, I can believe it!"

"He ain't no care, Mas'r Davy," said Mr. Peggotty in a solemn whisper—"keinder no care no-how for his life. When a man's wanted for rough sarvice in rough weather, he's theer. When there's hard duty to be done with danger in it, he steps for'ard afore all his mates. And yet he's as gentle as any child. There ain't a child in Yarmouth that doen't know him."

He gathered up the letters thoughtfully, smoothing them with his hand; put them into their little bundle; and placed it tenderly in his breast again. The face was gone from the door. I still saw the snow drifting in; but nothing else was there.

"Well!" he said, looking to his bag, "having seen you

to-night, Mas'r Davy (and that doos me good!), I shall away betimes to-morrow morning. You have seen what I've got heer;" putting his hand on where the little packet lay; "all that troubles me is, to think that any harm might come to me, afore that money was give back. If I was to die, and it was lost, or stole, or elseways made away with, and it was never know'd by him but what I'd took it, I believe the t'other wureld wouldn't hold me! I believe I must come back!"

He rose, and I rose too; we grasped each other by the hand again, before going out.

"I'd go ten thousand mile," he said, "I'd go till I dropped dead, to lay that money down afore him. If I do that, and find my Em'ly, I'm content. If I doen't find her, maybe she'll come to hear, sometime, as her loving uncle only ended his search for her when he ended his life; and if I know her, even that will turn her home at last!"

As he went out into the rigorous night, I saw the lonely figure flit away before us. I turned him hastily on some pretence, and held him in conversation until it was gone.

He spoke of a traveller's house on the Dover Road, where he knew he could find a clean, plain lodging for the night. I went with him over Westminster Bridge, and parted from him on the Surrey shore. Everything seemed, to my imagination, to be hushed in reverence for him, as he resumed his solitary journey through the snow.

I returned to the inn yard, and, impressed by my remembrance of the face, looked awfully around for it. It was not there. The snow had covered our late footprints; my new track was the only one to be seen; and even that began to die away (it snowed so fast) as I looked back over my shoulder.

CHAPTER XLI.

DORA'S AUNTS.

At last, an answer came from the two old ladies. They presented their compliments to Mr. Copperfield, and informed him that they had given his letter their best consideration, "with a view to the happiness of both parties"—which I thought rather an alarming expression, not only because of the use they had made of it in relation to the family difference before-mentioned, but because I had (and have all my life) observed that conventional phrases are a sort of fireworks, easily let off, and liable to take a great variety of shapes and colours not at all suggested by their original form. The Misses Spenlow added that they begged to forbear expressing, " through the medium of correspondence," an opinion on the subject of Mr. Copperfield's communication ; but that if Mr. Copperfield would do them the favour to call, upon a certain day (accompanied, if he thought proper, by a confidential friend), they would be happy to hold some conversation on the subject.

To this favour, Mr. Copperfield immediately replied, with his respectful compliments, that he would have the honour of waiting on the Misses Spenlow, at the time appointed ; accompanied, in accordance with their kind permission, by his friend Mr. Thomas Traddles of the Inner Court. Having dispatched which missive, Mr. Copperfield fell into a condition of strong nervous agitation ; and so remained until the day arrived.

It was a great augmentation of my uneasiness to be bereaved, at this eventful crisis, of the inestimable services of Miss Mills. But Mr. Mills, who was always doing something or other to annoy me—or I felt as if he were, which was the same thing—had brought his conduct to a climax, by taking it into his head that he would go to India. Why should he go to India, except to harass me? To be sure he had nothing to do with any other part of the world, and had a good deal to do with that part; being entirely in the Indian trade, whatever that was (I had floating dreams myself concerning golden shawls and elephants' teeth); having been at Calcutta in his youth; and designing now to go out there again, in the capacity of resident partner. But this was nothing to me. However, it was so much to him that for India he was bound, and Julia with him; and Julia went into the country to take leave of her relations; and the house was put into a perfect suit of bills, announcing that it was to be let or sold, and that the furniture (Mangle and all) was to be taken at a valuation. So, here was another earthquake of which I became the sport, before I had recovered from the shock of its predecessor!

I was in several minds how to dress myself on the important day; being divided between my desire to appear to advantage, and my apprehensions of putting on anything that might impair my severely practical character in the eyes of the Misses Spenlow. I endeavoured to hit a happy medium between these two extremes; my aunt approved the result; and Mr. Dick threw one of his shoes after Traddles and me, for luck, as we went down-stairs.

Excellent fellow as I knew Traddles to be, and warmly attached to him as I was, I could not help wishing, on that delicate occasion, that he had never contracted the habit of brushing his hair so very upright. It gave him a surprised look—not to say a hearth-broomy kind of expression—which, my apprehensions whispered, might be fatal to us.

I took the liberty of mentioning it to Traddles, as we

were walking to Putney; and saying that if he *would* smooth
it down a little—

"My dear Copperfield," said Traddles, lifting off his hat,
and rubbing his hair all kinds of ways, "nothing would give
me greater pleasure. But it won't."

"Won't be smoothed down?" said I.

"No," said Traddles. "Nothing will induce it. If I was
to carry a half-hundredweight upon it, all the way to Putney,
it would be up again the moment the weight was taken off.
You have no idea what obstinate hair mine is, Copperfield.
I am quite a fretful porcupine."

I was a little disappointed, I must confess, but thoroughly
charmed by his good-nature too. I told him how I esteemed
his good-nature; and said that his hair must have taken all
the obstinacy out of his character, for *he* had none.

"Oh!" returned Traddles, laughing, "I assure you, it's
quite an old story, my unfortunate hair. My uncle's wife
couldn't bear it. She said it exasperated her. It stood very
much in my way, too, when I first fell in love with Sophy.
Very much!"

"Did she object to it?"

"*She* didn't," rejoined Traddles; "but her eldest sister
—the one that's the Beauty—quite made game of it, I
understand. In fact, all the sisters laugh at it."

"Agreeable!" said I.

"Yes," returned Traddles with perfect innocence, "it's a
joke for us. They pretend that Sophy has a lock of it in
her desk, and is obliged to shut it in a clasped book, to keep
it down. We laugh about it."

"By-the-bye, my dear Traddles," said I, "your experience
may suggest something to me. When you became engaged
to the young lady whom you have just mentioned, did you
make a regular proposal to her family? Was there anything
like—what we are going through to-day, for instance?" I
added, nervously.

"Why," replied Traddles, on whose attentive face a

thoughtful shade had stolen, "it was rather a painful transaction, Copperfield, in my case. You see, Sophy being of so much use in the family, none of them could endure the thought of her ever being married. Indeed, they had quite settled among themselves that she never was to be married, and they called her the old maid. Accordingly, when I mentioned it, with the greatest precaution, to Mrs. Crewler—"

"The mama?" said I.

"The mama," said Traddles—"Reverend Horace Crewler —when I mentioned it with every possible precaution to Mrs. Crewler, the effect upon her was such that she gave a scream and became insensible. I couldn't approach the subject again, for months."

"You did at last?" said I.

"Well, the Reverend Horace did," said Traddles. "He is an excellent man, most exemplary in every way; and he pointed out to her that she ought, as a Christian, to reconcile herself to the sacrifice (especially as it was so uncertain), and to bear no uncharitable feeling towards me. As to myself, Copperfield, I give you my word, I felt a perfect bird of prey towards the family."

"The sisters took your part, I hope, Traddles?"

"Why, I can't say they did," he returned. "When we had comparatively reconciled Mrs. Crewler to it, we had to break it to Sarah. You recollect my mentioning Sarah, as the one that has something the matter with her spine?"

"Perfectly!"

"She clenched both her hands," said Traddles, looking at me in dismay; "shut her eyes; turned lead-colour; became perfectly stiff; and took nothing for two days but toast-and-water, administered with a tea-spoon."

"What a very unpleasant girl, Traddles!" I remarked.

"Oh, I beg your pardon, Copperfield!" said Traddles. "She is a very charming girl, but she has a great deal of feeling. In fact, they all have. Sophy told me afterwards, that the self-reproach she underwent while she was in attendance upon Sarah, no words could describe. I know it must have been severe, by my own feelings, Copperfield; which were like a criminal's. After Sarah was restored, we still had to break it to the other eight; and it produced various effects upon them of a most pathetic nature. The two little ones, whom Sophy educates, have only just left off de-testing me."

"At any rate, they are all reconciled to it now, I hope?" said I.

"Ye—yes, I should say they were, on the whole, resigned to it," said Traddles, doubtfully. "The fact is, we avoid mentioning the subject; and my unsettled prospects and indifferent circumstances are a great consolation to them. There will be a deplorable scene, whenever we are married. It will be much more like a funeral than a wedding. And they'll all hate me for taking her away!"

His honest face, as he looked at me with a serio-comic shake of his head, impresses me more in the remembrance than it did in the reality, for I was by this time in a state of such excessive trepidation and wandering of mind, as to be quite unable to fix my attention on anything. On our approaching the house where the Misses Spenlow lived, I was at such a discount in respect of my personal looks and presence of mind, that Traddles proposed a gentle stimulant in the form of a glass of ale. This having been adminis-tered at a neighbouring public-house, he conducted me, with tottering steps, to the Misses Spenlow's door.

I had a vague sensation of being, as it were, on view, when the maid opened it; and of wavering, somehow, across a hall with a weather-glass in it, into a quiet little drawing-room on the ground-floor, commanding a neat garden. Also of sitting down here, on a sofa, and seeing Traddles's hair start up, now his hat was removed, like one of those obtrusive little figures made of springs, that fly out of fictitious snuff-boxes when the lid is taken off. Also of hearing an

189

old-fashioned clock ticking away on the chimney-piece, and trying to make it keep time to the jerking of my heart,—which it wouldn't. Also of looking round the room for any sign of Dora, and seeing none. Also of thinking that Jip once barked in the distance, and was instantly choked by somebody. Ultimately I found myself backing Traddles into the fireplace, and bowing in great confusion to two dry little elderly ladies, dressed in black, and each looking wonderfully like a preparation in chip or tan of the late Mr. Spenlow.

"Pray," said one of the two little ladies, "be seated."

When I had done tumbling over Traddles, and had sat upon something which was not a cat—my first seat was—I so far recovered my sight, as to perceive that Mr. Spenlow had evidently been the youngest of the family ; that there was a disparity of six or eight years between the two sisters ; and that the younger appeared to be the manager of the conference, inasmuch as she had my letter in her hand—so familiar as it looked to me, and yet so odd!—and was referring to it through an eye-glass. They were dressed alike, but this sister wore her dress with a more youthful air than the other; and perhaps had a trifle more frill, or tucker, or brooch, or bracelet, or some little thing of that kind, which made her look more lively. They were both upright in their carriage, formal, precise, composed, and quiet. The sister who had not my letter, had her arms crossed on her breast, and resting on each other, like an Idol.

"Mr. Copperfield, I believe," said the sister who had got my letter, addressing herself to Traddles.

This was a frightful beginning. Traddles had to indicate that I was Mr. Copperfield, and I had to lay claim to myself, and they had to divest themselves of a preconceived opinion that Traddles was Mr. Copperfield, and altogether we were in a nice condition. To improve it, we all distinctly heard Jip give two short barks, and receive another choke.

"Mr. Copperfield!" said the sister with the letter.

Traddles and I in Conference with the Misses Spenlow

WE WAIT UPON DORA'S AUNTS.

I did something—bowed, I suppose—and was all attention, when the other sister struck in.

"My sister Lavinia," said she, "being conversant with matters of this nature, will state what we consider most calculated to promote the happiness of both parties."

I discovered afterwards that Miss Lavinia was an authority in affairs of the heart, by reason of there having anciently existed a certain Mr. Pidger, who played short whist, and was supposed to have been enamoured of her. My private opinion is, that this was entirely a gratuitous assumption, and that Pidger was altogether innocent of any such sentiments—to which he had never given any sort of expression that I could ever hear of. Both Miss Lavinia and Miss Clarissa had a superstition, however, that he would have declared his passion, if he had not been cut short in his youth (at about sixty) by over-drinking his constitution, and over-doing an attempt to set it right again by swilling Bath water. They had a lurking suspicion even, that he died of secret love; though I must say there was a picture of him in the house with a damask nose, which concealment did not appear to have ever preyed upon.

"We will not," said Miss Lavinia, "enter on the past history of this matter. Our poor brother Francis's death has cancelled that."

"We had not," said Miss Clarissa, "been in the habit of frequent association with our brother Francis; but there was no decided division or disunion between us. Francis took his road; we took ours. We considered it conducive to the happiness of all parties that it should be so. And it was so."

Each of the sisters leaned a little forward to speak, shook her head after speaking, and became upright again when silent. Miss Clarissa never moved her arms. She sometimes played tunes upon them with her fingers—minuets and marches, I should think—but never moved them.

"Our niece's position, or supposed position, is much

changed by our brother Francis's death," said Miss Lavinia; "and therefore we consider our brother's opinions as regarded her position as being changed too. We have no reason to doubt, Mr. Copperfield, that you are a young gentleman possessed of good qualities and honourable character; or that you have an affection—or are fully persuaded that you have an affection—for our niece."

I replied, as I usually did whenever I had a chance, that nobody had ever loved anybody else as I loved Dora. Traddles came to my assistance with a confirmatory murmur.

Miss Lavinia was going on to make some rejoinder, when Miss Clarissa, who appeared to be incessantly beset by a desire to refer to her brother Francis, struck in again:

"If Dora's mama," she said, "when she married our brother Francis, had at once said that there was not room for the family at the dinner-table, it would have been better for the happiness of all parties."

"Sister Clarissa," said Miss Lavinia. "Perhaps we needn't mind that now."

"Sister Lavinia," said Miss Clarissa, "it belongs to the subject. With your branch of the subject, on which alone you are competent to speak, I should not think of interfering. On this branch of the subject I have a voice and an opinion. It would have been better for the happiness of all parties, if Dora's mama, when she married our brother Francis, had mentioned plainly what her intentions were. We should then have known what we had to expect. We should have said 'pray do not invite us, at any time;' and all possibility of misunderstanding would have been avoided."

When Miss Clarissa had shaken her head, Miss Lavinia resumed: again referring to my letter through her eye-glass. They both had little bright round twinkling eyes, by the way, which were like birds' eyes. They were not unlike birds, altogether; having a sharp, brisk, sudden manner, and a little short, spruce way of adjusting themselves, like canaries.

Miss Lavinia, as I have said, resumed:

I INTERRUPT THE ORACLE.

"You ask permission of my sister Clarissa and myself, Mr. Copperfield, to visit here, as the accepted suitor of our niece."

"If our brother Francis," said Miss Clarissa, breaking out again, if I may call anything so calm a breaking out, "wished to surround himself with an atmosphere of Doctors' Commons, and of Doctors' Commons only, what right or desire had we to object? None, I am sure. We have ever been far from wishing to obtrude ourselves on any one. But why not say so? Let our brother Francis and his wife have their society. Let my sister Lavinia and myself have our society. We can find it for ourselves, I hope!"

As this appeared to be addressed to Traddles and me, both Traddles and I made some sort of reply. Traddles was inaudible. I think I observed, myself, that it was highly creditable to all concerned. I don't in the least know what I meant.

"Sister Lavinia," said Miss Clarissa, having now relieved her mind, "you can go on, my dear."

Miss Lavinia proceeded:

"Mr. Copperfield, my sister Clarissa and I have been very careful indeed in considering this letter; and we have not considered it without finally showing it to our niece, and discussing it with our niece. We have no doubt that you think you like her very much."

"Think, ma'am," I rapturously began, "oh!——"

But Miss Clarissa giving me a look (just like a sharp canary), as requesting that I would not interrupt the oracle, I begged pardon.

"Affection," said Miss Lavinia, glancing at her sister for corroboration, which she gave in the form of a little nod to every clause, "mature affection, homage, devotion, does not easily express itself. Its voice is low. It is modest and retiring, it lies in ambush, waits and waits. Such is the mature fruit. Sometimes a life glides away, and finds it still ripening in the shade."

DAVID COPPERFIELD.

Of course I did not understand then that this was an allusion to her supposed experience of the stricken Pidger; but I saw, from the gravity with which Miss Clarissa nodded her head, that great weight was attached to these words.

"The light—for I call them, in comparison with such sentiments, the light—inclinations of very young people," pursued Miss Lavinia, "are dust, compared to rocks. It is owing to the difficulty of knowing whether they are likely to endure or have any real foundation, that my sister Clarissa and myself have been very undecided how to act, Mr. Copperfield, and Mr.—— "

"Traddles," said my friend, finding himself looked at.

"I beg pardon. Of the Inner Temple, I believe?" said Miss Clarissa, again glancing at my letter.

Traddles said "Exactly so," and became pretty red in the face.

Now, although I had not received any express encouragement as yet, I fancied that I saw in the two little sisters, and particularly in Miss Lavinia, an intensified enjoyment of this new and fruitful subject of domestic interest, a settling down to make the most of it, a disposition to pet it, in which there was a good bright ray of hope. I thought I perceived that Miss Lavinia would have uncommon satisfaction in superintending two young lovers, like Dora and me; and that Miss Clarissa would have hardly less satisfaction in seeing her superintend us, and in chiming in with her own particular department of the subject whenever that impulse was strong upon her. This gave me courage to protest most vehemently that I loved Dora better than I could tell, or any one believe; that all my friends knew how I loved her; that my aunt, Agnes, Traddles, every one who knew me knew how I loved her, and how earnest my love had made me. For the truth of this, I appealed to Traddles. And Traddles, firing up as if he were plunging into a Parliamentary Debate, really did come out nobly: confirming me in good round terms, and in a plain sensible practical manner, that evidently made a favourable impression.

"I speak, if I may presume to say so, as one who has some little experience of such things," said Traddles, "being myself engaged to a young lady—one of ten, down in Devonshire—and seeing no probability, at present, of our engagement coming to a termination."

"You may be able to confirm what I have said, Mr. Traddles," observed Miss Lavinia, evidently taking a new interest in him, "of the affection that is modest and retiring; that waits and waits?"

"Entirely, ma'am," said Traddles.

Miss Clarissa looked at Miss Lavinia, and shook her head gravely. Miss Lavinia looked consciously at Miss Clarissa, and heaved a little sigh.

"Sister Lavinia," said Miss Clarissa, "take my smelling-bottle."

Miss Lavinia revived herself with a few whiffs of aromatic vinegar—Traddles and I looking on with great solicitude the while; and then went on to say, rather faintly:

"My sister and myself have been in great doubt, Mr. Traddles, what course we ought to take in reference to the likings, or imaginary likings, of such very young people as your friend Mr. Copperfield and our niece."

"Our brother Francis's child," remarked Miss Clarissa. "If our brother Francis's wife had found it convenient in her life-time (though she had an unquestionable right to act as she thought best) to invite the family to her dinner-table, we might have known our brother Francis's child better at the present moment. Sister Lavinia, proceed."

Miss Lavinia turned my letter, so as to bring the superscription towards herself, and referred through her eye-glass to some orderly-looking notes she had made on that part of it.

"It seems to us," said she, "prudent, Mr. Traddles, to bring these feelings to the test of our own observation. At present we know nothing of them, and are not in a situation to judge how much reality there may be in them. Therefore we are inclined so far to accede to Mr. Copperfield's proposal as to admit his visits here."

"I shall never, dear ladies," I exclaimed, relieved of an immense load of apprehension, "forget your kindness!"

"But," pursued Miss Lavinia,—"but, we would prefer to regard those visits, Mr. Traddles, as made, at present, to us. We must guard ourselves from recognising any positive engagement between Mr. Copperfield and our niece, until we have had an opportunity—"

"Until *you* have had an opportunity, sister Lavinia," said Miss Clarissa.

"Be it so," assented Miss Lavinia, with a sigh—"until I have had an opportunity of observing them."

"Copperfield," said Traddles, turning to me, "you feel, I am sure, that nothing could be more reasonable or considerate."

"Nothing!" cried I. "I am deeply sensible of it."

"In this position of affairs," said Miss Lavinia, again referring to her notes, "and admitting his visits on this understanding only, we must require from Mr. Copperfield a distinct assurance, on his word of honour, that no communication of any kind shall take place between him and our niece without our knowledge. That no project whatever shall be entertained with regard to our niece, without being first submitted to us—"

"To you, sister Lavinia," Miss Clarissa interposed.

"Be it so, Clarissa!" assented Miss Lavinia resignedly—"to me—and receiving our concurrence. We must make this a most express and serious stipulation, not to be broken on any account. We wished Mr. Copperfield to be accompanied by some confidential friend to-day," with an inclination of her head towards Traddles, who bowed, "in order that there might be no doubt or misconception on this subject. If Mr. Copperfield, or if you, Mr. Traddles, feel the least scruple, in giving this promise, I beg you to take time to consider it."

I exclaimed, in a state of high ecstatic fervour, that not a

moment's consideration could be necessary. I bound myself
by the required promise, in a most impassioned manner;
called upon Traddles to witness it; and denounced myself as
the most atrocious of characters if I ever swerved from it in
the least degree.

"Stay!" said Miss Lavinia, holding up her hand; "we
resolved, before we had the pleasure of receiving you two
gentlemen, to leave you alone for a quarter of an hour, to
consider this point. You will allow us to retire."

It was in vain for me to say that no consideration was
necessary. They persisted in withdrawing for the specified
time. Accordingly, these little birds hopped out with great
dignity; leaving me to receive the congratulations of Traddles,
and to feel as if I were translated to regions of exquisite
happiness. Exactly at the expiration of the quarter of an
hour, they reappeared with no less dignity than they had
disappeared. They had gone rustling away as if their little
dresses were made of autumn-leaves: and they came rustling
back, in like manner.

I then bound myself once more to the prescribed conditions.

"Sister Clarissa," said Miss Lavinia, "the rest is with you."

Miss Clarissa, unfolding her arms for the first time, took
the notes and glanced at them.

"We shall be happy," said Miss Clarissa, "to see Mr.
Copperfield to dinner, every Sunday, if it should suit his
convenience. Our hour is three."

I bowed.

"In the course of the week," said Miss Clarissa, "we shall
be happy to see Mr. Copperfield to tea. Our hour is half-
past six."

I bowed again.

"Twice in the week," said Miss Clarissa, "but, as a rule,
not oftener."

I bowed again.

"Miss Trotwood," said Miss Clarissa, "mentioned in Mr.
Copperfield's letter, will perhaps call upon us. When visiting

197

is better for the happiness of all parties, we are glad to receive visits, and return them. When it is better for the happiness of all parties that no visiting should take place (as in the case of our brother Francis, and his establishment) that is quite different."

I intimated that my aunt would be proud and delighted to make their acquaintance; though I must say I was not quite sure of their getting on very satisfactorily together. The conditions being now closed, I expressed my acknowledgments in the warmest manner; and, taking the hand first of Miss Clarissa, and then of Miss Lavinia, pressed it in each case, to my lips.

Miss Lavinia then arose, and begging Mr. Traddles to excuse us for a minute, requested me to follow her. I obeyed all in a tremble, and was conducted into another room. There, I found my blessed darling stopping her ears behind the door, with her dear little face against the wall; and Jip in the plate-warmer with his head tied up in a towel.

Oh! How beautiful she was in her black frock, and how she sobbed and cried at first, and wouldn't come out from behind the door! How fond we were of one another, when she did come out at last; and what a state of bliss I was in when we took Jip out of the plate-warmer, and restored him to the light, sneezing very much, and were all three reunited!

"My dearest Dora! Now, indeed, my own for ever!"

"Oh DON'T!" pleaded Dora. "Please!"

"Are you not my own for ever, Dora?"

"Oh yes, of course I am!" cried Dora, "but I am so frightened!"

"Frightened, my own?"

"Oh yes! I don't like him," said Dora. "Why don't he go?"

"Who, my life?"

"Your friend," said Dora. "It isn't any business of his. What a stupid he must be!"

"My love!" (There never was anything so coaxing as her childish ways.) "He is the best creature!"

"Oh, but we don't want any best creatures!" pouted Dora.

"My dear," I argued, "you will soon know him well, and like him of all things. And here is my aunt coming soon: and you'll like her of all things too, when you know her."

"No, please don't bring her!" said Dora, giving me a horrified little kiss, and folding her hands. "Don't. I know she's a naughty, mischief-making old thing! Don't let her come here, Doady!" which was a corruption of David.

Remonstrance was of no use, then; so I laughed, and admired, and was very much in love and very happy; and she showed me Jip's new trick of standing on his hind legs in a corner—which he did for about the space of a flash of lightning, and then fell down—and I don't know how long I should have stayed there, oblivious of Traddles, if Miss Lavinia had not come in to take me away. Miss Lavinia was very fond of Dora (she told me Dora was exactly like what she had been herself at her age—she must have altered a good deal), and she treated Dora just as if she had been a boy. I wanted to persuade Dora to come and see Traddles, but on my proposing it she ran off to her own room, and locked herself in; so I went to Traddles without her, and walked away with him on air.

"Nothing could be more satisfactory," said Traddles; "and they are very agreeable old ladies, I am sure. I shouldn't be at all surprised if you were to be married years before me, Copperfield."

"Does your Sophy play on any instrument, Traddles?" I inquired, in the pride of my heart.

"She knows enough of the piano to teach it to her little sisters," said Traddles.

"Does she sing at all?" I asked.

"Why, she sings ballads, sometimes, to freshen up the

199

others a little when they're out of spirits," said Traddles. " Nothing scientific."

" She doesn't sing to the guitar ? " said I.

" Oh dear no ! " said Traddles.

"Paint at all ? "

" Not at all," said Traddles.

I promised Traddles that he should hear Dora sing, and see some of her flower-painting. He said he should like it very much, and we went home arm in arm in great good humour and delight. I encouraged him to talk about Sophy on the way; which he did with a loving reliance on her that I very much admired. I compared her in my mind with Dora, with considerable inward satisfaction ; but I candidly admitted to myself that she seemed to be an excellent kind of girl for Traddles, too.

Of course my aunt was immediately made acquainted with the successful issue of the conference, and with all that had been said and done in the course of it. She was happy to see me so happy, and promised to call on Dora's aunts without loss of time. But she took such a long walk up and down our rooms that night, while I was writing to Agnes, that I began to think she meant to walk till morning.

My letter to Agnes was a fervent and grateful one, narrating all the good effects that had resulted from my following her advice. She wrote, by return of post, to me. Her letter was hopeful, earnest, and cheerful. She was always cheerful from that time.

I had my hands more full than ever, now. My daily journeys to Highgate considered, Putney was a long way off ; and I naturally wanted to go there as often as I could. The proposed tea-drinkings being quite impracticable, I compounded with Miss Lavinia for permission to visit every Saturday afternoon, without detriment to my privileged Sundays. So, the close of every week was a delicious time for me ; and I got through the rest of the week by looking forward to it.

OUR AUNTS EXCHANGE VISITS.

I was wonderfully relieved to find that my aunt and Dora's aunts rubbed on, all things considered, much more smoothly than I could have expected. My aunt made her promised visit within a few days of the conference; and within a few more days, Dora's aunts called upon her, in due state and form. Similar but more friendly exchanges took place afterwards, usually at intervals of three or four weeks. I know that my aunt distressed Dora's aunts very much, by utterly setting at naught the dignity of fly-conveyance, and walking out to Putney at extraordinary times, as shortly after breakfast or just before tea; likewise by wearing her bonnet in any manner that happened to be comfortable to her head, without at all deferring to the prejudices of civilisation on that subject. But Dora's aunts soon agreed to regard my aunt as an eccentric and somewhat masculine lady, with a strong understanding; and although my aunt occasionally ruffled the feathers of Dora's aunts, by expressing heretical opinions on various points of ceremony, she loved me too well not to sacrifice some of her little peculiarities to the general harmony.

The only member of our small society, who positively refused to adapt himself to circumstances, was Jip. He never saw my aunt without immediately displaying every tooth in his head, retiring under a chair, and growling incessantly: with now and then a doleful howl, as if she really were too much for his feelings. All kinds of treatment were tried with him—coaxing, scolding, slapping, bringing him to Buckingham Street (where he instantly dashed at the two cats, to the terror of all beholders); but he never could prevail upon himself to bear my aunt's society. He would sometimes think he had got the better of his objection, and be amiable for a few minutes; and then would put up his snub nose, and howl to that extent, that there was nothing for it but to blind him and put him in the plate-warmer. At length, Dora regularly muffled him in a towel and shut him up there, whenever my aunt was reported at the door.

One thing troubled me much, after we had fallen into this

quiet train. It was, that Dora seemed by one consent to be regarded like a pretty toy or plaything. My aunt, with whom she gradually became familiar, always called her Little Blossom; and the pleasure of Miss Lavinia's life was to wait upon her, curl her hair, make ornaments for her, and treat her like a pet child. What Miss Lavinia did, her sister did as a matter of course. It was very odd to me; but they all seemed to treat Dora, in her degree, much as Dora treated Jip in his.

I made up my mind to speak to Dora about this; and one day when we were out walking (for we were licensed by Miss Lavinia, after a while, to go out walking by ourselves), I said to her that I wished she could get them to behave towards her differently.

"Because you know, my darling," I remonstrated, "you are not a child."

"There!" said Dora. "Now you're going to be cross!"

"Cross, my love?"

"I am sure they're very kind to me," said Dora, "and I am very happy."

"Well! But, my dearest life!" said I, "you might be very happy, and yet be treated rationally."

Dora gave me a reproachful look—the prettiest look!—and then began to sob, saying, if I didn't like her, why had I ever wanted so much to be engaged to her? And why didn't I go away now, if I couldn't bear her?

What could I do, but kiss away her tears, and tell her how I doted on her, after that!

"I am sure I am very affectionate," said Dora; "you oughtn't to be cruel to me, Doady!"

"Cruel, my precious love! As if I would—or could—be cruel to you, for the world!"

"Then don't find fault with me," said Dora, making a rosebud of her mouth; "and I'll be good."

I was charmed by her presently asking me, of her own accord, to give her that cookery-book I had once spoken of, and to show her how to keep accounts, as I had once promised I would. I brought the volume with me on my next visit (I got it prettily bound, first, to make it look less dry and more inviting); and as we strolled about the Common, I showed her an old housekeeping-book of my aunt's, and gave her a set of tablets, and a pretty little pencil-case, and box of leads, to practise housekeeping with.

But the cookery-book made Dora's head ache, and the figures made her cry. They wouldn't add up, she said. So she rubbed them out, and drew little nosegays, and likenesses of me and Jip, all over the tablets.

Then I playfully tried verbal instruction in domestic matters, as we walked about on a Saturday afternoon. Sometimes, for example, when we passed a butcher's shop, I would say:

"Now suppose, my pet, that we were married, and you were going to buy a shoulder of mutton for dinner, would you know how to buy it?"

My pretty little Dora's face would fall, and she would make her mouth into a bud again, as if she would very much prefer to shut mine with a kiss.

"Would you know how to buy it, my darling?" I would repeat, perhaps, if I were very inflexible.

Dora would think a little, and then reply, perhaps, with great triumph:

"Why, the butcher would know how to sell it, and what need _I_ know? Oh, you silly Boy!"

So, when I once asked Dora, with an eye to the cookery-book, what she would do, if we were married, and I were to say I should like a nice Irish stew, she replied that she would tell the servant to make it; and then clapped her little hands together across my arm, and laughed in such a charming manner that she was more delightful than ever.

Consequently, the principal use to which the cookery-book was devoted, was being put down in the corner for Jip to stand upon. But Dora was so pleased, when she had trained him to stand upon it without offering to come off, and at the same time to hold the pencil-case in his mouth, that I was very glad I had bought it.

And we fell back on the guitar-case, and the flower-painting, and the songs about never leaving off dancing, Ta ra la! and were as happy as the week was long. I occasionally wished I could venture to hint to Miss Lavinia, that she treated the darling of my heart a little too much like a plaything; and I sometimes awoke, as it were, wondering to find that I had fallen into the general fault, and treated her like a plaything too—but not often.

CHAPTER XLII.

MISCHIEF.

I FEEL as if it were not for me to record, even though this manuscript is intended for no eyes but mine, how hard I worked at that tremendous shorthand, and all improvement appertaining to it, in my sense of responsibility to Dora and her aunts. I will only add, to what I have already written of my perseverance at this time of my life, and of a patient and continuous energy which then began to be matured within me, and which I know to be the strong part of my character, if it have any strength at all, that there, on looking back, I find the source of my success. I have been very fortunate in worldly matters; many men have worked much harder, and not succeeded half so well; but I never could have done what I have done, without the habits of punctuality, order, and diligence, without the determination to concentrate myself on one object at a time, no matter how quickly its successor should come upon its heels, which I then formed. Heaven knows I write this, in no spirit of self-laudation. The man who reviews his own life, as I do mine, in going on here, from page to page, had need to have been a good man indeed, if he would be spared the sharp consciousness of many talents neglected, many opportunities wasted, many erratic and perverted feelings constantly at war within his breast, and defeating him. I do not hold one natural gift, I dare say, that I have not abused. My meaning simply is, that whatever I have tried to do in life, I have tried with all my heart to do well; that whatever I have devoted myself to, I have devoted myself to completely; that in great aims and in small, I have always been thoroughly in earnest. I have never believed it possible that any natural or improved ability can claim immunity from the companionship of the steady, plain, hard-working qualities, and hope to gain its end. There is no such thing as such fulfilment on this earth. Some happy talent, and some fortunate opportunity, may form the two sides of the ladder on which some men mount, but the rounds of that ladder must be made of stuff to stand wear and tear; and there is no substitute for thorough-going, ardent, and sincere earnestness. Never to put one hand to anything on which I could throw my whole self; and never to affect depreciation of my work, whatever it was; I find, now, to have been my golden rules.

How much of the practice I have just reduced to precept, I owe to Agnes, I will not repeat here. My narrative proceeds to Agnes, with a thankful love.

She came on a visit of a fortnight to the Doctor's. Mr. Wickfield was the Doctor's old friend, and the Doctor wished to talk with him, and do him good. It had been matter of conversation with Agnes when she was last in town, and this visit was the result. She and her father came together. I was not much surprised to hear from her that she had engaged to find a lodging in the neighbourhood for Mrs. Heep, whose rheumatic complaint required change of air, and who would be charmed to have it in such company. Neither was I surprised when, on the very next day, Uriah, like a dutiful son, brought his worthy mother to take possession.

"You see, Master Copperfield," said he, as he forced himself upon my company for a turn in the Doctor's garden, "where a person loves, a person is a little jealous—leastways, anxious to keep an eye on the beloved one."

"Of whom are you jealous, now?" said I,

"Thanks to you, Master Copperfield," he returned, "of no one in particular just at present—no male person, at least."

"Do you mean that you are jealous of a female person?"

He gave me a sidelong glance out of his sinister red eyes, and laughed.

"Really, Master Copperfield," he said, "—I should say Mister, but I know you'll excuse the abit I've got into— you're so insinuating, that you draw me like a corkscrew! Well, I don't mind telling you," putting his fish-like hand on mine, "I'm not a lady's man in general, sir, and I never was, with Mrs. Strong."

His eyes looked green now, as they watched mine with a rascally cunning.

"What do you mean?" said I.

"Why, though I am a lawyer, Master Copperfield," he replied, with a dry grin, "I mean, just at present, what I say."

"And what do you mean by your look?" I retorted, quietly.

"By my look? Dear me, Copperfield, that's sharp practice! What do I mean by my look?"

"Yes," said I. "By your look."

He seemed very much amused, and laughed as heartily as it was in his nature to laugh. After some scraping of his chin with his hand, he went on to say, with his eyes cast downward—still scraping, very slowly:

"When I was but a numble clerk, she always looked down upon me. She was for ever having my Agnes backwards and forwards at her ouse, and she was for ever being a friend to you, Master Copperfield; but I was too far beneath her, myself, to be noticed."

"Well?" said I; "suppose you were!"

"—And beneath him too," pursued Uriah, very distinctly, and in a meditative tone of voice, as he continued to scrape his chin.

"Don't you know the Doctor better," said I, "than to

suppose him conscious of your existence, when you were not before him ? "

He directed his eyes at me in that sidelong glance again, and he made his face very lantern-jawed, for the greater convenience of scraping, as he answered :

" Oh dear, I am not referring to the Doctor ! Oh no, poor man ! I mean Mr. Maldon ! "

My heart quite died within me. All my old doubts, and apprehensions on that subject, all the Doctor's happiness and peace, all the mingled possibilities of innocence and compromise, that I could not unravel, I saw, in a moment, at the mercy of this fellow's twisting.

" He never could come into the office, without ordering and shoving me about," said Uriah. " One of your fine gentlemen he was ! I was very meek and umble—and I am. But I didn't like that sort of thing—and I don't ! "

He left off scraping his chin, and sucked in his cheeks until they seemed to meet inside ; keeping his sidelong glance upon me all the while.

" She is one of your lovely women, she is," he pursued, when he had slowly restored his face to its natural form ; " and ready to be no friend to such as me, I know. She's just the person as would put my Agnes up to higher sort of game. Now, I ain't one of your lady's men, Master Copperfield ; but I've had eyes in my ed, a pretty long time back. We umble ones have got eyes, mostly speaking—and we look out of 'em."

I endeavoured to appear unconscious and not disquieted, but, I saw in his face, with poor success.

" Now, I'm not a going to let myself be run down, Copperfield," he continued, raising that part of his countenance, where his red eyebrows would have been if he had had any, with malignant triumph, " and I shall do what I can to put a stop to this friendship. I don't approve of it. I don't mind acknowledging to you that I've got rather a grudging disposition, and want to keep off all intruders. I ain't a going, if I know it, to run the risk of being plotted against."

"You are always plotting, and delude yourself into the belief that everybody else is doing the like, I think," said I.

"Perhaps so, Master Copperfield," he replied. "But I've got a motive, as my fellow-partner used to say; and I go at it tooth and nail. I mustn't be put upon, as a numble person, too much. I can't allow people in my way. Really they must come out of the cart, Master Copperfield!"

"I don't understand you," said I.

"Don't you, though?" he returned, with one of his jerks. "I'm astonished at that, Master Copperfield, you being usually so quick! I'll try to be plainer, another time.—Is that Mr. Maldon a-norseback, ringing at the gate, sir?"

"It looks like him," I replied, as carelessly as I could.

Uriah stopped short, put his hands between his great knobs of knees, and doubled himself up with laughter. With perfectly silent laughter. Not a sound escaped from him. I was so repelled by his odious behaviour, particularly by this concluding instance, that I turned away without any ceremony; and left him doubled up in the middle of the garden, like a scarecrow in want of support.

It was not on that evening; but, as I well remember, on the next evening but one, which was a Saturday; that I took Agnes to see Dora. I had arranged the visit, beforehand, with Miss Lavinia; and Agnes was expected to tea.

I was in a flutter of pride and anxiety; pride in my dear little betrothed, and anxiety that Agnes should like her. All the way to Putney, Agnes being inside the stage-coach, and I outside, I pictured Dora to myself in every one of the pretty looks I knew so well; now making up my mind that I should like her to look exactly as she looked at such a time, and then doubting whether I should not prefer her looking as she looked at such another time; and almost worrying myself into a fever about it.

I was troubled by no doubt of her being very pretty, in

any case ; but it fell out that I had never seen her look so well. She was not in the drawing-room when I presented Agnes to her little aunts, but was shyly keeping out of the way. I knew where to look for her, now; and sure enough I found her stopping her ears again, behind the same dull old door. '

At first she wouldn't come at all; and then she pleaded for five minutes by my watch. When at length she put her arm through mine, to be taken to the drawing-room, her charming little face was flushed, and had never been so pretty. But, when we went into the room, and it turned pale, she was ten thousand times prettier yet.

Dora was afraid of Agnes. She had told me that she knew Agnes was " too clever." But when she saw her looking at once so cheerful and so earnest, and so thoughtful, and so good, she gave a faint little cry of pleased surprise, and just put her affectionate arms round Agnes's neck, and laid her innocent cheek against her face.

I never was so happy. I never was so pleased as when I saw those two sit down together, side by side. As when I saw my little darling looking up so naturally to those cordial eyes. As when I saw the tender, beautiful regard which Agnes cast upon her.

Miss Lavinia and Miss Clarissa partook, in their way, of my joy. It was the pleasantest tea-table in the world. Miss Clarissa presided. I cut and handed the sweet seed-cake— the little sisters had a bird-like fondness for picking up seeds and pecking at sugar; Miss Lavinia looked on with benignant patronage, as if our happy love were all her work; and we were perfectly contented with ourselves and one another.

The gentle cheerfulness of Agnes went to all their hearts. Her quiet interest in everything that interested Dora; her manner of making acquaintance with Jip (who responded instantly); her pleasant way, when Dora was ashamed to come over to her usual seat by me; her modest grace and ease, eliciting a crowd of blushing little marks of confidence from Dora; seemed to make our circle quite complete.

"I am so glad," said Dora, after tea, "that you like me. I didn't think you would; and I want, more than ever, to be liked, now Julia Mills is gone."

I have omitted to mention it, by-the-bye. Miss Mills had sailed, and Dora and I had gone aboard a great East India-man at Gravesend to see her; and we had had preserved ginger, and guava, and other delicacies of that sort for lunch; and we had left Miss Mills weeping on a camp-stool on the quarter-deck, with a large new diary under her arm, in which the original reflections awakened by the contemplation of Ocean were to be recorded under lock and key.

Agnes said, she was afraid, I must have given her an unpromising character; but Dora corrected that directly.

"Oh no!" she said, shaking her curls at me; "it was all praise. He thinks so much of your opinion, that I was quite afraid of it."

"My good opinion cannot strengthen his attachment to some people whom he knows," said Agnes, with a smile; "it is not worth their having."

"But please let me have it," said Dora, in her coaxing way, "if you can!"

We made merry about Dora's wanting to be liked, and Dora said I was a goose, and she didn't like me at any rate, and the short evening flew away on gossamer-wings. The time was at hand when the coach was to call for us. I was standing alone before the fire, when Dora came stealing softly in, to give me that usual precious little kiss before I went.

"Don't you think, if I had had her for a friend a long time ago, Doady," said Dora, her bright eyes shining very brightly, and her little right hand idly busying itself with one of the buttons of my coat, "I might have been more clever perhaps?"

"My love!" said I, "what nonsense!"

211

"Do you think it is nonsense?" returned Dora, without looking at me. "Are you sure it is?"

"Of course I am!"

"I have forgotten," said Dora, still turning the button round and round, "what relation Agnes is to you, you dear bad boy."

"No blood-relation," I replied; "but we were brought up together, like brother and sister."

"I wonder why you ever fell in love with me?" said Dora, beginning on another button of my coat.

"Perhaps because I couldn't see you, and not love you, Dora!"

"Suppose you had never seen me at all," said Dora, going to another button.

"Suppose we had never been born!" said I, gaily.

I wondered what she was thinking about, as I glanced in admiring silence at the little soft hand travelling up the row of buttons on my coat, and at the clustering hair that lay against my breast, and at the lashes of her downcast eyes, slightly rising as they followed her idle fingers. At length her eyes were lifted up to mine, and she stood on tiptoe to give me, more thoughtfully than usual, that precious little kiss—once, twice, three times—and went out of the room.

They all came back together within five minutes afterwards, and Dora's unusual thoughtfulness was quite gone then. She was laughingly resolved to put Jip through the whole of his performances, before the coach came. They took some time (not so much on account of their variety, as Jip's reluctance), and were still unfinished when it was heard at the door. There was a hurried but affectionate parting between Agnes and herself; and Dora was to write to Agnes (who was not to mind her letters being foolish, she said), and Agnes was to write to Dora; and they had a second parting at the coach-door, and a third when Dora, in spite of the remonstrances of Miss Lavinia, would come running out once more to remind Agnes at the coach-window about writing, and to shake her curls at me on the box.

The stage-coach was to put us down near Covent Garden, where we were to take another stage-coach for Highgate. I was impatient for the short walk in the interval, that Agnes might praise Dora to me. Ah! what praise it was! How lovingly and fervently did it commend the pretty creature I had won, with all her artless graces best displayed, to my most gentle care! How thoughtfully remind me, yet with no pretence of doing so, of the trust in which I held the orphan child!

Never, never, had I loved Dora so deeply and truly, as I loved her that night. When we had again alighted, and were walking in the starlight along the quiet road that led to the Doctor's house, I told Agnes it was her doing.

" When you were sitting by her," said I, " you seemed to be no less *her* guardian angel than mine ; and you seem so now, Agnes."

" A poor angel," she returned, " but faithful."

The clear tone of her voice, going straight to my heart, made it natural to me to say :

" The cheerfulness that belongs to you, Agnes (and to no one else that ever I have seen), is so restored, I have observed to-day, that I have begun to hope you are happier at home ? "

" I am happier in myself," she said ; " I am quite cheerful and light-hearted."

I glanced at the serene face looking upward, and thought it was the stars that made it seem so noble.

" There has been no change at home," said Agnes, after a few moments.

" No fresh reference," said I, " to—I wouldn't distress you, Agnes, but I cannot help asking—to what we spoke of, when we parted last ? "

" No, none," she answered.

" I have thought so much about it."

" You must think less about it. Remember that I confide

in simple love and truth at last. Have no apprehensions for me, Trotwood," she added, after a moment; "the step you dread my taking, I shall never take."

Although I think I had never really feared it, in any season of cool reflection, it was an unspeakable relief to me to have this assurance from her own truthful lips. I told her so, earnestly.

"And when this visit is over," said I,—"for we may not be alone another time,—how long is it likely to be, my dear Agnes, before you come to London again?"

"Probably a long time," she replied; "I think it will be best—for papa's sake—to remain at home. We are not likely to meet often, for some time to come; but I shall be a good correspondent of Dora's, and we shall frequently hear of one another that way."

We were now within the little court-yard of the Doctor's cottage. It was growing late. There was a light in the window of Mrs. Strong's chamber, and Agnes, pointing to it, bade me good-night.

"Do not be troubled," she said, giving me her hand, "by our misfortunes and anxieties. I can be happier in nothing than in your happiness. If you can ever give me help, rely upon it I will ask you for it. God bless you always!"

In her beaming smile, and in these last tones of her cheerful voice, I seemed again to see and hear my little Dora in her company. I stood awhile, looking through the porch at the stars, with a heart full of love and gratitude, and then walked slowly forth. I had engaged a bed at a decent alehouse close by, and was going out at the gate, when, happening to turn my head, I saw a light in the Doctor's study. A half-reproachful fancy came into my mind, that he had been working at the Dictionary without my help. With the view of seeing if this were so, and, in any case, of bidding him good-night, if he were yet sitting among his books, I turned back, and going softly across the hall, and gently opening the door, looked in.

URIAH POISONS DOCTOR STRONG'S MIND.

The first person whom I saw, to my surprise, by the sober light of the shaded lamp, was Uriah. He was standing close beside it, with one of his skeleton hands over his mouth, and the other resting on the Doctor's table. The Doctor sat in his study chair, covering his face with his hands. Mr. Wickfield, sorely troubled and distressed, was leaning forward, irresolutely touching the Doctor's arm.

For an instant, I supposed that the Doctor was ill. I hastily advanced a step under that impression, when I met Uriah's eye, and saw what was the matter. I would have withdrawn, but the Doctor made a gesture to detain me, and I remained.

"At any rate," observed Uriah, with a writhe of his ungainly person, "we may keep the door shut. We needn't make it known to ALL the town."

Saying which, he went on his toes to the door, which I had left open, and carefully closed it. He then came back, and took up his former position. There was an obtrusive show of compassionate zeal in his voice and manner, more intolerable—at least to me—than any demeanour he could have assumed.

"I have felt it incumbent upon me, Master Copperfield," said Uriah, "to point out to Doctor Strong what you and me have already talked about. You didn't exactly understand me, though?"

I gave him a look, but no other answer; and, going to my good old master, said a few words that I meant to be words of comfort and encouragement. He put his hand upon my shoulder, as it had been his custom to do when I was quite a little fellow, but did not lift his grey head.

"As you didn't understand me, Master Copperfield," resumed Uriah in the same officious manner, "I may take the liberty of umbly mentioning, being among friends, that I have called Doctor Strong's attention to the goings-on of Mrs. Strong. It's much against the grain with me, I assure you, Copperfield, to be concerned in anything so unpleasant;

but really, as it is, we're all mixing ourselves up with what oughtn't to be. That was what my meaning was, sir, when you didn't understand me."

I wonder now, when I recall his leer, that I did not collar him, and try to shake the breath out of his body.

" I dare say I didn't make myself very clear," he went on, " nor you neither. Naturally, we was both of us inclined to give such a subject a wide berth. Hows'ever, at last I have made up my mind to speak plain ; and I have mentioned to Doctor Strong that—did you speak, sir ? "

This was to the Doctor, who had moaned. The sound might have touched any heart, I thought, but it had no effect upon Uriah's.

" —mentioned to Doctor Strong," he proceeded, " that any one may see that Mr. Maldon, and the lovely and agreeable lady as is Doctor Strong's wife, are too sweet on one another. Really the time is come (we being at present all mixing ourselves up with what oughtn't to be), when Doctor Strong must be told that this was full as plain to everybody as the sun, before Mr. Maldon went to India ; that Mr. Maldon made excuses to come back, for nothing else ; and that he's always here, for nothing else. When you come in, sir, I was just putting it to my fellow-partner," towards whom he turned, " to say to Doctor Strong upon his word and honour, whether he'd ever been of this opinion long ago, or not. Come, Mr. Wickfield, sir ! Would you be so good as tell us ? Yes or no, sir ? Come, partner ! "

" For God's sake, my dear Doctor," said Mr. Wickfield, again laying his irresolute hand upon the Doctor's arm, " don't attach too much weight to any suspicions I may have entertained."

" There ! " cried Uriah, shaking his head. " What a melancholy confirmation : ain't it ? Him ! Such an old friend ! Bless your soul, when I was nothing but a clerk in his office, Copperfield, I've seen him twenty times, if I've seen him once, quite in a taking about it—quite put out, you know (and very proper in him as a father : I'm sure *I* can't blame him), to think that Miss Agnes was mixing herself up with what oughtn't to be."

"My dear Strong," said Mr. Wickfield in a tremulous voice, "my good friend, I needn't tell you that it has been my vice to look for some one master motive in everybody, and to try all actions by one narrow test. I may have fallen into such doubts as I have had, through this mistake."

"You have had doubts, Wickfield," said the Doctor, without lifting up his head. "You have had doubts."

"Speak up, fellow-partner," urged Uriah.

"I had, at one time, certainly," said Mr. Wickfield. "I —God forgive me—I thought *you* had."

"No, no, no!" returned the Doctor, in a tone of most pathetic grief.

"I thought, at one time," said Mr. Wickfield, "that you wished to send Maldon abroad to effect a desirable separation."

"No, no, no!" returned the Doctor. "To give Annie pleasure, by making some provision for the companion of her childhood. Nothing else."

"So I found," said Mr. Wickfield. "I couldn't doubt it, when you told me so. But I thought—I implore you to remember the narrow construction which has been my besetting sin—that, in a case where there was so much disparity in point of years—"

"That's the way to put it, you see, Master Copperfield!" observed Uriah, with fawning and offensive pity.

"—a lady of such youth, and such attractions, however real her respect for you, might have been influenced in marrying, by worldly considerations only. I made no allowance for innumerable feelings and circumstances that may have all tended to good. For Heaven's sake remember that!"

"How kind he puts it!" said Uriah, shaking his head.

"Always observing her from one point of view," said Mr. Wickfield; "but by all that is dear to you, my old friend, I entreat you to consider what it was; I am forced to confess now, having no escape—"

"No! There's no way out of it, Mr. Wickfield, sir," observed Uriah, "when it's got to this."

"—that I did," said Mr. Wickfield, glancing helplessly and distractedly at his partner, "that I did doubt her, and think her wanting in her duty to you; and that I did sometimes, if I must say all, feel averse to Agnes being in such a familiar relation towards her, as to see what I saw, or in my diseased theory fancied that I saw. I never mentioned this to any one. I never meant it to be known to any one. And though it is terrible to you to hear," said Mr. Wickfield, quite subdued, "if you knew how terrible it is for me to tell, you would feel compassion for me!"

The Doctor, in the perfect goodness of his nature, put out his hand. Mr. Wickfield held it for a little while in his, with his head bowed down.

"I am sure," said Uriah, writhing himself into the silence like a Conger-eel, "that this is a subject full of unpleasantness to everybody. But since we have got so far, I ought to take the liberty of mentioning that Copperfield has noticed it too."

I turned upon him, and asked him how he dared refer to me!

"Oh! it's very kind of you, Copperfield," returned Uriah, undulating all over, "and we all know what an amiable character yours is; but you know that the moment I spoke to you the other night, you knew what I meant. You know you knew what I meant, Copperfield. Don't deny it! You deny it with the best intentions; but don't do it, Copperfield."

I saw the mild eye of the good old Doctor turned upon me for a moment, and I felt that the confession of my old misgivings and remembrances was too plainly written in my face to be overlooked. It was of no use raging. I could not undo that. Say what I would, I could not unsay it.

We were silent again, and remained so, until the Doctor

rose and walked twice or thrice across the room. Presently he returned to where his chair stood; and, leaning on the back of it, and occasionally putting his handkerchief to his eyes, with a simple honesty that did him more honour, to my thinking, than any disguise he could have affected, said:

"I have been much to blame. I believe I have been very much to blame. I have exposed one whom I hold in my heart, to trials and aspersions—I call them aspersions, even to have been conceived in anybody's inmost mind—of which she never, but for me, could have been the object."

Uriah Heep gave a kind of snivel. I think to express sympathy.

"Of which my Annie," said the Doctor, "never, but for me, could have been the object. Gentlemen, I am old now, as you know; I do not feel, to-night, that I have much to live for. But my life—my Life—upon the truth and honour of the dear lady who has been the subject of this conversation!"

I do not think that the best embodiment of chivalry, the realisation of the handsomest and most romantic figure ever imagined by painter, could have said this with a more impressive and affecting dignity than the plain old Doctor did.

"But I am not prepared," he went on, "to deny—perhaps I may have been, without knowing it, in some degree prepared to admit—that I may have unwittingly ensnared that lady into an unhappy marriage. I am a man quite unaccustomed to observe; and I cannot but believe that the observation of several people, of different ages and positions, all too plainly tending in one direction (and that so natural), is better than mine."

I had often admired, as I have elsewhere described, his benignant manner towards his youthful wife; but the respectful tenderness he manifested in every reference to her on this occasion, and the almost reverential manner in which he put away from him the lightest doubt of her integrity, exalted him, in my eyes, beyond description.

"I married that lady," said the Doctor, "when she was

extremely young. I took her to myself when her character was scarcely formed. So far as it was developed, it had been my happiness to form it. I knew her father well. I knew her well. I had taught her what I could, for the love of all her beautiful and virtuous qualities. If I did her wrong; as I fear I did, in taking advantage (but I never meant it) of her gratitude and her affection; I ask pardon of that lady, in my heart!"

He walked across the room, and came back to the same place; holding the chair with a grasp that trembled, like his subdued voice, in its earnestness.

"I regarded myself as a refuge, for her, from the dangers and vicissitudes of life. I persuaded myself that, unequal though we were in years, she would live tranquilly and contentedly with me. I did not shut out of my consideration the time when I should leave her free, and still young and still beautiful, but with her judgment more matured—no, gentlemen—upon my truth!"

His homely figure seemed to be lightened up by his fidelity and generosity. Every word he uttered had a force that no other grace could have imparted to it.

"My life with this lady has been very happy. Until to-night, I have had uninterrupted occasion to bless the day on which I did her great injustice."

His voice, more and more faltering in the utterance of these words, stopped for a few moments; then he went on:

"Once awakened from my dream—I have been a poor dreamer, in one way or other, all my life—I see how natural it is that she should have some regretful feeling towards her old companion and her equal. That she does regard him with some innocent regret, with some blameless thoughts of what might have been, but for me, is, I fear, too true. Much that I have seen, but not noted, has come back upon me with new meaning, during this last trying hour. But, beyond this, gentlemen, the dear lady's name never must be coupled with a word, a breath, of doubt."

For a little while, his eye kindled and his voice was firm; for a little while he was again silent. Presently, he proceeded as before:

"It only remains for me, to bear the knowledge of the unhappiness I have occasioned, as submissively as I can. It is she who should reproach; not I. To save her from misconstruction, cruel misconstruction, that even my friends have not been able to avoid, becomes my duty. The more retired we live, the better I shall discharge it. And when the time comes—may it come soon, if it be His merciful pleasure!—when my death shall release her from constraint, I shall close my eyes upon her honoured face, with unbounded confidence and love; and leave her, with no sorrow then, to happier and brighter days."

I could not see him for the tears which his earnestness and goodness, so adorned by, and so adorning, the perfect simplicity of his manner, brought into my eyes. He had moved to the door, when he added:

"Gentlemen, I have shown you my heart. I am sure you will respect it. What we have said to-night is never to be said more. Wickfield, give me an old friend's arm upstairs!"

Mr. Wickfield hastened to him. Without interchanging a word they went slowly out of the room together, Uriah looking after them.

"Well, Master Copperfield!" said Uriah, meekly turning to me. "The thing hasn't took quite the turn that might have been expected, for the old Scholar—what an excellent man!—is as blind as a brickbat; but *this* family's out of the cart, I think!"

I needed but the sound of his voice to be so madly enraged as I never was before, and never have been since.

"You villain," said I, "what do you mean by entrapping me into your schemes? How dare you appeal to me just now, you false rascal, as if we had been in discussion together?"

As we stood, front to front, I saw so plainly, in the stealthy exultation of his face, what I already so plainly knew; I mean that he forced his confidence upon me, expressly to make me miserable, and had set a deliberate trap for me in this very matter; that I couldn't bear it. The whole of his lank cheek was invitingly before me, and I struck it with my open hand with that force that my fingers tingled as if I had burnt them.

He caught the hand in his, and we stood in that connexion, looking at each other. We stood so, a long time; long enough for me to see the white marks of my fingers die out of the deep red of his cheek, and leave it a deeper red.

"Copperfield," he said at length, in a breathless voice, "have you taken leave of your senses?"

"I have taken leave of you," said I, wresting my hand away. "You dog, I'll know no more of you."

"Won't you?" said he, constrained by the pain of his cheek to put his hand there. "Perhaps you won't be able to help it. Isn't this ungrateful of you, now?"

"I have shown you often enough," said I, "that I despise you. I have shown you now, more plainly, that I do. Why should I dread your doing your worst to all about you? What else do you ever do?"

He perfectly understood this allusion to the considerations that had hitherto restrained me in my communications with him. I rather think that neither the blow, nor the allusion, would have escaped me, but for the assurance I had had from Agnes that night. It is no matter.

There was another long pause. His eyes, as he looked at me, seemed to take every shade of colour that could make eyes ugly.

"Copperfield," he said, removing his hand from his cheek, "you have always gone against me. I know you always used to be against me at Mr. Wickfield's."

"You may think what you like," said I, still in a towering rage. "If it is not true, so much the worthier you."

"And yet I always liked you, Copperfield!" he rejoined.

I deigned to make him no reply; and, taking up my hat, was going out to bed, when he came between me and the door.

"Copperfield," he said, "there must be two parties to a quarrel. I won't be one."

"You may go to the devil!" said I.

"Don't say that!" he replied. "I know you'll be sorry afterwards. How can you make yourself so inferior to me, as to show such a bad spirit? But I forgive you."

"You forgive me!" I repeated disdainfully.

"I do, and you can't help yourself," replied Uriah. "To think of your going and attacking *me*, that have always been a friend to you! But there can't be a quarrel without two parties, and I won't be one. I will be a friend to you, in spite of you. So now you know what you've got to expect."

The necessity of carrying on this dialogue (his part in which was very slow; mine very quick) in a low tone, that the house might not be disturbed at an unseasonable hour, did not improve my temper; though my passion was cooling down. Merely telling him that I should expect from him what I always had expected, and had never yet been disappointed in, I opened the door upon him, as if he had been a great walnut put there to be cracked, and went out of the house. But he slept out of the house too, at his mother's lodging; and before I had gone many hundred yards, came up with me.

"You know, Copperfield," he said, in my ear (I did not turn my head), "you're in quite a wrong position;" which I felt to be true, and that made me chafe the more; "you can't make this a brave thing, and you can't help being forgiven. I don't intend to mention it to mother, nor to any living soul. I'm determined to forgive you. But I do wonder that you should lift your hand against a person that you knew to be so umble!"

I felt only less mean than he. He knew me better than I

knew myself. If he had retorted or openly exasperated me, it would have been a relief and a justification ; but he had put me on a slow fire, on which I lay tormented half the night.

In the morning, when I came out, the early church bell was ringing, and he was walking up and down with his mother. He addressed me as if nothing had happened, and I could do no less than reply. I had struck him hard enough to give him the toothache, I suppose. At all events his face was tied up in a black silk handkerchief, which, with his hat perched on the top of it, was far from improving his appearance. I heard that he went to a dentist's in London on the Monday morning, and had a tooth out. I hope it was a double one.

The Doctor gave out that he was not quite well; and remained alone, for a considerable part of every day, during the remainder of the visit. Agnes and her father had been gone a week, before we resumed our usual work. On the day preceding its resumption, the Doctor gave me with his own hands a folded note, not sealed. It was addressed to myself; and laid an injunction on me, in a few affectionate words, never to refer to the subject of that evening. I had confided it to my aunt, but to no one else. It was not a subject I could discuss with Agnes, and Agnes certainly had not the least suspicion of what had passed.

Neither, I felt convinced, had Mrs. Strong then. Several weeks elapsed before I saw the least change in her. It came on slowly, like a cloud when there is no wind. At first, she seemed to wonder at the gentle compassion with which the Doctor spoke to her, and at his wish that she should have her mother with her, to relieve the dull monotony of her life. Often, when we were at work, and she was sitting by, I would see her pausing and looking at him with that memorable face. Afterwards, I sometimes observed her rise, with her eyes full of tears, and go out of the room. Gradually, an unhappy shadow fell upon her beauty, and deepened every day. Mrs. Markleham was a regular inmate of the cottage then; but she talked and talked, and saw nothing.

As this change stole on Annie, once like sunshine in the Doctor's house, the Doctor became older in appearance, and more grave; but the sweetness of his temper, the placid kindness of his manner, and his benevolent solicitude for her, if they were capable of any increase, were increased. I saw him once, early on the morning of her birthday, when she came to sit in the window while we were at work (which she had always done, but now began to do with a timid and uncertain air that I thought very touching), take her forehead between his hands, kiss it, and go hurriedly away, too much moved to remain. I saw her stand where he had left her, like a statue; and then bend down her head, and clasp her hands, and weep, I cannot say how sorrowfully.

Sometimes, after that, I fancied that she tried to speak, even to me, in intervals when we were left alone. But she never uttered word. The Doctor always had some new project for her participating in amusements away from home, with her mother; and Mrs. Markleham, who was very fond of amusements, and very easily dissatisfied with anything else, entered into them with great good will, and was loud in her commendations. But Annie, in a spiritless unhappy way, only went whither she was led, and seemed to have no care for anything.

I did not know what to think. Neither did my aunt; who must have walked, at various times, a hundred miles in her uncertainty. What was strangest of all was, that the only real relief which seemed to make its way into the secret region of this domestic unhappiness, made its way there in the person of Mr. Dick.

What his thoughts were on the subject, or what his observation was, I am as unable to explain, as I dare say he would have been to assist me in the task. But, as I have recorded in the narrative of my school days, his veneration for the Doctor was unbounded; and there is a subtlety of perception in real attachment, even when it is borne towards man by one of the lower animals, which leaves the highest intellect behind. To this mind of the heart, if I may call it so, in Mr. Dick, some bright ray of the truth shot straight.

He had proudly resumed his privilege, in many of his spare hours, of walking up and down the garden with the Doctor; as he had been accustomed to pace up and down The Doctor's Walk at Canterbury. But matters were no sooner in this state, than he devoted all his spare time (and got up earlier to make it more) to these perambulations. If he had never been so happy as when the Doctor read that marvellous performance, the Dictionary, to him; he was now quite miserable unless the Doctor pulled it out of his pocket, and began. When the Doctor and I were engaged, he now fell into the custom of walking up and down with Mrs. Strong, and helping her to trim her favourite flowers, or weed the beds. I dare say he rarely spoke a dozen words in an hour: but his quiet interest, and his wistful face, found immediate response in both their breasts; each knew that the other liked him, and that he loved both; and he became what no one else could be—a link between them.

When I think of him, with his impenetrably wise face, walking up and down with the Doctor, delighted to be battered by the hard words in the Dictionary; when I think of him carrying huge watering-pots after Annie; kneeling down, in very paws of gloves, at patient microscopic work among the little leaves; expressing as no philosopher could have expressed, in everything he did, a delicate desire to be her friend; showering sympathy, trustfulness, and affection, out of every hole in the watering-pot; when I think of him never wandering in that better mind of his to which unhappiness addressed itself, never bringing the unfortunate King Charles into the garden, never wavering in his grateful service, never diverted from his knowledge that there was something wrong, or from his wish to set it right—I really feel almost ashamed of having known that he was not quite in his wits, taking account of the utmost I have done with mine.

"Nobody but myself, Trot, knows what that man is!" my aunt would proudly remark, when we conversed about it. "Dick will distinguish himself yet!"

I must refer to one other topic before I close this chapter. While the visit at the Doctor's was still in progress, I observed that the postman brought two or three letters every morning for Uriah Heep, who remained at Highgate until the rest went back, it being a leisure time; and that these were always directed in a business-like manner by Mr. Micawber, who now assumed a round legal hand. I was glad to infer, from these slight premises, that Mr. Micawber was doing well; and consequently was much surprised to receive, about this time, the following letter from his amiable wife:—

"CANTERBURY, *Monday Evening.*

"You will doubtless be surprised, my dear Mr. Copperfield, to receive this communication. Still more so, by its contents. Still more so, by the stipulation of implicit confidence which I beg to impose. But my feelings as a wife and mother require relief; and as I do not wish to consult my family (already obnoxious to the feelings of Mr. Micawber), I know no one of whom I can better ask advice than my friend and former lodger.

"You may be aware, my dear Mr. Copperfield, that between myself and Mr. Micawber (whom I will never desert), there has always been preserved a spirit of mutual confidence. Mr. Micawber may have occasionally given a bill without consulting me, or he may have misled me as to the period when that obligation would become due. This has actually happened. But, in general, Mr. Micawber has had no secrets from the bosom of affection—I allude to his wife—and has invariably, on our retirement to rest, recalled the events of the day.

"You will picture to yourself, my dear Mr. Copperfield, what the poignancy of my feelings must be, when I inform you that Mr. Micawber is entirely changed. He is reserved. He is secret. His life is a mystery to the partner of his joys and sorrows—I again allude to his wife—and if I should assure you that beyond knowing that it is passed from morning to night at the office, I now know less of it than I do of the man in the south, connected with whose mouth the thoughtless children repeat an idle tale respecting cold plum porridge, I should adopt a popular fallacy to express an actual fact.

"But this is not all. Mr. Micawber is morose. He is severe. He is estranged from our eldest son and daughter, he has no pride in his twins, he looks with an eye of coldness even on the unoffending stranger who last became a member of our circle. The pecuniary means of meeting our expenses, kept down to the utmost farthing, are obtained from him with great difficulty, and even under fearful threats that he will Settle himself (the exact expression); and he inexorably refuses to give any explanation whatever of this distracting policy.

"This is hard to bear. This is heart-breaking. If you will advise me, knowing my feeble powers such as they are, how you think it will be best to exert them in a dilemma so unwonted, you will add another friendly obligation to the many you have already rendered me. With loves from the children, and a smile from the happily-unconscious stranger, I remain, dear Mr. Copperfield,

> "Your afflicted,
>   "EMMA MICAWBER."

I did not feel justified in giving a wife of Mrs. Micawber's experience any other recommendation, than that she should try to reclaim Mr. Micawber by patience and kindness (as I knew she would in any case); but the letter set me thinking about him very much.

CHAPTER XLIII.

ONCE again, let me pause upon a memorable period of my life. Let me stand aside, to see the phantoms of those days go by me, accompanying the shadow of myself, in dim procession.

Weeks, months, seasons, pass along. They seem little more than a summer day and a winter evening. Now, the Common where I walk with Dora is all in bloom, a field of bright gold ; and now the unseen heather lies in mounds and bunches underneath a covering of snow. In a breath, the river that flows through our Sunday walks is sparkling in the summer sun, is ruffled by the winter wind, or thickened with drifting heaps of ice. Faster than ever river ran towards the sea, it flashes, darkens, and rolls away.

Not a thread changes in the house of the two little bird-like ladies. The clock ticks over the fireplace, the weather-glass hangs in the hall. Neither clock nor weather-glass is ever right ; but we believe in both, devoutly.

I have come legally to man's estate. I have attained the dignity of twenty-one. But this is a sort of dignity that may be thrust upon one. Let me think what I have achieved.

I have tamed that savage stenographic mystery. I make a respectable income by it. I am in high repute for my accomplishment in all pertaining to the art, and am joined with eleven others in reporting the debates in Parliament for a

Morning Newspaper. Night after night, I record predictions that never come to pass, professions that are never fulfilled, explanations that are only meant to mystify. I wallow in words. Britannia, that unfortunate female, is always before me, like a trussed fowl: skewered through and through with office-pens, and bound hand and foot with red tape. I am sufficiently behind the scenes to know the worth of political life. I am quite an Infidel about it, and shall never be converted.

My dear old Traddles has tried his hand at the same pursuit, but it is not in Traddles's way. He is perfectly good-humoured respecting his failure, and reminds me that he always did consider himself slow. He has occasional employment on the same newspaper, in getting up the facts of dry subjects, to be written about and embellished by more fertile minds. He is called to the bar; and with admirable industry and self-denial has scraped another hundred pounds together, to fee a conveyancer whose chambers he attends. A great deal of very hot port wine was consumed at his call; and, considering the figure, I should think the Inner Temple must have made a profit by it.

I have come out in another way. I have taken with fear and trembling to authorship. I wrote a little something, in secret, and sent it to a magazine, and it was published in the magazine. Since then, I have taken heart to write a good many trifling pieces. Now, I am regularly paid for them. Altogether, I am well off; when I tell my income on the fingers of my left hand, I pass the third finger and take in the fourth to the middle joint.

We have removed from Buckingham Street, to a pleasant little cottage very near the one I looked at, when my enthusiasm first came on. My aunt, however (who has sold the house at Dover, to good advantage), is not going to remain here, but intends removing herself to a still more tiny cottage close at hand. What does this portend? My marriage. Yes!

I AM GOING TO BE MARRIED.

Yes! I am going to be married to Dora! Miss Lavinia and Miss Clarissa have given their consent; and if ever canary birds were in a flutter, they are. Miss Lavinia, self-charged with the superintendence of my darling's wardrobe, is constantly cutting out brown-paper cuirasses, and differing in opinion from a highly respectable young man, with a long bundle, and a yard measure under his arm. A dressmaker, always stabbed in the breast with a needle and thread, boards and lodges in the house; and seems to me, eating, drinking, or sleeping, never to take her thimble off. They make a lay-figure of my dear. They are always sending for her to come and try something on. We can't be happy together for five minutes in the evening, but some intrusive female knocks at the door, and says, "Oh, if you please, Miss Dora, would you step up-stairs!"

Miss Clarissa and my aunt roam all over London, to find out articles of furniture for Dora and me to look at. It would be better for them to buy the goods at once, without this ceremony of inspection; for, when we go to see a kitchen fender and meat-screen, Dora sees a Chinese house for Jip, with little bells on the top, and prefers that. And it takes a long time to accustom Jip to his new residence, after we have bought it; whenever he goes in or out, he makes all the little bells ring, and is horribly frightened.

Peggotty comes up to make herself useful, and falls to work immediately. Her department appears to be, to clean everything over and over again. She rubs everything that can be rubbed, until it shines, like her own honest forehead, with perpetual friction. And now it is, that I begin to see her solitary brother passing through the dark streets at night, and looking, as he goes, among the wandering faces. I never speak to him at such an hour. I know too well, as his grave figure passes onward, what he seeks, and what he dreads.

Why does Traddles look so important when he calls upon me this afternoon in the Commons—where I still occasionally attend, for form's sake, when I have time? The realisation of my boyish day-dreams is at hand. I am going to take out the licence.

It is a little document to do so much; and Traddles contemplates it, as it lies upon my desk, half in admiration, half in awe. There are the names in the sweet old visionary connexion, David Copperfield and Dora Spenlow; and there, in the corner, is that Parental Institution, the Stamp Office, which is so benignantly interested in the various transactions of human life, looking down upon our Union; and there is the Archbishop of Canterbury invoking a blessing on us in print, and doing it as cheap as could possibly be expected.

Nevertheless, I am in a dream, a flustered, happy, hurried dream. I can't believe that it is going to be; and yet I can't believe but that every one I pass in the street, must have some kind of perception, that I am to be married the day after to-morrow. The Surrogate knows me, when I go down to be sworn, and disposes of me easily, as if there were a Masonic understanding between us. Traddles is not at all wanted, but is in attendance as my general backer.

"I hope the next time you come here, my dear fellow," I say to Traddles, "it will be on the same errand for yourself. And I hope it will be soon."

"Thank you for your good wishes, my dear Copperfield," he replies. "I hope so too. It's a satisfaction to know that she'll wait for me any length of time, and that she really is the dearest girl——"

"When are you to meet her at the coach?" I ask.

"At seven," says Traddles, looking at his plain old silver watch—the very watch he once took a wheel out of, at school, to make a water-mill. "That is about Miss Wickfield's time, is it not?"

"A little earlier. Her time is half-past eight."

"I assure you, my dear boy," says Traddles, "I am almost as pleased as if I were going to be married myself, to think that this event is coming to such a happy termination. And really the great friendship and consideration of personally associating Sophy with the joyful occasion, and inviting her to be a bridesmaid in conjunction with Miss Wickfield, demands my warmest thanks. I am extremely sensible of it."

I hear him, and shake hands with him; and we talk, and walk, and dine, and so on; but I don't believe it. Nothing is real.

Sophy arrives at the house of Dora's aunts, in due course. She has the most agreeable of faces,—not absolutely beautiful, but extraordinarily pleasant,—and is one of the most genial, unaffected, frank, engaging creatures I have ever seen. Traddles presents her to us with great pride; and rubs his hands for ten minutes by the clock, with every individual hair upon his head standing on tiptoe, when I congratulate him in a corner on his choice.

I have brought Agnes from the Canterbury coach, and her cheerful and beautiful face is among us for the second time. Agnes has a great liking for Traddles, and it is capital to see them meet, and to observe the glory of Traddles as he commends the dearest girl in the world to her acquaintance.

Still I don't believe it. We have a delightful evening, and are supremely happy: but I don't believe it yet. I can't collect myself. I can't check off my happiness as it takes place. I feel in a misty and unsettled kind of state; as if I had got up very early in the morning a week or two ago, and had never been to bed since. I can't make out when yesterday was. I seem to have been carrying the licence about, in my pocket, many months.

Next day, too, when we all go in a flock to see the house —our house—Dora's and mine—I am quite unable to regard myself as its master. I seem to be there, by permission of somebody else. I half expect the real master to come home presently, and say he is glad to see me. Such a beautiful little house as it is, with everything so bright and new; with the flowers on the carpets looking as if freshly gathered, and the green leaves on the paper as if they had just come out; with the spotless muslin curtains, and the blushing rose-coloured furniture, and Dora's garden hat with the blue ribbon—do I remember, now, how I loved her in such another hat when I first knew her!—already hanging on its little peg; the guitar-case quite at home on its heels in a corner; and everybody tumbling over Jip's Pagoda, which is much too big for the establishment.

Another happy evening, quite as unreal as all the rest of it, and I steal into the usual room before going away. Dora is not there. I suppose they have not done trying on yet. Miss Lavinia peeps in, and tells me mysteriously that she will not be long. She is rather long, notwithstanding: but by-and-by I hear a rustling at the door, and some one taps.

I say, "Come in!" but some one taps again.

I go to the door, wondering who it is; there, I meet a pair of bright eyes, and a blushing face; they are Dora's eyes and face, and Miss Lavinia has dressed her in to-morrow's dress, bonnet and all, for me to see. I take my little wife to my heart; and Miss Lavinia gives a little scream because I tumble the bonnet, and Dora laughs and cries at once, because I am so pleased; and I believe it less than ever.

"Do you think it pretty, Doady?" says Dora.

Pretty! I should rather think I did.

"And are you sure you like me very much?" says Dora.

The topic is fraught with such danger to the bonnet, that Miss Lavinia gives another little scream, and begs me to understand that Dora is only to be looked at, and on no account to be touched. So Dora stands in a delightful state of confusion for a minute or two, to be admired; and then takes off her bonnet—looking so natural without it!—and runs away with it in her hand; and comes dancing down again in her own familiar dress, and asks Jip if I have got a beautiful little wife, and whether he'll forgive her for being married, and kneels down to make him stand upon the cookery-book, for the last time in her single life.

I go home, more incredulous than ever, to a lodging that

I have hard by; and get up very early in the morning, to ride to the Highgate road and fetch my aunt.

I have never seen my aunt in such state. She is dressed in lavender-coloured silk, and has a white bonnet on, and is amazing. Janet has dressed her, and is there to look at me. Peggotty is ready to go to church, intending to behold the ceremony from the gallery. Mr. Dick, who is to give my darling to me at the altar, has had his hair curled. Traddles, whom I have taken up by appointment at the turnpike, presents a dazzling combination of cream colour and light blue; and both he and Mr. Dick have a general effect about them of being all gloves.

No doubt I see this, because I know it is so; but I am astray, and seem to see nothing. Nor do I believe anything whatever. Still, as we drive along in an open carriage, this fairy marriage is real enough to fill me with a sort of wondering pity for the unfortunate people who have no part in it, but are sweeping out the shops, and going to their daily occupations.

My aunt sits with my hand in hers all the way. When we stop a little way short of the church, to put down Peggotty, whom we have brought on the box, she gives it a squeeze, and me a kiss.

"God bless you, Trot! My own boy never could be dearer. I think of poor dear Baby this morning."

"So do I. And of all I owe to you, dear aunt."

"Tut, child!" says my aunt; and gives her hand in overflowing cordiality to Traddles, who then gives his to Mr. Dick, who then gives his to me, who then give mine to Traddles, and then we come to the church door.

The church is calm enough, I am sure; but it might be a steam-power loom in full action, for any sedative effect it has on me. I am too far gone for that.

The rest is all a more or less incoherent dream.

A dream of their coming in with Dora; of the pew-opener arranging us, like a drill-sergeant, before the altar rails; of my wondering, even then, why pew-openers must always be the most disagreeable females procurable, and whether there is any religious dread of a disastrous infection of good humour which renders it indispensable to set those vessels of vinegar upon the road to Heaven.

Of the clergyman and clerk appearing; of a few boatmen and some other people strolling in; of an ancient mariner behind me, strongly flavouring the church with rum; of the service beginning in a deep voice, and our all being very attentive.

Of Miss Lavinia, who acts as a semi-auxiliary bridesmaid being the first to cry, and of her doing homage (as I take it to the memory of Pidger, in sobs; of Miss Clarissa applying a smelling-bottle; of Agnes taking care of Dora; of my aunt endeavouring to represent herself as a model of stern ness, with tears rolling down her face; of little Dora trembling very much, and making her responses in faint whispers.

Of our kneeling down together, side by side; of Dora's trembling less and less, but always clasping Agnes by the hand; of the service being got through, quietly and gravely of our all looking at each other in an April state of smile and tears, when it is over; of my young wife being hysterical in the vestry, and crying for her poor papa, her dear papa.

Of her soon cheering up again, and our signing the register all round. Of my going into the gallery for Peggotty to bring *her* to sign it; of Peggotty's hugging me in a corner and telling me she saw my own dear mother married; of it being over, and our going away.

Of my walking so proudly and lovingly down the aisle with my sweet wife upon my arm, through a mist of half-seen people, pulpits, monuments, pews, fonts, organs, and church-windows, in which there flutter faint airs of association with my childish church at home, so long ago.

Of their whispering, as we pass, what a youthful couple we are, and what a pretty little wife she is. Of our all being so

I am Married

merry and talkative in the carriage going back. Of Sophy telling us that when she saw Traddles (whom I had entrusted with the licence) asked for it, she almost fainted, having been convinced that he would contrive to lose it, or to have his pocket picked. Of Agnes laughing gaily; and of Dora being so fond of Agnes that she will not be separated from her, but still keeps her hand.

Of there being a breakfast, with abundance of things, pretty and substantial, to eat and drink, whereof I partake, as I should do in any other dream, without the least perception of their flavour; eating and drinking, as I may say, nothing but love and marriage, and no more believing in the viands than in anything else.

Of my making a speech in the same dreamy fashion, without having an idea of what I want to say, beyond such as may be comprehended in the full conviction that I haven't said it. Of our being very sociably and simply happy (always in a dream though); and of Jip's having wedding cake, and its not agreeing with him afterwards.

Of the pair of hired post-horses being ready, and of Dora's going away to change her dress. Of my aunt and Miss Clarissa remaining with us; and our walking in the garden; and my aunt, who has made quite a speech at breakfast touching Dora's aunts, being mightily amused with herself, but a little proud of it too.

Of Dora's being ready, and of Miss Lavinia's hovering about her, loth to lose the pretty toy that has given her so much pleasant occupation. Of Dora's making a long series of surprised discoveries that she has forgotten all sorts of little things; and of everybody's running everywhere to fetch them.

Of their all closing about Dora, when at last she begins to say good-bye, looking, with their bright colours and ribbons, like a bed of flowers. Of my darling being almost smothered among the flowers, and coming out, laughing and crying both together, to my jealous arms.

Of my wanting to carry Jip (who is to go along with us), and Dora's saying, No, that she must carry him, or else he'll think she don't like him any more, now she is married, and will break his heart. Of our going, arm in arm, and Dora stopping and looking back, and saying, "If I have ever been cross or ungrateful to anybody, don't remember it!" and bursting into tears.

Of her waving her little hand, and our going away once more. Of her once more stopping and looking back, and hurrying to Agnes, and giving Agnes, above all the others, her last kisses and farewells.

We drive away together, and I awake from the dream. I believe it at last. It is my dear, dear, little wife beside me, whom I love so well!

"Are you happy now, you foolish boy?" says Dora, "and sure you don't repent?"

I have stood aside to see the phantoms of those days go by me. They are gone, and I resume the journey of my story.

CHAPTER XLIV.

IT was a strange condition of things, the honeymoon being over, and the bridesmaids gone home, when I found myself sitting down in my own small house with Dora; quite thrown out of employment, as I may say, in respect of the delicious old occupation of making love.

It seemed such an extraordinary thing to have Dora always there. It was so unaccountable not to be obliged to go out to see her, not to have any occasion to be tormenting myself about her, not to have to write to her, not to be scheming and devising opportunities of being alone with her. Sometimes of an evening, when I looked up from my writing, and saw her seated opposite, I would lean back in my chair, and think how queer it was that there we were, alone together as a matter of course—nobody's business any more—all the romance of our engagement put away upon a shelf, to rust —no one to please but one another—one another to please, for life.

When there was a debate, and I was kept out very late, it seemed so strange to me, as I was walking home, to think that Dora was at home! It was such a wonderful thing, at first, to have her coming softly down to talk to me as I ate my supper. It was such a stupendous thing to know for certain that she put her hair in papers. It was altogether such an astonishing event to see her do it!

I doubt whether two young birds could have known less

239

about keeping house, than I and my pretty Dora did. We had a servant, of course. She kept house for us. I have still a latent belief that she must have been Mrs. Crupp's daughter in disguise, we had such an awful time of it with Mary Anne.

Her name was Paragon. Her nature was represented to us, when we engaged her, as being feebly expressed in her name. She had a written character, as large as a proclamation; and, according to this document, could do everything of a domestic nature that ever I heard of, and a great many things that I never did hear of. She was a woman in the prime of life; of a severe countenance; and subject (particularly in the arms) to a sort of perpetual measles or fiery rash. She had a cousin in the Life Guards, with such long legs that he looked like the afternoon shadow of somebody else. His shell-jacket was as much too little for him as he was too big for the premises. He made the cottage smaller than it need have been, by being so very much out of proportion to it. Besides which, the walls were not thick, and whenever he passed the evening at our house, we always knew of it by hearing one continual growl in the kitchen.

Our treasure was warranted sober and honest. I am therefore willing to believe that she was in a fit when we found her under the boiler; and that the deficient tea-spoons were attributable to the dustman.

But she preyed upon our minds dreadfully. We felt our inexperience, and were unable to help ourselves. We should have been at her mercy, if she had had any; but she was a remorseless woman, and had none. She was the cause of our first little quarrel.

"My dearest life," I said one day to Dora, "do you think Mary Anne has any idea of time?"

"Why, Doady?" inquired Dora, looking up, innocently, from her drawing.

"My love, because it's five, and we were to have dined at four."

THE AWFUL MARY ANNE.

Dora glanced wistfully at the clock, and hinted that she thought it was too fast.

"On the contrary, my love," said I, referring to my watch, "it's a few minutes too slow."

My little wife came and sat upon my knee, to coax me to be quiet, and drew a line with her pencil down the middle of my nose; but I couldn't dine off that, though it was very agreeable.

"Don't you think, my dear," said I, "it would be better for you to remonstrate with Mary Anne?"

"Oh no, please! I couldn't, Doady!" said Dora.

"Why not, my love?" I gently asked.

"Oh, because I am such a little goose," said Dora, "and she knows I am!"

I thought this sentiment so incompatible with the establishment of any system of check on Mary Anne, that I frowned a little.

"Oh, what ugly wrinkles in my bad boy's forehead!" said Dora, and still being on my knee, she traced them with her pencil; putting it to her rosy lips to make it mark blacker, and working at my forehead with a quaint little mockery of being industrious, that quite delighted me in spite of myself.

"There's a good child," said Dora, "it makes its face so much prettier to laugh."

"But, my love," said I.

"No, no! please!" cried Dora, with a kiss, "don't be a naughty Blue Beard! Don't be serious!"

"My precious wife," said I, "we must be serious sometimes. Come! Sit down on this chair, close beside me! Give me the pencil! There! Now let us talk sensibly. You know, dear;" what a little hand it was to hold, and what a tiny wedding-ring it was to see! "You know, my love, it is not exactly comfortable to have to go out without one's dinner. Now, is it?"

"N—n—no!" replied Dora, faintly.

"My love, how you tremble!"

241

"Because I KNOW you're going to scold me," exclaimed Dora, in a piteous voice.

"My sweet, I am only going to reason."

"Oh, but reasoning is worse than scolding!" exclaimed Dora, in despair. "I didn't marry to be reasoned with. If you meant to reason with such a poor little thing as I am, you ought to have told me so, you cruel boy!"

I tried to pacify Dora, but she turned away her face, and shook her curls from side to side, and said "You cruel, cruel boy!" so many times, that I really did not exactly know what to do: so I took a few turns up and down the room in my uncertainty, and came back again.

"Dora, my darling!"

"No, I am not your darling. Because you *must* be sorry that you married me, or else you wouldn't reason with me!" returned Dora.

I felt so injured by the inconsequential nature of this charge, that it gave me courage to be grave.

"Now, my own Dora," said I, "you are very childish, and are talking nonsense. You must remember, I am sure, that I was obliged to go out yesterday when dinner was half over; and that, the day before, I was made quite unwell by being obliged to eat underdone veal in a hurry; to-day, I don't dine at all—and I am afraid to say how long we waited for breakfast—and *then* the water didn't boil. I don't mean to reproach you, my dear, but this is not comfortable."

"Oh, you cruel, cruel boy, to say I am a disagreeable wife!" cried Dora.

"Now, my dear Dora, you must know that I never said that!"

"You said I wasn't comfortable!" said Dora.

"I said the housekeeping was not comfortable."

"It's exactly the same thing!" cried Dora. And she evidently thought so, for she wept most grievously.

I took another turn across the room, full of love for my pretty wife, and distracted by self-accusatory inclinations to knock my head against the door. I sat down again, and said :

"I am not blaming you, Dora. We have both a great deal to learn. I am only trying to show you, my dear, that you must—you really must" (I was resolved not to give this up) "accustom yourself to look after Mary Anne. Likewise to act a little for yourself, and me."

"I wonder, I do, at your making such ungrateful speeches," sobbed Dora. "When you know that the other day, when you said you would like a little bit of fish, I went out myself, miles and miles, and ordered it, to surprise you."

"And it was very kind of you, my own darling," said I. "I felt it so much that I wouldn't on any account have even mentioned that you bought a Salmon—which was too much for two. Or that it cost one pound six—which was more than we can afford."

"You enjoyed it very much," sobbed Dora. "And you said I was a Mouse."

"And I'll say so again, my love," I returned, "a thousand times!"

But I had wounded Dora's soft little heart, and she was not to be comforted. She was so pathetic in her sobbing and bewailing, that I felt as if I had said I don't know what to hurt her. I was obliged to hurry away; I was kept out late; and I felt all night such pangs of remorse as made me miserable. I had the conscience of an assassin, and was haunted by a vague sense of enormous wickedness.

It was two or three hours past midnight when I got home. I found my aunt, in our house, sitting up for me.

"Is anything the matter, aunt?" said I, alarmed.

"Nothing, Trot," she replied. "Sit down, sit down. Little Blossom has been rather out of spirits, and I have been keeping her company. That's all."

I leaned my head upon my hand; and felt more sorry and downcast, as I sat looking at the fire, than I could have supposed possible so soon after the fulfilment of my brightest hopes. As I sat thinking, I happened to meet my aunt's eyes, which were resting on my face. There was an anxious expression in them, but it cleared directly.

"I assure you, aunt," said I, "I have been quite unhappy myself all night, to think of Dora's being so. But I had no other intention than to speak to her tenderly and lovingly about our home-affairs."

My aunt nodded encouragement.

"You must have patience, Trot," said she.

"Of course. Heaven knows I don't mean to be unreasonable, aunt!"

"No, no," said my aunt. "But Little Blossom is a very tender little blossom, and the wind must be gentle with her."

I thanked my good aunt, in my heart, for her tenderness towards my wife; and I was sure that she knew I did.

"Don't you think, aunt," said I, after some further contemplation of the fire, "that you could advise and counsel Dora a little, for our mutual advantage, now and then?"

"Trot," returned my aunt, with some emotion, "no! Don't ask me such a thing."

Her tone was so very earnest that I raised my eyes in surprise.

"I look back on my life, child," said my aunt, "and I think of some who are in their graves, with whom I might have been on kinder terms. If I judged harshly of other people's mistakes in marriage, it may have been because I had bitter reason to judge harshly of my own. Let that pass. I have been a grumpy, frumpy, wayward sort of a woman, a good many years. I am still, and I always shall be. But you and I have done one another some good, Trot —at all events, you have done me good, my dear; and division must not come between us, at this time of day."

"Division between *us!*" cried I.

"Child, child!" said my aunt, smoothing her dress, "how soon it might come between us, or how unhappy I might make our Little Blossom, if I meddled in anything, a prophet couldn't say. I want our pet to like me, and be as gay as a butterfly. Remember your own home, in that second marriage; and never do both me and her the injury you have hinted at!"

I comprehended, at once, that my aunt was right; and I comprehended the full extent of her generous feeling towards my dear wife.

"These are early days, Trot," she pursued, "and Rome was not built in a day, nor in a year. You have chosen freely for yourself;" a cloud passed over her face for a moment, I thought; "and you have chosen a very pretty and a very affectionate creature. It will be your duty, and it will be your pleasure too—of course I know that; I am not delivering a lecture—to estimate her (as you chose her) by the qualities she has, and not by the qualities she may not have. The latter you must develop in her, if you can. And if you cannot, child," here my aunt rubbed her nose, "you must just accustom yourself to do without 'em. But remember, my dear, your future is between you two. No one can assist you; you are to work it out for yourselves. This is marriage, Trot; and Heaven bless you both in it, for a pair of babes in the wood as you are!"

My aunt said this in a sprightly way, and gave me a kiss to ratify the blessing.

"Now," said she, "light my little lantern, and see me into my bandbox by the garden path;" for there was a communication between our cottages in that direction. "Give Betsey Trotwood's love to Blossom, when you come back; and whatever you do, Trot, never dream of setting Betsey up as a scarecrow, for if *I* ever saw her in the glass, she's quite grim enough and gaunt enough in her private capacity!"

With this my aunt tied her head up in a handkerchief, with which she was accustomed to make a bundle of it on such occasions; and I escorted her home. As she stood in her garden, holding up her little lantern to light me back, I thought her observation of me had an anxious air again;

but I was too much occupied in pondering on what she had said, and too much impressed—for the first time, in reality—by the conviction that Dora and I had indeed to work out our future for ourselves, and that no one could assist us, to take much notice of it.

Dora came stealing down in her little slippers, to meet me, now that I was alone; and cried upon my shoulder, and said I had been hard-hearted and she had been naughty; and I said much the same thing in effect, I believe; and we made it up, and agreed that our first little difference was to be our last, and that we were never to have another if we lived a hundred years.

The next domestic trial we went through, was the Ordeal of Servants. Mary Anne's cousin deserted into our coal-hole, and was brought out, to our great amazement, by a piquet of his companions in arms, who took him away handcuffed in a procession that covered our front-garden with ignominy. This nerved me to get rid of Mary Anne, who went so mildly, on receipt of wages, that I was surprised, until I found out about the tea-spoons, and also about the little sums she had borrowed in my name of the tradespeople without authority. After an interval of Mrs. Kidgerbury—the oldest inhabitant of Kentish Town, I believe, who went out charing, but was too feeble to execute her conceptions of that art—we found another treasure, who was one of the most amiable of women, but who generally made a point of falling either up or down the kitchen stairs with the tray, and almost plunged into the parlour, as into a bath, with the tea-things. The ravages committed by this unfortunate rendering her dismissal necessary, she was succeeded (with intervals of Mrs. Kidgerbury) by a long line of Incapables; terminating in a young person of genteel appearance, who went to Greenwich Fair in Dora's bonnet. After whom I remember nothing but an average equality of failure.

Everybody we had anything to do with seemed to cheat us. Our appearance in a shop was a signal for the damaged goods to be brought out immediately. If we bought a lobster, it was full of water. All our meat turned out to be tough, and there was hardly any crust to our loaves. In search of the principle on which joints ought to be roasted, to be roasted enough, and not too much, I myself referred to the Cookery Book, and found it there established as the allowance of a quarter of an hour to every pound, and say a quarter over. But the principle always failed us by some curious fatality, and we never could hit any medium between redness and cinders.

I had reason to believe that in accomplishing these failures we incurred a far greater expense than if we had achieved a series of triumphs. It appeared to me, on looking over the tradesmen's books, as if we might have kept the basement story paved with butter, such was the extensive scale of our consumption of that article. I don't know whether the Excise returns of the period may have exhibited any increase in the demand for pepper; but if our performances did not affect the market, I should say several families must have left off using it. And the most wonderful fact of all was, that we never had anything in the house.

As to the washerwoman pawning the clothes, and coming in a state of penitent intoxication to apologise, I suppose that might have happened several times to anybody. Also the chimney on fire, the parish engine, and perjury on the part of the Beadle. But I apprehend that we were personally unfortunate in engaging a servant with a taste for cordials, who swelled our running account for porter at the public-house by such inexplicable items as " quartern rum shrub (Mrs. C.) ;" " Half-quartern gin and cloves (Mrs. C.) ;" " Glass rum and peppermint (Mrs. C.)"—the parentheses always referring to Dora, who was supposed, it appeared on explanation, to have imbibed the whole of these refreshments.

One of our first feats in the housekeeping way was a little dinner to Traddles. I met him in town, and asked him to walk out with me that afternoon. He readily consenting,

I wrote to Dora, saying I would bring him home. It was pleasant weather, and on the road we made my domestic happiness the theme of conversation. Traddles was very full of it; and said, that, picturing himself with such a home, and Sophy waiting and preparing for him, he could think of nothing wanting to complete his bliss.

I could not have wished for a prettier little wife at the opposite end of the table, but I certainly could have wished, when we sate down, for a little more room. I did not know how it was, but though there were only two of us, we were at once always cramped for room, and yet had always room enough to lose everything in. I suspect it may have been because nothing had a place of its own, except Jip's pagoda, which invariably blocked up the main thoroughfare. On the present occasion, Traddles was so hemmed in by the pagoda and the guitar-case, and Dora's flower-painting, and my writing-table, that I had serious doubts of the possibility of his using his knife and fork; but he protested, with his own good-humour, "Oceans of room, Copperfield! I assure you, Oceans!"

There was another thing I could have wished; namely, that Jip had never been encouraged to walk about the table-cloth during dinner. I began to think there was something disorderly in his being there at all, even if he had not been in the habit of putting his foot in the salt or the melted-butter. On this occasion he seemed to think he was introduced expressly to keep Traddles at bay; and he barked at my old friend, and made short runs at his plate, with such undaunted pertinacity, that he may be said to have engrossed the conversation.

However, as I knew how tender-hearted my dear Dora was, and how sensitive she would be to any slight upon her favourite, I hinted no objection. For similar reasons I made no allusion to the skirmishing plates upon the floor; or to the disreputable appearance of the castors, which were all at sixes and sevens, and looked drunk; or to the further blockade of Traddles by wandering vegetable dishes and jugs. I could

Our Housekeeping

not help wondering in my own mind, as I contemplated the boiled leg of mutton before me, previous to carving it, how it came to pass that our joints of meat were of such extra-ordinary shapes—and whether our butcher contracted for all the deformed sheep that came into the world; but I kept my reflections to myself.

"My love," said I to Dora, "what have you got in that dish?"

I could not imagine why Dora had been making tempting little faces at me, as if she wanted to kiss me.

"Oysters, dear," said Dora, timidly.

"Was that *your* thought?" said I, delighted.

"Ye-yes, Doady," said Dora.

"There never was a happier one!" I exclaimed, laying down the carving-knife and fork. "There is nothing Traddles likes so much!"

"Ye-yes, Doady," said Dora, "and so I bought a beautiful little barrel of them, and the man said they were very good. But I—I am afraid there's something the matter with them. They don't seem right." Here Dora shook her head, and diamonds twinkled in her eyes.

"They are only opened in both shells," said I. "Take the top one off, my love."

"But it won't come off," said Dora, trying very hard, and looking very much distressed.

"Do you know, Copperfield," said Traddles, cheerfully examining the dish, "I think it is in consequence—they are capital oysters, but I *think* it is in consequence—of their never having been opened."

They never had been opened; and we had no oyster-knives —and couldn't have used them if we had; so we looked at the oysters and ate the mutton. At least we ate as much of it as was done, and made up with capers. If I had per-mitted him, I am satisfied that Traddles would have made a perfect savage of himself, and eaten a plateful of raw meat, to express enjoyment of the repast; but I would hear of no such immolation on the altar of friendship; and we had a course of bacon instead; there happening, by good fortune, to be cold bacon in the larder.

My poor little wife was in such affliction when she thought I should be annoyed, and in such a state of joy when she found I was not, that the discomfiture I had subdued very soon vanished, and we passed a happy evening; Dora sitting with her arm on my chair while Traddles and I discussed a glass of wine, and taking every opportunity of whispering in my ear that it was so good of me not to be a cruel, cross old boy. By and bye she made tea for us; which it was so pretty to see her do, as if she was busying herself with a set of doll's tea-things, that I was not particular about the quality of the beverage. Then Traddles and I played a game or two at cribbage; and Dora singing to the guitar the while, it seemed to me as if our courtship and marriage were a tender dream of mine, and the night when I first listened to her voice were not yet over.

When Traddles went away, and I came back into the parlour from seeing him out, my wife planted her chair close to mine, and sat down by my side.

"I am very sorry," she said. "Will you try to teach me, Doady?"

"I must teach myself first, Dora," said I. "I am as bad as you, love."

"Ah! But you can learn," she returned; "and you are a clever, clever man!"

"Nonsense, mouse!" said I.

"I wish," resumed my wife, after a long silence, "that I could have gone down into the country for a whole year, and lived with Agnes!"

Her hands were clasped upon my shoulder, and her chin rested on them, and her blue eyes looked quietly into mine.

"Why so?" I asked.

"I think she might have improved me, and I think I might have learned from *her*," said Dora.

MY CHILD-WIFE.

"All in good time, my love. Agnes has had her father to take care of for these many years, you should remember. Even when she was quite a child, she was the Agnes whom we know," said I.

"Will you call me a name I want you to call me?" inquired Dora, without moving.

"What is it?" I asked with a smile.

"It's a stupid name," she said, shaking her curls for a moment. "Child-wife."

I laughingly asked my child-wife what her fancy was in desiring to be so called. She answered without moving, otherwise than as the arm I twined about her may have brought her blue eyes nearer to me:

"I don't mean, you silly fellow, that you should use the name instead of Dora. I only mean that you should think of me that way. When you are going to be angry with me, say to yourself, 'it's only my child-wife!' When I am very disappointing, say, 'I knew, a long time ago, that she would make but a child-wife!' When you miss what I should like to be, and I think can never be, say, 'still my foolish child-wife loves me!' For indeed I do."

I had not been serious with her; having no idea, until now, that she was serious herself. But her affectionate nature was so happy in what I now said to her with my whole heart, that her face became a laughing one before her glittering eyes were dry. She was soon my child-wife indeed; sitting down on the floor outside the Chinese House, ringing all the little bells one after another, to punish Jip for his recent bad behaviour; while Jip lay blinking in the doorway with his head out, even too lazy to be teased.

This appeal of Dora's made a strong impression on me. I look back on the time I write of; I invoke the innocent figure that I dearly loved, to come out from the mists and shadows of the past, and turn its gentle head towards me once again; and I can still declare that this one little speech was constantly in my memory. I may not have used it to

251

the best account; I was young and inexperienced; but I never turned a deaf ear to its artless pleading.

Dora told me, shortly afterwards, that she was going to be a wonderful housekeeper. Accordingly, she polished the tablets, pointed the pencil, bought an immense account-book, carefully stitched up with a needle and thread all the leaves of the Cookery Book which Jip had torn, and made quite a desperate little attempt " to be good," as she called it. But the figures had the old obstinate propensity—they *would not* add up. When she had entered two or three laborious items in the account-book, Jip would walk over the page, wagging his tail, and smear them all out. Her own little right-hand middle finger got steeped to the very bone in ink; and I think that was the only decided result obtained.

Sometimes, of an evening, when I was at home and at work—for I wrote a good deal now, and was beginning in a small way to be known as a writer—I would lay down my pen, and watch my child-wife trying to be good. First of all, she would bring out the immense account-book, and lay it down upon the table, with a deep sigh. Then she would open it at the place where Jip had made it illegible last night, and call Jip up to look at his misdeeds. This would occasion a diversion in Jip's favour, and some inking of his nose, perhaps, as a penalty. Then she would tell Jip to lie down on the table instantly, " like a lion "—which was one of his tricks, though I cannot say the likeness was striking —and, if he were in an obedient humour, he would obey. Then she would take up a pen, and begin to write, and find a hair in it. Then she would take up another pen, and begin to write, and find that it spluttered. Then she would take up another pen, and begin to write, and say in a low voice, " Oh, it's a talking pen, and will disturb Doady ! " And then she would give it up as a bad job, and put the account-book away, after pretending to crush the lion with it.

Or, if she were in a very sedate and serious state of mind, she would sit down with the tablets, and a little basket of bills and other documents, which looked more like curl-papers than anything else, and endeavour to get some result out of them. After severely comparing one with another, and making entries on the tablets, and blotting them out, and counting all the fingers of her left hand over and over again, backwards and forwards, she would be so vexed and discouraged, and would look so unhappy, that it gave me pain to see her bright face clouded—and for me!—and I would go softly to her, and say:

"What's the matter, Dora?"

Dora would look up hopelessly, and reply, "They won't come right. They make my head ache so. And they won't do anything I want!"

Then I would say, "Now let us try together. Let me show you, Dora."

Then I would commence a practical demonstration, to which Dora would pay profound attention, perhaps for five minutes; when she would begin to be dreadfully tired, and would lighten the subject by curling my hair, or trying the effect of my face with my shirt-collar turned down. If I tacitly checked this playfulness, and persisted, she would look so scared and disconsolate, as she became more and more bewildered, that the remembrance of her natural gaiety when I first strayed into her path, and of her being my child-wife, would come reproachfully upon me; and I would lay the pencil down, and call for the guitar.

I had a great deal of work to do, and had many anxieties, but the same considerations made me keep them to myself. I am far from sure, now, that it was right to do this, but I did it for my child-wife's sake. I search my breast, and I commit its secrets, if I know them, without any reservation to this paper. The old unhappy loss or want of something had, I am conscious, some place in my heart; but not to the embitterment of my life. When I walked alone in the fine weather, and thought of the summer days when all the air had been filled with my boyish enchantment, I did miss something of the realisation of my dreams; but I thought it was a softened glory of the Past, which nothing could have thrown upon the present time. I did feel, sometimes, for a little while, that I could have wished my wife had been my counsellor: had had more character and purpose, to sustain me, and improve me by; had been endowed with power to fill up the void which somewhere seemed to be about me; but I felt as if this were an unearthly consummation of my happiness, that never had been meant to be, and never could have been.

I was a boyish husband as to years. I had known the softening influence of no other sorrows or experiences than those recorded in these leaves. If I did any wrong, as I may have done much, I did it in mistaken love, and in my want of wisdom. I write the exact truth. It would avail me nothing to extenuate it now.

Thus it was that I took upon myself the toils and cares of our life, and had no partner in them. We lived much as before, in reference to our scrambling household arrangements; but I had got used to those, and Dora I was pleased to see was seldom vexed now. She was bright and cheerful in the old childish way, loved me dearly, and was happy with her old trifles.

When the debates were heavy—I mean as to length, not quality, for in the last respect they were not often otherwise —and I went home late, Dora would never rest when she heard my footsteps, but would always come down-stairs to meet me. When my evenings were unoccupied by the pursuit for which I had qualified myself with so much pains, and I was engaged in writing at home, she would sit quietly near me, however late the hour, and be so mute, that I would often think she had dropped asleep. But generally, when I raised my head, I saw her blue eyes looking at me with the quiet attention of which I have already spoken.

"Oh, what a weary boy!" said Dora one night, when I met her eyes as I was shutting up my desk.

"What a weary girl!" said I. "That's more tc the purpose. You must go to bed another time, my love. It's far too late for you."

"No, don't send me to bed!" pleaded Dora, coming to my side. "Pray, don't do that!"

"Dora!"

To my amazement she was sobbing on my neck.

"Not well, my dear! not happy!"

"Yes! quite well, and very happy!" said Dora. "But say you'll let me stop, and see you write."

"Why, what a sight for such bright eyes at midnight!" I replied.

"Are they bright, though?" returned Dora, laughing. "I'm so glad they're bright."

"Little Vanity!" said I.

But it was not vanity; it was only harmless delight in my admiration. I knew that very well, before she told me so.

"If you think them pretty, say I may always stop, and see you write!" said Dora. "*Do* you think them pretty?"

"Very pretty."

"Then let me always stop and see you write."

"I am afraid that won't improve their brightness, Dora."

"Yes it will! Because, you clever boy, you'll not forget me then, while you are full of silent fancies. Will you mind it, if I say something very, very silly?—more than usual?" inquired Dora, peeping over my shoulder into my face.

"What wonderful thing is that?" said I.

"Please let me hold the pens," said Dora. "I want to have something to do with all those many hours when you are so industrious. May I hold the pens?"

The remembrance of her pretty joy when I said Yes, brings tears into my eyes. The next time I sat down to write, and regularly afterwards, she sat in her old place, with a spare bundle of pens at her side. Her triumph in this connexion with my work, and her delight when I wanted a new pen—which I very often feigned to do—suggested to me a new way of pleasing my child-wife. I occasionally made a pretence of wanting a page or two of manuscript copied. Then Dora was in her glory. The preparations she made for this great work, the aprons she put on, the bibs she borrowed from the kitchen to keep off the ink, the time she took, the innumerable stoppages she made to have a laugh with Jip as if he understood it all, her conviction that her work was incomplete unless she signed her name at the end, and the way in which she would bring it to me, like a school-copy, and then, when I praised it, clasp me round the neck, are touching recollections to me, simple as they might appear to other men.

She took possession of the keys soon after this, and went jingling about the house with the whole bunch in a little basket, tied to her slender waist. I seldom found that the places to which they belonged were locked, or that they were of any use except as a plaything for Jip—but Dora was pleased, and that pleased me. She was quite satisfied that a good deal was effected by this make-belief of housekeeping; and was as merry as if we had been keeping a baby-house, for a joke.

So we went on. Dora was hardly less affectionate to my aunt than to me, and often told her of the time when she was afraid she was "a cross old thing." I never saw my aunt unbend more systematically to any one. She courted Jip, though Jip never responded; listened, day after day, to the guitar, though I am afraid she had no taste for music; never attacked the Incapables, though the temptation must have been severe; went wonderful distances on foot to purchase, as surprises, any trifles that she found out Dora wanted; and never came in by the garden, and missed her from the room, but she would call out, at the foot of the stairs, in a voice that sounded cheerfully all over the house:

"Where's Little Blossom?"

CHAPTER XLV.

MR. DICK FULFILS MY AUNT'S PREDICTIONS.

It was some time now, since I had left the Doctor. Living in his neighbourhood, I saw him frequently; and we all went to his house on two or three occasions to dinner or tea. The Old Soldier was in permanent quarters under the Doctor's roof. She was exactly the same as ever, and the same immortal butterflies hovered over her cap.

Like some other mothers, whom I have known in the course of my life, Mrs. Markleham was far more fond of pleasure than her daughter was. She required a great deal of amusement, and, like a deep old soldier, pretended, in consulting her own inclinations, to be devoting herself to her child. The Doctor's desire that Annie should be entertained, was therefore particularly acceptable to this excellent parent; who expressed unqualified approval of his discretion.

I have no doubt, indeed, that she probed the Doctor's wound without knowing it. Meaning nothing but a certain matured frivolity and selfishness, not always inseparable from full-blown years, I think she confirmed him in his fear that he was a constraint upon his young wife, and that there was no congeniality of feeling between them, by so strongly commending his design of lightening the load of her life.

"My dear soul," she said to him one day when I was present, "you know there is no doubt it would be a little pokey for Annie to be always shut up here."

The Doctor nodded his benevolent head.

"When she comes to her mother's age," said Mrs. Markleham, with a flourish of her fan, "then it'll be another thing. You might put ME into a Jail, with genteel society and a rubber, and I should never care to come out. But I am not Annie, you know; and Annie is not her mother."

"Surely, surely," said the Doctor.

"You are the best of creatures—no, I beg your pardon!" for the Doctor made a gesture of deprecation, "I must say before your face, as I always say behind your back, you are the best of creatures; but of course you don't—now do you?—enter into the same pursuits and fancies as Annie."

"No," said the Doctor, in a sorrowful tone.

"No, of course not," retorted the Old Soldier. "Take your Dictionary, for example. What a useful work a Dictionary is! What a necessary work! The meanings of words! Without Doctor Johnson, or somebody of that sort, we might have been at this present moment calling an Italian-iron a bedstead. But we can't expect a Dictionary—especially when it's making—to interest Annie, can we?"

The Doctor shook his head.

"And that's why I *so* much approve," said Mrs. Markleham, tapping him on the shoulder with her shut-up fan, "of your thoughtfulness. It shows that you don't expect, as many elderly people do expect, old heads on young shoulders. You have studied Annie's character, and you understand it. *That's* what I find so charming!"

Even the calm and patient face of Doctor Strong expressed some little sense of pain, I thought, under the infliction of these compliments.

"Therefore, my dear Doctor," said the Soldier, giving him several affectionate taps, "you may command me, at all times and seasons. Now, do understand that I am entirely at your service. I am ready to go with Annie to operas, concerts, exhibitions, all kinds of places; and you shall never find that I am tired. Duty, my dear Doctor, before every consideration in the universe!"

THE OLD SOLDIER ON DUTY.

She was as good as her word. She was one of those people who can bear a great deal of pleasure, and she never flinched in her perseverance in the cause. She seldom got hold of the newspaper (which she settled herself down in the softest chair in the house to read through an eye-glass, every day, for two hours), but she found out something that she was certain Annie would like to see. It was in vain for Annie to protest that she was weary of such things. Her mother's remonstrance always was, "Now, my dear Annie, I am sure you know better; and I must tell you, my love, that you are not making a proper return for the kindness of Doctor Strong."

This was usually said in the Doctor's presence, and appeared to me to constitute Annie's principal inducement for withdrawing her objections when she made any. But in general she resigned herself to her mother, and went where the Old Soldier would.

It rarely happened now that Mr. Maldon accompanied them. Sometimes my aunt and Dora were invited to do so, and accepted the invitation. Sometimes Dora only was asked. The time had been when I should have been uneasy in her going; but reflection on what had passed that former night in the Doctor's study, had made a change in my mistrust. I believed that the Doctor was right, and I had no worse suspicions.

My aunt rubbed her nose sometimes when she happened to be alone with me, and said she couldn't make it out; she wished they were happier; she didn't think our military friend (so she always called the Old Soldier) mended the matter at all. My aunt further expressed her opinion, "that if our military friend would cut off those butterflies, and give 'em to the chimney-sweepers for May-day, it would look like the beginning of something sensible on her part."

But her abiding reliance was on Mr. Dick. That man had evidently an idea in his head, she said; and if he could only once pen it up into a corner, which was his great difficulty, he would distinguish himself in some extraordinary manner.

Unconscious of this prediction, Mr. Dick continued to occupy precisely the same ground in reference to the Doctor and to Mrs. Strong. He seemed neither to advance nor to recede. He appeared to have settled into his original foundation, like a building ; and I must confess that my faith in his ever moving, was not much greater than if he had been a building.

But one night, when I had been married some months, Mr. Dick put his head into the parlour, where I was writing alone (Dora having gone out with my aunt to take tea with the two little birds), and said, with a significant cough :

"You couldn't speak to me without inconveniencing yourself, Trotwood, I am afraid ?"

"Certainly, Mr. Dick," said I ; "come in !"

"Trotwood," said Mr. Dick, laying his finger on the side of his nose, after he had shaken hands with me. "Before I sit down, I wish to make an observation. You know your aunt ?"

"A little," I replied.

"She is the most wonderful woman in the world, sir !"

After the delivery of this communication, which he shot out of himself as if he were loaded with it, Mr. Dick sat down with greater gravity than usual, and looked at me.

"Now, boy," said Mr. Dick, "I am going to put a question to you."

"As many as you please," said I.

"What do you consider me, sir ?" asked Mr. Dick, folding his arms.

"A dear old friend," said I.

"Thank you, Trotwood," returned Mr. Dick, laughing, and reaching across in high glee to shake hands with me. "But I mean, boy," resuming his gravity, "what do you consider me in this respect ?" touching his forehead.

I was puzzled how to answer, but he helped me with a word.

A CONVERSATION WITH MR. DICK.

" Weak ? " said Mr. Dick.

" Well," I replied, dubiously. " Rather so."

" Exactly ! " cried Mr. Dick, who seemed quite enchanted by my reply. " That is, Trotwood, when they took some of the trouble out of you-know-who's head, and put it you know where, there was a——— " Mr. Dick made his two hands revolve very fast about each other a great number of times, and then brought them into collision, and rolled them over and over one another, to express confusion. " There was that sort of thing done to me somehow. Eh ? "

I nodded at him, and he nodded back again.

" In short, boy," said Mr. Dick, dropping his voice to a whisper, " I am simple."

I would have qualified that conclusion, but he stopped me.

" Yes I am ! She pretends I am not. She won't hear of it ; but I am. I know I am. If she hadn't stood my friend, sir, I should have been shut up, to lead a dismal life these many years. But I'll provide for her ! I never spend the copying money. I put it in a box. I have made a will. I'll leave it all to her. She shall be rich—noble ! "

Mr. Dick took out his pocket-handkerchief, and wiped his eyes. He then folded it up with great care, pressed it smooth between his two hands, put it in his pocket, and seemed to put my aunt away with it.

" Now you are a scholar, Trotwood," said Mr. Dick. " You are a fine scholar. You know what a learned man, what a great man, the Doctor is. You know what honour he has always done me. Not proud in his wisdom. Humble, humble—condescending even to poor Dick, who is simple and knows nothing. I have sent his name up, on a scrap of paper, to the kite, along the string, when it has been in the sky, among the larks. The kite has been glad to receive it, sir, and the sky has been brighter with it."

I delighted him by saying, most heartily, that the Doctor was deserving of our best respect and highest esteem.

" And his beautiful wife is a star," said Mr. Dick. " A

261

shining star. I have seen her shine, sir. But," bringing his chair nearer, and laying one hand upon my knee—"clouds, sir—clouds."

I answered the solicitude which his face expressed, by conveying the same expression into my own, and shaking my head.

"What clouds?" said Mr. Dick.

He looked so wistfully into my face, and was so anxious to understand, that I took great pains to answer him slowly and distinctly, as I might have entered on an explanation to a child.

"There is some unfortunate division between them," I replied. "Some unhappy cause of separation. A secret. It may be inseparable from the discrepancy in their years. It may have grown up out of almost nothing."

Mr. Dick, who told off every sentence with a thoughtful nod, paused when I had done, and sat considering, with his eyes upon my face, and his hand upon my knee.

"Doctor not angry with her, Trotwood?" he said, after some time.

"No. Devoted to her."

"Then, I have got it, boy!" said Mr. Dick.

The sudden exultation with which he slapped me on the knee, and leaned back in his chair, with his eyebrows lifted up as high as he could possibly lift them, made me think him farther out of his wits than ever. He became as suddenly grave again, and leaning forward as before, said—first respectfully taking out his pocket-handkerchief, as if it really did represent my aunt:

"Most wonderful woman in the world, Trotwood. Why has *she* done nothing to set things right?"

"Too delicate and difficult a subject for such interference," I replied.

"Fine scholar," said Mr. Dick, touching me with his finger. "Why has *he* done nothing?"

For the same reason," I returned.

MR. DICK'S BRIGHT IDEA.

"Then, I have got it, boy!" said Mr. Dick. And he stood up before me, more exultingly than before, nodding his head, and striking himself repeatedly upon the breast, until one might have supposed that he had nearly nodded and struck all the breath out of his body.

"A poor fellow with a craze, sir," said Mr. Dick, "a simpleton, a weak-minded person—present company, you know!" striking himself again, "may do what wonderful people may not do. I'll bring them together, boy. I'll try. They'll not blame *me*. They'll not object to *me*. They'll not mind what *I* do, if it's wrong. I'm only Mr. Dick. And who minds Dick? Dick's nobody! Whoo!" He blew a slight, contemptuous breath, as if he blew himself away.

It was fortunate he had proceeded so far with his mystery, for we heard the coach stop at the little garden gate, which brought my aunt and Dora home.

"Not a word, boy!" he pursued in a whisper; "leave all the blame with Dick—simple Dick—mad Dick. I have been thinking, sir, for some time, that I was getting it, and now I have got it. After what you have said to me, I am sure I have got it. All right!"

Not another word did Mr. Dick utter on the subject; but he made a very telegraph of himself for the next half-hour (to the great disturbance of my aunt's mind), to enjoin inviolable secrecy on me.

To my surprise, I heard no more about it for some two or three weeks, though I was sufficiently interested in the result of his endeavours; descrying a strange gleam of good sense—I say nothing of good feeling, for that he always exhibited—in the conclusion to which he had come. At last I began to believe, that, in the flighty and unsettled state of his mind, he had either forgotten his intention or abandoned it.

One fair evening, when Dora was not inclined to go out, my aunt and I strolled up to the Doctor's cottage. It was autumn, when there were no debates to vex the evening air; and I remember how the leaves smelt like our garden at

Blunderstone as we trod them under foot, and how the old, unhappy feeling, seemed to go by, on the sighing wind.

It was twilight when we reached the cottage. Mrs. Strong was just coming out of the garden, where Mr. Dick yet lingered, busy with his knife, helping the gardener to point some stakes. The Doctor was engaged with some one in his study; but the visitor would be gone directly, Mrs. Strong said, and begged us to remain and see him. We went into the drawing-room with her, and sat down by the darkening window. There was never any ceremony about the visits of such old friends and neighbours as we were.

We had not sat here many minutes, when Mrs. Markleham, who usually contrived to be in a fuss about something, came bustling in, with her newspaper in her hand, and said, out of breath, " My goodness gracious, Annie, why didn't you tell me there was some one in the Study ! "

" My dear mama," she quietly returned, " how could I know that you desired the information ? "

" Desired the information ! " said Mrs. Markleham, sinking on the sofa. " I never had such a turn in all my life ! "

' Have you been to the Study, then, mama ? " asked Annie.

" *Been* to the Study, my dear ! " she returned emphatically. " Indeed I have ! I came upon the amiable creature—if you'll imagine my feelings, Miss Trotwood and David—in the act of making his will."

Her daughter looked round from the window quickly.

" In the act, my dear Annie," repeated Mrs. Markleham, spreading the newspaper on her lap like a table-cloth, and patting her hands upon it, " of making his last Will and Testament. The foresight and affection of the dear ! I must tell you how it was. I really must, in justice to the darling —for he is nothing less !—tell you how it was. Perhaps you know, Miss Trotwood, that there is never a candle lighted in this house, until one's eyes are literally falling out of one's head with being stretched to read the paper. And that there is not a chair in this house, in which a paper can be what call, read, except one in the Study. This took me to the Study, where I saw a light. I opened the door. In company with the dear Doctor were two professional people, evidently connected with the law, and they were all three standing at the table : the darling Doctor pen in hand 'This simply expresses then,' said the Doctor—Annie, my love, attend to the very words—'this simply expresses then, gentlemen, the confidence I have in Mrs. Strong, and gives her all unconditionally?' One of the professional people replied, 'And gives her all unconditionally.' Upon that, with the natural feelings of a mother, I said, 'Good God, I beg your pardon!' fell over the door-step, and came away through the little back passage where the pantry is."

Mrs. Strong opened the window, and went out into the verandah, where she stood leaning against a pillar.

"But now isn't it, Miss Trotwood, isn't it, David, invigorating," said Mrs. Markleham, mechanically following her with her eyes, "to find a man at Doctor Strong's time of life, with the strength of mind to do this kind of thing? It only shows how right I was. I said to Annie, when Doctor Strong paid a very flattering visit to myself, and made her the subject of a declaration and an offer, I said, 'My dear, there is no doubt whatever, in my opinion, with reference to a suitable provision for you, that Doctor Strong will do more than he binds himself to do.'"

Here the bell rang, and we heard the sound of the visitors' feet as they went out.

"It's all over, no doubt," said the Old Soldier, after listening; "the dear creature has signed, sealed, and delivered, and his mind's at rest. Well it may be! What a mind! Annie, my love, I am going to the Study with my paper, for I am a poor creature without news. Miss Trotwood, David, pray come and see the Doctor."

I was conscious of Mr. Dick's standing in the shadow of the room, shutting up his knife, when we accompanied her to the Study; and of my aunt's rubbing her nose violently, by the way, as a mild vent for her intolerance of our military friend; but who got first into the Study, or how Mrs. Markleham settled herself in a moment in her easy chair, or how my aunt and I came to be left together near the door (unless her eyes were quicker than mine, and she held me back), I have forgotten if I ever knew. But this I know,— that we saw the Doctor before he saw us, sitting at his table, among the folio volumes in which he delighted, resting his head calmly on his hand. That, in the same moment, we saw Mrs. Strong glide in, pale and trembling. That Mr. Dick supported her on his arm. That he laid his other hand upon the Doctor's arm, causing him to look up with an abstracted air. That, as the Doctor moved his head, his wife dropped down on one knee at his feet, and, with her hands imploringly lifted, fixed upon his face the memorable look I had never forgotten. That at this sight Mrs. Markleham dropped the newspaper, and stared more like a figure-head intended for a ship to be called The Astonishment, than anything else I can think of.

The gentleness of the Doctor's manner and surprise, the dignity that mingled with the supplicating attitude of his wife, the amiable concern of Mr. Dick, and the earnestness with which my aunt said to herself, "*That* man mad!" (triumphantly expressive of the misery from which she had saved him)—I see and hear, rather than remember, as I write about it.

"Doctor!" said Mr. Dick. "What is it that's amiss? Look here!"

"Annie!" cried the Doctor. "Not at my feet, my dear!"

"Yes!" she said. "I beg and pray that no one will leave the room! Oh, my husband and father, break this long silence. Let us both know what it is that has come between us!"

Mrs. Markleham, by this time recovering the power of speech, and seeming to swell with family pride and motherly indignation, here exclaimed, "Annie, get up immediately, and

Mr. Dick fulfils my Aunt's Prediction

don't disgrace everybody belonging to you by humbling your-self like that, unless you wish to see me go out of my mind on the spot!"

"Mama!" returned Annie. "Waste no words on me, for my appeal is to my husband, and even you are nothing here."

"Nothing!" exclaimed Mrs. Markleham. "Me, nothing! The child has taken leave of her senses. Please to get me a glass of water!"

I was too attentive to the Doctor and his wife, to give any heed to this request; and it made no impression on anybody else; so Mrs. Markleham panted, stared, and fanned herself.

"Annie!" said the Doctor, tenderly taking her in his hands. "My dear! If any unavoidable change has come, in the sequence of time, upon our married life, you are not to blame. The fault is mine, and only mine. There is no change in my affection, admiration, and respect. I wish to make you happy. I truly love and honour you. Rise, Annie, pray!"

But she did not rise. After looking at him for a little while, she sank down closer to him, laid her arm across his knee, and dropping her head upon it, said:

"If I have any friend here, who can speak one word for me, or for my husband in this matter; if I have any friend here, who can give a voice to any suspicion that my heart has sometimes whispered to me; if I have any friend here, who honours my husband, or has ever cared for me, and has anything within his knowledge, no matter what it is, that may help to mediate between us,—I implore that friend to speak!"

There was a profound silence. After a few moments of painful hesitation, I broke the silence.

"Mrs. Strong," I said, "there is something within my knowledge, which I have been earnestly entreated by Doctor Strong to conceal, and have concealed until to-night. But I believe the time has come when it would be mistaken faith and delicacy to conceal it any longer, and when your appeal absolves me from his injunction."

She turned her face towards me for a moment, and I knew that I was right. I could not have resisted its entreaty, if the assurance that it gave me had been less convincing.

"Our future peace," she said, "may be in your hands. I trust it confidently to your not suppressing anything. I know beforehand that nothing you, or any one, can tell me, will show my husband's noble heart in any other light than one. Howsoever it may seem to you to touch me, disregard that. I will speak for myself, before him, and before God afterwards."

Thus earnestly besought, I made no reference to the Doctor for his permission, but, without any other compromise of the truth than a little softening of the coarseness of Uriah Heep, related plainly what had passed in that same room that night. The staring of Mrs. Markleham during the whole narration, and the shrill, sharp interjections with which she occasionally interrupted it, defy description.

When I had finished, Annie remained, for some few moments, silent, with her head bent down as I have described. Then, she took the Doctor's hand (he was sitting in the same attitude as when we had entered the room), and pressed it to her breast, and kissed it. Mr. Dick softly raised her; and she stood, when she began to speak, leaning on him, and looking down upon her husband—from whom she never turned her eyes.

"All that has ever been in my mind, since I was married," she said in a low, submissive, tender voice, "I will lay bare before you. I could not live and have one reservation, knowing what I know now."

"Nay, Annie," said the Doctor, mildly, "I have never doubted you, my child. There is no need; indeed there is no need, my dear."

"There is great need," she answered, in the same way, "that I should open my whole heart before the soul of generosity and truth, whom, year by year, and day by day, I have loved and venerated more and more, as Heaven knows!"

"Really," interrupted Mrs. Markleham, "if I have any discretion at all—"

("Which you haven't, you Marplot," observed my aunt, in an indignant whisper.)

"—I must be permitted to observe that it cannot be requisite to enter into these details."

"No one but my husband can judge of that, mama," said Annie, without removing her eyes from his face, "and he will hear me. If I say anything to give you pain, mama, forgive me. I have borne pain first, often and long, myself."

"Upon my word!" gasped Mrs. Markleham.

"When I was very young," said Annie, "quite a little child, my first associations with knowledge of any kind were inseparable from a patient friend and teacher—the friend of my dead father—who was always dear to me. I can remember nothing that I know, without remembering him. He stored my mind with its first treasures, and stamped his character upon them all. They never could have been, I think, as good as they have been to me, if I had taken them from any other hands."

"Makes her mother nothing!" exclaimed Mrs. Markleham.

"Not so, mama," said Annie; "but I make him what he was. I must do that. As I grew up, he occupied the same place still. I was proud of his interest: deeply, fondly, gratefully attached to him. I looked up to him I can hardly describe how—as a father, as a guide, as one whose praise was different from all other praise, as one in whom I could have trusted and confided, if I had doubted all the world. You know, mama, how young and inexperienced I was, when you presented him before me, of a sudden, as a lover."

"I have mentioned the fact, fifty times at least, to everybody here!" said Mrs. Markleham.

("Then hold your tongue, for the Lord's sake, and don't mention it any more!" muttered my aunt.)

"It was so great a change: so great a loss, I felt it at

first," said Annie, still preserving the same look and tone, "that I was agitated and distressed. I was but a girl; and when so great a change came in the character in which I had so long looked up to him, I think I was sorry. But nothing could have made him what he used to be again; and I was proud that he should think me so worthy, and we were married."

"—At Saint Alphage, Canterbury," observed Mrs. Markleham.

("Confound the woman!" said my aunt, "she *won't* be quiet!")

"I never thought," proceeded Annie, with a heightened colour, "of any worldly gain that my husband would bring to me. My young heart had no room in its homage for any such poor reference. Mama, forgive me when I say that it was *you* who first presented to my mind the thought that any one could wrong me, and wrong him, by such a cruel suspicion."

"Me!" cried Mrs. Markleham.

("Ah! You, to be sure!" observed my aunt, "and you can't fan it away, my military friend!")

"It was the first unhappiness of my new life," said Annie. "It was the first occasion of every unhappy moment I have known. These moments have been more, of late, than I can count; but not—my generous husband!—not for the reason you suppose; for in my heart there is not a thought, a recollection, or a hope, that any power could separate from you!"

She raised her eyes, and clasped her hands, and looked as beautiful and true, I thought, as any Spirit. The Doctor looked on her, henceforth, as stedfastly as she on him.

"Mama is blameless," she went on, "of having ever urged you for herself, and she is blameless in intention every way, I am sure,—but when I saw how many importunate claims were pressed upon you in my name; how you were traded on in my name; how generous you were, and how Mr. Wickfield, who had your welfare very much at heart, resented it; the first sense of my exposure to the mean suspicion that my tenderness was bought—and sold to you, of all men, on earth —fell upon me, like unmerited disgrace, in which I forced you to participate. I cannot tell you what it was—mama cannot imagine what it was—to have this dread and trouble always on my mind, yet know in my own soul that on my marriage-day I crowned the love and honour of my life!"

"A specimen of the thanks one gets," cried Mrs. Markleham, in tears, "for taking care of one's family! I wish I was a Turk!"

("I wish you were, with all my heart—and in your native country!" said my aunt.)

"It was at that time that mama was most solicitous about my Cousin Maldon. I had liked him:" she spoke softly, but without any hesitation: "very much. We had been little lovers once. If circumstances had not happened otherwise, I might have come to persuade myself that I really loved him, and might have married him, and been most wretched. There can be no disparity in marriage like unsuitability of mind and purpose."

I pondered on those words, even while I was studiously attending to what followed, as if they had some particular interest, or some strange application that I could not divine. "There can be no disparity in marriage like unsuitability of mind and purpose"—"no disparity in marriage like unsuitability of mind and purpose."

"There is nothing," said Annie, "that we have in common. I have long found that there is nothing. If I were thankful to my husband for no more, instead of for so much, I should be thankful to him for having saved me from the first mistaken impulse of my undisciplined heart."

She stood quite still, before the Doctor, and spoke with an earnestness that thrilled me. Yet her voice was just as quiet as before.

"When he was waiting to be the object of your munificence,

so freely bestowed for my sake, and when I was unhappy in the mercenary shape I was made to wear, I thought it would have become him better to have worked his own way on. I thought that if I had been he, I would have tried to do it, at the cost of almost any hardship. But I thought no worse of him, until the night of his departure for India. That night I knew he had a false and thankless heart. I saw a double meaning, then, in Mr. Wickfield's scrutiny of me. I perceived, for the first time, the dark suspicion that shadowed my life."

"Suspicion, Annie!" said the Doctor. "No, no, no!"

"In your mind there was none, I know, my husband!" she returned. "And when I came to you, that night, to lay down all my load of shame and grief, and knew that I had to tell, that, underneath your roof, one of my own kindred, to whom you had been a benefactor, for the love of me, had spoken to me words that should have found no utterance, even if I had been the weak and mercenary wretch he thought me—my mind revolted from the taint the very tale conveyed. It died upon my lips, and from that hour till now has never passed them."

Mrs. Markleham, with a short groan, leaned back in her easy chair; and retired behind her fan, as if she were never coming out any more.

"I have never, but in your presence, interchanged a word with him from that time; then, only when it has been necessary for the avoidance of this explanation. Years have passed since he knew from me, what his situation here was. The kindnesses you have secretly done for his advancement, and then disclosed to me, for my surprise and pleasure, have been, you will believe, but aggravations of the unhappiness and burden of my secret."

She sunk down gently at the Doctor's feet, though he did his utmost to prevent her; and said, looking up, tearfully, into his face:

"Do not speak to me yet! Let me say a little more!

Right or wrong, if this were to be done again, I think I should do just the same. You never can know what it was to be devoted to you, with those old associations; to find that any one could be so hard as to suppose that the truth of my heart was bartered away, and to be surrounded by appearances confirming that belief. I was very young, and had no adviser. Between mama and me, in all relating to you, there was a wide division. If I shrunk into myself, hiding the disrespect I had undergone, it was because I honoured you so much, and so much wished that you should honour me!"

"Annie, my pure heart!" said the Doctor, "my dear girl!"

"A little more! a very few words more! I used to think there were so many whom you might have married, who would not have brought such charge and trouble on you, and who would have made your home a worthier home. I used to be afraid that I had better have remained your pupil, and almost your child. I used to fear that I was so unsuited to your learning and wisdom. If all this made me shrink within myself (as indeed it did), when I had that to tell, it was still because I honoured you so much, and hoped that you might one day honour me."

"That day has shone this long time, Annie," said the Doctor, "and can have but one long night, my dear."

"Another word! I afterwards meant—stedfastly meant, and purposed to myself—to bear the whole weight of knowing the unworthiness of one to whom you had been so good. And now a last word, dearest and best of friends! The cause of the late change in you, which I have seen with so much pain and sorrow, and have sometimes referred to my old apprehension—at other times to lingering suppositions nearer to the truth—has been made clear to-night; and by an accident I have also come to know, to-night, the full measure of your noble trust in me, even under that mistake. I do not hope that any love and duty I may render in return, will ever make me worthy of your priceless confidence; but with all this knowledge fresh upon me, I can lift my eyes to this dear face, revered as a father's, loved as a husband's, sacred to me in my childhood as a friend's, and solemnly declare that in my lightest thought I had never wronged you; never wavered in the love and the fidelity I owe you!"

She had her arms around the Doctor's neck, and he leant his head down over her, mingling his grey hair with her dark brown tresses.

"Oh, hold me to your heart, my husband! Never cast me out! Do not think or speak of disparity between us, for there is none, except in all my many imperfections. Every succeeding year I have known this better, as I have esteemed you more and more. Oh, take me to your heart, my husband, for my love was founded on a rock, and it endures!"

In the silence that ensued, my aunt walked gravely up to Mr. Dick, without at all hurrying herself, and gave him a hug and a sounding kiss. And it was very fortunate, with a view to his credit, that she did so; for I am confident that I detected him at that moment in the act of making preparations to stand on one leg, as an appropriate expression of delight.

"You are a very remarkable man, Dick!" said my aunt, with an air of unqualified approbation; "and never pretend to be anything else, for I know better!"

With that, my aunt pulled him by the sleeve, and nodded to me; and we three stole quietly out of the room, and came away.

"That's a settler for our military friend, at any rate," said my aunt, on the way home. "I should sleep the better for that, if there was nothing else to be glad of!"

"She was quite overcome, I am afraid," said Mr. Dick, with great commiseration.

"What! Did you ever see a crocodile overcome?" inquired my aunt.

"I don't think I ever saw a crocodile," returned Mr. Dick, mildly.

"There never would have been anything the matter, if it

274

hadn't been for that old Animal," said my aunt, with strong emphasis. "It's very much to be wished that some mothers would leave their daughters alone after marriage, and not be so violently affectionate. They seem to think the only return that can be made them for bringing an unfortunate young woman into the world—God bless my soul, as if she asked to be brought, or wanted to come!—is full liberty to worry her out of it again. What are you thinking of, Trot?"

I was thinking of all that had been said. My mind was still running on some of the expressions used. "There can be no disparity in marriage like unsuitability of mind and purpose." "The first mistaken impulse of an undisciplined heart." "My love was founded on a rock." But we were at home; and the trodden leaves were lying under-foot, and the autumn wind was blowing.

CHAPTER XLVI.

INTELLIGENCE.

I MUST have been married, if I may trust to my imperfect memory for dates, about a year or so, when one evening, as I was returning from a solitary walk, thinking of the book I was then writing—for my success had steadily increased with my steady application, and I was engaged at that time upon my first work of fiction—I came past Mrs. Steerforth's house. I had often passed it before, during my residence in that neighbourhood, though never when I could choose another road. Howbeit, it did sometimes happen that it was not easy to find another, without making a long circuit; and so I had passed that way, upon the whole, pretty often.

I had never done more than glance at the house, as I went by with a quickened step. It had been uniformly gloomy and dull. None of the best rooms abutted on the road; and the narrow, heavily-framed old-fashioned windows, never cheerful under any circumstances, looked very dismal, close shut, and with their blinds always drawn down. There was a covered way across a little paved court, to an entrance that was never used; and there was one round staircase window, at odds with all the rest, and the only one unshaded by a blind, which had the same unoccupied blank look. I do not remember that I ever saw a light in all the house. If I had been a casual passer-by, I should have probably supposed that some childless person lay dead in it. If I had happily possessed no knowledge of the place, and had seen it often in that changeless state, I should have pleased my fancy with many ingenious speculations, I dare say.

As it was, I thought as little of it as I might. But my mind could not go by it and leave it, as my body did; and it usually awakened a long train of meditations. Coming before me on this particular evening that I mention, mingled with the childish recollections and later fancies, the ghosts of half-formed hopes, the broken shadows of disappointments dimly seen and understood, the blending of experience and imagination, incidental to the occupation with which my thoughts had been busy, it was more than commonly suggestive. I fell into a brown study as I walked on, and a voice at my side made me start.

It was a woman's voice, too. I was not long in recollecting Mrs. Steerforth's little parlour-maid, who had formerly worn blue ribbons in her cap. She had taken them out now, to adapt herself, I suppose, to the altered character of the house; and wore but one or two disconsolate bows of sober brown.

"If you please, sir, would you have the goodness to walk in, and speak to Miss Dartle?"

"Has Miss Dartle sent you for me?" I inquired.

"Not to-night, sir, but it's just the same. Miss Dartle saw you pass a night or two ago; and I was to sit at work on the staircase, and when I saw you pass again, to ask you to step in and speak to her."

I turned back, and inquired of my conductor, as we went along, how Mrs. Steerforth was. She said her lady was but poorly, and kept her own room a good deal.

When we arrived at the house, I was directed to Miss Dartle in the garden, and left to make my presence known to her myself. She was sitting on a seat at one end of a kind of terrace, overlooking the great city. It was a sombre evening, with a lurid light in the sky; and as I saw the prospect scowling in the distance, with here and there some larger object starting up into the sullen glare, I fancied it was no inapt companion to the memory of this fierce woman.

She saw me as I advanced, and rose for a moment to receive me. I thought her, then, still more colourless and thin than when I had seen her last; the flashing eyes still brighter, and the scar still plainer.

Our meeting was not cordial. We had parted angrily on the last occasion; and there was an air of disdain about her, which she took no pains to conceal.

"I am told you wish to speak to me, Miss Dartle," said I, standing near her, with my hand upon the back of the seat, and declining her gesture of invitation to sit down.

"If you please," said she. "Pray has this girl been found?"

"No."

"And yet she has run away!"

I saw her thin lips working while she looked at me, as if they were eager to load her with reproaches.

"Run away?" I repeated.

"Yes! From him," she said, with a laugh. "If she is not found, perhaps she never will be found. She may be dead!"

The vaunting cruelty with which she met my glance, I never saw expressed in any other face that ever I have seen.

"To wish her dead," said I, "may be the kindest wish that one of her own sex could bestow upon her. I am glad that time has softened you so much, Miss Dartle."

She condescended to make no reply, but, turning on me with another scornful laugh, said:

"The friends of this excellent and much-injured young lady are friends of yours. You are their champion, and assert their rights. Do you wish to know what is known of her?"

"Yes," said I.

She rose with an ill-favoured smile, and taking a few steps towards a wall of holly that was near at hand, dividing the lawn from a kitchen-garden, said, in a louder voice, "Come here!"—as if she were calling to some unclean beast.

"You will restrain any demonstrative championship or vengeance in this place, of course, Mr. Copperfield?" said she, looking over her shoulder at me with the same expression.

I inclined my head, without knowing what she meant; and she said, " Come here ! " again ; and returned, followed by the respectable Mr. Littimer, who, with undiminished respectability, made me a bow, and took up his position behind her. The air of wicked grace: of triumph, in which, strange to say, there was yet something feminine and alluring : with which she reclined upon the seat between us, and looked at me, was worthy of a cruel Princess in a Legend.

" Now," said she, imperiously, without glancing at him, and touching the old wound as it throbbed : perhaps, in this instance, with pleasure rather than pain. " Tell Mr. Copperfield about the flight."

" Mr. James and myself, ma'am—— "

" Don't address yourself to me ! " she interrupted with a frown.

" Mr. James and myself, sir—— "

" Nor to me, if you please," said I.

Mr. Littimer, without being at all discomposed, signified by a slight obeisance, that anything that was most agreeable to us was most agreeable to him ; and began again :

" Mr. James and myself have been abroad with the young woman, ever since she left Yarmouth under Mr. James's protection. We have been in a variety of places, and seen a deal of foreign country. We have been in France, Switzerland, Italy—in fact, almost all parts."

He looked at the back of the seat, as if he were addressing himself to that ; and softly played upon it with his hands, as if he were striking chords upon a dumb piano.

" Mr. James took quite uncommonly to the young woman ; and was more settled, for a length of time, than I have known him to be since I have been in his service. The young woman was very improvable, and spoke the languages ; and wouldn't have been known for the same country-person. I noticed that she was much admired wherever we went."

Miss Dartle put her hand upon her side. I saw him steal a glance at her, and slightly smile to himself.

"Very much admired, indeed, the young woman was. What with her dress; what with the air and sun; what with being made so much of; what with this, that, and the other; her merits really attracted general notice."

He made a short pause. Her eyes wandered restlessly over the distant prospect, and she bit her nether lip to stop that busy mouth.

Taking his hands from the seat, and placing one of them within the other, as he settled himself on one leg, Mr. Littimer proceeded, with his eyes cast down, and his respectable head a little advanced, and a little on one side:

"The young woman went on in this manner for some time, being occasionally low in her spirits, until I think she began to weary Mr. James by giving way to her low spirits and tempers of that kind; and things were not so comfortable. Mr. James he began to be restless again. The more restless he got, the worse she got; and I must say, for myself, that I had a very difficult time of it indeed between the two. Still matters were patched up here, and made good there, over and over again; and altogether lasted, I am sure, for a longer time than anybody could have expected."

Recalling her eyes from the distance, she looked at me again now, with her former air. Mr. Littimer, clearing his throat behind his hand with a respectable short cough, changed legs, and went on:

"At last, when there had been, upon the whole, a good many words and reproaches, Mr. James he set off one morning, from the neighbourhood of Naples, where we had a villa (the young woman being very partial to the sea), and, under pretence of coming back in a day or so, left it in charge with me to break it out, that, for the general happiness of all concerned, he was"—here an interruption of the short cough —"gone. But Mr. James, I must say, certainly did behave extremely honourable; for he proposed that the young woman should marry a very respectable person, who was fully prepared to overlook the past, and who was, at least, as good as anybody the young woman could have aspired to in a regular way: her connexions being very common."

He changed legs again, and wetted his lips. I was convinced that the scoundrel spoke of himself, and I saw my conviction reflected in Miss Dartle's face.

"This I also had it in charge to communicate. I was willing to do anything to relieve Mr. James from his difficulty, and to restore harmony between himself and an affectionate parent, who has undergone so much on his account. Therefore I undertook the commission. The young woman's violence when she came to, after I broke the fact of his departure, was beyond all expectations. She was quite mad, and had to be held by force; or, if she couldn't have got to a knife, or got to the sea, she'd have beaten her head against the marble floor."

Miss Dartle, leaning back upon the seat, with a light of exultation in her face, seemed almost to caress the sounds this fellow had uttered.

"But when I came to the second part of what had been entrusted to me," said Mr. Littimer, rubbing his hands, uneasily, "which anybody might have supposed would have been, at all events, appreciated as a kind intention, then the young woman came out in her true colours. A more outrageous person I never did see. Her conduct was surprisingly bad. She had no more gratitude, no more feeling, no more patience, no more reason in her, than a stock or a stone. If I hadn't been upon my guard, I am convinced she would have had my blood."

"I think the better of her for it," said I, indignantly.

Mr. Littimer bent his head, as much as to say, "Indeed, sir? But you're young!" and resumed his narrative.

"It was necessary, in short, for a time, to take away everything nigh her, that she could do herself, or anybody else, an injury with, and to shut her up close. Notwithstanding which, she got out in the night; forced the lattice of a window, that I had nailed up myself; dropped on a vine

281

that was trailed below; and never has been seen or heard of, to my knowledge, since."

"She is dead, perhaps," said Miss Dartle, with a smile, as if she could have spurned the body of the ruined girl.

"She may have drowned herself, miss," returned Mr. Littimer, catching at an excuse for addressing himself to somebody. "It's very possible. Or, she may have had assistance from the boatmen, and the boatmen's wives and children. Being given to low company, she was very much in the habit of talking to them on the beach, Miss Dartle, and sitting by their boats. I have known her do it, when Mr. James has been away, whole days. Mr. James was far from pleased to find out once, that she had told the children she was a boatman's daughter, and that in her own country, long ago, she had roamed about the beach, like them."

Oh, Emily! Unhappy beauty! What a picture rose before me of her sitting on the far-off shore, among the children like herself when she was innocent, listening to little voices such as might have called her Mother had she been a poor man's wife; and to the great voice of the sea, with its eternal "Never more!"

"When it was clear that nothing could be done, Miss Dartle—"

"Did I tell you not to speak to me?" she said, with stern contempt.

"You spoke to me, miss," he replied. "I beg your pardon. But it is my service to obey."

"Do your service," she returned. "Finish your story, and go!"

"When it was clear," he said, with infinite respectability, and an obedient bow, "that she was not to be found, I went to Mr. James, at the place where it had been agreed that I should write to him, and informed him of what had occurred. Words passed between us in consequence, and I felt it due to my character to leave him. I could bear, and I have borne, a great deal from Mr. James; but he insulted me too far.

He hurt me. Knowing the unfortunate difference between himself and his mother, and what her anxiety of mind was likely to be, I took the liberty of coming home to England, and relating— "

"For money which I paid him," said Miss Dartle to me.

"Just so, ma'am—and relating what I knew. I am not aware," said Mr. Littimer, after a moment's reflection, "that there is anything else. I am at present out of employment, and should be happy to meet with a respectable situation."

Miss Dartle glanced at me, as though she would inquire if there were anything that I desired to ask. As there was something which had occurred to my mind, I said in reply :

"I could wish to know from this—creature," I could not bring myself to utter any more conciliatory word, "whether they intercepted a letter that was written to her from home, or whether he supposes that she received it."

He remained calm and silent, with his eyes fixed on the ground, and the tip of every finger of his right hand delicately poised against the tip of every finger of his left.

Miss Dartle turned her head disdainfully towards him.

"I beg your pardon, miss," he said, awakening from his abstraction, "but, however submissive to you, I have my position, though a servant. Mr. Copperfield and you, miss, are different people. If Mr. Copperfield wishes to know anything from me, I take the liberty of reminding Mr. Copperfield that he can put a question to me. I have a character to maintain."

After a momentary struggle with myself, I turned my eyes upon him, and said, "You have heard my question. Consider it addressed to yourself, if you choose. What answer do you make?"

"Sir," he rejoined, with an occasional separation and reunion of those delicate tips, "my answer must be qualified; because, to betray Mr. James's confidence to his mother, and to betray it to you, are two different actions. It is not probable, I consider, that Mr. James would encourage the receipt of letters likely to increase low spirits and unpleasantness; but further than that, sir, I should wish to avoid going."

"Is that all?" inquired Miss Dartle of me.

I indicated that I had nothing more to say. "Except," I added, as I saw him moving off, "that I understand this fellow's part in the wicked story, and that, as I shall make it known to the honest man who has been her father from her childhood, I would recommend him to avoid going too much into public."

He had stopped the moment I began, and had listened with his usual repose of manner.

"Thank you, sir. But you'll excuse me if I say, sir, that there are neither slaves nor slave-drivers in this country, and that people are not allowed to take the law into their own hands. If they do, it is more to their own peril, I believe, than to other people's. Consequently speaking, I am not at all afraid of going wherever I may wish, sir."

With that, he made a polite bow; and, with another to Miss Dartle, went away through the arch in the wall of holly by which he had come. Miss Dartle and I regarded each other for a little while in silence; her manner being exactly what it was, when she had produced the man.

"He says besides," she observed, with a slow curling of her lip, "that his master, as he hears, is coasting Spain; and this done, is away to gratify his seafaring tastes till he is weary. But this is of no interest to you. Between these two proud persons, mother and son, there is a wider breach than before; and little hope of its healing, for they are one at heart, and time makes each more obstinate and imperious. Neither is this of any interest to you; but it introduces what I wish to say. This devil whom you make an angel of, I mean this low girl whom he picked out of the tide-mud," with her black eyes full upon me, and her passionate finger up, "may be alive —for I believe some common things are hard to die. If she is, you will desire to have a pearl of such price found and taken care of. We desire that, too; that he may not by any chance be made her prey again. So far, we are united in one interest; and that is why I, who would do her any mischief that so coarse a wretch is capable of feeling, have sent for you to hear what you have heard."

I saw, by the change in her face, that some one was advancing behind me. It was Mrs. Steerforth, who gave me her hand more coldly than of yore, and with an augmentation of her former stateliness of manner; but still, I perceived—and I was touched by it—with an ineffaceable remembrance of my old love for her son. She was greatly altered. Her fine figure was far less upright, her handsome face was deeply marked, and her hair was almost white. But when she sat down on the seat, she was a handsome lady still; and well I knew the bright eye with its lofty look, that had been a light in my very dreams at school.

" Is Mr. Copperfield informed of everything, Rosa?"

" Yes."

" And has he heard Littimer himself?"

" Yes; I have told him why you wished it."

" You are a good girl. I have had some slight correspondence with your former friend, sir," addressing me, " but it has not restored his sense of duty or natural obligation. Therefore I have no other object in this, than what Rosa has mentioned. If, by the course which may relieve the mind of the decent man you brought here (for whom I am sorry—I can say no more), my son may be saved from again falling into the snares of a designing enemy, well!"

She drew herself up, and sat looking straight before her, far away.

" Madam," I said respectfully, " I understand. I assure you I am in no danger of putting any strained construction on your motives. But I must say, even to you, having known this injured family from childhood, that if you suppose the girl, so deeply wronged, has not been cruelly deluded, and would not rather die a hundred deaths than take a cup of water from your son's hand now, you cherish a terrible mistake."

"Well, Rosa, well!" said Mrs. Steerforth, as the other was about to interpose, "it is no matter. Let it be. You are married, sir, I am told?"

I answered that I had been some time married.

"And are doing well? I hear little in the quiet life I lead, but I understand you are beginning to be famous."

"I have been very fortunate," I said, "and find my name connected with some praise."

"You have no mother?"—in a softened voice.

"No."

"It is a pity," she returned. "She would have been proud of you. Good night!"

I took the hand she held out with a dignified, unbending air, and it was as calm in mine as if her breast had been at peace. Her pride could still its very pulses, it appeared, and draw the placid veil before her face, through which she sat looking straight before her on the far distance.

As I moved away from them along the terrace, I could not help observing how steadily they both sat gazing on the prospect, and how it thickened and closed around them. Here and there, some early lamps were seen to twinkle in the distant city; and in the eastern quarter of the sky the lurid light still hovered. But, from the greater part of the broad valley interposed, a mist was rising like a sea, which, mingling with the darkness, made it seem as if the gathering waters would encompass them. I have reason to remember this, and think of it with awe; for before I looked upon those two again, a stormy sea had risen to their feet.

Reflecting on what had been thus told me, I felt it right that it should be communicated to Mr. Peggotty. On the following evening I went into London in quest of him. He was always wandering about from place to place, with his one object of recovering his niece before him; but was more in London than elsewhere. Often and often, now, had I seen him in the dead of night passing along the streets, searching, among the few who loitered out of doors at those untimely hours, for what he dreaded to find.

He kept a lodging over the little chandler's shop in Hungerford Market, which I have had occasion to mention more than once, and from which he first went forth upon his errand of mercy. Hither I directed my walk. On making inquiry for him, I learned from the people of the house that he had not gone out yet, and I should find him in his room up-stairs.

He was sitting reading by a window in which he kept a few plants. The room was very neat and orderly. I saw in a moment that it was always kept prepared for her reception, and that he never went out but he thought it possible he might bring her home. He had not heard my tap at the door, and only raised his eyes when I laid my hand upon his shoulder.

"Mas'r Davy! Thankee, sir! thankee hearty, for this visit! Sit ye down. You're kindly welcome, sir!"

"Mr. Peggotty," said I, taking the chair he handed me, "don't expect much! I have heard some news."

"Of Em'ly!"

He put his hand, in a nervous manner, on his mouth, and turned pale, as he fixed his eyes on mine.

"It gives no clue to where she is; but she is not with him."

He sat down, looking intently at me, and listened in profound silence to all I had to tell. I well remember the sense of dignity, beauty even, with which the patient gravity of his face impressed me, when, having gradually removed his eyes from mine, he sat looking downward, leaning his forehead on his hand. He offered no interruption, but remained throughout perfectly still. He seemed to pursue her figure through the narrative, and to let every other shape go by him, as if it were nothing.

When I had done, he shaded his face, and continued silent. I looked out of the window for a little while, and occupied myself with the plants.

DAVID COPPERFIELD.

"How do you fare to feel about it, Mas'r Davy?" he inquired at length.

"I think that she is living," I replied.

"I doen't know. Maybe the first shock was too rough, and in the wildness of her art——! That there blue water as she used to speak on. Could she have thowt o' that so many year, because it was to be her grave!"

He said this, musing, in a low, frightened voice; and walked across the little room.

"And yet," he added, "Mas'r Davy, I have felt so sure as she was living—I have know'd, awake and sleeping, as it was so trew that I should find her—I have been so led on by it, and held up by it—that I doen't believe I can have been deceived. No! Em'ly's alive!"

He put his hand down firmly on the table, and set his sunburnt face into a resolute expression.

"My niece, Em'ly, is alive, sir!" he said, stedfastly. "I doen't know wheer it comes from, or how 'tis, but *I am told* as she's alive!"

He looked almost like a man inspired, as he said it. I waited for a few moments, until he could give me his undivided attention; and then proceeded to explain the precaution, that, it had occurred to me last night, it would be wise to take.

"Now, my dear friend—" I began.

"Thankee, thankee, kind sir," he said, grasping my hand in both of his.

"If she should make her way to London, which is likely—for where could she lose herself so readily as in this vast city; and what would she wish to do, but lose and hide herself, if she does not go home?—"

"And she won't go home," he interposed, shaking his head mournfully. "If she had left of her own accord, she might; not as 't was, sir."

"If she should come here," said I, "I believe there is one person, here, more likely to discover her than any other in

the world. Do you remember—hear what I say, with fortitude
—think of your great object!—do you remember Martha?"

"Of our town?"

I needed no other answer than his face.

"Do you know that she is in London?"

"I have seen her in the streets," he answered with a
shiver.

"But you don't know," said I, "that Emily was charitable
to her, with Ham's help, long before she fled from home.
Nor, that, when we met one night, and spoke together in the
room yonder, over the way, she listened at the door."

"Mas'r Davy!" he replied in astonishment. "That night
when it snew so hard?"

"That night. I have never seen her since. I went back,
after parting from you, to speak to her, but she was gone. I
was unwilling to mention her to you then, and I am now;
but she is the person of whom I speak, and with whom I
think we should communicate. Do you understand?"

"Too well, sir," he replied. We had sunk our voices,
almost to a whisper, and continued to speak in that tone.

"You say you have seen her. Do you think that you could
find her? I could only hope to do so by chance."

"I think, Mas'r Davy, I know wheer to look."

"It is dark. Being together, shall we go out now, and try
to find her to-night?"

He assented, and prepared to accompany me. Without
appearing to observe what he was doing, I saw how carefully
he adjusted the little room, put a candle ready and the means
of lighting it, arranged the bed, and finally took out of a
drawer one of her dresses (I remember to have seen her wear
it), neatly folded with some other garments, and a bonnet,
which he placed upon a chair. He made no allusion to these
clothes, neither did I. There they had been waiting for her,
many and many a night, no doubt.

"The time was, Mas'r Davy," he said, as we came down-
stairs, "when I thowt this girl, Martha, a'most like the

289

dirt underneath my Em'ly's feet. God forgive me, there's a difference now!"

As we went along, partly to hold him in conversation, and partly to satisfy myself, I asked him about Ham. He said, almost in the same words as formerly, that Ham was just the same, "wearing away his life with kiender no care nohow for 't; but never murmuring, and liked by all."

I asked him what he thought Ham's state of mind was, in reference to the cause of their misfortunes? Whether he believed it was dangerous? What he supposed, for example, Ham would do, if he and Steerforth ever should encounter?

"I doen't know, sir," he replied. "I have thowt of it oftentimes, but I can't arrize myself of it, no matters."

I recalled to his remembrance the morning after her departure, when we were all three on the beach. "Do you recollect," said I, "a certain wild way in which he looked out to sea, and spoke about 'the end of it'?"

"Sure I do!" said he.

"What do you suppose he meant?"

"Mas'r Davy," he replied, "I've put the question to myself a mort o' times, and never found no answer. And theer's one curious thing—that, though he is so pleasant, I wouldn't fare to feel comfortable to try and get his mind upon 't. He never said a wured to me as warn't as dootiful as dootiful could be, and it ain't likely as he'd begin to speak any other ways now; but it's fur from being fleet water in his mind, where them thowts lays. It's deep, sir, and I can't see down."

"You are right," said I, "and that has sometimes made me anxious."

"And me too, Mas'r Davy," he rejoined. "Even more so, I do assure you, than his ventersome ways, though both belongs to the alteration in him. I doen't know as he'd do violence under any circumstances, but I hope as them two may be kep asunders."

We had come, through Temple Bar, into the city. Conversing no more now, and walking at my side, he yielded himself up to the one aim of his devoted life, and went on, with that hushed concentration of his faculties which would have made his figure solitary in a multitude. We were not far from Blackfriars Bridge, when he turned his head and pointed to a solitary female figure flitting along the opposite side of the street. I knew it, readily, to be the figure that we sought.

We crossed the road, and were pressing on towards her, when it occurred to me that she might be more disposed to feel a woman's interest in the lost girl, if we spoke to her in a quieter place, aloof from the crowd, and where we should be less observed. I advised my companion, therefore, that we should not address her yet, but follow her; consulting in this, likewise, an indistinct desire I had, to know where she went.

He acquiescing, we followed at a distance : never losing sight of her, but never caring to come very near, as she frequently looked about. Once she stopped to listen to a band of music : and then we stopped too.

She went on a long way. Still we went on. It was evident, from the manner in which she held her course, that she was going to some fixed destination ; and this, and her keeping in the busy streets, and I suppose the strange fascination in the secrecy and mystery of so following any one, made me adhere to my first purpose. At length she turned into a dull, dark street, where the noise and crowd were lost ; and I said, " We may speak to her now ; " and, mending our pace, we went after her.

CHAPTER XLVII.

MARTHA.

We were now down in Westminster. We had turned back
to follow her, having encountered her coming towards us,
and Westminster Abbey was the point at which she passed
from the lights and noise of the leading streets. She proceeded so quickly, when she got free of the two currents of
passengers setting towards and from the bridge, that, between
this and the advance she had of us when she struck off, we
were in the narrow water-side street by Millbank before we
came up with her. At that moment she crossed the road,
as if to avoid the footsteps that she heard so close behind,
and, without looking back, passed on even more rapidly.

A glimpse of the river through a dull gateway, where some
waggons were housed for the night, seemed to arrest my feet.
I touched my companion without speaking, and we both for-
bore to cross after her, and both followed on that opposite
side of the way; keeping as quietly as we could in the shadow
of the houses, but keeping very near her.

There was, and is when I write, at the end of that low-
lying street, a dilapidated little wooden building, probably an
obsolete old ferry-house. Its position is just at that point
where the street ceases, and the road begins to lie between
a row of houses and the river. As soon as she came here,
and saw the water, she stopped as if she had come to her

292

destination; and presently went slowly along by the brink of the river, looking intently at it.

All the way here, I had supposed that she was going to some house; indeed, I had vaguely entertained the hope that the house might be in some way associated with the lost girl. But, that one dark glimpse of the river, through the gateway, had instinctively prepared me for her going no farther.

The neighbourhood was a dreary one at that time; as oppressive, sad, and solitary by night, as any about London. There were neither wharves nor houses on the melancholy waste of road near the great blank Prison. A sluggish ditch deposited its mud at the prison walls. Coarse grass and rank weeds straggled over all the marshy land in the vicinity. In one part, carcases of houses, inauspiciously begun and never finished, rotted away. In another, the ground was cumbered with rusty iron monsters of steam-boilers, wheels, cranks, pipes, furnaces, paddles, anchors, diving-bells, windmill-sails, and I know not what strange objects, accumulated by some speculator, and grovelling in the dust, underneath which—having sunk into the soil of their own weight in wet weather—they had the appearance of vainly trying to hide themselves. The clash and glare of sundry fiery Works upon the river-side, arose by night to disturb everything except the heavy and unbroken smoke that poured out of their chimneys. Slimy gaps and causeways, winding among old wooden piles, with a sickly substance clinging to the latter, like green hair, and the rags of last year's handbills offering rewards for drowned men fluttering above high-water mark, led down through the ooze and slush to the ebb tide. There was a story that one of the pits dug for the dead in the time of the Great Plague was hereabout; and a blighting influence seemed to have proceeded from it over the whole place. Or else it looked as if it had gradually decomposed into that nightmare condition, out of the overflowings of the polluted stream.

As if she were a part of the refuse it had cast out, and left to corruption and decay, the girl we had followed strayed down to the river's brink, and stood in the midst of this night-picture, lonely and still, looking at the water.

There were some boats and barges astrand in the mud, and these enabled us to come within a few yards of her without being seen. I then signed to Mr. Peggotty to remain where he was, and emerged from their shade to speak to her. I did not approach her solitary figure without trembling; for this gloomy end to her determined walk, and the way in which she stood, almost within the cavernous shadow of the iron bridge, looking at the lights crookedly reflected in the strong tide, inspired a dread within me.

I think she was talking to herself. I am sure, although absorbed in gazing at the water, that her shawl was off her shoulders, and that she was muffling her hands in it, in an unsettled and bewildered way, more like the action of a sleep-walker than a waking person. I know, and never can forget, that there was that in her wild manner which gave me no assurance but that she would sink before my eyes, until I had her arm within my grasp.

At the same moment I said "Martha!"

She uttered a terrified scream, and struggled with me with such strength that I doubt if I could have held her alone. But a stronger hand than mine was laid upon her; and when she raised her frightened eyes and saw whose it was, she made but one more effort and dropped down between us. We carried her away from the water to where there were some dry stones, and there laid her down, crying and moaning. In a little while she sat among the stones, holding her wretched head with both her hands.

"Oh, the river!" she cried passionately. "Oh, the river!"

"Hush, hush!" said I. "Calm yourself."

But she still repeated the same words, continually exclaiming, "Oh, the river!" over and over again.

"I know it's like me!" she exclaimed. "I know that I belong to it. I know that it's the natural company of such as I am! It comes from country places, where there was

The River

nce no harm in it—and it creeps through the dismal streets, efiled and miserable—and it goes away, like my life, to a reat sea, that is always troubled—and I feel that I must go ith it!"

I have never known what despair was, except in the tone f those words.

"I can't keep away from it. I can't forget it. It haunts ie day and night. It's the only thing in all the world that am fit for, or that's fit for me. Oh, the dreadful river!"

The thought passed through my mind that in the face f my companion, as he looked upon her without speech or notion, I might have read his niece's history, if I had known othing of it. I never saw, in any painting or reality, horror nd compassion so impressively blended. He shook as if he vould have fallen; and his hand—I touched it with my own, or his appearance alarmed me—was deadly cold.

"She is in a state of frenzy," I whispered to him. "She ill speak differently in a little time."

I don't know what he would have said in answer. He nade some motion with his mouth, and seemed to think he ad spoken; but he had only pointed to her with his out-tretched hand.

A new burst of crying came upon her now, in which she nce more hid her face among the stones, and lay before us, prostrate image of humiliation and ruin. Knowing that this tate must pass, before we could speak to her with any hope, I ventured to restrain him when he would have raised her, nd we stood by in silence until she became more tranquil.

"Martha," said I then, leaning down, and helping her to ise—she seemed to want to rise as if with the intention of going away, but she was weak, and leaned against a boat. 'Do you know who this is, who is with me?"

She said faintly, "Yes."

"Do you know that we have followed you a long way to-night?"

She shook her head. She looked neither at him nor at

me, but stood in a humble attitude, holding her bonnet and shawl in one hand, without appearing conscious of them, and pressing the other, clenched, against her forehead.

"Are you composed enough," said I, "to speak on the subject which so interested you—I hope Heaven may remember it!—that snowy night?"

Her sobs broke out afresh, and she murmured some inarticulate thanks to me for not having driven her away from the door.

"I want to say nothing for myself," she said, after a few moments. "I am bad, I am lost. I have no hope at all. But tell him, sir," she had shrunk away from him, "if you don't feel too hard to me to do it, that I never was in any way the cause of his misfortune."

"It has never been attributed to you," I returned, earnestly responding to her earnestness.

"It was you, if I don't deceive myself," she said, in a broken voice, "that came into the kitchen, the night she took such pity on me; was so gentle to me; didn't shrink away from me like all the rest, and gave me such kind help! Was it you, sir?"

"It was," said I.

"I should have been in the river long ago," she said, glancing at it with a terrible expression, "if any wrong to her had been upon my mind. I never could have kept out of it a single winter's night, if I had not been free of any share in that!"

"The cause of her flight is too well understood," I said. "You are innocent of any part in it, we thoroughly believe, —we know."

"Oh I might have been much the better for her, if I had had a better heart!" exclaimed the girl, with most forlorn regret; "for she was always good to me! She never spoke a word to me but what was pleasant and right. Is it likely I would try to make her what I am myself, knowing what I am myself so well? When I lost everything that makes life dear, the worst of all my thoughts was that I was parted for ever from her!"

Mr. Peggotty, standing with one hand on the gunwale of the boat, and his eyes cast down, put his disengaged hand before his face.

"And when I heard what had happened before that snowy night, from some belonging to our town," cried Martha, "the bitterest thought in all my mind was, that the people would remember she once kept company with me, and would say I had corrupted her! When, Heaven knows, I would have died to have brought back her good name!"

Long unused to any self-control, the piercing agony of her remorse and grief was terrible.

"To have died, would not have been much—what can I say?—I would have lived!" she cried. "I would have lived to be old, in the wretched streets—and to wander about, avoided, in the dark—and to see the day break on the ghastly line of houses, and remember how the same sun used to shine into my room, and wake me once—I would have done even that to save her!"

Sinking on the stones, she took some in each hand, and clenched them up, as if she would have ground them. She writhed into some new posture constantly: stiffening her arms, twisting them before her face, as though to shut out from her eyes the little light there was, and drooping her head, as if it were heavy with insupportable recollections.

"What shall I ever do!" she said, fighting thus with her despair. "How can I go on as I am, a solitary curse to myself, a living disgrace to every one I come near!" Suddenly she turned to my companion. "Stamp upon me, kill me! When she was your pride, you would have thought I had done her harm if I had brushed against her in the street. You can't believe—why should you?—a syllable that comes out of my lips. It would be a burning shame upon you, even now, if she and I exchanged a word. I don't complain. I don't say she and I are alike. I know there is a long, long way between us. I only say, with all my guilt and wretchedness upon my head, that I am grateful to her from my soul, and love her. Oh don't think that all the power I had of loving anything, is quite worn out! Throw me away, as all the world does. Kill me for being what I am, and having ever known her; but don't think that of me!"

He looked upon her, while she made this supplication, in a wild distracted manner; and, when she was silent, gently raised her.

"Martha," said Mr. Peggotty, "God forbid as I should judge you. Forbid as I, of all men, should do that, my girl! You doen't know half the change that's come, in course of time, upon me, when you think it likely. Well!" he paused a moment, then went on. "You doen't understand how 'tis that this here gentleman and me has wished to speak to you. You doen't understand what 'tis we has afore us. Listen now!"

His influence upon her was complete. She stood, shrinkingly, before him, as if she were afraid to meet his eyes; but her passionate sorrow was quite hushed and mute.

"If you heerd," said Mr. Peggotty, "owt of what passed between Mas'r Davy and me, th' night when it snew so hard, you know as I have been—wheer not—fur to seek my dear niece. My dear niece," he repeated steadily. "Fur she's more dear to me now, Martha, than ever she was dear afore."

She put her hands before her face; but otherwise remained quiet.

"I have heerd her tell," said Mr. Peggotty, "as you was early left fatherless and motherless, with no friend fur to take, in a rough seafaring-way, their place. Maybe you can guess that if you'd had such a friend, you'd have got into a way of being fond of him in course of time, and that my niece was kiender daughter-like to me."

As she was silently trembling, he put her shawl carefully about her, taking it up from the ground for that purpose.

"Whereby," said he, "I know, both as she would go to

the wureld's furdest end with me, if she could once see me again; and that she would fly to the wureld's furdest end to keep off seeing me. For though she ain't no call to doubt my love, and doen't—and doen't," he repeated, with a quiet assurance of the truth of what he said, "there's shame steps in, and keeps betwixt us."

I read, in every word of his plain impressive way of delivering himself, new evidence of his having thought of this one topic, in every feature it presented.

"According to our reckoning," he proceeded, "Mas'r Davy's here, and mine, she is like, one day, to make her own poor solitary course to London. We believe—Mas'r Davy, me, and all of us—that you are as innocent of everything that has befel her, as the unborn child. You've spoke of her being pleasant, kind, and gentle to you. Bless her, I knew she was! I knew she always was, to all. You're thankful to her, and you love her. Help us all you can to find her, and may Heaven reward you!"

She looked at him hastily, and for the first time, as if she were doubtful of what he had said.

"Will you trust me?" she asked, in a low voice of astonishment.

"Full and free!" said Mr. Peggotty.

"To speak to her, if I should ever find her; shelter her, if I have any shelter to divide with her; and then, without her knowledge, come to you, and bring you to her?" she asked hurriedly.

We both replied together, "Yes!"

She lifted up her eyes, and solemnly declared that she would devote herself to this task, fervently and faithfully. That she would never waver in it, never be diverted from it, never relinquish it while there was any chance of hope. If she were not true to it, might the object she now had in life, which bound her to something devoid of evil, in its passing away from her, leave her more forlorn and more despairing, if that were possible, than she had been upon the river's brink that night; and then might all help, human and Divine, renounce her evermore!

She did not raise her voice above her breath, or address us, but said this to the night sky; then stood profoundly quiet, looking at the gloomy water.

We judged it expedient, now, to tell her all we knew; which I recounted at length. She listened with great attention, and with a face that often changed, but had the same purpose in all its varying expressions. Her eyes occasionally filled with tears, but those she repressed. It seemed as if her spirit were quite altered, and she could not be too quiet.

She asked when all was told, where we were to be communicated with, if occasion should arise. Under a dull lamp in the road, I wrote our two addresses on a leaf of my pocket-book, which I tore out and gave to her, and which she put in her poor bosom. I asked her where she lived herself. She said, after a pause, in no place long. It were better not to know.

Mr. Peggotty suggesting to me, in a whisper, what had already occurred to myself, I took out my purse; but I could not prevail upon her to accept any money, nor could I exact any promise from her that she would do so at another time. I represented to her that Mr. Peggotty could not be called, for one in his condition, poor; and that the idea of her engaging in this search, while depending on her own resources, shocked us both. She continued stedfast. In this particular, his influence upon her was equally powerless with mine. She gratefully thanked him, but remained inexorable.

"There may be work to be got," she said. "I'll try."

"At least take some assistance," I returned, "until you have tried."

"I could not do what I have promised, for money," she replied. "I could not take it, if I was starving. To give me money would be to take away your trust, to take away the object that you have given me, to take away the only certain thing that saves me from the river."

SOMETHING WORTH LIVING FOR.

"In the name of the great Judge," said I, "before whom you and all of us must stand at His dread time, dismiss that terrible idea! We can all do some good, if we will."

She trembled, and her lip shook, and her face was paler, as she answered:

"It has been put into your hearts, perhaps, to save a wretched creature for repentance. I am afraid to think so; it seems too bold. If any good should come of me, I might begin to hope; for nothing but harm has ever come of my deeds yet. I am to be trusted, for the first time in a long while, with my miserable life, on account of what you have given me to try for. I know no more, and I can say no more."

Again she repressed the tears that had begun to flow; and, putting out her trembling hand, and touching Mr. Peggotty, as if there was some healing virtue in him, went away along the desolate road. She had been ill, probably for a long time. I observed, upon that closer opportunity of observation, that she was worn and haggard, and that her sunken eyes expressed privation and endurance.

We followed her at a short distance, our way lying in the same direction, until we came back into the lighted and populous streets. I had such implicit confidence in her declaration, that I then put it to Mr. Peggotty, whether it would not seem, in the onset, like distrusting her, to follow her any farther. He being of the same mind, and equally reliant on her, we suffered her to take her own road, and took ours, which was towards Highgate. He accompanied me a good part of the way; and when we parted, with a prayer for the success of this fresh effort, there was a new and thoughtful compassion in him that I was at no loss to interpret.

It was midnight when I arrived at home. I had reached my own gate, and was standing listening for the deep bell of Saint Paul's, the sound of which I thought had been borne towards me among the multitude of striking clocks, when

I was rather surprised to see that the door of my aunt's cottage was open, and that a faint light in the entry was shining out across the road.

Thinking that my aunt might have relapsed into one of her old alarms, and might be watching the progress of some imaginary conflagration in the distance, I went to speak to her. It was with very great surprise that I saw a man standing in her little garden.

He had a glass and bottle in his hand, and was in the act of drinking. I stopped short, among the thick foliage outside, for the moon was up now, though obscured; and I recognised the man whom I had once supposed to be a delusion of Mr. Dick's, and had once encountered with my aunt in the streets of the city.

He was eating as well as drinking, and seemed to eat with a hungry appetite. He seemed curious regarding the cottage, too, as if it were the first time he had seen it. After stooping to put the bottle on the ground, he looked up at the windows, and looked about; though with a covert and impatient air, as if he was anxious to be gone.

The light in the passage was obscured for a moment, and my aunt came out. She was agitated, and told some money into his hand. I heard it chink.

" What's the use of this ? " he demanded.

" I can spare no more," returned my aunt.

" Then I can't go," said he. " Here ! You may take it back ! "

" You bad man," returned my aunt, with great emotion; "how can you use me so ? But why do I ask ? It is because you know how weak I am ! What have I to do, to free myself for ever of your visits, but to abandon you to your deserts ? "

" And why don't you abandon me to my deserts ? " said he.

" *You* ask me why ! " returned my aunt. " What a heart you must have ! "

He stood moodily rattling the money, and shaking his head, until at length he said :

I SEE MY AUNT'S STRANGE VISITOR.

"Is this all you mean to give me, then?"

"It is all I *can* give you," said my aunt. "You know I have had losses, and am poorer than I used to be. I have told you so. Having got it, why do you give me the pain of looking at you for another moment, and seeing what you have become?"

"I have become shabby enough, if you mean that," he said. "I lead the life of an owl."

"You stripped me of the greater part of all I ever had," said my aunt. "You closed my heart against the whole world, years and years. You treated me falsely, ungratefully, and cruelly. Go, and repent of it. Don't add new injuries to the long, long list of injuries you have done me!"

"Aye!" he returned. "It's all very fine!—Well! I must do the best I can, for the present, I suppose."

In spite of himself, he appeared abashed by my aunt's indignant tears, and came slouching out of the garden. Taking two or three quick steps, as if I had just come up, I met him at the gate, and went in as he came out. We eyed one another narrowly in passing, and with no favour.

"Aunt," said I, hurriedly. "This man alarming you again! Let me speak to him. Who is he?"

"Child," returned my aunt, taking my arm, "come in, and don't speak to me for ten minutes."

We sat down in her little parlour. My aunt retired behind the round green fan of former days, which was screwed on the back of a chair, and occasionally wiped her eyes, for about a quarter of an hour. Then she came out, and took her seat beside me.

"Trot," said my aunt, calmly, "it's my husband."

"Your husband, aunt? I thought he had been dead!"

"Dead to me," returned my aunt, "but living."

I sat in silent amazement.

"Betsey Trotwood don't look a likely subject for the tender passion," said my aunt, composedly, "but the time was, Trot, when she believed in that man most entirely.

303

When she loved him, Trot, right well. When there was no proof of attachment and affection that she would not have given him. He repaid her by breaking her fortune, and nearly breaking her heart. So she put all that sort of sentiment, once and for ever, in a grave, and filled it up, and flattened it down."

"My dear good aunt!"

"I left him," my aunt proceeded, laying her hand as usual on the back of mine, "generously. I may say at this distance of time, Trot, that I left him generously. He had been so cruel to me, that I might have effected a separation on easy terms for myself; but I did not. He soon made ducks and drakes of what I gave him, sank lower and lower, married another woman, I believe, became an adventurer, a gambler, and a cheat. What he is now, you see. But he was a fine-looking man when I married him," said my aunt, with an echo of her old pride and admiration in her tone; "and I believed him—I was a fool!—to be the soul of honour!"

She gave my hand a squeeze, and shook her head.

"He is nothing to me now, Trot, less than nothing. But, sooner than have him punished for his offences (as he would be if he prowled about in this country), I give him more money than I can afford, at intervals when he reappears, to go away. I was a fool when I married him; and I am so far an incurable fool on that subject, that, for the sake of what I once believed him to be, I wouldn't have even this shadow of my idle fancy hardly dealt with. For I was in earnest, Trot, if ever a woman was."

My aunt dismissed the matter with a heavy sigh, and smoothed her dress.

"There, my dear!" she said. "Now, you know the beginning, middle, and end, and all about it. We won't mention the subject to one another any more; neither, of course, will you mention it to anybody else. This is my grumpy, frumpy story, and we'll keep it to ourselves, Trot!"

CHAPTER XLVIII.

DOMESTIC.

I LABOURED hard at my book, without allowing it to interfere with the punctual discharge of my newspaper duties; and it came out and was very successful. I was not stunned by the praise which sounded in my ears, notwithstanding that I was keenly alive to it, and thought better of my own performance, I have little doubt, than anybody else did. It has always been in my observation of human nature, that a man who has any good reason to believe in himself never flourishes himself before the faces of other people in order that they may believe in him. For this reason, I retained my modesty in very self-respect; and the more praise I got, the more I tried to deserve.

It is not my purpose, in this record, though in all other essentials it is my written memory, to pursue the history of my own fictions. They express themselves, and I leave them to themselves. When I refer to them, incidentally, it is only as a part of my progress.

Having some foundation for believing, by this time, that nature and accident had made me an author, I pursued my vocation with confidence. Without such assurance I should certainly have left it alone, and bestowed my energy on some other endeavour. I should have tried to find out what nature and accident really had made me, and to be that, and nothing else.

305

DAVID COPPERFIELD.

I had been writing, in the newspaper and elsewhere, so prosperously, that when my new success was achieved, I considered myself reasonably entitled to escape from the dreary debates. One joyful night, therefore, I noted down the music of the parliamentary bagpipes for the last time, and I have never heard it since; though I still recognise the old drone in the newspapers, without any substantial variation (except, perhaps, that there is more of it) all the livelong session.

I now write of the time when I had been married, I suppose, about a year and a half. After several varieties of experiment, we had given up the housekeeping as a bad job. The house kept itself, and we kept a page. The principal function of this retainer was to quarrel with the cook; in which respect he was a perfect Whittington, without his cat, or the remotest chance of being made Lord Mayor.

He appears to me to have lived in a hail of saucepan-lids. His whole existence was a scuffle. He would shriek for help on the most improper occasions,—as when we had a little dinner party, or a few friends in the evening,—and would come tumbling out of the kitchen, with iron missiles flying after him. We wanted to get rid of him, but he was very much attached to us, and wouldn't go. He was a tearful boy, and broke into such deplorable lamentations, when a cessation of our connexion was hinted at, that we were obliged to keep him. He had no mother—no anything in the way of a relative, that I could discover, except a sister, who fled to America the moment we had taken him off her hands; and he became quartered on us like a horrible young changeling. He had a lively perception of his own unfortunate state, and was always rubbing his eyes with the sleeve of his jacket, or stooping to blow his nose on the extreme corner of a little pocket-handkerchief, which he never *would* take completely out of his pocket, but always economised and secreted.

This unlucky page, engaged in an evil hour at six pounds ten per annum, was a source of continual trouble to me. I watched him as he grew—and *he* grew like scarlet beans—

with painful apprehensions of the time when he would begin to shave; even of the days when he would be bald or grey. I saw no prospect of ever getting rid of him; and, projecting myself into the future, used to think what an inconvenience he would be when he was an old man.

I never expected anything less, than this unfortunate's manner of getting me out of my difficulty. He stole Dora's watch, which, like everything else belonging to us, had no particular place of its own; and, converting it into money, spent the produce (he was always a weak-minded boy) in incessantly riding up and down between London and Uxbridge outside the coach. He was taken to Bow Street, as well as I remember, on the completion of his fifteenth journey; when four-and-sixpence, and a second-hand fife which he couldn't play, were found upon his person.

The surprise and its consequences would have been much less disagreeable to me if he had not been penitent. But he was very penitent indeed, and in a peculiar way—not in the lump, but by instalments. For example : the day after that on which I was obliged to appear against him, he made certain revelations touching a hamper in the cellar, which we believed to be full of wine, but which had nothing in it except bottles and corks. We supposed he had now eased his mind, and told the worst he knew of the cook; but, a day or two afterwards, his conscience sustained a new twinge, and he disclosed how she had a little girl, who, early every morning, took away our bread; and also how he himself had been suborned to maintain the milkman in coals. In two or three days more, I was informed by the authorities of his having led to the discovery of sirloins of beef among the kitchen-stuff, and sheets in the rag-bag. A little while afterwards, he broke out in an entirely new direction, and confessed to a knowledge of burglarious intentions as to our premises, on the part of the pot-boy, who was immediately taken up. I got to be so ashamed of being such a victim, that I would have given him any money to hold his tongue, or would have offered a round bribe for his being permitted to run away. It was an aggravating circumstance in the case that he had no idea of this, but conceived that he was making me amends in every new discovery : not to say, heaping obligations on my head.

At last I ran away myself, whenever I saw an emissary of the police approaching with some new intelligence ; and lived a stealthy life until he was tried and ordered to be transported. Even then he couldn't be quiet, but was always writing us letters; and wanted so much to see Dora before he went away, that Dora went to visit him, and fainted when she found herself inside the iron bars. In short, I had no peace of my life until he was expatriated, and made (as I afterwards heard) a shepherd of, "up the country" somewhere; I have no geographical idea where.

All this led me into some serious reflections, and presented our mistakes in a new aspect; as I could not help communicating to Dora one evening, in spite of my tenderness for her.

"My love," said I, "it is very painful to me to think that our want of system and management, involves not only ourselves (which we have got used to), but other people."

"You have been silent for a long time, and now you are going to be cross!" said Dora.

"No, my dear, indeed! Let me explain to you what I mean."

"I think I don't want to know," said Dora.

"But I want you to know, my love. Put Jip down."

Dora put his nose to mine, and said "Boh!" to drive my seriousness away; but, not succeeding, ordered him into his Pagoda, and sat looking at me, with her hands folded, and a most resigned little expression of countenance.

"The fact is, my dear," I began, "there is contagion in us. We infect every one about us."

I might have gone on in this figurative manner, if Dora's face had not admonished me that she was wondering with all her might whether I was going to propose any new kind of vaccination, or other medical remedy, for this unwholesome state of ours. Therefore I checked myself, and made my meaning plainer.

"It is not merely, my pet," said I, "that we lose money and comfort, and even temper sometimes, by not learning to be more careful; but that we incur the serious responsibility of spoiling every one who comes into our service, or has any dealings with us. I begin to be afraid that the fault is not entirely on one side, but that these people all turn out ill because we don't turn out very well ourselves."

"Oh, what an accusation," exclaimed Dora, opening her eyes wide; "to say that you ever saw me take gold watches! Oh!"

"My dearest," I remonstrated, "don't talk preposterous nonsense! Who has made the least allusion to gold watches?"

"You did," returned Dora. "You know you did. You said I hadn't turned out well, and compared me to him."

"To whom?" I asked.

"To the page," sobbed Dora. "Oh, you cruel fellow, to compare your affectionate wife to a transported page! Why didn't you tell me your opinion of me before we were married? Why didn't you say, you hard-hearted thing, that you were convinced I was worse than a transported page? Oh, what a dreadful opinion to have of me! Oh, my goodness!"

"Now, Dora, my love," I returned, gently trying to remove the handkerchief she pressed to her eyes, "this is not only very ridiculous of you, but very wrong. In the first place, it's not true."

"You always said he was a story-teller," sobbed Dora. "And now you say the same of me! Oh, what shall I do! What shall I do!"

"My darling girl," I retorted, "I really must entreat you to be reasonable, and listen to what I did say, and do say. My dear Dora, unless we learn to do our duty to those whom we employ, they will never learn to do their duty to us. I am afraid we present opportunities to people to do wrong, that never ought to be presented. Even if we were as lax as we are, in all our arrangements, by choice—which we are not—even if we liked it, and found it agreeable to be so—which we don't—I am persuaded we should have no right to go on in this way. We are positively corrupting people. We are bound to think of that. I can't help thinking of it, Dora. It is a reflection I am unable to dismiss, and it sometimes makes me very uneasy. There, dear, that's all. Come now. Don't be foolish!"

Dora would not allow me, for a long time, to remove the handkerchief. She sat sobbing and murmuring behind it, that, if I was uneasy, why had I ever been married? Why hadn't I said, even the day before we went to church, that I knew I should be uneasy, and I would rather not? If I couldn't bear her, why didn't I send her away to her aunts at Putney, or to Julia Mills in India? Julia would be glad to see her, and would not call her a transported page; Julia never had called her anything of the sort. In short, Dora was so afflicted, and so afflicted me by being in that condition, that I felt it was of no use repeating this kind of effort, though never so mildly, and I must take some other course.

What other course was left to take? To "form her mind?" This was a common phrase of words which had a fair and promising sound, and I resolved to form Dora's mind.

I began immediately. When Dora was very childish, and I would have infinitely preferred to humour her, I tried to be grave—and disconcerted her, and myself too. I talked to her on the subjects which occupied my thoughts; and I read Shakespeare to her—and fatigued her to the last degree. I accustomed myself to giving her, as it were quite casually, little scraps of useful information, or sound opinion —and she started from them when I let them off, as if they had been crackers. No matter how incidentally or naturally I endeavoured to form my little wife's mind, I could not help seeing that she always had an instinctive perception of what I was about, and became a prey to the keenest apprehensions. In particular, it was clear to me, that she thought Shakespeare a terrible fellow. The formation went on very slowly.

I pressed Traddles into the service without his knowledge; and whenever he came to see us, exploded my mines upon him for the edification of Dora at second hand. The amount of practical wisdom I bestowed upon Traddles in this manner was immense, and of the best quality; but it had no other effect upon Dora than to depress her spirits, and make her always nervous with the dread that it would be her turn next. I found myself in the condition of a schoolmaster, a trap, a pitfall; of always playing spider to Dora's fly, and always pouncing out of my hole to her infinite disturbance.

Still, looking forward through this intermediate stage, to the time when there should be a perfect sympathy between Dora and me, and when I should have " formed her mind" to my entire satisfaction, I persevered, even for months. Finding at last, however, that, although I had been all this time a very porcupine or hedgehog, bristling all over with determination, I had effected nothing, it began to occur to me that perhaps Dora's mind was already formed.

On further consideration this appeared so likely, that I abandoned my scheme, which had had a more promising appearance in words than in action; resolving henceforth to be satisfied with my child-wife, and to try to change her into nothing else by any process. I was heartily tired of being sagacious and prudent by myself, and of seeing my darling under restraint; so, I bought a pretty pair of earrings for her, and a collar for Jip, and went home one day to make myself agreeable.

Dora was delighted with the little presents, and kissed me joyfully; but, there was a shadow between us, however slight, and I had made up my mind that it should not be there. If there must be such a shadow anywhere, I would keep it for the future in my own breast.

I sat down by my wife on the sofa, and put the ear-rings in her ears; and then I told her that I feared we had not been quite as good company lately, as we used to be, and that the fault was mine. Which I sincerely felt, and which indeed it was.

"The truth is, Dora, my life," I said, "I have been trying to be wise."

"And to make me wise too," said Dora, timidly. "Haven't you, Doady?"

I nodded assent to the pretty inquiry of the raised eyebrows, and kissed the parted lips.

"It's of not a bit of use," said Dora, shaking her head, until the ear-rings rang again. "You know what a little thing I am, and what I wanted you to call me from the first. If you can't do so, I am afraid you'll never like me. Are you sure you don't think, sometimes, it would have been better to have—"

"Done what, my dear?" For she made no effort to proceed.

"Nothing!" said Dora.

"Nothing?" I repeated.

She put her arms round my neck, and laughed, and called herself by her favourite name of a goose, and hid her face on my shoulder in such a profusion of curls that it was quite a task to clear them away and see it.

"Don't I think it would have been better to have done nothing, than to have tried to form my little wife's mind?" said I, laughing at myself. "Is that the question? Yes, indeed, I do."

"Is that what you have been trying?" cried Dora. "Oh what a shocking boy!"

"But I shall never try any more," said I. "For I love her dearly as she is."

"Without a story—really?" inquired Dora, creeping closer to me.

"Why should I seek to change," said I, "what has been

so precious to me for so long? You never can show better than as your own natural self, my sweet Dora; and we'll try no conceited experiments, but go back to our old way, and be happy."

"And be happy!" returned Dora. "Yes! All day! And you won't mind things going a tiny morsel wrong, sometimes?"

"No, no," said I. "We must do the best we can."

"And you won't tell me, any more, that we make other people bad," coaxed Dora; "will you? Because you know it's so dreadfully cross!"

"No, no," said I.

"It's better for me to be stupid than uncomfortable, isn't it?" said Dora.

"Better to be naturally Dora than anything else in the world."

"In the world! Ah, Doady, it's a large place!"

She shook her head, turned her delighted bright eyes up to mine, kissed me, broke into a merry laugh, and sprang away to put on Jip's new collar.

So ended my last attempt to make any change in Dora. I had been unhappy in trying it; I could not endure my own solitary wisdom; I could not reconcile it with her former appeal to me as my child-wife. I resolved to do what I could, in a quiet way, to improve our proceedings myself; but, I foresaw that my utmost would be very little, or I must degenerate into the spider again, and be for ever lying in wait.

And the shadow I have mentioned, that was not to be between us any more, but was to rest wholly on my own heart. How did that fall?

The old unhappy feeling pervaded my life. It was deepened, if it were changed at all; but it was as undefined as ever, and addressed me like a strain of sorrowful music faintly heard in the night. I loved my wife dearly, and I was happy; but the happiness I had vaguely anticipated, once,

was not the happiness I enjoyed, and there was alway
something wanting.

In fulfilment of the compact I have made with myself, to
reflect my mind on this paper, I again examine it, closely
and bring its secrets to the light. What I missed, I still
regarded—I always regarded—as something that had been
a dream of my youthful fancy; that was incapable of realisation; that I was now discovering to be so, with some natural
pain, as all men did. But, that it would have been better
for me if my wife could have helped me more, and shared
the many thoughts in which I had no partner; and that
this might have been; I knew.

Between these two irreconcileable conclusions: the one
that what I felt was general and unavoidable; the other
that it was particular to me, and might have been different;
I balanced curiously, with no distinct sense of their opposition to each other. When I thought of the airy dreams
of youth that are incapable of realisation, I thought of the
better state preceding manhood that I had outgrown. And
then the contented days with Agnes, in the dear old house,
arose before me, like spectres of the dead, that might have
some renewal in another world, but never never more could
be reanimated here.

Sometimes, the speculation came into my thoughts, What
might have happened, or what would have happened, if
Dora and I had never known each other? But, she was so
incorporated with my existence, that it was the idlest of
all fancies, and would soon rise out of my reach and sight,
like gossamer floating in the air.

I always loved her. What I am describing, slumbered,
and half awoke, and slept again, in the innermost recesses
of my mind. There was no evidence of it in me; I know
of no influence it had in anything I said or did. I bore
the weight of all our little cares, and all my projects.
Dora held the pens; and we both felt that our shares were
adjusted as the case required. She was truly fond of me,

314

and proud of me; and when Agnes wrote a few earnest words in her letters to Dora, of the pride and interest with which my old friends heard of my growing reputation, and read my book as if they heard me speaking its contents, Dora read them out to me with tears of joy in her bright eyes, and said I was a dear old clever, famous boy.

"The first mistaken impulse of an undisciplined heart." Those words of Mrs. Strong's were constantly recurring to me, at this time; were almost always present to my mind. I awoke with them, often, in the night; I remember to have even read them, in dreams, inscribed upon the walls of houses. For I knew, now, that my own heart was undisciplined when it first loved Dora; and that if it had been disciplined, it never could have felt, when we were married, what it had felt in its secret experience.

"There can be no disparity in marriage, like unsuitability of mind and purpose." Those words I remembered too. I had endeavoured to adapt Dora to myself, and found it impracticable. It remained for me to adapt myself to Dora; to share with her what I could, and be happy; to bear on my own shoulders what I must, and be still happy. This was the discipline to which I tried to bring my heart, when I began to think. It made my second year much happier than my first; and, what was better still, made Dora's life all sunshine.

But, as that year wore on, Dora was not strong. I had hoped that lighter hands than mine would help to mould her character, and that a baby-smile upon her breast might change my child-wife to a woman. It was not to be. The spirit fluttered for a moment on the threshold of its little prison, and, unconscious of captivity, took wing.

"When I can run about again, as I used to do, aunt," said Dora, "I shall make Jip race. He is getting quite slow and lazy."

"I suspect, my dear," said my aunt, quietly working by her side, "he has a worse disorder than that. Age, Dora."

"Do you think he is old?" said Dora, astonished. "Oh, how strange it seems that Jip should be old!"

"It's a complaint we are all liable to, Little One, as we get on in life," said my aunt, cheerfully; "I don't feel more free from it than I used to be, I assure you."

"But Jip," said Dora, looking at him with compassion, "even little Jip! Oh, poor fellow!"

"I dare say he'll last a long time yet, Blossom," said my aunt, patting Dora on the cheek, as she leaned out of her couch to look at Jip, who responded by standing on his hind legs, and baulking himself in various asthmatic attempts to scramble up by the head and shoulders. "He must have a piece of flannel in his house this winter, and I shouldn't wonder if he came out quite fresh again, with the flowers in the spring. Bless the little dog!" exclaimed my aunt. "If he had as many lives as a cat, and was on the point of losing 'em all, he'd bark at me with his last breath, I believe!"

Dora had helped him up on the sofa; where he really was defying my aunt to such a furious extent, that he couldn't keep straight, but barked himself sideways. The more my aunt looked at him, the more he reproached her; for, she had lately taken to spectacles, and for some inscrutable reason he considered the glasses personal.

Dora made him lie down by her, with a good deal of persuasion; and when he was quiet, drew one of his long ears through and through her hand, repeating thoughtfully, "Even little Jip! Oh, poor fellow!"

"His lungs are good enough," said my aunt, gaily, "and his dislikes are not at all feeble. He has a good many years before him, no doubt. But if you want a dog to race with, Little Blossom, he has lived too well for that, and I'll give you one."

"Thank you, aunt," said Dora, faintly. "But don't, please!"

"No?" said my aunt, taking off her spectacles.

DORA AND JIP.

"I couldn't have any other dog but Jip," said Dora. "It would be so unkind to Jip! Besides, I couldn't be such friends with any other dog but Jip; because he wouldn't have known me before I was married, and wouldn't have barked at Doady when he first came to our house. I couldn't care for any other dog but Jip, I am afraid, aunt."

"To be sure!" said my aunt, patting her cheek again. "You are right."

"You are not offended," said Dora, "are you?"

"Why, what a sensitive pet it is!" cried my aunt, bending over her affectionately. "To think that I could be offended!"

"No, no, I didn't really think so," returned Dora; "but I am a little tired, and it made me silly for a moment—I am always a silly little thing, you know; but it made me more silly—to talk about Jip. He has known me in all that has happened to me, haven't you, Jip? And I couldn't bear to slight him, because he was a little altered—could I, Jip?"

Jip nestled closer to his mistress, and lazily licked her hand.

"You are not so old, Jip, are you, that you'll leave your mistress yet?" said Dora. "We may keep one another company a little longer!"

My pretty Dora! When she came down to dinner on the ensuing Sunday, and was so glad to see old Traddles (who always dined with us on Sunday), we thought she would be "running about as she used to do," in a few days. But they said, wait a few days more, and then, wait a few days more; and still she neither ran nor walked. She looked very pretty, and was very merry; but the little feet that used to be so nimble when they danced round Jip, were dull and motionless.

I began to carry her down-stairs every morning, and up-stairs every night. She would clasp me round the neck and laugh, the while, as if I did it for a wager. Jip would

317

bark and caper round us, and go on before, and look back
on the landing, breathing short, to see that we were coming
My aunt, the best and most cheerful of nurses, would trudge
after us, a moving mass of shawls and pillows. Mr. Dick
would not have relinquished his post of candle-bearer to any
one alive. Traddles would be often at the bottom of the
staircase, looking on, and taking charge of sportive messages
from Dora to the dearest girl in the world. We made quite
a gay procession of it, and my child-wife was the gayest there

But, sometimes, when I took her up, and felt that she
was lighter in my arms, a dead blank feeling came upon me
as if I were approaching to some frozen region yet unseen
that numbed my life. I avoided the recognition of this
feeling by any name, or by any communing with myself
until one night, when it was very strong upon me, and my
aunt had left her with a parting cry of " Good-night
Little Blossom," I sat down at my desk alone, and cried to
think, Oh what a fatal name it was, and how the blossom
withered in its bloom upon the tree!

CHAPTER XLIX.

I RECEIVED one morning by the post, the following letter, dated Canterbury, and addressed to me at Doctors' Commons; which I read with some surprise:

" My DEAR SIR,

" Circumstances beyond my individual control have, for a considerable lapse of time, effected a severance of that intimacy which, in the limited opportunities conceded to me in the midst of my professional duties, of contemplating the scenes and events of the past, tinged by the prismatic hues of memory, has ever afforded me, as it ever must continue to afford, gratifying emotions of no common description. This fact, my dear sir, combined with the distinguished elevation to which your talents have raised you, deters me from presuming to aspire to the liberty of addressing the companion of my youth, by the familiar appellation of Copperfield! It is sufficient to know that the name to which I do myself the honour to refer, will ever be treasured among the muniments of our house (I allude to the archives connected with our former lodgers, preserved by Mrs. Micawber), with sentiments of personal esteem amounting to affection.

" It is not for one situated, through his original errors and a fortuitous combination of unpropitious events, as is the foundered Bark (if he may be allowed to assume so

319

maritime a denomination), who now takes up the pen to address you—it is not, I repeat, for one so circumstanced, to adopt the language of compliment, or of congratulation. That, he leaves to abler and to purer hands.

"If your more important avocations should admit of your ever tracing these imperfect characters thus far—which may be, or may not be, as circumstances arise—you will naturally inquire by what object am I influenced, then, in inditing the present missive? Allow me to say that I fully defer to the reasonable character of that inquiry, and proceed to develop it: premising that it is *not* an object of a pecuniary nature.

"Without more directly referring to any latent ability that may possibly exist on my part, of wielding the thunderbolt, or directing the devouring and avenging flame in any quarter, I may be permitted to observe, in passing, that my brightest visions are for ever dispelled—that my peace is shattered and my power of enjoyment destroyed—that my heart is no longer in the right place—and that I no more walk erect before my fellow-man. The canker is in the flower. The cup is bitter to the brim. The worm is at his work, and will soon dispose of his victim. The sooner the better. But I will not digress.

"Placed in a mental position of peculiar painfulness, beyond the assuaging reach even of Mrs. Micawber's influence, though exercised in the tripartite character of woman, wife, and mother, it is my intention to fly from myself for a short period, and devote a respite of eight-and-forty hours to revisiting some metropolitan scenes of past enjoyment. Among other havens of domestic tranquillity and peace of mind, my feet will naturally tend towards the King's Bench Prison. In stating that I shall be (D.V.) on the outside of the south wall of that place of incarceration on civil process, the day after to-morrow, at seven in the evening, precisely, my object in this epistolary communication is accomplished.

"I do not feel warranted in soliciting my former friend Mr. Copperfield, or my former friend Mr. Thomas Traddles of the Inner Temple, if that gentleman is still existent and forthcoming, to condescend to meet me, and renew (so far as may be) our past relations of the olden time. I confine myself to throwing out the observation, that, at the hour and place I have indicated, may be found such ruined vestiges as yet

> "Remain,
>> "Of
>>> "A
>>>> "Fallen Tower,
>>>>> "WILKINS MICAWBER.

"P.S. It may be advisable to superadd to the above, the statement that Mrs. Micawber is *not* in confidential possession of my intentions."

I read the letter over several times. Making due allowance for Mr. Micawber's lofty style of composition, and for the extraordinary relish with which he sat down and wrote long letters on all possible and impossible occasions, I still believed that something important lay hidden at the bottom of this roundabout communication. I put it down, to think about it; and took it up again, to read it once more; and was still pursuing it, when Traddles found me in the height of my perplexity.

"My dear fellow," said I, "I never was better pleased to see you. You come to give me the benefit of your sober judgment at a most opportune time. I have received a very singular letter, Traddles, from Mr. Micawber."

"No?" cried Traddles. "You don't say so? And I have received one from Mrs. Micawber!"

With that, Traddles, who was flushed with walking, and whose hair, under the combined effects of exercise and excitement, stood on end as if he saw a cheerful ghost, produced his letter and made an exchange with me. I watched him

into the heart of Mr. Micawber's letter, and returned th
elevation of eyebrows with which he said "'Wielding th
thunderbolt, or directing the devouring and avenging flame!
Bless me, Copperfield!"—and then entered on the perusal c
Mrs. Micawber's epistle.

It ran thus:

"My best regards to Mr. Thomas Traddles, and if h
should still remember one who formerly had the happiness c
being well acquainted with him, may I beg a few moment
of his leisure time? I assure Mr. T. T. that I would no
intrude upon his kindness, were I in any other position tha
on the confines of distraction.

"Though harrowing to myself to mention, the alienatio
of Mr. Micawber (formerly so domesticated) from his wife an
family, is the cause of my addressing my unhappy appeal t
Mr. Traddles, and soliciting his best indulgence. Mr. T. ca
form no adequate idea of the change in Mr. Micawber'
conduct, of his wildness, of his violence. It has graduall
augmented, until it assumes the appearance of aberration o
intellect. Scarcely a day passes, I assure Mr. Traddles, o
which some paroxysm does not take place. Mr. T. will no
require me to depict my feelings, when I inform him that
have become accustomed to hear Mr. Micawber assert that h
has sold himself to the D. Mystery and secrecy have lon
been his principal characteristic, have long replaced unlimite
confidence. The slightest provocation, even being asked i
there is anything he would prefer for dinner, causes him t
express a wish for a separation. Last night, on bein
childishly solicited for twopence, to buy 'lemon-stunners'—
local sweetmeat—he presented an oyster-knife at the twins!

"I entreat Mr. Traddles to bear with me in entering int
these details. Without them, Mr. T. would indeed find i
difficult to form the faintest conception of my heart-rendin
situation.

"May I now venture to confide to Mr. T. the purport o

my letter? Will he now allow me to throw myself on his friendly consideration? Oh yes, for I know his heart!

"The quick eye of affection is not easily blinded, when of the female sex. Mr. Micawber is going to London. Though he studiously concealed his hand, this morning before break-fast, in writing the direction-card which he attached to the little brown valise of happier days, the eagle-glance of matri-monial anxiety detected d, o, n, distinctly traced. The West-End destination of the coach, is the Golden Cross. Dare I fervently implore Mr. T. to see my misguided husband, and to reason with him? Dare I ask Mr. T. to endeavour to step in between Mr. Micawber and his agonised family? Oh no, for that would be too much!

"If Mr. Copperfield should yet remember one unknown to fame, will Mr. T. take charge of my unalterable regards and similar entreaties? In any case, he will have the benevolence *to consider this communication strictly private, and on no account whatever to be alluded to, however distantly, in the presence of Mr. Micawber.* If Mr. T. should ever reply to it (which I cannot but feel to be *most* improbable), a letter addressed to M. E., Post Office, Canterbury, will be fraught with less painful consequences than any addressed immediately to one, who subscribes herself, in extreme distress,

"Mr. Thomas Traddles's respectful friend and suppliant,
"EMMA MICAWBER."

"What do you think of that letter?" said Traddles, cast-ing his eyes upon me, when I had read it twice.

"What do you think of the other?" said I. For he was still reading it with knitted brows.

"I think that the two together, Copperfield," replied Traddles, "mean more than Mr. and Mrs. Micawber usually mean in their correspondence—but I don't know what. They are both written in good faith, I have no doubt, and without any collusion. Poor thing!" he was now alluding to Mrs. Micawber's letter, and we were standing side by side comparing the two; "it will be a charity to write to her, at all events, and tell her that we will not fail to see Mr. Micawber."

I acceded to this, the more readily, because I now reproached myself with having treated her former letter rather lightly. It had set me thinking a good deal at the time, as I have mentioned in its place; but my absorption in my own affairs, my experience of the family, and my hearing nothing more, had gradually ended in my dismissing the subject. I had often thought of the Micawbers, but chiefly to wonder what "pecuniary liabilities" they were establishing in Canterbury, and to recall how shy Mr. Micawber was of me when he became clerk to Uriah Heep.

However, I now wrote a comforting letter to Mrs. Micawber, in our joint names, and we both signed it. As we walked into town to post it, Traddles and I held a long conference, and launched into a number of speculations, which I need not repeat. We took my aunt into our counsels in the afternoon; but our only decided conclusion was, that we would be very punctual in keeping Mr. Micawber's appointment.

Although we appeared at the stipulated place a quarter of an hour before the time, we found Mr. Micawber already there. He was standing with his arms folded, over against the wall, looking at the spikes on the top, with a sentimental expression, as if they were the interlacing boughs of trees that had shaded him in his youth.

When we accosted him, his manner was something more confused, and something less genteel than of yore. He had relinquished his legal suit of black for the purposes of this excursion, and wore the old surtout and tights, but not quite with the old air. He gradually picked up more and more of it as we conversed with him; but, his very eye-glass seemed to hang less easily, and his shirt-collar, though still of the old formidable dimensions, rather drooped.

"Gentlemen!" said Mr. Micawber, after the first salutations, "you are friends in need, and friends indeed. Allow me to offer my inquiries with reference to the physical welfare of Mrs. Copperfield *in esse*, and Mrs. Traddles *in posse*,—presuming, that is to say, that my friend Mr. Traddles is not yet united to the object of his affections, for weal and for woe."

We acknowledged his politeness, and made suitable replies. He then directed our attention to the wall, and was beginning, "I assure you, gentlemen," when I ventured to object to that ceremonious form of address, and to beg that he would speak to us in the old way.

"My dear Copperfield," he returned, pressing my hand, "your cordiality overpowers me. This reception of a shattered fragment of the Temple once called Man—if I may be permitted so to express myself—bespeaks a heart that is an honour to our common nature. I was about to observe that I again behold the serene spot where some of the happiest hours of my existence fleeted by."

"Made so, I am sure, by Mrs. Micawber," said I. "I hope she is well?"

"Thank you," returned Mr. Micawber, whose face clouded at this reference, "she is but so-so. And this," said Mr. Micawber, nodding his head sorrowfully, "is the Bench! Where, for the first time in many revolving years, the overwhelming pressure of pecuniary liabilities was not proclaimed, from day to day, by importunate voices declining to vacate the passage; where there was no knocker on the door for any creditor to appeal to; where personal service of process was not required, and detainers were merely lodged at the gate! Gentlemen," said Mr. Micawber, "when the shadow of that iron-work on the summit of the brick structure has been reflected on the gravel of the Parade, I have seen my children thread the mazes of the intricate pattern, avoiding the dark marks. I have been familiar with every stone in the place. If I betray weakness, you will know how to excuse me."

"We have all got on in life since then, Mr. Micawber," said I.

"Mr. Copperfield," returned Mr. Micawber, bitterly, "when

I was an inmate of that retreat I could look my fellow-man in the face, and punch his head if he offended me. My fellow-man and myself are no longer on those glorious terms!"

Turning from the building in a downcast manner, Mr. Micawber accepted my proffered arm on one side, and the proffered arm of Traddles on the other, and walked away between us.

"There are some landmarks," observed Mr. Micawber, looking fondly back over his shoulder, "on the road to the tomb, which, but for the impiety of the aspiration, a man would wish never to have passed. Such is the Bench in my chequered career."

"Oh, you are in low spirits, Mr. Micawber," said Traddles.

"I am, sir," interposed Mr. Micawber.

"I hope," said Traddles, "it is not because you have conceived a dislike to the law—for I am a lawyer myself, you know."

Mr. Micawber answered not a word.

"How is our friend Heep, Mr. Micawber?" said I, after a silence.

"My dear Copperfield," returned Mr. Micawber, bursting into a state of much excitement, and turning pale, "if you ask after my employer as *your* friend, I am sorry for it; if you ask after him as *my* friend, I sardonically smile at it. In whatever capacity you ask after my employer, I beg, without offence to you, to limit my reply to this—that whatever his state of health may be, his appearance is foxy: not to say diabolical. You will allow me, as a private individual, to decline pursuing a subject which has lashed me to the utmost verge of desperation in my professional capacity."

I expressed my regret for having innocently touched upon a theme that roused him so much. "May I ask," said I, "without any hazard of repeating the mistake, how my old friends Mr. and Miss Wickfield are?"

"Miss Wickfield," said Mr. Micawber, now turning red,

I INVITE MR. MICAWBER TO HIGHGATE.

"is, as she always is, a pattern, and a bright example. My dear Copperfield, she is the only starry spot in a miserable existence. My respect for that young lady, my admiration of her character, my devotion to her for her love and truth, and goodness!—Take me," said Mr. Micawber, "down a turning, for, upon my soul, in my present state of mind I am not equal to this!"

We wheeled him off into a narrow street, where he took out his pocket-handkerchief, and stood with his back to a wall. If I looked as gravely at him as Traddles did, he must have found our company by no means inspiriting.

"It is my fate," said Mr. Micawber, unfeignedly sobbing, but doing even that, with a shadow of the old expression of doing something genteel; "it is my fate, gentlemen, that the finer feelings of our nature have become reproaches to me. My homage to Miss Wickfield, is a flight of arrows in my bosom. You had better leave me, if you please, to walk the earth as a vagabond. The worm will settle *my* business in double-quick time."

Without attending to this invocation, we stood by, until he put up his pocket-handkerchief, pulled up his shirt-collar, and, to delude any person in the neighbourhood who might have been observing him, hummed a tune with his hat very much on one side. I then mentioned—not knowing what might be lost if we lost sight of him yet—that it would give me great pleasure to introduce him to my aunt, if he would ride out to Highgate, where a bed was at his service.

"You shall make us a glass of your own punch, Mr. Micawber," said I, "and forget whatever you have on your mind, in pleasanter reminiscences."

"Or, if confiding anything to friends will be more likely to relieve you, you shall impart it to us, Mr. Micawber," said Traddles, prudently.

"Gentlemen," returned Mr. Micawber, "do with me as you will! I am a straw upon the surface of the deep, and am tossed in all directions by the elephants—I beg your pardon; I should have said the elements."

We walked on, arm-in-arm, again; found the coach in the act of starting; and arrived at Highgate without encountering any difficulties by the way. I was very uneasy and very uncertain in my mind what to say or do for the best—so was Traddles, evidently. Mr. Micawber was for the most part plunged into deep gloom. He occasionally made an attempt to smarten himself, and hum the fag-end of a tune; but his relapses into profound melancholy were only made the more impressive by the mockery of a hat exceedingly on one side, and a shirt-collar pulled up to his eyes.

We went to my aunt's house rather than to mine, because of Dora's not being well. My aunt presented herself on being sent for, and welcomed Mr. Micawber with gracious cordiality. Mr. Micawber kissed her hand, retired to the window, and pulling out his pocket-handkerchief, had a mental wrestle with himself.

Mr. Dick was at home. He was by nature so exceedingly compassionate of any one who seemed to be ill at ease, and was so quick to find any such person out, that he shook hands with Mr. Micawber, at least half-a-dozen times in five minutes. To Mr. Micawber, in his trouble, this warmth, on the part of a stranger, was so extremely touching, that he could only say, on the occasion of each successive shake, "My dear sir, you overpower me!" Which gratified Mr. Dick so much, that he went at it again with greater vigour than before.

"The friendliness of this gentleman," said Mr. Micawber to my aunt, "if you will allow me, ma'am, to cull a figure of speech from the vocabulary of our coarser national sports— floors me. To a man who is struggling with a complicated burden of perplexity and disquiet, such a reception is trying, I assure you."

"My friend Mr. Dick," replied my aunt, proudly, "is not a common man."

"That I am convinced of," said Mr. Micawber. "My

dear sir!" for Mr. Dick was shaking hands with him again; "I am deeply sensible of your cordiality!"

"How do you find yourself?" said Mr. Dick, with an anxious look.

"Indifferent, my dear sir," returned Mr. Micawber, sighing.

"You must keep up your spirits," said Mr. Dick, "and make yourself as comfortable as possible."

Mr. Micawber was quite overcome by these friendly words, and by finding Mr. Dick's hand again within his own. "It has been my lot," he observed, "to meet, in the diversified panorama of human existence, with an occasional oasis, but never with one so green, so gushing, as the present!"

At another time I should have been amused by this; but I felt that we were all constrained and uneasy, and I watched Mr. Micawber so anxiously, in his vacillations between an evident disposition to reveal something, and a counter-disposition to reveal nothing, that I was in a perfect fever. Traddles, sitting on the edge of his chair, with his eyes wide open, and his hair more emphatically erect than ever, stared by turns at the ground and at Mr. Micawber, without so much as attempting to put in a word. My aunt, though I saw that her shrewdest observation was concentrated on her new guest, had more useful possession of her wits than either of us; for she held him in conversation, and made it necessary for him to talk, whether he liked it or not.

"You are a very old friend of my nephew's, Mr. Micawber," said my aunt. "I wish I had had the pleasure of seeing you before."

"Madam," returned Mr. Micawber, "I wish I had had the honour of knowing you at an earlier period. I was not always the wreck you at present behold."

"I hope Mrs. Micawber and your family are well, sir," said my aunt.

Mr. Micawber inclined his head. "They are as well, ma'am," he desperately observed, after a pause, "as Aliens and Outcasts can ever hope to be."

"Lord bless you, sir!" exclaimed my aunt in her abrupt way. "What are you talking about?"

"The subsistence of my family, ma'am," returned Mr. Micawber, "trembles in the balance. My employer——"

Here Mr. Micawber provokingly left off; and began to peel the lemons that had been under my directions set before him, together with all the other appliances he used in making punch.

"Your employer, you know," said Mr. Dick, jogging his arm as a gentle reminder.

"My good sir," returned Mr. Micawber, "you recall me. I am obliged to you." They shook hands again. "My employer, ma'am—Mr. Heep—once did me the favour to observe to me, that if I were not in the receipt of the stipendiary emoluments appertaining to my engagement with him, I should probably be a mountebank about the country, swallowing a sword-blade, and eating the devouring element. For anything that I can perceive to the contrary, it is still probable that my children may be reduced to seek a livelihood by personal contortion, while Mrs. Micawber abets their unnatural feats, by playing the barrel-organ."

Mr. Micawber, with a random but expressive flourish of his knife, signified that these performances might be expected to take place after he was no more; then resumed his peeling with a desperate air.

My aunt leaned her elbow on the little round table that she usually kept beside her, and eyed him attentively. Notwithstanding the aversion with which I regarded the idea of entrapping him into any disclosure he was not prepared to make voluntarily, I should have taken him up at this point, but for the strange proceedings in which I saw him engaged; whereof his putting the lemon-peel into the kettle, the sugar into the snuffer-tray, the spirit into the empty jug, and confidently attempting to pour boiling water out of a candle-stick, were among the most remarkable. I saw that a crisis was at hand, and it came. He clattered all his means and implements together, rose from his chair, pulled out his pocket-handkerchief, and burst into tears.

"My dear Copperfield," said Mr. Micawber, behind his handkerchief, "this is an occupation, of all others, requiring an untroubled mind, and self-respect. I cannot perform it. It is out of the question."

"Mr. Micawber," said I, "what is the matter? Pray speak out. You are among friends."

"Among friends, sir!" repeated Mr. Micawber; and all he had reserved came breaking out of him. "Good heavens, it is principally because I *am* among friends that my state of mind is what it is. What is the matter, gentlemen? What is *not* the matter? Villany is the matter; baseness is the matter; deception, fraud, conspiracy, are the matter; and the name of the whole atrocious mass is—HEEP!"

My aunt clapped her hands, and we all started up as if we were possessed.

"The struggle is over!" said Mr. Micawber, violently gesticulating with his pocket-handkerchief, and fairly striking out from time to time with both arms, as if he were swimming under superhuman difficulties. "I will lead this life no longer. I am a wretched being, cut off from everything that makes life tolerable. I have been under a Taboo in that infernal scoundrel's service. Give me back my wife, give me back my family, substitute Micawber for the petty wretch who walks about in the boots at present on my feet, and call upon me to swallow a sword to-morrow, and I'll do it. With an appetite!"

I never saw a man so hot in my life. I tried to calm him, that we might come to something rational; but he got hotter and hotter, and wouldn't hear a word.

"I'll put my hand in no man's hand," said Mr. Micawber, gasping, puffing, and sobbing, to that degree that he was like a man fighting with cold water, "until I have—blown to fragments—the—a—detestable—serpent—HEEP! I'll partake of no one's hospitality, until I have—a—moved Mount

Vesuvius—to eruption—on—a—the abandoned rascal—HEEP! Refreshment—a—underneath this roof—particularly punch —would—a—choke me—unless—I had—previously—choked the eyes—out of the head—a—of—interminable cheat, and liar—HEEP! I—a—I'll know nobody—and—a—say nothing —and—a—live nowhere—until I have crushed—to—a—undiscoverable atoms—the—transcendent and immortal hypocrite and perjurer—HEEP!"

I really had some fear of Mr. Micawber's dying on the spot. The manner in which he struggled through these inarticulate sentences, and, whenever he found himself getting near the name of Heep, fought his way on to it, dashed at it in a fainting state, and brought it out with a vehemence little less than marvellous, was frightful; but now, when he sank into a chair, steaming, and looked at us, with every possible colour in his face that had no business there, and an endless procession of lumps following one another in hot haste up his throat, whence they seemed to shoot into his forehead, he had the appearance of being in the last extremity. I would have gone to his assistance, but he waved me off, and wouldn't hear a word.

"No, Copperfield!—No communication—a—until—Miss Wickfield—a—redress from wrongs inflicted by consummate scoundrel—HEEP!" (I am quite convinced he could not have uttered three words, but for the amazing energy with which this word inspired him when he felt it coming.) "Inviolable secret—a—from the whole world—a—no exceptions—this day week—a—at breakfast time—a—everybody present—including aunt—a—and extremely friendly gentleman—to be at the hotel at Canterbury—a—where—Mrs. Micawber and myself—Auld Lang Syne in chorus—and—a—will expose intolerable ruffian, HEEP! No more to say—a—or listen to persuasion—go immediately—not capable—a—bear society—upon the track of devoted and doomed traitor—HEEP!"

With this last repetition of the magic word that had kept him going at all, and in which he surpassed all his previous efforts, Mr. Micawber rushed out of the house; leaving us in a state of excitement, hope, and wonder, that reduced us to a condition little better than his own. But even then his passion for writing letters was too strong to be resisted; for while we were yet in the height of our excitement, hope, and wonder, the following pastoral note was brought to me from a neighbouring tavern, at which he had called to write it:—

"Most secret and confidential.

"MY DEAR SIR,

"I beg to be allowed to convey, through you, my apologies to your excellent aunt for my late excitement. An explosion of a smouldering volcano long suppressed, was the result of an internal contest more easily conceived than described.

"I trust I rendered tolerably intelligible my appointment for the morning of this day week, at the house of public entertainment at Canterbury, where Mrs. Micawber and myself had once the honour of uniting our voices to yours, in the well-known strain of the Immortal exciseman nurtured beyond the Tweed.

"The duty done, and act of reparation performed, which can alone enable me to contemplate my fellow-mortal, I shall be known no more. I shall simply require to be deposited in that place of universal resort, where

"'Each in his narrow cell for ever laid,
"'The rude forefathers of the hamlet sleep,'

"—With the plain Inscription,
"WILKINS MICAWBER."

CHAPTER L.

MR. PEGGOTTY'S DREAM COMES TRUE.

By this time, some months had passed since our interview on the bank of the river with Martha. I had never seen her since, but she had communicated with Mr. Peggotty on several occasions. Nothing had come of her zealous intervention; nor could I infer, from what he told me, that any clue had ever been obtained, for a moment, to Emily's fate. I confess that I began to despair of her recovery, and gradually to sink deeper and deeper into the belief that she was dead.

His conviction remained unchanged. So far as I know—and I believe his honest heart was transparent to me—he never wavered again, in his solemn certainty of finding her. His patience never tired. And, although I trembled for the agony it might one day be to him to have his strong assurance shivered at a blow, there was something so religious in it, so affectingly expressive of its anchor being in the purest depths of his fine nature, that the respect and honour in which I held him were exalted every day.

His was not a lazy trustfulness that hoped, and did no more. He had been a man of sturdy action all his life, and he knew that in all things wherein he wanted help he must do his own part faithfully, and help himself. I have known him set out in the night, on a misgiving that the light might not be, by some accident, in the window of the old boat, and walk to Yarmouth. I have known him, on reading something

334

in the newspaper, that might apply to her, take up his stick, and go forth on a journey of three or four score miles. He made his way by sea to Naples, and back, after hearing the narrative to which Miss Dartle had assisted me. All his journeys were ruggedly performed; for he was always steadfast in a purpose of saving money for Emily's sake, when she should be found. In all this long pursuit, I never heard him repine; I never heard him say he was fatigued, or out of heart.

Dora had often seen him since our marriage, and was quite fond of him. I fancy his figure before me now, standing near her sofa, with his rough cap in his hand, and the blue eyes of my child-wife raised, with a timid wonder, to his face. Sometimes of an evening, about twilight, when he came to talk with me, I would induce him to smoke his pipe in the garden, as we slowly paced to and fro together; and then, the picture of his deserted home, and the comfortable air it used to have in my childish eyes of an evening when the fire was burning, and the wind moaning round it, came most vividly into my mind.

One evening, at this hour, he told me that he had found Martha waiting near his lodging on the preceding night when he came out, and that she had asked him not to leave London on any account, until he should have seen her again.

"Did she tell you why?" I inquired.

"I asked her, Mas'r Davy," he replied, "but it is but few words as she ever says, and she on'y got my promise and so went away."

"Did she say when you might expect to see her again?" I demanded.

"No, Mas'r Davy," he returned, drawing his hand thoughtfully down his face. "I asked that too; but it was more (she said) than she could tell."

As I had long forborne to encourage him with hopes that hung on threads, I made no other comment on this information than that I supposed he would see her soon. Such speculations as it engendered within me I kept to myself, and those were faint enough.

I was walking alone in the garden, one evening, about a fortnight afterwards. I remember that evening well. It was the second in Mr. Micawber's week of suspense. There had been rain all day, and there was a damp feeling in the air. The leaves were thick upon the trees and heavy with wet; but the rain had ceased, though the sky was still dark; and the hopeful birds were singing cheerfully. As I walked to and fro in the garden, and the twilight began to close around me, their little voices were hushed; and that peculiar silence which belongs to such an evening in the country when the lightest trees are quite still, save for the occasional droppings from their boughs, prevailed.

There was a little green perspective of trellis-work and ivy at the side of our cottage, through which I could see, from the garden where I was walking, into the road before the house. I happened to turn my eyes towards this place, as I was thinking of many things; and I saw a figure beyond, dressed in a plain cloak. It was bending eagerly towards me, and beckoning.

"Martha!" said I, going to it.

"Can you come with me?" she inquired, in an agitated whisper. "I have been to him, and he is not at home. I wrote down where he was to come, and left it on his table with my own hand. They said he would not be out long. I have tidings for him. Can you come directly?"

My answer was to pass out at the gate immediately. She made a hasty gesture with her hand, as if to entreat my patience and my silence, and turned towards London, whence, as her dress betokened, she had come expeditiously on foot.

I asked her if that were not our destination? On her motioning Yes, with the same hasty gesture as before, I stopped an empty coach that was coming by, and we got into it. When I asked her where the coachman was to drive, she answered, "Anywhere near Golden Square! And quick!"—

then shrunk into a corner, with one trembling hand before her face, and the other making the former gesture, as if she could not bear a voice.

Now much disturbed, and dazzled with conflicting gleams of hope and dread, I looked at her for some explanation. But, seeing how strongly she desired to remain quiet, and feeling that it was my own natural inclination too, at such a time, I did not attempt to break the silence. We proceeded without a word being spoken. Sometimes she glanced out of the window, as though she thought we were going slowly, though indeed we were going fast; but otherwise remained exactly as at first.

We alighted at one of the entrances to the Square she had mentioned, where I directed the coach to wait, not knowing but that we might have some occasion for it. She laid her hand on my arm, and hurried me on to one of the sombre streets, of which there are several in that part, where the houses were once fair dwellings in the occupation of single families, but have, and had, long degenerated into poor lodgings let off in rooms. Entering at the open door of one of these, and releasing my arm, she beckoned me to follow her up the common staircase, which was like a tributary channel to the street.

The house swarmed with inmates. As we went up, doors of rooms were opened and people's heads put out; and we passed other people on the stairs, who were coming down. In glancing up from the outside, before we entered, I had seen women and children lolling at the windows over flower-pots; and we seemed to have attracted their curiosity, for these were principally the observers who looked out of their doors. It was a broad panelled staircase, with massive balustrades of some dark wood; cornices above the doors, ornamented with carved fruit and flowers; and broad seats in the windows. But all these tokens of past grandeur were miserably decayed and dirty; rot, damp, and age, had weakened the flooring, which in many places was unsound and even unsafe. Some attempts had been made, I noticed, to infuse new blood into this dwindling frame, by repairing the costly old wood-work here and there with common deal; but it was like the marriage of a reduced old noble to a plebeian pauper, and each party to the ill-assorted union shrunk away from the other. Several of the back windows on the staircase had been darkened or wholly blocked up. In those that remained, there was scarcely any glass; and, through the crumbling frames by which the bad air seemed always to come in, and never to go out, I saw, through other glassless windows, into other houses in a similar condition, and looked giddily down into a wretched yard, which was the common dust-heap of the mansion.

We proceeded to the top-story of the house. Two or three times, by the way, I thought I observed in the indistinct light the skirts of a female figure going up before us. As we turned to ascend the last flight of stairs between us and the roof, we caught a full view of this figure pausing for a moment, at a door. Then it turned the handle, and went in.

"What's this!" said Martha, in a whisper. "She has gone into my room. I don't know her!"

I knew her. I had recognised her with amazement, for Miss Dartle.

I said something to the effect that it was a lady whom I had seen before, in a few words, to my conductress; and had scarcely done so when we heard her voice in the room, though not, from where we stood, what she was saying. Martha, with an astonished look, repeated her former action, and softly led me up the stairs; and then, by a little back door which seemed to have no lock, and which she pushed open with a touch, into a small empty garret with a low sloping roof: little better than a cupboard. Between this, and the room she had called hers, there was a small door of communication, standing partly open. Here we stopped, breathless with our ascent, and she placed her hand lightly on my lips. I could only see, of the room beyond, that it was pretty large; that there was a bed in it; and that there were some common pictures of ships upon the walls. I could not see Miss Dartle, or the person whom we had heard her address. Certainly, my companion could not, for my position was the best.

A dead silence prevailed for some moments. Martha kept one hand on my lips, and raised the other in a listening attitude.

"It matters little to me her not being at home," said Rosa Dartle, haughtily, "I know nothing of her. It is you I come to see."

"Me?" replied a soft voice.

At the sound of it, a thrill went through my frame. For it was Emily's!

"Yes," returned Miss Dartle, "I have come to look at you. What? You are not ashamed of the face that has done so much?"

The resolute and unrelenting hatred of her tone, its cold stern sharpness, and its mastered rage, presented her before me, as if I had seen her standing in the light. I saw the flashing black eyes, and the passion-wasted figure; and I saw the scar, with its white track cutting through her lips, quivering and throbbing as she spoke.

"I have come to see," she said, "James Steerforth's fancy; the girl who ran away with him, and is the town-talk of the commonest people of her native place; the bold, flaunting, practised companion of persons like James Steerforth. I want to know what such a thing is like."

There was a rustle, as if the unhappy girl, on whom she heaped these taunts, ran towards the door, and the speaker swiftly interposed herself before it. It was succeeded by a moment's pause.

When Miss Dartle spoke again, it was through her set teeth, and with a stamp upon the ground.

"Stay there!" she said, "or I'll proclaim you to the house, and the whole street! If you try to evade *me*, I'll stop you, if it's by the hair, and raise the very stones against you!"

A frightened murmur was the only reply that reached my ears. A silence succeeded. I did not know what to do. Much as I desired to put an end to the interview, I felt that I had no right to present myself; that it was for Mr. Peggotty alone to see her and recover her. Would he never come? I thought, impatiently.

"So!" said Rosa Dartle, with a contemptuous laugh, "I see her at last! Why, he was a poor creature to be taken by that delicate mock-modesty, and that hanging head!"

"Oh, for Heaven's sake, spare me!" exclaimed Emily. "Whoever you are, you know my pitiable story, and for Heaven's sake spare me, if you would be spared yourself!"

"If *I* would be spared!" returned the other fiercely; "what is there in common between *us*, do you think?"

"Nothing but our sex," said Emily, with a burst of tears.

"And that," said Rosa Dartle, "is so strong a claim, preferred by one so infamous, that if I had any feeling in my breast but scorn and abhorrence of you, it would freeze it up. Our sex! You are an honour to our sex!"

"I have deserved this," cried Emily, "but it's dreadful! Dear, dear lady, think what I have suffered, and how I am fallen! Oh, Martha, come back! Oh, home, home!"

Miss Dartle placed herself in a chair, within view of the door, and looked downward, as if Emily were crouching on the floor before her. Being now between me and the light, I could see her curled lip, and her cruel eyes intently fixed on one place, with a greedy triumph.

"Listen to what I say!" she said; "and reserve your false arts for your dupes. Do you hope to move *me* by your tears? No more than you could charm me by your smiles, you purchased slave."

"Oh, have some mercy on me!" cried Emily. "Show me some compassion, or I shall die mad!"

"It would be no great penance," said Rosa Dartle, "for your crimes. Do you know what you have done? Do you ever think of the home you have laid waste?"

"Oh, is there ever night or day, when I don't think of it!" cried Emily; and now I could just see her, on her knees, with her head thrown back, her pale face looking upward, her hands wildly clasped and held out, and her hair streaming about her. "Has there ever been a single minute, waking or sleeping, when it hasn't been before me, just as it used to be in the lost days when I turned my back upon it for ever and for ever! Oh, home, home! Oh dear, dear uncle, if you ever could have known the agony your love would cause me when I fell away from good, you never would have shown it to me so constant, much as you felt it; but would have been angry to me, at least once in my life, that I might have had some comfort! I have none, none, no comfort upon earth, for all of them were always fond of me!" She dropped on her face, before the imperious figure in the chair, with an imploring effort to clasp the skirt of her dress.

Rosa Dartle sat looking down upon her, as inflexible as a figure of brass. Her lips were tightly compressed, as if she knew that she must keep a strong constraint upon herself—I write what I sincerely believe—or she would be tempted to strike the beautiful form with her foot. I saw her, distinctly, and the whole power of her face and character seemed forced into that expression.—Would he never come?

"The miserable vanity of these earth-worms!" she said, when she had so far controlled the angry heavings of her breast, that she could trust herself to speak. "*Your* home! Do you imagine that I bestow a thought on it, or suppose you could do any harm to that low place, which money would not pay for, and handsomely? *Your* home! You were a part of the trade of your home, and were bought and sold like any other vendible thing your people dealt in."

"Oh not that!" cried Emily. "Say anything of me; but don't visit my disgrace and shame, more than I have done, on folks who are as honourable as you! Have some respect for them, as you are a lady, if you have no mercy for me."

"I speak," she said, not deigning to take any heed of this

appeal, and drawing away her dress from the contamination of Emily's touch, "I speak of *his* home—where I live. Here," she said, stretching out her hand with her contemptuous laugh, and looking down upon the prostrate girl, "is a worthy cause of division between lady-mother and gentleman-son; of grief in a house where she wouldn't have been admitted as a kitchen-girl; of anger, and repining, and reproach. This piece of pollution, picked up from the waterside, to be made much of for an hour, and then tossed back to her original place!"

"No! no!" cried Emily, clasping her hands together. "When he first came into my way—that the day had never dawned upon me, and he had met me being carried to my grave! —I had been brought up as virtuous as you or any lady, and was going to be the wife of as good a man as you or any lady in the world can ever marry. If you live in his home and know him, you know, perhaps, what his power with a weak, vain girl might be. I don't defend myself, but I know well, and he knows well, or he will know when he comes to die, and his mind is troubled with it, that he used all his power to deceive me, and that I believed him, trusted him, and loved him!"

Rosa Dartle sprang up from her seat; recoiled; and in recoiling struck at her, with a face of such malignity, so darkened and disfigured by passion, that I had almost thrown myself between them. The blow, which had no aim, fell upon the air. As she now stood panting, looking at her with the utmost detestation that she was capable of expressing, and trembling from head to foot with rage and scorn, I thought I had never seen such a sight, and never could see such another.

"*You* love him? *You?*" she cried, with her clenched hand, quivering as if it only wanted a weapon to stab the object of her wrath.

Emily had shrunk out of my view. There was no reply.

"And tell that to *me*" she added, "with your shameful

lips? Why don't they whip these creatures? If I could order it to be done, I would have this girl whipped to death."

And so she would, I have no doubt. I would not have trusted her with the rack itself, while that furious look lasted.

She slowly, very slowly, broke into a laugh, and pointed at Emily with her hand, as if she were a sight of shame for gods and men.

"*She* love!" she said. "That carrion! And he ever cared for her, she'd tell me. Ha, ha! The liars that these traders are!"

Her mockery was worse than her undisguised rage. Of the two, I would have much preferred to be the object of the latter. But, when she suffered it to break loose, it was only for a moment. She had chained it up again, and however it might tear her within, she subdued it to herself.

"I came here, you pure fountain of love," she said, "to see —as I began by telling you—what such a thing as you was like. I was curious. I am satisfied. Also to tell you, that you had best seek that home of yours, with all speed, and hide your head among those excellent people who are expecting you, and whom your money will console. When it's all gone, you can believe, and trust, and love again, you know! I thought you a broken toy that had lasted its time; a worthless spangle that was tarnished, and thrown away. But, finding you true gold, a very lady, and an ill-used innocent, with a fresh heart full of love and trustfulness—which you look like, and is quite consistent with your story!—I have something more to say. Attend to it; for what I say I'll do. Do you hear me, you fairy spirit? What I say, I mean to do!"

Her rage got the better of her again, for a moment; but it passed over her face like a spasm, and left her smiling.

"Hide yourself," she pursued, "if not at home, somewhere. Let it be somewhere beyond reach; in some obscure life—or, better still, in some obscure death. I wonder, if your loving heart will not break, you have found no way of helping it to be still! I have heard of such means sometimes. I believe they may be easily found."

A low crying, on the part of Emily, interrupted her here. She stopped, and listened to it as if it were music.

"I am of a strange nature, perhaps," Rosa Dartle went on; "but I can't breathe freely in the air you breathe. I find it sickly. Therefore, I will have it cleared; I will have it purified of you. If you live here to-morrow, I'll have your story and your character proclaimed on the common stair. There are decent women in the house, I am told; and it is a pity such a light as you should be among them, and concealed. If, leaving here, you seek any refuge in this town in any character but your true one (which you are welcome to bear, without molestation from me), the same service shall be done you, if I hear of your retreat. Being assisted by a gentleman who not long ago aspired to the favour of your hand, I am sanguine as to that."

Would he never, never come? How long was I to bear this? How long could I bear it?

"Oh me, oh me!" exclaimed the wretched Emily, in a tone that might have touched the hardest heart, I should have thought; but there was no relenting in Rosa Dartle's smile. "What, what, shall I do!"

"Do?" returned the other. "Live happy in your own reflections! Consecrate your existence to the recollection of James Steerforth's tenderness—he would have made you his serving-man's wife, would he not?—or to feeling grateful to the upright and deserving creature who would have taken you as his gift. Or, if those proud remembrances, and the consciousness of your own virtues, and the honourable position to which they have raised you in the eyes of everything that wears the human shape, will not sustain you, marry that good man, and be happy in his condescension. If this will not do either, die! There are doorways and dust-heaps for such deaths, and such despair—find one, and take your flight to Heaven!"

Mr. Peggotty's Dream comes true

THE LONELY WANDERINGS END.

I heard a distant foot upon the stairs. I knew it, I was certain. It was his, thank God!

She moved slowly from before the door when she said this, and passed out of my sight.

"But mark!" she added, slowly and sternly, opening the other door to go away, "I am resolved, for reasons that I have and hatreds that I entertain, to cast you out, unless you withdraw from my reach altogether, or drop your pretty mask. This is what I had to say; and what I say, I mean to do!"

The foot upon the stairs came nearer—nearer—passed her as she went down—rushed into the room!

"Uncle!"

A fearful cry followed the word. I paused a moment, and, looking in, saw him supporting her insensible figure in his arms. He gazed for a few seconds in the face; then stooped to kiss it—oh, how tenderly!—and drew a handkerchief before it.

"Mas'r Davy," he said, in a low tremulous voice, when it was covered, "I thank my Heav'nly Father as my dream's come true! I thank Him hearty for having guided of me, in His own ways, to my darling!"

With those words he took her up in his arms; and, with the veiled face lying on his bosom, and addressed towards his own, carried her, motionless and unconscious, down the stairs.

CHAPTER LI.

THE BEGINNING OF A LONGER JOURNEY.

IT was yet early in the morning of the following day, when, as I was walking in my garden with my aunt (who took little other exercise now, being so much in attendance on my dear Dora), I was told that Mr. Peggotty desired to speak with me. He came into the garden to meet me half-way, on my going towards the gate; and bared his head, as it was always his custom to do when he saw my aunt, for whom he had a high respect. I had been telling her all that had happened over-night. Without saying a word, she walked up with a cordial face, shook hands with him, and patted him on the arm. It was so expressively done, that she had no need to say a word. Mr. Peggotty understood her quite as well as if she had said a thousand.

"I'll go in now, Trot," said my aunt, "and look after Little Blossom, who will be getting up presently."

"Not along of my being heer, ma'am, I hope?" said Mr. Peggotty. "Unless my wits is gone a bahd's neezing"—by which Mr. Peggotty meant to say, bird's-nesting—"this morning, 'tis along of me as you're a going to quit us?"

"You have something to say, my good friend," returned my aunt, "and will do better without me."

"By your leave, ma'am," returned Mr. Peggotty, "I should take it kind, pervising you doen't mind my clicketten, if you'd bide heer."

346

"Would you?" said my aunt, with short good-nature. "Then I am sure I will!"

So, she drew her arm through Mr. Peggotty's, and walked with him to a leafy little summer-house there was at the bottom of the garden, where she sat down on a bench, and I beside her. There was a seat for Mr. Peggotty too, but he preferred to stand, leaning his hand on the small rustic table. As he stood, looking at his cap for a little while before beginning to speak, I could not help observing what power and force of character his sinewy hand expressed, and what a good and trusty companion it was to his honest brow and iron-grey hair.

"I took my dear child away last night," Mr. Peggotty began, as he raised his eyes to ours, "to my lodging, wheer I have a long time been expecting of her and preparing fur her. It was hours afore she knowed me right; and when she did, she kneeled down at my feet, and kiender said to me, as if it was her prayers, how it all come to be. You may believe me, when I heerd her voice, as I had heerd at home so playful— and see her humbled, as it might be in the dust our Saviour wrote in with his blessed hand—I felt a wownd go to my 'art, in the midst of all its thankfulness."

He drew his sleeve across his face, without any pretence of concealing why; and then cleared his voice.

"It warn't for long as I felt that; for she was found. I had on'y to think as she was found, and it was gone. I doen't know why I do so much as mention of it now, I'm sure. I didn't have it in my mind a minute ago, to say a word about myself; but it come up so nat'ral, that I yielded to it afore I was aweer."

"You are a self-denying soul," said my aunt, "and will have your reward."

Mr. Peggotty, with the shadows of the leaves playing athwart his face, made a surprised inclination of the head towards my aunt, as an acknowledgment of her good opinion; then, took up the thread he had relinquished.

"When my Em'ly took flight," he said, in stern wrath for the moment, "from the house wheer she was made a pris'ner by that theer spotted snake as Mas'r Davy see,—and his story's trew, and may GOD confound him!—she took flight in the night. It was a dark night, with a many stars a shining. She was wild. She ran along the sea beach, believing the old boat was theer; and calling out to us to turn away our faces, for she was a coming by. She heerd herself a crying out, like as if it was another person; and cut herself on them sharp-pinted stones and rocks, and felt it no more than if she had been rock herself. Ever so fur she run, and there was fire afore her eyes, and roarings in her ears. Of a sudden—or so she thowt, you unnerstand—the day broke, wet and windy, and she was lying b'low a heap of stone upon the shore, and a woman was a speaking to her, saying, in the language of that country, what was it as had gone so much amiss?"

He saw everything he related. It passed before him, as he spoke, so vividly, that, in the intensity of his earnestness, he presented what he described to me, with greater distinctness than I can express. I can hardly believe, writing now long afterwards, but that I was actually present in these scenes; they are impressed upon me with such an astonishing air of fidelity.

"As Em'ly's eyes—which was heavy—see this woman better," Mr. Peggotty went on, "she know'd as she was one of them as she had often talked to on the beach. Fur, though she had run (as I have said) ever so fur in the night, she had oftentimes wandered long ways, partly afoot, partly in boats and carriages, and know'd all that country, 'long the coast, miles and miles. She hadn't no children of her own, this woman, being a young wife; but she was a looking to have one afore long. And may my prayers go up to Heaven that 'twill be a happ'ness to her, and a comfort, and a honour, all her life! May it love her and be dootiful to her, in her old age; helpful of her at the last; a Angel to her heer, and heerafter!"

" Amen ! " said my aunt.

" She had been summat timorous and down," said Mr. Peggotty, " and had sat, at first, a little way off, at her spinning, or such work as it was, when Em'ly talked to the children. But Em'ly had took notice of her, and had gone and spoke to her ; and as the young woman was partial to the children herself, they had soon made friends. Sermuchser, that when Em'ly went that way, she always giv Em'ly flowers. This was her as now asked what it was that had gone so much amiss. Em'ly told her, and she—took her home. She did indeed. . She took her home," said Mr. Peggotty, covering his face.

He was more affected by this act of kindness, than I had ever seen him affected by anything since the night she went away. My aunt and I did not attempt to disturb him.

" It was a little cottage, you may suppose," he said, presently, " but she found space for Em'ly in it,—her husband was away at sea,—and she kep it secret, and prevailed upon such neighbours as she had (they was not many near) to keep it secret too. Em'ly was took bad with fever, and what is very strange to me is,—maybe 'tis not so strange to scholars,—the language of that country went out of her head, and she could only speak her own, that no one unnerstood. She recollects, as if she had dreamed it, that she lay there, always a talking her own tongue, always believing as the old boat was round the next pint in the bay, and begging and imploring of 'em to send theer and tell how she was dying, and bring back a message of forgiveness, if it was on'y a wured. A'most the whole time, she thowt,— now, that him as I made mention on just now was lurking for her unnerneath the winder : now that him as had brought her to this was in the room,—and cried to the good young woman not to give her up, and know'd at the same time, that she couldn't unnerstand, and dreaded that she must be took away. Likewise the fire was afore her eyes, and the roarings in her ears ; and there was no to-day, nor yesterday, nor yet to-morrow; but everything in her life as ever had been, or as ever could be, and everything as never had been, and as never could be, was a crowding on her all at once, and nothing clear nor welcome, and yet she sang and laughed about it! How long this lasted, I doen't know; but then there come a sleep; and in that sleep, from being a many times stronger than her own self, she fell into the weakness of the littlest child."

Here he stopped, as if for relief from the terrors of his own description. After being silent for a few moments, he pursued his story.

"It was a pleasant arternoon when she awoke; and so quiet, that there warn't a sound but the rippling of that blue sea without a tide, upon the shore. It was her belief, at first, that she was at home upon a Sunday morning; but, the vine leaves as she see at the winder, and the hills beyond, warn't home, and contradicted of her. Then, come in her friend, to watch alongside of her bed; and then she know'd as the old boat warn't round that next pint in the bay no more, but was fur off; and know'd where she was, and why; and broke out a crying on that good young woman's bosom, wheer I hope her baby is a lying now, a cheering of her with its pretty eyes!"

He could not speak of this good friend of Emily's without a flow of tears. It was in vain to try. He broke down again, endeavouring to bless her!

"That done my Em'ly good," he resumed, after such emotion as I could not behold without sharing in; and as to my aunt, she wept with all her heart; "that done Em'ly good, and she begun to mend. But, the language of that country was quite gone from her, and she was forced to make signs. So she went on, getting better from day to day, slow, but sure, and trying to learn the names of common things—names as she seemed never to have heerd in all her life—till one evening come, when she was a setting at her window, looking at a little girl at play upon the beach. And of a sudden this child held out her hand, and said, what would be in English, 'Fisherman's daughter, here's a shell!'—for you are to unnerstand that they used at first to call her 'Pretty lady,' as the general way in that country is, and that she had taught 'em to call her 'Fisherman's daughter' instead. The child says of a sudden, 'Fisherman's daughter, here's a shell!' Then Em'ly unnerstands her; and she answers, bursting out a crying; and it all comes back!

"When Em'ly got strong again," said Mr. Peggotty, after another short interval of silence, "she casts about to leave that good young creetur, and get to her own countty. The husband was come home, then; and the two together put her aboard a small trader bound to Leghorn, and from that to France. She had a little money, but it was less than little as they would take for all they done. I'm a'most glad on it, though they was so poor. What they done, is laid up wheer neither moth nor rust doth corrupt, and wheer thieves do not break through nor steal. Mas'r Davy, it'll outlast all the treasure in the wureld.

"Em'ly got to France, and took service to wait on travelling ladies at a inn in the port. Theer, theer come, one day, that snake.—Let him never come nigh me. I doen't know what hurt I might do him!—Soon as she see him, without him seeing her, all her fear and wildness returned upon her, and she fled afore the very breath he draw'd. She come to England, and was set ashore at Dover.

"I doen't know," said Mr. Peggotty, "for sure, when her 'art begun to fail her; but all the way to England she had thowt to come to her dear home. Soon as she got to England she turned her face tow'rds it. But, fear of not being forgiv, fear of being pinted at, fear of some of us being dead along of her, fear of many things, turned her from it, kiender by force, upon the road: 'Uncle, uncle,' she says to me, 'the fear of not being worthy to do, what my torn and bleeding breast so longed to do, was the most fright'ning fear of all! I turned back, when my 'art was full of prayers that I might crawl to the old doorstep, in the night, kiss it, lay my wicked face upon it, and theer be found dead in the morning.'

"She come," said Mr. Peggotty, dropping his voice to an awe-stricken whisper, "to London. She—as had never seen it in her life—alone—without a penny—young—so pretty —come to London. A'most the moment as she lighted heer, all so desolate, she found (as she believed) a friend; a decent woman as spoke to her about the needlework as she had been brought up to do, about finding plenty of it fur her, about a lodging for the night, and making secret inquiration concerning of me and all at home, to-morrow. When my child," he said aloud, and with an energy of gratitude that shook him from head to foot, "stood upon the brink of more than I can say or think on—Martha, trew to her promise, saved her."

I could not repress a cry of joy.

"Mas'r Davy!" said he, griping my hand in that strong hand of his, "it was you as first made mention of her to me. I thankee, sir! She was arnest. She had know'd of her bitter knowledge wheer to watch and what to do. She had done it. And the Lord was above all! She come, white and hurried, upon Em'ly in her sleep. She says to her, 'Rise up from worse than death, and come with me!' Them belonging to the house would have stopped her, but they might as soon have stopped the sea. 'Stand away from me,' she says, 'I am a ghost that calls her from beside her open grave!' She told Em'ly she had seen me, and know'd I loved her, and forgive her. She wrapped her, hasty, in her clothes. She took her, faint and trembling, on her arm. She heeded no more what they said, than if she had had no ears. She walked among 'em with my child, minding only her; and brought her safe out, in the dead of the night, from that black pit of ruin!

"She attended on Em'ly," said Mr. Peggotty, who had released my hand, and put his own hand on his heaving chest; "she attended to my Em'ly, lying wearied out, and wandering betwixt whiles, till late next day. Then she went in search of me; then in search of you, Mas'r Davy. She didn't tell Em'ly what she come out fur, lest her 'art should fail, and she should think of hiding of herself. How the cruel lady know'd of her being theer, I can't say. Whether him as I have spoke so much of, chanced to see 'em going theer, or whether (which is most like to my thinking) he had heerd it from the woman, I doen't greatly ask myself. My niece is found.

"All night long," said Mr. Peggotty, "we have been together, Em'ly and me. 'Tis little (considering the time) as she has said, in wureds, through them broken-hearted tears; 'tis less as I have seen of her dear face, as grow'd into a woman's at my hearth. But, all night long, her arms has been about my neck; and her head has laid heer; and we knows full well, as we can put our trust in one another ever more."

He ceased to speak, and his hand upon the table rested there in perfect repose, with a resolution in it that might have conquered lions.

"It was a gleam of light upon me, Trot," said my aunt, drying her eyes, "when I formed the resolution of being godmother to your sister Betsey Trotwood, who disappointed me; but, next to that, hardly anything would have given me greater pleasure, than to be godmother to that good young creature's baby!"

Mr. Peggotty nodded his understanding of my aunt's feelings, but could not trust himself with any verbal reference to the subject of her commendation. We all remained silent, and occupied with our own reflections (my aunt drying her eyes, and now sobbing convulsively, and now laughing and calling herself a fool); until I spoke.

"You have quite made up your mind," said I to Mr. Peggotty, "as to the future, good friend? I need scarcely ask you."

"Quite, Mas'r Davy," he returned; "and told Em'ly. Theer's mighty countries, fur from heer. Our future life lays over the sea."

"They will emigrate together, aunt," said I.

"Yes!" said Mr. Peggotty, with a hopeful smile. "No one can't reproach my darling in Australia. We will begin a new life over theer!"

I asked him if he yet proposed to himself any time for going away.

"I was down at the Docks early this morning, sir," he returned, "to get information concerning of them ships. In about six weeks or two months from now, there'll be one sailing—I see her this morning—went aboard—and we shall take our passage in her."

"Quite alone?" I asked.

"Aye, Mas'r Davy!" he returned. "My sister, you see, she's that fond of you and yourn, and that accustomed to think on'y of her own country, that it wouldn't be hardly fair to let her go. Besides which, theer's one she has in charge, Mas'r Davy, as doen't ought to be forgot."

"Poor Ham!" said I.

"My good sister takes care of his house, you see, ma'am, and he takes kindly to her," Mr. Peggotty explained for my aunt's better information. "He'll set and talk to her with a calm spirit, wen it's like he couldn't bring himself to open his lips to another. Poor fellow!" said Mr. Peggotty, shaking his head, "theer's not so much left him, that he could spare the little as he has!"

"And Mrs. Gummidge?" said I.

"Well, I've had a mort of con-sideration, I do tell you," returned Mr. Peggotty, with a perplexed look which gradually cleared as he went on, "concerning of Missis Gummidge. You see, wen Missis Gummidge falls a thinking of the old 'un, she an't what you may call good company. Betwixt you and me, Mas'r Davy—and you, ma'am—wen Mrs. Gummidge takes to wimicking,"—our old county word for crying,—"she's liable to be considered to be, by them as didn't know the old 'un, peevish-like. Now I *did* know the old 'un," said Mr. Peggotty, "and I know'd his merits, so I unnerstan' her; but 'tan't entirely so, you see, with others —nat'rally can't be!"

My aunt and I both acquiesced.

"Wheerby," said Mr. Peggotty, "my sister might—I doen't say she would, but might—find Missis Gummidge give her a leetle trouble now-and-again. Therefur 'tan't my intentions to moor Missis Gummidge 'long with them, but to find a Bein' fur her wheer she can fisherate for herself." (A Bein' signifies, in that dialect, a home, and to fisherate is to provide.) "Fur which purpose," said Mr. Peggotty, "I means to make her a 'lowance afore I go, as'll leave her pretty comfort'ble. She's the faithfullest of creeturs. 'Tan't to be expected, of course, at her time of life, and being lone and lorn, as the good old Mawther is to be knocked about aboardship, and in the woods and wilds of a new and fur-away country. So that's what I'm a going to do with *her*."

He forgot nobody. He thought of everybody's claims and strivings, but his own.

"Em'ly," he continued, "will keep along with me—poor child, she's sore in need of peace and rest!—until such time as we goes upon our voyage. She'll work at them clothes, as must be made; and I hope her troubles will begin to seem longer ago than they was, wen she finds herself once more by her rough but loving uncle."

My aunt nodded confirmation of this hope, and imparted great satisfaction to Mr. Peggotty.

"Theer's one thing furder, Mas'r Davy," said he, putting his hand in his breast-pocket, and gravely taking out the little paper bundle I had seen before, which he unrolled on the table. "Theer's these heer bank-notes—fifty pound, and ten. To them I wish to add the money as she come away with. I've asked her about that (but not saying why), and have added of it up; I an't a scholar. Would you be so kind as see how 'tis?"

He handed me, apologetically for his scholarship, a piece of paper, and observed me while I looked it over. It was quite right.

"Thankee, sir," he said, taking it back. "This money, if you doen't see objections, Mas'r Davy, I shall put up jest afore I go, in a cover d'rected to him; and put that up in another, d'rected to his mother. I shall tell her, in no more wureds than I speak to you, what it's the price on; and that I'm gone, and past receiving of it back."

I told him that I thought it would be right to do so—that I was thoroughly convinced it would be, since he felt it to be right.

"I said that theer was on'y one thing furder," he proceeded with a grave smile, when he had made up his little bundle again, and put it in his pocket; "but theer was two. I warn't sure in my mind, wen I come out this morning, as I could go and break to Ham, of my own self, what had so thankfully happened. So I writ a letter while I was out, and put it in the post-office, telling of 'em how all was as 'tis, and that I should come down to-morrow to unload my mind of what little needs a doing of down theer, and, most-like, take my farewell leave of Yarmouth."

"And do you wish me to go with you?" said I, seeing that he left something unsaid.

"If you could do me that kind favour, Mas'r Davy," he replied, "I know the sight on you would cheer 'em up a bit."

My little Dora being in good spirits, and very desirous that I should go—as I found on talking it over with her—I readily pledged myself to accompany him in accordance with his wish. Next morning, consequently, we were on the Yarmouth coach, and again travelling over the old ground.

As we passed along the familiar street at night—Mr. Peggotty, in despite of all my remonstrances, carrying my bag—I glanced into Omer and Joram's shop, and saw my old friend Mr. Omer there, smoking his pipe. I felt reluctant to be present, when Mr. Peggotty first met his sister and Ham; and made Mr. Omer my excuse for lingering behind.

"How is Mr. Omer after this long time?" said I, going in.

He fanned away the smoke of his pipe, that he might get a better view of me, and soon recognised me with great delight.

"I should get up, sir, to acknowledge such an honour as this visit," said he, "only my limbs are rather out of sorts, and I am wheeled about. With the exception of my limbs and my breath, hows'ever, I am as hearty as a man can be, I'm thankful to say."

I congratulated him on his contented looks and his good spirits, and saw, now, that his easy chair went on wheels.

"It's an ingenious thing, ain't it?" he inquired, following the direction of my glance, and polishing the elbow with his arm. "It runs as light as a feather, and tracks as true as a mail-coach. Bless you, my little Minnie—my grand-daughter you know, Minnie's child—puts her little strength against the back, gives it a shove, and away we go, as clever and merry as ever you see anything! And I tell you what—it's a most uncommon chair to smoke a pipe in."

I never saw such a good old fellow to make the best of a thing, and find out the enjoyment of it, as Mr. Omer. He was as radiant, as if his chair, his asthma, and the failure of his limbs, were the various branches of a great invention for enchancing the luxury of a pipe.

"I see more of the world, I can assure you," said Mr. Omer, "in this chair, than ever I see out of it. You'd be surprised at the number of people that looks in of a day to have a chat. You really would! There's twice as much in the newspaper, since I've taken to this chair, as there used to be. As to general reading, dear me, what a lot of it I do get through! That's what I feel so strong, you know! If it had been my eyes, what should I have done? If it had been my ears, what should I have done? Being my limbs, what does it signify? Why, my limbs only made my breath shorter when I used 'em. And now, if I want to go out into the street or down to the sands, I've only got to call Dick, Joram's youngest 'prentice, and away I go in my own carriage, like the Lord Mayor of London."

He half suffocated himself with laughing here.

"Lord bless you!" said Mr. Omer, resuming his pipe, "a man must take the fat with the lean; that's what he must make up his mind to, in this life. Joram does a fine business. Ex-cellent business!"

"I am very glad to hear it," said I.

"I knew you would be," said Mr. Omer. "And Joram and Minnie are like valentines. What more can a man expect? What's his limbs to *that!*"

His supreme contempt for his own limbs, as he sat smoking, was one of the pleasantest oddities I have ever encountered.

"And since I've took to general reading, you've took to general writing, eh, sir?" said Mr. Omer, surveying me admiringly. "What a lovely work that was of yours! What expressions in it! I read it every word—every word. And as to feeling sleepy! Not at all!"

I laughingly expressed my satisfaction, but I must confess that I thought this association of ideas significant.

"I give you my word and honour, sir," said Mr. Omer, "that when I lay that book upon the table, and look at it outside; compact in three separate and indiwidual wollumes —one, two, three; I am as proud as Punch to think that I once had the honour of being connected with your family. And dear me, it's a long time ago, now, ain't it? Over at Blunderstone. With a pretty little party laid along with the other party. And you quite a small party then, yourself. Dear, dear!"

I changed the subject by referring to Emily. After assuring him that I did not forget how interested he had always been in her, and how kindly he had always treated her, I gave him a general account of her restoration to her uncle by the aid of Martha; which I knew would please the old man. He listened with the utmost attention, and said, feelingly, when I had done:

"I am rejoiced at it, sir! It's the best news I have heard for many a day. Dear, dear, dear! And what's going to be undertook for that unfortunate young woman, Martha, now?"

"You touch a point that my thoughts have been dwelling on since yesterday," said I, "but on which I can give you no information yet, Mr. Omer. Mr. Peggotty has not alluded to it, and I have a delicacy in doing so. I am sure he has not forgotten it. He forgets nothing that is disinterested and good."

"Because you know," said Mr. Omer, taking himself up, where he had left off, "whatever *is* done, I should wish to be a member of. Put me down for anything you may consider right, and let me know. I never could think the girl all bad, and I am glad to find she's not. So will my daughter Minnie be. Young women are contradictory creatures in some things—her mother was just the same as her—but their hearts are soft and kind. It's all show with Minnie, about Martha. Why she should consider it necessary to make any show, I don't undertake to tell you. But it's all show, bless you. She'd do her any kindness in private. So, put me down for whatever you may consider right, will you be so good? and drop me a line where to forward it. Dear me!" said Mr. Omer, "when a man is drawing on to a time of life, where the two ends of life meet; when he finds himself, however hearty he is, being wheeled about for the second time, in a speeches of go-cart; he should be over-rejoiced to do a kindness if he can. He wants plenty. And I don't speak of myself, particular," said Mr. Omer, "because, sir, the way I look at it is, that we are all drawing on to the bottom of the hill, whatever age we are, on account of time never standing still for a single moment. So let us always do a kindness, and be over-rejoiced. To be sure!"

359

He knocked the ashes out of his pipe, and put it on a ledge in the back of his chair, expressly made for its reception.

"There's Em'ly's cousin, him that she was to have been married to," said Mr. Omer, rubbing his hands feebly, "as fine a fellow as there is in Yarmouth! He'll come and talk or read to me, in the evening, for an hour together sometimes. That's a kindness, I should call it! All his life's a kindness."

"I am going to see him now," said I.

"Are you?" said Mr. Omer. "Tell him I was hearty, and sent my respects. Minnie and Joram's at a ball. They would be as proud to see you as I am, if they was at home. Minnie won't hardly go out at all, you see, 'on account of father,' as she says. So I swore to-night, that if she didn't go, I'd go to bed at six. In consequence of which," Mr. Omer shook himself and his chair, with laughter at the success of his device, "she and Joram's at a ball."

I shook hands with him, and wished him good night.

"Half a minute, sir," said Mr. Omer. "If you was to go without seeing my little elephant, you'd lose the best of sights. You never see such a sight! Minnie!"

A musical little voice answered, from somewhere up-stairs, "I am coming, grandfather!" and a pretty little girl with long, flaxen, curling hair, soon came running into the shop.

"This is my little elephant, sir," said Mr. Omer, fondling the child. "Siamese breed, sir. Now, little elephant!"

The little elephant set the door of the parlour open, enabling me to see that, in these latter days, it was converted into a bedroom for Mr. Omer, who could not be easily conveyed up-stairs; and then hid her pretty forehead, and tumbled her long hair, against the back of Mr. Omer's chair.

"The elephant butts, you know, sir," said Mr. Omer, winking, "when he goes at a object. Once, elephant. Twice. Three times!"

At this signal, the little elephant, with a dexterity that was next to marvellous in so small an animal, whisked the

360

chair round with Mr. Omer in it, and rattled it off, pell-mell, into the parlour, without touching the doorpost : Mr. Omer indescribably enjoying the performance, and looking back at me on the road as if it were the triumphant issue of his life's exertions.

After a stroll about the town, I went to Ham's house. Peggotty had now removed here for good ; and had let her own house to the successor of Mr. Barkis in the carrying business, who had paid her very well for the goodwill, cart, and horse. I believe the very same slow horse that Mr. Barkis drove, was still at work.

I found them in the neat kitchen, accompanied by Mrs. Gummidge, who had been fetched from the old boat by Mr. Peggotty himself. I doubt if she could have been induced to desert her post, by any one else. He had evidently told them all. Both Peggotty and Mrs. Gummidge had their aprons to their eyes, and Ham had just stepped out "to take a turn on the beach." He presently came home, very glad to see me ; and I hope they were all the better for my being there. We spoke, with some approach to cheerfulness, of Mr. Peggotty's growing rich in a new country, and of the wonders he would describe in his letters. We said nothing of Emily by name, but distantly referred to her more than once. Ham was the serenest of the party.

But, Peggotty told me, when she lighted me to a little chamber where the Crocodile book was lying ready for me on the table, that he always was the same. She believed (she told me, crying) that he was broken-hearted ; though he was as full of courage as of sweetness, and worked harder and better than any boat-builder in any yard in all that part. There were times, she said, of an evening, when he talked of their old life in the boat-house ; and then he mentioned Emily as a child. But, he never mentioned her as a woman.

I thought I had read in his face that he would like to speak to me alone. I therefore resolved to put myself in his way next evening, as he came home from his work. Having settled this with myself, I fell asleep. That night, for the first time in all those many nights, the candle was taken out of the window, Mr. Peggotty swung in his old hammock in the old boat, and the wind murmured with the old sound round his head.

All next day, he was occupied in disposing of his fishing-boat and tackle; in packing up, and sending to London by waggon, such of his little domestic possessions as he thought would be useful to him; and in parting with the rest, or bestowing them on Mrs. Gummidge. She was with him all day. As I had a sorrowful wish to see the old place once more, before it was locked up, I engaged to meet them there in the evening. But I so arranged it, as that I should meet Ham first.

It was easy to come in his way, as I knew where he worked. I met him at a retired part of the sands, which I knew he would cross, and turned back with him, that he might have leisure to speak to me if he really wished. I had not mistaken the expression of his face. We had walked but a little way together, when he said, without looking at me:

"Mas'r Davy, have you seen her?"

"Only for a moment, when she was in a swoon," I softly answered.

We walked a little farther, and he said:

"Mas'r Davy, shall you see her, d'ye think?"

"It would be too painful to her, perhaps," said I.

"I have thowt of that," he replied. "So 'twould, sir, so 'twould."

"But, Ham," said I, gently, "if there is anything that I could write to her, for you, in case I could not tell it; if there is anything you would wish to make known to her through me; I should consider it a sacred trust."

"I am sure on't. I thankee, sir, most kind! I think theer is something I could wish said or wrote."

"What is it?"

We walked a little farther in silence, and then he spoke.

"'Tan't that I forgive her. 'Tan't that so much. 'Tis more as I beg of her to forgive me, for having pressed my affections upon her. Odd times, I think that if I hadn't had her promise fur to marry me, sir, she was that trustful of me, in a friendly way, that she'd have told me what was struggling in her mind, and would have counselled with me, and I might have saved her."

I pressed his hand. "Is that all?"

"Theer's yet a something else," he returned, "if I can say it, Mas'r Davy."

We walked on, farther than we had walked yet, before he spoke again. He was not crying when he made the pauses I shall express by lines. He was merely collecting himself to speak very plainly.

"I loved her—and I love the mem'ry of her—too deep— to be able to lead her to believe of my own self as I'm a happy man. I could only be happy—by forgetting of her— and I'm afeerd I couldn't hardly bear as she should be told I done that. But if you, being so full of learning, Mas'r Davy, could think of anything to say as might bring her to believe I wasn't greatly hurt: still loving of her, and mourning for her: anything as might bring her to believe as I was not tired of my life, and yet was hoping fur to see her without blame, wheer the wicked cease from troubling and the weary are at rest—anything as would ease her sorrowful mind, and yet not make her think as I could ever marry, or as 'twas possible that any one could ever be to me what she was—I should ask of you to say that—with my prayers for her— that was so dear."

I pressed his manly hand again, and told him I would charge myself to do this as well as I could.

"I thankee, sir," he answered. "'Twas kind of you to meet me. 'Twas kind of you to bear him company down. Mas'r Davy, I unnerstan' very well, though my aunt will come to Lon'on afore they sail, and they'll unite once more, that I am not like to see him agen. I fare to feel sure on't. We doen't say so, but so 'twill be, and better so. The last you see on him—the very last—will you give him the lovingest duty and thanks of the orphan, as he was ever more than a father to?"

This I also promised, faithfully.

"I thankee agen, sir," he said, heartily shaking hands. "I know wheer you're a going. Good-bye!"

With a slight wave of his hand, as though to explain to me that he could not enter the old place, he turned away. As I looked after his figure, crossing the waste in the moonlight, I saw him turn his face towards a strip of silvery light upon the sea, and pass on, looking at it, until he was a shadow in the distance.

The door of the boat-house stood open when I approached; and, on entering, I found it emptied of all its furniture, saving one of the old lockers, on which Mrs. Gummidge, with a basket on her knee, was seated, looking at Mr. Peggotty. He leaned his elbow on the rough chimney-piece, and gazed upon a few expiring embers in the grate; but he raised his head, hopefully, on my coming in, and spoke in a cheery manner.

"Come, according to promise, to bid farewell to 't, eh, Mas'r Davy?" he said, taking up the candle. "Bare enough, now, an't it?"

"Indeed you have made good use of the time," said I.

"Why, we have not been idle, sir. Missis Gummidge has worked like a—I doen't know what Missis Gummidge an't worked like," said Mr. Peggotty, looking at her, at a loss for a sufficiently approving simile.

Mrs. Gummidge, leaning on her basket, made no observation.

"Theer's the very locker that you used to sit on, 'long with Em'ly!" said Mr. Peggotty, in a whisper. "I'm a going to carry it away with me, last of all. And heer's your old little bedroom, see, Mas'r Davy? A'most as bleak to-night, as 'art could wish!"

GOOD IN MRS. GUMMIDGE.

In truth, the wind, though it was low, had a solemn sound, and crept around the deserted house with a whispered wailing that was very mournful. Everything was gone, down to the little mirror with the oyster-shell frame. I thought of myself, lying here, when that first great change was being wrought at home. I thought of the blue-eyed child who had enchanted me. I thought of Steerforth: and a foolish, fearful fancy came upon me of his being near at hand, and liable to be met at any turn.

"'Tis like to be long," said Mr. Peggotty, in a low voice, "afore the boat finds new tenants. They look upon 't down heer, as being unfort'nate now!"

"Does it belong to anybody in the neighbourhood?" I asked.

"To a mast-maker up town," said Mr. Peggotty. "I'm a going to give the key to him to-night."

We looked into the other little room, and came back to Mrs. Gummidge, sitting on the locker, whom Mr. Peggotty, putting the light on the chimney-piece, requested to rise, that he might carry it outside the door before extinguishing the candle.

"Dan'l," said Mrs. Gummidge, suddenly deserting her basket, and clinging to his arm, "my dear Dan'l, the parting words I speak in this house is, I mustn't be left behind. Doen't ye think of leaving me behind, Dan'l! Oh, doen't ye ever do it!"

Mr. Peggotty, taken aback, looked from Mrs. Gummidge to me, and from me to Mrs. Gummidge, as if he had been awakened from a sleep.

"Doen't ye, dearest Dan'l, doen't ye!" cried Mrs. Gummidge, fervently. "Take me 'long with you, Dan'l, take me 'long with you and Em'ly! I'll be your servant, constant and trew. If there's slaves in them parts where you're a going, I'll be bound to you for one, and happy, but doen't ye leave me behind, Dan'l, that's a deary dear!"

"My good soul," said Mr. Peggotty, shaking his head,

"you doen't know what a long voyage, and what a hard life 'tis!"

"Yes I do, Dan'l! I can guess!" cried Mrs. Gummidge. "But my parting words under this roof is, I shall go into the house and die, if I am not took. I can dig, Dan'l. I can work. I can live hard. I can be loving and patient now—more than you think, Dan'l, if you'll on'y try me. I wouldn't touch the 'lowance, not if I was dying of want, Dan'l Peggotty; but I'll go with you and Em'ly, if you'll on'y let me, to the world's end! I know how 'tis; I know you think that I am lone and lorn; but, deary love, 'tan't so no more! I ain't sat here, so long, a watching, and a thinking of your trials, without some good being done me. Mas'r Davy, speak to him for me! I knows his ways, and Em'ly's, and I knows their sorrows, and can be a comfort to 'em, some odd times, and labour for 'em allus! Dan'l, deary Dan'l, let me go 'long with you!"

And Mrs. Gummidge took his hand, and kissed it with a homely pathos and affection, in a homely rapture of devotion and gratitude, that he well deserved.

We brought the locker out, extinguished the candle, fastened the door on the outside, and left the old boat close shut up, a dark speck in the cloudy night. Next day, when we were returning to London outside the coach, Mrs. Gummidge and her basket were on the seat behind, and Mrs. Gummidge was happy.

CHAPTER LII.

I ASSIST AT AN EXPLOSION.

WHEN the time Mr. Micawber had appointed so mysteriously, was within four-and-twenty hours of being come, my aunt and I consulted how we should proceed; for my aunt was very unwilling to leave Dora. Ah! how easily I carried Dora up and down stairs, now!

We were disposed, notwithstanding Mr. Micawber's stipulation for my aunt's attendance, to arrange that she should stay at home, and be represented by Mr. Dick and me. In short, we had resolved to take this course, when Dora again unsettled us by declaring that she never would forgive herself, and never would forgive her bad boy, if my aunt remained behind, on any pretence.

"I won't speak to you," said Dora, shaking her curls at my aunt. "I'll be disagreeable! I'll make Jip bark at you all day. I shall be sure that you really are a cross old thing, if you don't go!"

"Tut, Blossom!" laughed my aunt. "You know you can't do without me!"

"Yes, I can," said Dora. "You are no use to me at all. You never run up and down stairs for me, all day long. You never sit and tell me stories about Doady, when his shoes were worn out, and he was covered with dust—oh, what a poor little mite of a fellow! You never do anything at all

367

to please me, do you, dear?" Dora made haste to kiss my aunt, and say, "Yes, you do! I'm only joking!"—lest my aunt should think she really meant it.

"But, aunt," said Dora, coaxingly, "now listen. You must go. I shall tease you, till you let me have my own way about it. I shall lead my naughty boy *such* a life, if he don't make you go. I shall make myself *so* disagreeable—and so will Jip! You'll wish you had gone, like a good thing, for ever and ever so long, if you don't go. Besides," said Dora, putting back her hair, and looking wonderingly at my aunt and me, "why shouldn't you both go? I am not very ill indeed. Am I?"

"Why, what a question!" cried my aunt.

"What a fancy!" said I.

"Yes! I know I am a silly little thing!" said Dora, slowly looking from one of us to the other, and then putting up her pretty lips to kiss us as she lay upon her couch. "Well, then, you must both go, or I shall not believe you; and then I shall cry!"

I saw, in my aunt's face, that she began to give way now, and Dora brightened again, as she saw it too.

"You'll come back with so much to tell me, that it'll take at least a week to make me understand!" said Dora. "Because I *know* I shan't understand, for a length of time, if there's any business in it. And there's sure to be some business in it! If there's anything to add up, besides, I don't know when I shall make it out; and my bad boy will look *so* miserable all the time. There! Now you'll go, won't you? You'll only be gone one night, and Jip will take care of me while you are gone. Doady will carry me up-stairs before you go, and I won't come down again till you come back; and you shall take Agnes a dreadfully scolding letter from me, because she has never been to see us!"

We agreed, without any more consultation, that we would both go, and that Dora was a little Impostor, who feigned to be rather unwell, because she liked to be petted. She was greatly pleased, and very merry; and we four, that is to say my aunt, Mr. Dick, Traddles, and I, went down to Canterbury by the Dover mail that night.

At the hotel where Mr. Micawber had requested us to await him, which we got into, with some trouble, in the middle of the night, I found a letter, importing that he would appear in the morning punctually at half-past nine. After which, we went shivering, at that uncomfortable hour, to our respective beds, through various close passages; which smelt as if they had been steeped, for ages, in a solution of soup and stables.

Early in the morning, I sauntered through the dear old tranquil streets, and again mingled with the shadows of the venerable gateways and churches. The rooks were sailing about the cathedral towers; and the towers themselves, overlooking many a long unaltered mile of the rich country and its pleasant streams, were cutting the bright morning air, as if there were no such thing as change on earth. Yet the bells, when they sounded, told me sorrowfully of change in everything; told me of their own age, and my pretty Dora's youth; and of the many, never old, who had lived and loved and died, while the reverberations of the bells had hummed through the rusty armour of the Black Prince hanging up within, and, motes upon the deep of Time, had lost themselves in air, as circles do in water.

I looked at the old house from the corner of the street, but did not go nearer to it, lest, being observed, I might unwittingly do any harm to the design I had come to aid. The early sun was striking edgewise on its gables and lattice-windows, touching them with gold; and some beams of its old peace seemed to touch my heart.

I strolled into the country for an hour or so, and then returned by the main street, which in the interval had shaken off its last night's sleep. Among those who were stirring in the shops, I saw my ancient enemy, the butcher, now advanced to top-boots and a baby, and in business for himself. He

369

was nursing the baby, and appeared to be a benignant member of society.

We all became very anxious and impatient, when we sat down to breakfast. As it approached nearer and nearer to half-past nine o'clock, our restless expectation of Mr. Micawber increased. At last we made no more pretence of attending to the meal, which, except with Mr. Dick, had been a mere form from the first; but my aunt walked up and down the room, Traddles sat upon the sofa affecting to read the paper with his eyes on the ceiling; and I looked out of the window to give early notice of Mr. Micawber's coming. Nor had I long to watch, for, at the first chime of the half-hour, he appeared in the street.

"Here he is," said I, "and not in his legal attire!"

My aunt tied the strings of her bonnet (she had come down to breakfast in it), and put on her shawl, as if she were ready for anything that was resolute and uncompromising. Traddles buttoned his coat with a determined air. Mr. Dick, disturbed by these formidable appearances, but feeling it necessary to imitate them, pulled his hat, with both hands, as firmly over his ears as he possibly could; and instantly took it off again, to welcome Mr. Micawber.

"Gentlemen, and madam," said Mr. Micawber, "good morning! My dear sir," to Mr. Dick, who shook hands with him violently, "you are extremely good."

"Have you breakfasted?" said Mr. Dick. "Have a chop!"

"Not for the world, my good sir!" cried Mr. Micawber, stopping him on his way to the bell; "appetite and myself, Mr. Dixon, have long been strangers."

Mr. Dixon was so well pleased with his new name, and appeared to think it so very obliging in Mr. Micawber to confer it upon him, that he shook hands with him again, and laughed rather childishly.

"Dick," said my aunt, "attention!"

Mr. Dick recovered himself, with a blush.

"Now, sir," said my aunt to Mr. Micawber, as she put on her gloves, "we are ready for Mount Vesuvius, or anything else, as soon as *you* please."

"Madam," returned Mr. Micawber, "I trust you will shortly witness an eruption. Mr. Traddles, I have your permission, I believe, to mention here that we have been in communication together ?"

"It is undoubtedly the fact, Copperfield," said Traddles, to whom I looked in surprise. "Mr. Micawber has consulted me, in reference to what he has in contemplation; and I have advised him to the best of my judgment."

"Unless I deceive myself, Mr. Traddles," pursued Mr. Micawber, "what I contemplate is a disclosure of an important nature."

"Highly so," said Traddles.

"Perhaps, under such circumstances, madam and gentlemen," said Mr. Micawber, "you will do me the favour to submit yourselves, for the moment, to the direction of one, who, however unworthy to be regarded in any other light but as a Waif and Stray upon the shore of human nature, is still your fellow-man, though crushed out of his original form by individual errors, and the accumulative force of a combination of circumstances ?"

"We have perfect confidence in you, Mr. Micawber," said I, "and will do what you please."

"Mr. Copperfield," returned Mr. Micawber, "your confidence is not, at the existing juncture, ill-bestowed. I would beg to be allowed a start of five minutes by the clock; and then to receive the present company, inquiring for Miss Wickfield, at the office of Wickfield and Heep, whose Stipendiary I am."

My aunt and I looked at Traddles, who nodded his approval.

"I have no more," observed Mr. Micawber, "to say at present."

With which, to my infinite surprise, he included us all in

a comprehensive bow, and disappeared; his manner being extremely distant, and his face extremely pale.

Traddles only smiled, and shook his head (with his hair standing upright on the top of it), when I looked to him for an explanation; so I took out my watch, and, as a last resource, counted off the five minutes. My aunt, with her own watch in her hand, did the like. When the time was expired, Traddles gave her his arm; and we all went out together to the old house without saying one word on the way.

We found Mr. Micawber at his desk, in the turret office on the ground floor, either writing, or pretending to write, hard. The large office-ruler was stuck into his waistcoat, and was not so well concealed but that a foot or more of that instrument protruded from his bosom, like a new kind of shirt-frill.

As it appeared to me that I was expected to speak, I said aloud :

" How do you do, Mr. Micawber ? "

" Mr. Copperfield," said Mr. Micawber, gravely, " I hope I see you well ? "

" Is Miss Wickfield at home ? " said I.

" Mr. Wickfield is unwell in bed, sir, of a rheumatic fever," he returned; " but Miss Wickfield, I have no doubt, will be happy to see old friends. Will you walk in, sir ? "

He preceded us to the dining-room—the first room I had entered in that house—and flinging open the door of Mr. Wickfield's former office, said, in a sonorous voice :

" Miss Trotwood, Mr. David Copperfield, Mr. Thomas Traddles, and Mr. Dixon ! "

I had not seen Uriah Heep since the time of the blow. Our visit astonished him, evidently; not the less, I dare say, because it astonished ourselves. He did not gather his eyebrows together, for he had none worth mentioning; but he frowned to that degree that he almost closed his small eyes, while the hurried raising of his gristly hand to his chin betrayed some trepidation or surprise. This was only when we were in the act of entering his room, and when I caught a glance at him over my aunt's shoulder. A moment afterwards, he was as fawning and as humble as ever.

"Well, I am sure," he said. "This is indeed an unexpected pleasure! To have, as I may say, all friends round Saint Paul's at once, is a treat unlooked for! Mr. Copperfield, I hope I see you well, and—if I may umbly express self so—friendly towards them as is ever your friends, whether or not. Mrs. Copperfield, sir, I hope she's getting on. We have been made quite uneasy by the poor accounts we have had of her state, lately, I do assure you."

I felt ashamed to let him take my hand, but I did not know yet what else to do.

"Things are changed in this office, Miss Trotwood, since I was an umble clerk, and held your pony; ain't they?" said Uriah, with his sickliest smile. "But *I* am not changed, Miss Trotwood."

"Well, sir," returned my aunt, "to tell you the truth, I think you are pretty constant to the promise of your youth; if that's any satisfaction to you."

"Thank you, Miss Trotwood," said Uriah, writhing in his ungainly manner, "for your good opinion! Micawber, tell 'em to let Miss Agnes know—and mother. Mother will be quite in a state, when she sees the present company!" said Uriah, setting chairs.

"You are not busy, Mr. Heep?" said Traddles, whose eye the cunning red eye accidentally caught, as it at once scrutinised and evaded us.

"No, Mr. Traddles," replied Uriah, resuming his official seat, and squeezing his bony hands, laid palm to palm, between his bony knees. "Not so much so as I could wish. But lawyers, sharks, and leeches, are not easily satisfied, you know! Not but what myself and Micawber have our hands pretty full in general, on account of Mr. Wickfield's being hardly fit for any occupation, sir. But it's a pleasure as well as a duty, I am sure, to work for *him*. You've not been intimate with Mr. Wickfield, I think, Mr. Traddles? I believe I've only had the honour of seeing you once myself?"

"No, I have not been intimate with Mr. Wickfield," returned Traddles; "or I might perhaps have waited on you long ago, Mr. Heep."

There was something in the tone of this reply, which made Uriah look at the speaker again, with a very sinister and suspicious expression. But, seeing only Traddles, with his good-natured face, simple manner, and hair on end, he dismissed it as he replied, with a jerk of his whole body, but especially his throat:

"I am sorry for that, Mr. Traddles. You would have admired him as much as we all do. His little failings would only have endeared him to you the more. But if you would like to hear my fellow-partner eloquently spoken of, I should refer you to Copperfield. The family is a subject he's very strong upon, if you never heard him."

I was prevented from disclaiming the compliment (if I should have done so, in any case), by the entrance of Agnes, now ushered in by Mr. Micawber. She was not quite so self-possessed as usual, I thought; and had evidently undergone anxiety and fatigue. But her earnest cordiality, and her quiet beauty, shone with the gentler lustre for it.

I saw Uriah watch her while she greeted us; and he reminded me of an ugly and rebellious genie watching a good spirit. In the meanwhile, some slight sign passed between Mr. Micawber and Traddles; and Traddles, unobserved except by me, went out.

"Don't wait, Micawber," said Uriah.

Mr. Micawber, with his hand upon the ruler in his breast, stood erect before the door, most unmistakably contemplating one of his fellow-men, and that man his employer.

"What are you waiting for?" said Uriah. "Micawber! did you hear me tell you not to wait?"

"Yes!" replied the immovable Mr. Micawber.

"Then why *do* you wait?" said Uriah.

"Because I—in short choose," replied Mr. Micawber, with a burst.

Uriah's cheeks lost colour, and an unwholesome paleness, still faintly tinged by his pervading red, overspread them. He looked at Mr. Micawber attentively, with his whole face breathing short and quick in every feature.

"You are a dissipated fellow, as all the world knows," he said, with an effort at a smile, "and I am afraid you'll oblige me to get rid of you. Go along! I'll talk to you presently."

"If there is a scoundrel on this earth," said Mr. Micawber, suddenly breaking out again with the utmost vehemence, "with whom I have already talked too much, that scoundrel's name is—HEEP!"

Uriah fell back, as if he had been struck or stung. Looking slowly round upon us with the darkest and wickedest expression that his face could wear, he said, in a lower voice:

"Oho! This is a conspiracy! You have met here, by appointment! You are playing Booty with my clerk, are you, Copperfield? Now, take care. You'll make nothing of this. We understand each other, you and me. There's no love between us. You were always a puppy with a proud stomach, from your first coming here; and you envy me my rise, do you? None of your plots against me; I'll counterplot you! Micawber, you be off. I'll talk to you presently."

"Mr. Micawber," said I, "there is a sudden change in this fellow, in more respects than the extraordinary one of his speaking the truth in one particular, which assures me that he is brought to bay. Deal with him as he deserves!"

"You are a precious set of people, ain't you?" said Uriah, in the same low voice, and breaking out into a clammy heat, which he wiped from his forehead, with his long lean hand, "to buy over my clerk, who is the very scum of society,—as you yourself were, Copperfield, you know it, before any one

had charity on you,—to defame me with his lies? Miss
Trotwood, you had better stop this; or I'll stop your
husband shorter than will be pleasant to you. I won't know
your story professionally, for nothing, old lady! Miss Wickfield, if you have any love for your father, you had better
not join that gang. I'll ruin him, if you do. Now, come!
I have got some of you under the harrow. Think twice,
before it goes over you. Think twice, you, Micawber, if you
don't want to be crushed. I recommend you to take yourself
off, and be talked to presently, you fool! while there's time
to retreat! Where's mother?" he said, suddenly appearing to
notice, with alarm, the absence of Traddles, and pulling down
the bell-rope. "Fine doings in a person's own house!"

"Mrs. Heep is here, sir," said Traddles, returning with
that worthy mother of a worthy son. "I have taken the
liberty of making myself known to her."

"Who are you to make yourself known?" retorted Uriah.
"And what do you want here?"

"I am the agent and friend of Mr. Wickfield, sir," said
Traddles, in a composed business-like way. "And I have a
power of attorney from him in my pocket, to act for him
in all matters."

"The old ass has drunk himself into a state of dotage,"
said Uriah, turning uglier than before, "and it has been got
from him by fraud!"

"Something has been got from him by fraud, I know,"
returned Traddles quietly; "and so do you, Mr. Heep. We
will refer that question, if you please, to Mr. Micawber."

"Ury—!" Mrs. Heep began, with an anxious gesture.

"You hold your tongue, mother," he returned; "least
said, soonest mended."

"But, my Ury—"

"Will you hold your tongue, mother, and leave it to me?"

Though I had long known that his servility was false, and
all his pretences knavish and hollow, I had had no adequate
conception of the extent of his hypocrisy, until I now saw

him with his mask off. The suddenness with which he dropped it, when he perceived that it was useless to him; the malice, insolence, and hatred he revealed; the leer with which he exulted, even at this moment, in the evil he had done—all this time being desperate too, and at his wits' end for the means of getting the better of us—though perfectly consistent with the experience I had of him, at first took even me by surprise, who had known him so long, and disliked him so heartily.

I say nothing of the look he conferred on me, as he stood eyeing us, one after another; for I had always understood that he hated me, and I remembered the marks of my hand upon his cheek. But when his eyes passed on to Agnes, and I saw the rage with which he felt his power over her slipping away, and the exhibition, in their disappointment, of the odious passions that had led him to aspire to one whose virtues he could never appreciate or care for, I was shocked by the mere thought of her having lived, an hour, within sight of such a man.

After some rubbing of the lower part of his face, and some looking at us with those bad eyes, over his gristly fingers, he made one more address to me, half whining, and half abusive.

"You think it justifiable, do you, Copperfield, you who pride yourself so much on your honour and all the rest of it, to sneak about my place, eaves-dropping with my clerk? If it had been *me*, I shouldn't have wondered; for I don't make myself out a gentleman (though I never was in the streets either, as you were, according to Micawber), but being *you!*—And you're not afraid of doing this, either? You don't think at all of what I shall do, in return; or of getting yourself into trouble for conspiracy and so forth? Very well. We shall see! Mr. What's-your-name, you were going to refer some question to Micawber. There's your referee. Why don't you make him speak? He has learnt his lesson, I see."

Seeing that what he said had no effect on me or any of

us, he sat on the edge of his table with his hands in his pockets, and one of his splay feet twisted round the other leg, waiting doggedly for what might follow.

Mr. Micawber, whose impetuosity I had restrained thus far with the greatest difficulty, and who had repeatedly interposed with the first syllable of Scoun-drel! without getting to the second, now burst forward, drew the ruler from his breast (apparently as a defensive weapon), and produced from his pocket a foolscap document, folded in the form of a large letter. Opening this packet, with his old flourish, and glancing at the contents, as if he cherished an artistic admiration of their style of composition, he began to read as follows:

"'Dear Miss Trotwood and gentlemen——'"

"Bless and save the man!" exclaimed my aunt in a low voice. "He'd write letters by the ream, if it was a capital offence!"

Mr. Micawber, without hearing her, went on.

"'In appearing before you to denounce probably the most consummate Villain that has ever existed,'" Mr. Micawber, without looking off the letter, pointed the ruler, like a ghostly truncheon, at Uriah Heep, "'I ask no consideration for myself. The victim, from my cradle, of pecuniary liabilities to which I have been unable to respond, I have ever been the sport and toy of debasing circumstances. Ignominy, Want, Despair, and Madness, have, collectively or separately, been the attendants of my career.'"

The relish with which Mr. Micawber described himself, as a prey to these dismal calamities, was only to be equalled by the emphasis with which he read his letter; and the kind of homage he rendered to it with a roll of his head, when he thought he had hit a sentence very hard indeed.

"'In an accumulation of Ignominy, Want, Despair, and Madness, I entered the office—or, as our lively neighbour the Gaul would term it, the Bureau—of the Firm, nominally conducted under the appellation of Wickfield and—Heep, but, in reality, wielded by—HEEP alone. HEEP, and only HEEP, is the mainspring of that machine. HEEP, and only HEEP, is the Forger and the Cheat.'"

Uriah, more blue than white at these words, made a dart at the letter, as if to tear it in pieces. Mr. Micawber, with a perfect miracle of dexterity or luck, caught his advancing knuckles with the ruler, and disabled his right hand. It dropped at the wrist, as if it were broken. The blow sounded as if it had fallen on wood.

"The Devil take you!" said Uriah, writhing in a new way with pain. "I'll be even with you."

"Approach me again, you—you—you HEEP of infamy," gasped Mr. Micawber, "and if your head is human, I'll break it. Come on, come on!"

I think I never saw anything more ridiculous—I was sensible of it, even at the time—than Mr. Micawber making broad-sword guards with the ruler, and crying, "Come on!" while Traddles and I pushed him back into a corner, from which, as often as we got him into it, he persisted in emerging again.

His enemy, muttering to himself, after wringing his wounded hand for some time, slowly drew off his neck-kerchief and bound it up; then, held it in his other hand, and sat upon his table with his sullen face looking down.

Mr. Micawber, when he was sufficiently cool, proceeded with his letter.

"'The stipendiary emoluments in consideration of which I entered into the service of—HEEP,'" always pausing before that word and uttering it with astonishing vigour, "'were not defined, beyond the pittance, of twenty-two shillings and six per week. The rest was left contingent on the value of my professional exertions; in other and more expressive words, on the baseness of my nature, the cupidity of my motives, the poverty of my family, the general moral (or rather immoral) resemblance between myself and—HEEP. Need I say, that it soon became necessary for me to solicit

from—HEEP—pecuniary advances towards the support of Mrs
Micawber, and our blighted but rising family? Need I say
that this necessity had been foreseen by—HEEP? That those
advances were secured by I O U's and other similar acknow
ledgments, known to the legal institutions of this country
And that I thus became immeshed in the web he had spun
for my reception?'"

Mr. Micawber's enjoyment of his epistolary powers, in
describing this unfortunate state of things, really seemed to
outweigh any pain or anxiety that the reality could have
caused him. He read on:

"'Then it was that—HEEP—began to favour me with just
so much of his confidence, as was necessary to the discharge
of his infernal business. Then it was that I began, if I may
so Shakespearingly express myself, to dwindle, peak, and pine
I found that my services were constantly called into requi
sition for the falsification of business, and the mystification
of an individual whom I will designate as Mr. W. That
Mr. W. was imposed upon, kept in ignorance, and deluded
in every possible way; yet, that all this while, the ruffian—
HEEP—was professing unbounded gratitude to, and unbounded
friendship for, that much-abused gentleman. This was bad
enough; but, as the philosophic Dane observes, with that
universal applicability which distinguishes the illustrious
ornament of the Elizabethan Era, worse remains behind!'"

Mr. Micawber was so very much struck by this happy
rounding off with a quotation, that he indulged himself, and
us, with a second reading of the sentence, under pretence of
having lost his place.

"'It is not my intention,'" he continued, reading on, "'to
enter on a detailed list, within the compass of the present
epistle (though it is ready elsewhere), of the various malpractices of a minor nature, affecting the individual whom I
have denominated Mr. W., to which I have been a tacitly
consenting party. My object, when the contest within myself
between stipend and no stipend, baker and no baker, existence

and non-existence, ceased, was to take advantage of my opportunities to discover and expose the major malpractices committed, to that gentleman's grievous wrong and injury, by—HEEP. Stimulated by the silent monitor within, and by a no less touching and appealing monitor without—to whom I will briefly refer as Miss W.—I entered on a not unlaborious task of clandestine investigation, protracted now, to the best of my knowledge, information, and belief, over a period exceeding twelve calendar months.'"

He read this passage, as if it were from an Act of Parliament; and appeared majestically refreshed by the sound of the words.

"'My charges against—HEEP,'" he read on, glancing at him, and drawing the ruler into a convenient position under his left arm, in case of need, "'are as follows.'"

We all held our breath, I think. I am sure Uriah held his.

"'First,'" said Mr. Micawber. "'When Mr. W.'s faculties and memory for business became, through causes into which it is not necessary or expedient for me to enter, weakened and confused,—HEEP—designedly perplexed and complicated the whole of the official transactions. When Mr. W. was least fit to enter on business,—HEEP was always at hand to force him to enter on it. He obtained Mr. W.'s signature under such circumstances to documents of importance, representing them to be other documents of no importance. He induced Mr. W. to empower him to draw out, thus, one particular sum of trust-money, amounting to twelve six fourteen, two and nine, and employed it to meet pretended business charges and deficiencies which were either already provided for, or had never really existed. He gave this proceeding, throughout, the appearance of having originated in Mr. W.'s own dishonest intention, and of having been accomplished by Mr. W.'s own dishonest act; and has used it, ever since, to torture and constrain him.'"

"You shall prove this, you Copperfield!" said Uriah, with a threatening shake of the head. "All in good time!"

"Ask—HEEP—Mr. Traddles, who lived in his house after him," said Mr. Micawber, breaking off from the letter; "will you?"

"The fool himself—and lives there now," said Uriah, disdainfully.

"Ask—HEEP—if he ever kept a pocket-book in that house," said Mr. Micawber; "will you?"

I saw Uriah's lank hand stop, involuntarily, in the scraping of his chin.

"Or ask him," said Mr. Micawber, "if he ever burnt one there. If he says Yes, and asks you where the ashes are, refer him to Wilkins Micawber, and he will hear of something not at all to his advantage!"

The triumphant flourish with which Mr. Micawber delivered himself of these words, had a powerful effect in alarming the mother; who cried out in much agitation:

"Ury, Ury! Be umble, and make terms, my dear!"

"Mother!" he retorted, "will you keep quiet? You're in a fright, and don't know what you say or mean. Umble!" he repeated, looking at me, with a snarl; "I've umbled some of 'em for a pretty long time back, umble as I was!"

Mr. Micawber, genteelly adjusting his chin in his cravat, presently proceeded with his composition.

"'Second. HEEP has, on several occasions, to the best of my knowledge, information, and belief—'"

"But *that* won't do," muttered Uriah, relieved. "Mother, you keep quiet."

"We will endeavour to provide something that WILL do, and do for you finally, sir, very shortly," replied Mr. Micawber.

"'Second. HEEP has, on several occasions, to the best of my knowledge, information, and belief, systematically forged, to various entries, books, and documents, the signature of Mr. W.; and has distinctly done so in one instance, capable of proof by me. To wit, in manner following, that is to say:'"

FORGERY.

Again, Mr. Micawber had a relish in this formal piling up of words, which, however ludicrously displayed in his case, was, I must say, not at all peculiar to him. I have observed it, in the course of my life, in numbers of men. It seems to me to be a general rule. In the taking of legal oaths, for instance, deponents seem to enjoy themselves mightily when they come to several good words in succession, for the expression of one idea; as, that they utterly detest, abominate, and abjure, or so forth; and the old anathemas were made relishing on the same principle. We talk about the tyranny of words, but we like to tyrannise over them too; we are fond of having a large superfluous establishment of words to wait upon us on great occasions; we think it looks important, and sounds well. As we are not particular about the meaning of our liveries on state occasions, if they be but fine and numerous enough, so, the meaning or necessity of our words is a secondary consideration, if there be but a great parade of them. And as individuals get into trouble by making too great a show of liveries, or as slaves when they are too numerous rise against their masters, so I think I could mention a nation that has got into many great difficulties, and will get into many greater, from maintaining too large a retinue of words.

Mr. Micawber read on, almost smacking his lips:

"'To wit, in manner following, that is to say. Mr. W. being infirm, and it being within the bounds of probability that his decease might lead to some discoveries, and to the downfall of—HEEP's—power over the W. family,—as I, Wilkins Micawber, the undersigned, assume—unless the filial affection of his daughter could be secretly influenced from allowing any investigation of the partnership affairs to be ever made, the said—HEEP—deemed it expedient to have a bond ready by him, as from Mr. W., for the before-mentioned sum of twelve six fourteen, two and nine, with interest, stated therein to have been advanced by—HEEP—to Mr. W. to save Mr. W. from dishonour; though really the sum was never advanced by him, and has long been replaced. The signatures to this instrument purporting to be executed by Mr. W. and attested by Wilkins Micawber, are forgeries by—HEEP. I have, in my possession, in his hand and pocket-book, several similar imitations of Mr. W.'s signature, here and there defaced by fire, but legible to any one. I never attested any such document. And I have the document itself, in my possession.'"

Uriah Heep, with a start, took out of his pocket a bunch of keys, and opened a certain drawer; then, suddenly bethought himself of what he was about, and turned again towards us, without looking in it.

"'And I have the document,'" Mr. Micawber read again, looking about as if it were the text of a sermon, "'in my possession,'—that is to say, I had, early this morning, when this was written, but have since relinquished it to Mr. Traddles."

"It is quite true," assented Traddles.

"Ury, Ury!" cried the mother, "be umble and make terms. I know my son will be umble, gentlemen, if you'll give him time to think. Mr. Copperfield, I'm sure you know that he was always very umble, sir!"

It was singular to see how the mother still held to the old trick, when the son had abandoned it as useless.

"Mother," he said, with an impatient bite at the handkerchief in which his hand was wrapped, "you had better take and fire a loaded gun at me."

"But I love you, Ury," cried Mrs. Heep. And I have no doubt she did; or that he loved her, however strange it may appear; though, to be sure, they were a congenial couple. "And I can't bear to hear you provoking the gentleman, and endangering of yourself more. I told the gentleman at first, when he told me up-stairs it was come to light, that I would answer for your being umble, and making amends. Oh, see how umble *I* am, gentlemen, and don't mind him!"

"Why, there's Copperfield, mother," he angrily retorted,

pointing his lean finger at me, against whom all his animosity was levelled, as the prime mover in the discovery ; and I did not undeceive him ; " there's Copperfield, would have given you a hundred pound to say less than you've blurted out ! "

" I can't help it, Ury," cried his mother. " I can't see you running into danger, through carrying your head so high. Better be umble, as you always was."

He remained for a little, biting the handkerchief, and then said to me with a scowl :

" What more have you got to bring forward ? If anything, go on with it. What do you look at me for ? "

Mr. Micawber promptly resumed his letter, glad to revert to a performance with which he was so highly satisfied.

" ' Third. And last. I am now in a condition to show, by—HEEP's—false books, and—HEEP's—real memoranda, beginning with the partially destroyed pocket-book (which I was unable to comprehend, at the time of its accidental discovery by Mrs. Micawber, on our taking possession of our present abode, in the locker or bin devoted to the reception of the ashes calcined on our domestic hearth), that the weaknesses, the faults, the very virtues, the parental affections, and the sense of honour, of the unhappy Mr. W. have been for years acted on by, and warped to the base purposes of—HEEP. That Mr. W. has been for years deluded and plundered, in every conceivable manner, to the pecuniary aggrandisement of the avaricious, false, and grasping—HEEP. That the engrossing object of—HEEP—was, next to gain, to subdue Mr. and Miss W. (of his ulterior views in reference to the latter I say nothing) entirely to himself. That his last act, completed but a few months since, was to induce Mr. W. to execute a relinquishment of his share in the partnership, and even a bill of sale on the very furniture of his house, in consideration of a certain annuity, to be well and truly paid by—HEEP—on the four common quarter-days in each and every year. That these meshes ; beginning with alarming and falsified accounts of the estate of which Mr. W. is the receiver, at a period when Mr. W. had launched into imprudent and ill-judged speculations, and may not have had the money, for which he was morally and legally responsible, in hand; going on with pretended borrowings of money at enormous interest, really coming from—Heep—and by—Heep—fraudulently obtained or withheld from Mr. W. himself, on pretence of such speculations or otherwise; perpetuated by a miscellaneous catalogue of unscrupulous chicaneries—gradually thickened, until the unhappy Mr. W. could see no world beyond. Bankrupt, as he believed, alike in circumstances, in all other hope, and in honour, his sole reliance was upon the monster in the garb of man,'"—Mr. Micawber made a good deal of this, as a new turn of expression,—"'who, by making himself necessary to him, had achieved his destruction. All this I undertake to show. Probably much more!'"

I whispered a few words to Agnes, who was weeping, half joyfully, half sorrowfully, at my side; and there was a movement among us, as if Mr. Micawber had finished. He said, with exceeding gravity, "Pardon me," and proceeded, with a mixture of the lowest spirits and the most intense enjoyment, to the peroration of his letter.

"'I have now concluded. It merely remains for me to substantiate these accusations; and then, with my ill-starred family, to disappear from the landscape on which we appear to be an incumbrance. That is soon done. It may be reasonably inferred that our baby will first expire of inanition, as being the frailest member of our circle; and that our twins will follow next in order. So be it! For myself, my Canterbury Pilgrimage has done much; imprisonment on civil process, and want, will soon do more. I trust that the labour and hazard of an investigation—of which the smallest results have been slowly pieced together, in the pressure of arduous avocations, under grinding penurious apprehensions, at rise of morn, at dewy eve, in the shadows of night, under the watchful eye of one whom it were superfluous to call Demon

386

—combined with the struggle of parental Poverty to turn it, when completed, to the right account, may be as the sprinkling of a few drops of sweet water on my funereal pyre. I ask no more. Let it be, in justice, merely said of me, as of a gallant and eminent naval Hero, with whom I have no pretensions to cope, that what I have done, I did, in despite of mercenary and selfish objects,

> "For England, home, and Beauty."

> " 'Remaining always, &c. &c., WILKINS MICAWBER.' "

Much affected, but still intensely enjoying himself, Mr. Micawber folded up his letter, and handed it with a bow to my aunt, as something she might like to keep.

There was, as I had noticed on my first visit long ago, an iron safe in the room. The key was in it. A hasty suspicion seemed to strike Uriah; and, with a glance at Mr. Micawber, he went to it, and threw the doors clanking open. It was empty.

"Where are the books?" he cried, with a frightful face. "Some thief has stolen the books!"

Mr. Micawber tapped himself with the ruler. "*I* did, when I got the key from you as usual—but a little earlier —and opened it this morning."

"Don't be uneasy," said Traddles. "They have come into my possession. I will take care of them, under the authority I mentioned."

"You receive stolen goods, do you?" cried Uriah.

"Under such circumstances," answered Traddles, "yes."

What was my astonishment when I beheld my aunt, who had been profoundly quiet and attentive, make a dart at Uriah Heep, and seize him by the collar with both hands!

"You know what *I* want?" said my aunt.

"A strait-waistcoat," said he.

"No. My property!" returned my aunt. "Agnes, my dear, as long as I believed it had been really made away with by your father, I wouldn't—and, my dear, I didn't, even to

Trot, as he knows—breathe a syllable of its having been placed here for investment. But now I know this fellow's answerable for it, and I'll have it! Trot, come and take it away from him!"

Whether my aunt supposed, for the moment, that he kept her property in his neck-kerchief, I am sure I don't know; but she certainly pulled at it as if she thought so. I hastened to put myself between them, and to assure her that we would all take care that he should make the utmost restitution of everything he had wrongly got. This, and a few moments' reflection, pacified her; but she was not at all disconcerted by what she had done (though I cannot say as much for her bonnet), and resumed her seat composedly.

During the last few minutes, Mrs. Heep had been clamouring to her son to be "umble;" and had been going down on her knees to all of us in succession, and making the wildest promises. Her son sat her down in his chair; and, standing sulkily by her, holding her arm with his hand, but not rudely, said to me, with a ferocious look:

"What do you want done?"

"I will tell you what must be done," said Traddles.

"Has that Copperfield no tongue?" muttered Uriah. "I would do a good deal for you if you could tell me, without lying, that somebody had cut it out."

"My Uriah means to be umble!" cried his mother. "Don't mind what he says, good gentlemen!"

"What must be done," said Traddles, "is this. First, the deed of relinquishment, that we have heard of, must be given over to me now—here."

"Suppose I haven't got it," he interrupted.

"But you have," said Traddles; "therefore, you know, we won't suppose so." And I cannot help avowing that this was the first occasion on which I really did justice to the clear head, and the plain, patient, practical good sense, of my old schoolfellow. "Then," said Traddles, "you must prepare to disgorge all that your rapacity has become possessed of, and to make restoration to the last farthing. All the partner-ship books and papers must remain in our possession; all your books and papers; all money accounts and securities, of both kinds. In short, everything here."

"Must it? I don't know that," said Uriah. "I must have time to think about that."

"Certainly," replied Traddles; "but, in the meanwhile, and until everything is done to our satisfaction, we shall maintain possession of these things; and beg you—in short, compel you—to keep your own room, and hold no communi-cation with any one."

"I won't do it!" said Uriah, with an oath.

"Maidstone Jail is a safer place of detention," observed Traddles; "and though the law may be longer in righting us, and may not be able to right us so completely as you can, there is no doubt of its punishing *you*. Dear me, you know that quite as well as I! Copperfield, will you go round to the Guildhall, and bring a couple of officers?"

Here, Mrs. Heep broke out again, crying on her knees to Agnes to interfere in their behalf, exclaiming that he was very humble, and it was all true, and if he didn't do what we wanted, she would, and much more to the same purpose; being half frantic with fears for her darling. To inquire what he might have done, if he had had any boldness, would be like inquiring what a mongrel cur might do, if it had the spirit of a tiger. He was a coward, from head to foot; and showed his dastardly nature through his sullenness and mor-tification, as much as at any time of his mean life.

"Stop!" he growled to me; and wiped his hot face with his hand. "Mother, hold your noise. Well! Let 'em have that deed. Go and fetch it!"

"Do you help her, Mr. Dick," said Traddles, "if you please."

Proud of his commission, and understanding it, Mr. Dick accompanied her as a shepherd's dog might accompany a sheep. But Mrs. Heep gave him little trouble; for she not only returned with the deed, but with the box in which it was, where we found a banker's book and some other papers that were afterwards serviceable.

"Good!" said Traddles, when this was brought. "Now, Mr. Heep, you can retire to think: particularly observing, if you please, that I declare to you, on the part of all present, that there is only one thing to be done; that it is what I have explained; and that it must be done without delay."

Uriah, without lifting his eyes from the ground, shuffled across the room with his hand to his chin, and pausing at the door, said:

"Copperfield, I have always hated you. You've always been an upstart, and you've always been against me."

"As I think I told you once before," said I, "it is you who have been, in your greed and cunning, against all the world. It may be profitable to you to reflect, in future, that there never were greed and cunning in the world yet, that did not do too much, and over-reach themselves. It is as certain as death."

"Or as certain as they used to teach at school (the same school where I picked up so much umbleness), from nine o'clock to eleven, that labour was a curse; and from eleven o'clock to one, that it was a blessing and a cheerfulness, and a dignity, and I don't know what all, eh?" said he with a sneer. "You preach, about as consistent as they did. Won't umbleness go down? I shouldn't have got round my gentleman fellow-partner without it, I think.—Micawber, you old bully, I'll pay *you!*"

Mr. Micawber, supremely defiant of him and his extended finger, and making a great deal of his chest until he had slunk out at the door, then addressed himself to me, and proffered me the satisfaction of "witnessing the re-establishment of mutual confidence between himself and Mrs. Micawber." After which, he invited the company generally to the contemplation of that affecting spectacle.

"The veil that has long been interposed between Mrs. Micawber and myself, is now withdrawn," said Mr. Micawber;

*Restoration of Mutual Confidence between
Mr. and Mrs. Micawber*

"and my children and the Author of their Being can once more come in contact on equal terms."

As we were all very grateful to him, and all desirous to show that we were, as well as the hurry and disorder of our spirits would permit, I dare say we should all have gone, but that it was necessary for Agnes to return to her father, as yet unable to bear more than the dawn of hope; and for some one else to hold Uriah in safe keeping. So Traddles remained for the latter purpose, to be presently relieved by Mr. Dick; and Mr. Dick, my aunt, and I, went home with Mr. Micawber. As I parted hurriedly from the dear girl to whom I owed so much, and thought from what she had been saved, perhaps, that morning—her better resolution notwithstanding—I felt devoutly thankful for the miseries of my younger days which had brought me to the knowledge of Mr. Micawber.

His house was not far off; and as the street-door opened into the sitting-room, and he bolted in with a precipitation quite his own, we found ourselves at once in the bosom of the family. Mr. Micawber exclaiming, "Emma! my life!" rushed into Mrs. Micawber's arms. Mrs. Micawber shrieked, and folded Mr. Micawber in her embrace. Miss Micawber, nursing the unconscious stranger of Mrs. Micawber's last letter to me, was sensibly affected. The stranger leaped. The twins testified their joy by several inconvenient but innocent demonstrations. Master Micawber, whose disposition appeared to have been soured by early disappointment, and whose aspect had become morose, yielded to his better feelings, and blubbered.

"Emma!" said Mr. Micawber. "The cloud is past from my mind. Mutual confidence, so long preserved between us once, is restored, to know no further interruption. Now, welcome poverty!" cried Mr. Micawber, shedding tears. "Welcome misery, welcome houselessness, welcome hunger, rags, tempest, and beggary! Mutual confidence will sustain us to the end!"

With these expressions, Mr. Micawber placed Mrs. Micawber in a chair, and embraced the family all round; welcoming a variety of bleak prospects, which appeared, to the best of my judgment, to be anything but welcome to them; and calling upon them to come out into Canterbury and sing a chorus, as nothing else was left for their support.

But Mrs. Micawber having, in the strength of her emotions, fainted away, the first thing to be done, even before the chorus could be considered complete, was to recover her. This, my aunt and Mr. Micawber did; and then my aunt was introduced, and Mrs. Micawber recognised me.

"Excuse me, dear Mr. Copperfield," said the poor lady, giving me her hand, "but I am not strong; and the removal of the late misunderstanding between Mr. Micawber and myself was at first too much for me."

"Is this all your family, ma'am?" said my aunt.

"There are no more at present," returned Mrs. Micawber.

"Good gracious, I didn't mean that, ma'am," said my aunt. "I mean are all these yours?"

"Madam," replied Mr. Micawber, "it is a true bill."

"And that eldest young gentleman, now," said my aunt, musing, "what has *he* been brought up to?"

"It was my hope when I came here," said Mr. Micawber, "to have got Wilkins into the Church: or perhaps I shall express my meaning more strictly, if I say the Choir. But there was no vacancy for a tenor in the venerable Pile for which this city is so justly eminent; and he has—in short, he has contracted a habit of singing in public-houses, rather than in sacred edifices."

"But he means well," said Mrs. Micawber, tenderly.

"I dare say, my love," rejoined Mr. Micawber, "that he means particularly well; but I have not yet found that he carries out his meaning, in any given direction whatsoever."

Master Micawber's moroseness of aspect returned upon him again, and he demanded, with some temper, what he was to do? Whether he had been born a carpenter, or a coach-painter, any more than he had been born a bird? Whether he could go into the next street, and open a chemist's shop? Whether he could rush to the next assizes, and proclaim himself a lawyer? Whether he could come out by force at the opera, and succeed by violence? Whether he could do anything, without being brought up to something?

My aunt mused a little while, and then said:

"Mr. Micawber, I wonder you have never turned your thoughts to emigration."

"Madam," returned Mr. Micawber, "it was the dream of my youth, and the fallacious aspiration of my riper years." I am thoroughly persuaded, by the bye, that he had never thought of it in his life.

"Aye?" said my aunt, with a glance at me. "Why, what a thing it would be for yourselves and your family, Mr. and Mrs. Micawber, if you were to emigrate now."

"Capital, madam, capital," urged Mr. Micawber, gloomily.

"That is the principal, I may say the only difficulty, my dear Mr. Copperfield," assented his wife.

"Capital?" cried my aunt. "But you are doing us a great service—have done us a great service, I may say, for surely much will come out of the fire—and what could we do for you, that would be half so good as to find the capital?"

"I could not receive it as a gift," said Mr. Micawber, full of fire and animation, "but if a sufficient sum could be advanced, say at five per cent. interest per annum, upon my personal liability—say my notes of hand, at twelve, eighteen, and twenty-four months, respectively, to allow time for something to turn up——"

"Could be? Can be and shall be, on your own terms," returned my aunt, "if you say the word. Think of this now, both of you. Here are some people David knows, going out to Australia shortly. If you decide to go, why shouldn't you go in the same ship? You may help each other. Think of this now, Mr. and Mrs. Micawber. Take your time, and weigh it well."

"There is but one question, my dear ma'am, I could wish to ask," said Mrs. Micawber. "The climate, I believe, is healthy?"

"Finest in the world!" said my aunt.

"Just so," returned Mrs. Micawber. "Then my question arises. Now, *are* the circumstances of the country such, that a man of Mr. Micawber's abilities would have a fair chance of rising in the social scale? I will not say, at present, might he aspire to be Governor, or anything of that sort; but would there be a reasonable opening for his talents to develop themselves—that, would be amply sufficient—and find their own expansion?"

"No better opening anywhere," said my aunt, "for a man who conducts himself well, and is industrious."

"For a man who conducts himself well," repeated Mrs. Micawber, with her clearest business manner, "and is industrious. Precisely. It is evident to me that Australia is the legitimate sphere of action for Mr. Micawber!"

"I entertain the conviction, my dear madam," said Mr. Micawber, "that it is, under existing circumstances, the land, the only land, for myself and family; and that something of an extraordinary nature will turn up on that shore. It is no distance—comparatively speaking; and though consideration is due to the kindness of your proposal, I assure you that is a mere matter of form."

Shall I ever forget how, in a moment, he was the most sanguine of men, looking on to fortune; or how Mrs. Micawber presently discoursed about the habits of the kangaroo! Shall I ever recall that street of Canterbury on a market day, without recalling him, as he walked back with us; expressing, in the hardy roving manner he assumed, the unsettled habits of a temporary sojourner in the land; and looking at the bullocks, as they came by, with the eye of an Australian farmer!

CHAPTER LIII.

I must pause yet once again. Oh, my child-wife, there is a figure in the moving crowd before my memory, quiet and still, saying in its innocent love and childish beauty, Stop to think of me—turn to look upon the Little Blossom, as it flutters to the ground!

I do. All else grows dim, and fades away. I am again with Dora, in our cottage. I do not know how long she has been ill. I am so used to it in feeling, that I cannot count the time. It is not really long, in weeks or months; but, in my usage and experience, it is a weary, weary while.

They have left off telling me to "wait a few days more." I have begun to fear, remotely, that the day may never shine, when I shall see my child-wife running in the sunlight with her old friend Jip.

He is, as it were suddenly, grown very old. It may be, that he misses in his mistress, something that enlivened him and made him younger; but he mopes, and his sight is weak, and his limbs are feeble, and my aunt is sorry that he objects to her no more, but creeps near her as he lies on Dora's bed—she sitting at the bedside—and mildly licks her hand.

Dora lies smiling on us, and is beautiful, and utters no hasty or complaining word. She says that we are very good to her; that her dear old careful boy is tiring himself out, she knows; that my aunt has no sleep, yet is always wakeful, active, and kind. Sometimes, the little bird-like ladies come to see her; and then we talk about our wedding-day, and all that happy time.

What a strange rest and pause in my life there seems to be—and in all life, within doors and without—when I sit in the quiet, shaded, orderly room, with the blue eyes of my child-wife turned towards me, and her little fingers twining round my hand! Many and many an hour I sit thus; but, of all those times, three times come the freshest on my mind.

It is morning; and Dora, made so trim by my aunt's hands, shows me how her pretty hair *will* curl upon the pillow yet, and how long and bright it is, and how she likes to have it loosely gathered in that net she wears.

"Not that I am vain of it, now, you mocking boy," she says, when I smile; "but because you used to say you thought it so beautiful; and because, when I first began to think about you, I used to peep in the glass, and wonder whether you would like very much to have a lock of it. Oh what a foolish fellow you were, Doady, when I gave you one!"

"That was on the day when you were painting the flowers I had given you, Dora, and when I told you how much in love I was."

"Ah! but I didn't like to tell *you*," says Dora, "*then*, how I had cried over them, because I believed you really liked me! When I can run about again as I used to do, Doady, let us go and see those places where we were such a silly couple, shall we? And take some of the old walks? And not forget poor papa?"

"Yes, we will, and have some happy days. So you must make haste to get well, my dear."

"Oh, I shall soon do that! I am so much better, you don't know!"

It is evening; and I sit in the same chair, by the same bed, with the same face turned towards me. We have been silent, and there is a smile upon her face. I have ceased to carry my light burden up and down stairs now. She lies here all the day.

"Doady!"

"My dear Dora!"

"You won't think what I am going to say, unreasonable, after what you told me, such a little while ago, of Mr. Wickfield's not being well? I want to see Agnes. Very much I want to see her."

"I will write to her, my dear."

"Will you?"

"Directly."

"What a good, kind boy! Doady, take me on your arm. Indeed, my dear, it's not a whim. It's not a foolish fancy. I want, very much indeed, to see her!"

"I am certain of it. I have only to tell her so, and she is sure to come."

"You are very lonely when you go down-stairs, now?" Dora whispers, with her arm about my neck.

"How can I be otherwise, my own love, when I see your empty chair?"

"My empty chair!" She clings to me for a little while, in silence. "And you really miss me, Doady?" looking up, and brightly smiling. "Even poor, giddy, stupid me?"

"My heart, who is there upon earth that I could miss so much?"

"Oh, husband! I am so glad, yet so sorry!" creeping closer to me, and folding me in both her arms. She laughs and sobs, and then is quiet, and quite happy.

"Quite!" she says. "Only give Agnes my dear love, and tell her that I want very, very much to see her; and I have nothing left to wish for."

"Except to get well again, Dora."

"Ah, Doady! Sometimes I think—you know I always was a silly little thing!—that that will never be!"

"Don't say so, Dora! Dearest love, don't think so!"

397

"I won't, if I can help it, Doady. But I am very happy; though my dear boy is so lonely by himself, before his child-wife's empty chair!"

It is night; and I am with her still. Agnes has arrived; has been among us, for a whole day and an evening. She, my aunt, and I, have sat with Dora since the morning, all together. We have not talked much, but Dora has been perfectly contented and cheerful. We are now alone.

Do I know, now, that my child-wife will soon leave me? They have told me so; they have told me nothing new to my thoughts; but I am far from sure that I have taken that truth to heart. I cannot master it. I have withdrawn by myself, many times to-day, to weep. I have remembered Who wept for a parting between the living and the dead. I have bethought me of all that gracious and compassionate history. I have tried to resign myself, and to console myself; and that, I hope, I may have done imperfectly; but what I cannot firmly settle in my mind is, that the end will absolutely come. I hold her hand in mine, I hold her heart in mine, I see her love for me, alive in all its strength. I cannot shut out a pale lingering shadow of belief that she will be spared.

"I am going to speak to you, Doady. I am going to say something I have often thought of saying, lately. You won't mind?" with a gentle look.

"Mind, my darling?"

"Because I don't know what you will think, or what you may have thought sometimes. Perhaps you have often thought the same. Doady, dear, I am afraid I was too young."

I lay my face upon the pillow by her, and she looks into my eyes, and speaks very softly. Gradually, as she goes on, I feel, with a stricken heart, that she is speaking of herself as past.

"I am afraid, dear, I was too young. I don't mean in

years only, but in experience, and thoughts, and everything. I was such a silly little creature! I am afraid it would have been better, if we had only loved each other as a boy and girl, and forgotten it. I have begun to think I was not fit to be a wife."

I try to stay my tears, and to reply, "Oh, Dora, love, as fit as I to be a husband!"

"I don't know," with the old shake of her curls. "Perhaps! But, if I had been more fit to be married, I might have made you more so, too. Besides, you are very clever, and I never was."

"We have been very happy, my sweet Dora."

"I was very happy, very. But, as years went on, my dear boy would have wearied of his child-wife. She would have been less and less a companion for him. He would have been more and more sensible of what was wanting in his home. She wouldn't have improved. It is better as it is."

"Oh, Dora, dearest, dearest, do not speak to me so. Every word seems a reproach!"

"No, not a syllable!" she answers, kissing me. "Oh, my dear, you never deserved it, and I loved you far too well, to say a reproachful word to you, in earnest—it was all the merit I had, except being pretty—or you thought me so. Is it lonely, down-stairs, Doady?"

"Very! Very!"

"Don't cry! Is my chair there?"

"In its old place."

"Oh, how my poor boy cries! Hush, hush! Now, make me one promise. I want to speak to Agnes. When you go down-stairs, tell Agnes so, and send her up to me; and while I speak to her, let no one come—not even aunt. I want to speak to Agnes by herself. I want to speak to Agnes, quite alone."

I promise that she shall, immediately; but I cannot leave her, for my grief.

"I said that it was better as it is!" she whispers, as she holds me in her arms. "Oh, Doady, after more years, you never could have loved your child-wife better than you do; and, after more years, she would so have tried and disappointed you, that you might not have been able to love her half so well! I know I was too young and foolish. It is much better as it is!"

Agnes is down-stairs, when I go into the parlour; and I give her the message. She disappears, leaving me alone with Jip.

His Chinese house is by the fire; and he lies within it, on his bed of flannel, querulously trying to sleep. The bright moon is high and clear. As I look out on the night, my tears fall fast, and my undisciplined heart is chastened heavily —heavily.

I sit down by the fire, thinking with a blind remorse of all those secret feelings I have nourished since my marriage. I think of every little trifle between me and Dora, and feel the truth, that trifles make the sum of life. Ever rising from the sea of my remembrance, is the image of the dear child as I knew her first, graced by my young love, and by her own, with every fascination wherein such love is rich. Would it, indeed, have been better if we had loved each other as a boy and girl, and forgotten it? Undisciplined heart, reply!

How the time wears, I know not; until I am recalled by my child-wife's old companion. More restless than he was, he crawls out of his house, and looks at me, and wanders to the door, and whines to go up-stairs.

"Not to-night, Jip! Not to-night!"

He comes very slowly back to me, licks my hand, and lifts his dim eyes to my face.

"Oh, Jip! It may be, never again!"

He lies down at my feet, stretches himself out as if to sleep, and with a plaintive cry, is dead.

My Child-Wife's old Companion

"Oh, Agnes! Look, look, here!

—That face, so full of pity, and of grief, that rain of tears, that awful mute appeal to me, that solemn hand upraised towards Heaven!

"Agnes?"

It is over. Darkness comes before my eyes; and, for a time, all things are blotted out of my remembrance.

CHAPTER LIV.

THIS is not the time at which I am to enter on the state of my mind beneath its load of sorrow. I came to think that the Future was walled up before me, that the energy and action of my life were at an end, that I never could find any refuge but in the grave. I came to think so, I say, but not in the first shock of my grief. It slowly grew to that. If the events I go on to relate, had not thickened around me, in the beginning to confuse, and in the end to augment, my affliction, it is possible (though I think not probable), that I might have fallen at once into this condition. As it was, an interval occurred before I fully knew my own distress; an interval, in which I even supposed that its sharpest pangs were past; and when my mind could soothe itself by resting on all that was most innocent and beautiful, in the tender story that was closed for ever.

When it was first proposed that I should go abroad, or how it came to be agreed among us that I was to seek the restoration of my peace in change and travel, I do not, even now, distinctly know. The spirit of Agnes so pervaded all we thought, and said, and did, in that time of sorrow, that I assume I may refer the project to her influence. But her influence was so quiet that I know no more.

And now, indeed, I began to think that in my old association of her with the stained-glass window in the church, a

402

prophetic foreshadowing of what she would be to me, in the calamity that was to happen in the fulness of time, had found a way into my mind. In all that sorrow, from the moment, never to be forgotten, when she stood before me with her upraised hand, she was like a sacred presence in my lonely house. When the Angel of Death alighted there, my child-wife fell asleep—they told me so when I could bear to hear it—on her bosom, with a smile. From my swoon, I first awoke to a consciousness of her compassionate tears, her words of hope and peace, her gentle face bending down as from a purer region nearer Heaven, over my undisciplined heart, and softening its pain.

Let me go on.

I was to go abroad. That seemed to have been determined among us from the first. The ground now covering all that could perish of my departed wife, I waited only for what Mr. Micawber called the "final pulverisation of Heep," and for the departure of the emigrants.

At the request of Traddles, most affectionate and devoted of friends in my trouble, we returned to Canterbury: I mean my aunt, Agnes, and I. We proceeded by appointment straight to Mr. Micawber's house; where, and at Mr. Wickfield's, my friend had been labouring ever since our explosive meeting. When poor Mrs. Micawber saw me come in, in my black clothes, she was sensibly affected. There was a great deal of good in Mrs. Micawber's heart, which had not been dunned out of it in all those many years.

"Well, Mr. and Mrs. Micawber," was my aunt's first salutation after we were seated. "Pray, have you thought about that emigration proposal of mine?"

"My dear madam," returned Mr. Micawber, "perhaps I cannot better express the conclusion at which Mrs. Micawber, your humble servant, and I may add our children, have jointly and severally arrived, than by borrowing the language of an illustrious poet, to reply that our Boat is on the shore, and our Bark is on the sea."

"That's right," said my aunt. "I augur all sorts of good from your sensible decision."

"Madam, you do us a great deal of honour," he rejoined. He then referred to a memorandum. "With respect to the pecuniary assistance enabling us to launch our frail canoe on the ocean of enterprise, I have reconsidered that important business point; and would beg to propose my notes of hand —drawn, it is needless to stipulate, on stamps of the amounts respectively required by the various Acts of Parliament applying to such securities—at eighteen, twenty-four, and thirty months. The proposition I originally submitted, was twelve, eighteen, and twenty-four; but I am apprehensive that such an arrangement might not allow sufficient time for the requisite amount of—Something—to turn up. We might not," said Mr. Micawber, looking round the room as if it represented several hundred acres of highly cultivated land, "on the first responsibility becoming due, have been successful in our harvest, or we might not have got our harvest in. Labour, I believe, is sometimes difficult to obtain in that portion of our colonial possessions where it will be our lot to combat with the teeming soil."

"Arrange it in any way you please, sir," said my aunt.

"Madam," he replied, "Mrs. Micawber and myself are deeply sensible of the very considerate kindness of our friends and patrons. What I wish is, to be perfectly business-like, and perfectly punctual. Turning over, as we are about to turn over, an entirely new leaf; and falling back, as we are now in the act of falling back, for a Spring of no common magnitude; it is important to my sense of self-respect, besides being an example to my son, that these arrangements should be concluded as between man and man."

I don't know that Mr. Micawber attached any meaning to this last phrase; I don't know that anybody ever does, or did; but he appeared to relish it uncommonly, and repeated, with an impressive cough, "as between man and man."

"I propose," said Mr. Micawber, "Bills—a convenience to

the mercantile world, for which, I believe, we are originally indebted to the Jews, who appear to me to have had a devilish deal too much to do with them ever since—because they are negotiable. But if a Bond, or any other description of security, would be preferred, I should be happy to execute any such instrument. As between man and man."

My aunt observed, that in a case where both parties were willing to agree to anything, she took it for granted there would be no difficulty in settling this point. Mr. Micawber was of her opinion.

"In reference to our domestic preparations, madam," said Mr. Micawber, with some pride, "for meeting the destiny to which we are now understood to be self-devoted, I beg to report them. My eldest daughter attends at five every morning in a neighbouring establishment, to acquire the process—if process it may be called—of milking cows. My younger children are instructed to observe, as closely as circumstances will permit, the habits of the pigs and poultry maintained in the poorer parts of this city : a pursuit from which they have, on two occasions, been brought home, within an inch of being run over. I have myself directed some attention, during the past week, to the art of baking ; and my son Wilkins has issued forth with a walking-stick and driven cattle, when permitted, by the rugged hirelings who had them in charge, to render any voluntary service in that direction—which I regret to say, for the credit of our nature, was not often ; he being generally warned, with imprecations, to desist."

"All very right indeed," said my aunt, encouragingly. "Mrs. Micawber has been busy, too, I have no doubt."

"My dear madam," returned Mrs. Micawber, with her business-like air, "I am free to confess, that I have not been actively engaged in pursuits immediately connected with cultivation or with stock, though well aware that both will claim my attention on a foreign shore. Such opportunities as I have been enabled to alienate from my domestic duties,

I have devoted to corresponding at some length with my family. For I own it seems to me, my dear Mr. Copperfield," said Mrs. Micawber, who always fell back on me (I suppose from old habit) to whomsoever else she might address her discourse at starting, "that the time is come when the past should be buried in oblivion; when my family should take Mr. Micawber by the hand, and Mr. Micawber should take my family by the hand; when the lion should lie down with the lamb, and my family be on terms with Mr. Micawber."

I said I thought so too.

"This, at least, is the light, my dear Mr. Copperfield," pursued Mrs. Micawber, "in which *I* view the subject. When I lived at home with my papa and mama, my papa was accustomed to ask, when any point was under discussion in our limited circle, 'In what light does my Emma view the subject?' That my papa was too partial, I know; still, on such a point as the frigid coldness which has ever subsisted between Mr. Micawber and my family, I necessarily have formed an opinion, delusive though it may be."

"No doubt. Of course you have, ma'am," said my aunt.

"Precisely so," assented Mrs. Micawber. "Now, I may be wrong in my conclusions; it is very likely that I am; but my individual impression is, that the gulf between my family and Mr. Micawber may be traced to an apprehension, on the part of my family, that Mr. Micawber would require pecuniary accommodation. I cannot help thinking," said Mrs. Micawber, with an air of deep sagacity, "that there are members of my family who have been apprehensive that Mr. Micawber would solicit them for their names.—I do not mean to be conferred in Baptism upon our children, but to be inscribed on Bills of Exchange, and negotiated in the Money Market."

The look of penetration with which Mrs. Micawber announced this discovery, as if no one had ever thought of it before, seemed rather to astonish my aunt; who abruptly replied, " Well, ma'am, upon the whole, I shouldn't wonder if you were right!"

" Mr. Micawber being now on the eve of casting off the pecuniary shackles that have so long enthralled him," said Mrs. Micawber, " and of commencing a new career in a country where there is sufficient range for his abilities,—which, in my opinion, is exceedingly important; Mr. Micawber's abilities peculiarly requiring space,—it seems to me that my family should signalise the occasion by coming forward. What I could wish to see, would be a meeting between Mr. Micawber and my family at a festive entertainment, to be given at my family's expense; where Mr. Micawber's health and prosperity being proposed, by some leading member of my family, Mr. Micawber might have an opportunity of developing his views."

" My dear," said Mr. Micawber, with some heat, " it may be better for me to state distinctly, at once, that if I were to develop my views to that assembled group, they would possibly be found of an offensive nature; my impression being that your family are, in the aggregate, impertinent Snobs; and, in detail, unmitigated Ruffians."

" Micawber," said Mrs. Micawber, shaking her head, " no! You have never understood them, and they have never understood you."

Mr. Micawber coughed.

" They have never understood you, Micawber," said his wife. " They may be incapable of it. If so, that is their mis. fortune. I can pity their misfortune."

" I am extremely sorry, my dear Emma," said Mr. Micawber, relenting, " to have been betrayed into any expressions that might, even remotely, have the appearance of being strong expressions. All I would say, is, that I can go abroad without your family coming forward to favour me,—in short, with a parting Shove of their cold shoulders; and that, upon the whole, I would rather leave England with such impetus as I possess, than derive any acceleration of it from that

407

quarter. At the same time, my dear, if they should condescend to reply to your communications—which our joint experience renders most improbable—far be it from me to be a barrier to your wishes."

The matter being thus amicably settled, Mr. Micawber gave Mrs. Micawber his arm, and glancing at the heap of books and papers lying before Traddles on the table, said they would leave us to ourselves; which they ceremoniously did.

"My dear Copperfield," said Traddles, leaning back in his chair when they were gone, and looking at me with an affection that made his eyes red, and his hair all kinds of shapes, "I don't make any excuse for troubling you with business, because I know you are deeply interested in it, and it may divert your thoughts. My dear boy, I hope you are not worn out?

"I am quite myself," said I, after a pause. "We have more cause to think of my aunt than of any one. You know how much she has done."

"Surely, surely," answered Traddles. "Who can forget it!"

"But even that is not all," said I. "During the last fortnight, some new trouble has vexed her; and she has been in and out of London every day. Several times she has gone out early, and been absent until evening. Last night, Traddles, with this journey before her, it was almost midnight before she came home. You know what her consideration for others is. She will not tell me what has happened to distress her."

My aunt, very pale, and with deep lines in her face, sat immovable until I had finished; when some stray tears found their way to her cheeks, and she put her hand on mine.

"It's nothing, Trot; it's nothing. There will be no more of it. You shall know by and by. Now, Agnes, my dear, let us attend to these affairs."

"I must do Mr. Micawber the justice to say," Traddles began, "that although he would appear not to have worked to any good account for himself, he is a most untiring man when he works for other people. I never saw such a fellow. If he always goes on in the same way, he must be, virtually, about two hundred years old, at present. The heat into which he has been continually putting himself; and the distracted and impetuous manner in which he has been diving, day and night, among papers and books; to say nothing of the immense number of letters he has written me between this house and Mr. Wickfield's, and often across the table when he has been sitting opposite, and might much more easily have spoken; is quite extraordinary."

"Letters!" cried my aunt. "I believe he dreams in letters!"

"There's Mr. Dick, too," said Traddles, "has been doing wonders! As soon as he was released from overlooking Uriah Heep, whom he kept in such charge as *I* never saw exceeded, he began to devote himself to Mr. Wickfield. And really his anxiety to be of use in the investigations we have been making, and his real usefulness in extracting, and copying, and fetching, and carrying, have been quite stimulating to us."

"Dick is a very remarkable man," exclaimed my aunt; "and I always said he was. Trot, you know it."

"I am happy to say, Miss Wickfield," pursued Traddles, at once with great delicacy and with great earnestness, "that in your absence Mr. Wickfield has considerably improved. Relieved of the incubus that had fastened upon him for so long a time, and of the dreadful apprehensions under which he had lived, he is hardly the same person. At times, even his impaired power of concentrating his memory and attention on particular points of business, has recovered itself very much; and he has been able to assist us in making some things clear, that we should have found very difficult indeed, if not hopeless, without him. But, what I have to do is to come to results; which are short enough; not to gossip on all the hopeful circumstances I have observed, or I shall never have done."

409

His natural manner and agreeable simplicity made it transparent that he said this to put us in good heart, and to enable Agnes to hear her father mentioned with greater confidence ; but it was not the less pleasant for that.

"Now, let me see," said Traddles, looking among the papers on the table. " Having counted our funds, and reduced to order a great mass of unintentional confusion in the first place, and of wilful confusion and falsification in the second, we take it to be clear that Mr. Wickfield might now wind up his business, and his agency-trust, and exhibit no deficiency or defalcation whatever."

" Oh, thank Heaven !" cried Agnes, fervently.

" But," said Traddles, " the surplus that would be left as his means of support—and I suppose the house to be sold, even in saying this—would be so small, not exceeding in all probability some hundreds of pounds, that perhaps, Miss Wickfield, it would be best to consider whether he might not retain his agency of the estate to which he has so long been receiver. His friends might advise him, you know ; now he is free. You yourself, Miss Wickfield—Copperfield—I— "

" I have considered it, Trotwood," said Agnes, looking to me, " and I feel that it ought not to be, and must not be ; even on the recommendation of a friend to whom I am so grateful, and owe so much."

" I will not say that I recommend it," observed Traddles. " I think it right to suggest it. No more."

" I am happy to hear you say so," answered Agnes, steadily, " for it gives me hope, almost assurance, that we think alike. Dear Mr. Traddles and dear Trotwood, papa once free with honour, what could I wish for ! I have always aspired, if I could have released him from the toils in which he was held, to render back some little portion of the love and care I owe him, and to devote my life to him. It has been, for years, the utmost height of my hopes. To take our future on myself, will be the next great happiness

—the next to his release from all trust and responsibility—
that I can know."

" Have you thought how, Agnes ? "

" Often ! I am not afraid, dear Trotwood. I am certain
of success. So many people know me here, and think kindly
of me, that I am certain. Don't mistrust me. Our wants
are not many. If I rent the dear old house, and keep a
school, I shall be useful and happy."

The calm fervour of her cheerful voice brought back so
vividly, first the dear old house itself, and then my solitary
home, that my heart was too full for speech. Traddles pretended for a little while to be busily looking among the
papers.

" Next, Miss Trotwood," said Traddles, " that property of
yours."

" Well, sir," sighed my aunt. " All I have got to say
about it, is, that if it's gone, I can bear it ; and if it's not
gone, I shall be glad to get it back."

" It was originally, I think, eight thousand pounds,
Consols ? " said Traddles.

" Right ! " replied my aunt.

" I can't account for more than five," said Traddles, with
an air of perplexity.

" —thousand, do you mean ? " inquired my aunt, with
uncommon composure, " or pounds ? "

" Five thousand pounds," said Traddles.

" It was all there was," returned my aunt. " I sold three,
myself. One, I paid for your articles, Trot, my dear ; and
the other two I have by me. When I lost the rest, I
thought it wise to say nothing about that sum, but to keep
it secretly for a rainy day. I wanted to see how you would
come out of the trial, Trot ; and you came out nobly—
persevering, self-reliant, self-denying ! So did Dick. Don't
speak to me, for I find my nerves a little shaken ! "

Nobody would have thought so, to see her sitting upright,
with her arms folded ; but she had wonderful self-command.

411

"Then I am delighted to say," cried Traddles, beaming with joy, "that we have recovered the whole money!"

"Don't congratulate me, anybody!" exclaimed my aunt. "How so, sir?"

"You believed it had been misappropriated by Mr. Wickfield?" said Traddles.

"Of course I did," said my aunt, "and was therefore easily silenced. Agnes, not a word!"

"And indeed," said Traddles, "it was sold, by virtue of the power of management he held from you; but I needn't say by whom sold, or on whose actual signature. It was afterwards pretended to Mr. Wickfield, by that rascal,—and proved, too, by figures,—that he had possessed himself of the money (on general instructions, *he* said) to keep other deficiencies and difficulties from the light. Mr. Wickfield, being so weak and helpless in his hands as to pay you, afterwards, several sums of interest on a pretended principal which he knew did not exist, made himself, unhappily, a party to the fraud."

"And at last took the blame upon himself," added my aunt; "and wrote me a mad letter, charging himself with robbery, and wrong unheard of. Upon which I paid him a visit early one morning, called for a candle, burnt the letter, and told him if he ever could right me and himself, to do it; and if he couldn't, to keep his own counsel for his daughter's sake.—If anybody speaks to me, I'll leave the house!"

We all remained quiet; Agnes covering her face.

"Well, my dear friend," said my aunt, after a pause, "and you have really extorted the money back from him?"

"Why, the fact is," returned Traddles, "Mr. Micawber had so completely hemmed him in, and was always ready with so many new points if an old one failed, that he could not escape from us. A most remarkable circumstance is, that I really don't think he grasped this sum even so much for the gratification of his avarice, which was inordinate, as in the hatred he felt for Copperfield. He said so to me, plainly. He said he would even have spent as much, to baulk or injure Copperfield."

"Ha!" said my aunt, knitting her brows thoughtfully, and glancing at Agnes. "And what's become of him?"

"I don't know. He left here," said Traddles, "with his mother, who had been clamouring, and beseeching, and disclosing, the whole time. They went away by one of the London night coaches, and I know no more about him; except that his malevolence to me at parting was audacious. He seemed to consider himself hardly less indebted to me, than to Mr. Micawber; which I consider (as I told him) quite a compliment."

"Do you suppose he has any money, Traddles?" I asked.

"Oh dear, yes, I should think so," he replied, shaking his head, seriously. "I should say he must have pocketed a good deal, in one way or other. But, I think you would find, Copperfield, if you had an opportunity of observing his course, that money would never keep that man out of mischief. He is such an incarnate hypocrite, that whatever object he pursues, he must pursue crookedly. It's his only compensation for the outward restraints he puts upon himself. Always creeping along the ground to some small end or other, he will always magnify every object in the way; and consequently will hate and suspect everybody that comes, in the most innocent manner, between him and it. So, the crooked courses will become crookeder, at any moment, for the least reason, or for none. It's only necessary to consider his history here," said Traddles, "to know that."

"He's a monster of meanness!" said my aunt.

"Really I don't know about that," observed Traddles, thoughtfully. "Many people can be very mean, when they give their minds to it."

"And now, touching Mr. Micawber," said my aunt.

"Well, really," said Traddles, cheerfully, "I must, once more, give Mr. Micawber high praise. But for his having

413

been so patient and persevering for so long a time, we never could have hoped to do anything worth speaking of. And I think we ought to consider that Mr. Micawber did right, for right's sake, when we reflect what terms he might have made with Uriah Heep himself, for his silence."

"I think so too," said I.

"Now, what would you give him?" inquired my aunt.

"Oh! Before you come to that," said Traddles, a little disconcerted, "I am afraid I thought it discreet to omit (not being able to carry everything before me) two points, in making this lawless adjustment—for it's perfectly lawless from beginning to end—of a difficult affair. Those I. O. U.'s, and so forth, which Mr. Micawber gave him for the advances he had—"

"Well! They must be paid," said my aunt.

"Yes, but I don't know when they may be proceeded on, or where they are," rejoined Traddles, opening his eyes; "and I anticipate, that, between this time and his departure, Mr. Micawber will be constantly arrested, or taken in execution."

"Then he must be constantly set free again, and taken out of execution," said my aunt. "What's the amount altogether?"

"Why, Mr. Micawber has entered the transactions—he calls them transactions—with great form, in a book," rejoined Traddles, smiling; "and he makes the amount a hundred and three pounds, five."

"Now, what shall we give him, that sum included?" said my aunt. "Agnes, my dear, you and I can talk about division of it afterwards. What should it be? Five hundred pounds?"

Upon this, Traddles and I both struck in at once. We both recommended a small sum in money, and the payment, without stipulation to Mr. Micawber, of the Uriah claims as they came in. We proposed that the family should have their passage and their outfit, and a hundred pounds; and

414

that Mr. Micawber's arrangement for the repayment of the advances should be gravely entered into, as it might be wholesome for him to suppose himself under that responsibility. To this, I added the suggestion, that I should give some explanation of his character and history to Mr. Peggotty, who I knew could be relied on; and that to Mr. Peggotty should be quietly entrusted the discretion of advancing another hundred. I further proposed to interest Mr. Micawber in Mr. Peggotty, by confiding so much of Mr. Peggotty's story to him as I might feel justified in relating, or might think expedient; and to endeavour to bring each of them to bear upon the other, for the common advantage. We all entered warmly into these views; and I may mention at once, that the principals themselves did so, shortly afterwards, with perfect good will and harmony.

Seeing that Traddles now glanced anxiously at my aunt again, I reminded him of the second and last point to which he had adverted.

"You and your aunt will excuse me, Copperfield, if I touch upon a painful theme, as I greatly fear I shall," said Traddles, hesitating; "but I think it necessary to bring it to your recollection. On the day of Mr. Micawber's memorable denunciation, a threatening allusion was made by Uriah Heep to your aunt's—husband."

My aunt, retaining her stiff position, and apparent composure, assented with a nod.

"Perhaps," observed Traddles, "it was mere purposeless impertinence?"

"No," returned my aunt.

"There was—pardon me—really such a person, and at all in his power?" hinted Traddles.

"Yes, my good friend," said my aunt.

Traddles, with a perceptible lengthening of his face, explained that he had not been able to approach this subject; that it had shared the fate of Mr. Micawber's liabilities, in not being comprehended in the terms he had made; that we were no longer of any authority with Uriah Heep; and that if he could do us, or any of us, any injury or annoyance, no doubt he would.

My aunt remained quiet; until again some stray tears found their way to her cheeks.

"You are quite right," she said. "It was very thoughtful to mention it."

"Can I—or Copperfield—do anything?" asked Traddles, gently.

"Nothing," said my aunt. "I thank you many times. Trot, my dear, a vain threat! Let us have Mr. and Mrs. Micawber back. And don't any of you speak to me!" With that she smoothed her dress, and sat, with her upright carriage, looking at the door.

"Well, Mr. and Mrs. Micawber!" said my aunt, when they entered. "We have been discussing your emigration, with many apologies to you for keeping you out of the room so long; and I'll tell you what arrangements we propose."

These she explained to the unbounded satisfaction of the family,—children and all being then present,—and so much to the awakening of Mr. Micawber's punctual habits in the opening stage of all bill transactions, that he could not be dissuaded from immediately rushing out, in the highest spirits, to buy the stamps for his notes of hand. But, his joy received a sudden check; for within five minutes, he returned in the custody of a sheriff's officer, informing us, in a flood of tears, that all was lost. We, being quite prepared for this event, which was of course a proceeding of Uriah Heep's, soon paid the money; and in five minutes more Mr. Micawber was seated at the table, filling up the stamps with an expression of perfect joy, which only that congenial employment, or the making of punch, could impart in full completeness to his shining face. To see him at work on the stamps, with the relish of an artist, touching them like pictures, looking at them sideways, taking weighty notes of dates and amounts in his pocket-book, and contemplating them when finished, with a high sense of their precious value, was a sight indeed.

"Now, the best thing you can do, sir, if you'll allow me to advise you," said my aunt, after silently observing him, "is to abjure that occupation for evermore."

"Madam," replied Mr. Micawber, "it is my intention to register such a vow on the virgin page of the future. Mrs. Micawber will attest it. I trust," said Mr. Micawber, solemnly, "that my son Wilkins will ever bear in mind, that he had infinitely better put his fist in the fire, than use it to handle the serpents that have poisoned the life-blood of his unhappy parent!" Deeply affected, and changed in a moment to the image of despair, Mr. Micawber regarded the serpents with a look of gloomy abhorrence (in which his late admiration of them was not quite subdued), folded them up and put them in his pocket.

This closed the proceedings of the evening. We were weary with sorrow and fatigue, and my aunt and I were to return to London on the morrow. It was arranged that the Micawbers should follow us, after effecting a sale of their goods to a broker; that Mr. Wickfield's affairs should be brought to a settlement, with all convenient speed, under the direction of Traddles; and that Agnes should also come to London, pending those arrangements. We passed the night at the old house, which, freed from the presence of the Heeps, seemed purged of a disease; and I lay in my old room, like a shipwrecked wanderer come home.

We went back next day to my aunt's house—not to mine; and when she and I sat alone, as of old, before going to bed, she said:

"Trot, do you really wish to know what I have had upon my mind lately?"

"Indeed I do, aunt. If there ever was a time when I felt unwilling that you should have a sorrow or anxiety which I could not share, it is now."

"You have had sorrow enough, child," said my aunt, affectionately, "without the addition of *my* little miseries. I could have no other motive, Trot, in keeping anything from you."

"I know that well," said I. "But tell me now."

"Would you ride with me a little way to-morrow morning?" asked my aunt.

"Of course."

"At nine," said she. "I'll tell you then, my dear."

At nine, accordingly, we went out in a little chariot, and drove to London. We drove a long way through the streets until we came to one of the large hospitals. Standing hard by the building was a plain hearse. The driver recognised my aunt, and in obedience to a motion of her hand at the window, drove slowly off; we following.

"You understand it now, Trot," said my aunt. "He is gone!"

"Did he die in the hospital?"

"Yes."

She sat immovable beside me; but, again I saw the stray tears on her face.

"He was there once before," said my aunt presently. "He was ailing a long time—a shattered, broken man, these many years. When he knew his state in this last illness, he asked them to send for me. He was sorry then. Very sorry."

"You went, I know, aunt."

"I went. I was with him a good deal afterwards."

"He died the night before we went to Canterbury?" said I.

My aunt nodded. "No one can harm him now," she said. "It was a vain threat."

We drove away, out of town, to the churchyard at Hornsey. "Better here than in the streets," said my aunt. "He was born here."

We alighted; and followed the plain coffin to a corner I

remember well, where the service was read consigning it to the dust.

"Six-and-thirty years ago, this day, my dear," said my aunt, as we walked back to the chariot, "I was married. God forgive us all!"

We took our seats in silence; and so she sat beside me for a long time, holding my hand. At length she suddenly burst into tears, and said:

"He was a fine-looking man when I married him, Trot— and he was sadly changed!"

It did not last long. After the relief of tears, she soon became composed, and even cheerful. Her nerves were a little shaken, she said, or she would not have given way to it. God forgive us all!

So we rode back to her little cottage at Highgate, where we found the following short note, which had arrived by that morning's post from Mr. Micawber:

> "Canterbury,
> "Friday.

"My dear Madam, and Copperfield,

"The fair land of promise lately looming on the horizon is again enveloped in impenetrable mists, and for ever withdrawn from the eyes of a drifting wretch whose Doom is sealed!

"Another writ has been issued (in His Majesty's High Court of King's Bench at Westminster), in another cause of HEEP v. MICAWBER, and the defendant in that cause is the prey of the sheriff having legal jurisdiction in this bailiwick.

> "'Now's the day, and now's the hour,
> See the front of battle lower,
> See approach proud EDWARD'S power—
> Chains and slavery!'

Consigned to which, and to a speedy end (for mental torture is not supportable beyond a certain point, and that point I feel I have attained), my course is run. Bless you, bless you!

Some future traveller, visiting, from motives of curiosity, not unmingled, let us hope, with sympathy, the place of confinement allotted to debtors in this city, may, and I trust will, Ponder, as he traces on its wall, inscribed with a rusty nail,

> " The obscure initials
>> " W. M.

"P.S. I re-open this to say that our common friend, Mr. Thomas Traddles (who has not yet left us, and is looking extremely well), has paid the debt and costs, in the noble name of Miss Trotwood; and that myself and family are at the height of earthly bliss."

CHAPTER LV.

I now approach an event in my life, so indelible, so awful, so bound by an infinite variety of ties to all that has preceded it, in these pages, that, from the beginning of my narrative, I have seen it growing larger and larger as I advanced, like a great tower in a plain, and throwing its fore-cast shadow even on the incidents of my childish days.

For years after it occurred, I dreamed of it often. I have started up so vividly impressed by it, that its fury has yet seemed raging in my quiet room, in the still night. I dream of it sometimes, though at lengthened and uncertain intervals, to this hour. I have an association between it and a stormy wind, or the lightest mention of a sea-shore, as strong as any of which my mind is conscious. As plainly as I behold what happened, I will try to write it down. I do not recall it, but see it done; for it happens again before me.

The time drawing on rapidly for the sailing of the emigrant-ship, my good old nurse (almost broken-hearted for me, when we first met) came up to London. I was constantly with her, and her brother, and the Micawbers (they being very much together); but Emily I never saw.

One evening when the time was close at hand, I was alone with Peggotty and her brother. Our conversation turned on Ham. She described to us how tenderly he had taken leave of her, and how manfully and quietly he had borne himself.

421

Most of all, of late, when she believed he was most tried. It was a subject of which the affectionate creature never tired; and our interest in hearing the many examples which she, who was so much with him, had to relate, was equal to hers in relating them.

My aunt and I were at that time vacating the two cottages at Highgate; I intending to go abroad, and she to return to her house at Dover. We had a temporary lodging in Covent Garden. As I walked home to it, after this evening's conversation, reflecting on what had passed between Ham and myself when I was last at Yarmouth, I wavered in the original purpose I had formed, of leaving a letter for Emily when I should take leave of her uncle on board the ship, and thought it would be better to write to her now. She might desire, I thought, after receiving my communication, to send some parting word by me to her unhappy lover. I ought to give her the opportunity.

I therefore sat down in my room, before going to bed, and wrote to her. I told her that I had seen him, and that he had requested me to tell her what I have already written in its place in these sheets. I faithfully repeated it. I had no need to enlarge upon it, if I had had the right. Its deep fidelity and goodness were not to be adorned by me or any man. I left it out, to be sent round in the morning; with a line to Mr. Peggotty, requesting him to give it to her; and went to bed at day-break.

I was weaker than I knew then; and, not falling asleep until the sun was up, lay late, and unrefreshed, next day. I was roused by the silent presence of my aunt at my bedside. I felt it in my sleep, as I suppose we all do feel such things.

"Trot, my dear," she said, when I opened my eyes, "I couldn't make up my mind to disturb you. Mr. Peggotty is here; shall he come up?"

I replied yes, and he soon appeared.

"Mas'r Davy," he said, when we had shaken hands, "I

giv Em'ly your letter, sir, and she writ this heer; and begged of me fur to ask you to read it, and if you see no hurt in't, to be so kind as take charge on't."

"Have you read it?" said I.

He nodded sorrowfully. I opened it, and read as follows:

"I have got your message. Oh, what can I write, to thank you for your good and blessed kindness to me!

"I have put the words close to my heart. I shall keep them till I die. They are sharp thorns, but they are such comfort. I have prayed over them, oh, I have prayed so much. When I find what you are, and what uncle is, I think what God must be, and can cry to him.

"Good-bye for ever. Now, my dear, my friend, good-bye for ever in this world. In another world, if I am forgiven, I may wake a child and come to you. All thanks and blessings. Farewell, evermore."

This, blotted with tears, was the letter.

"May I tell her as you doen't see no hurt in't, and as you'll be so kind as take charge on't, Mas'r Davy?" said Mr. Peggotty, when I had read it.

"Unquestionably," said I—"but I am thinking—"

"Yes, Mas'r Davy?"

"I am thinking," said I, "that I'll go down again to Yarmouth. There's time, and to spare, for me to go and come back before the ship sails. My mind is constantly running on him, in his solitude; to put this letter of her writing in his hand at this time, and to enable you to tell her, in the moment of parting, that he has got it, will be a kindness to both of them. I solemnly accepted his commission, dear good fellow, and cannot discharge it too completely. The journey is nothing to me. I am restless, and shall be better in motion. I'll go down to-night."

Though he anxiously endeavoured to dissuade me, I saw that he was of my mind; and this, if I had required to be confirmed in my intention, would have had the effect. He went round to the coach-office, at my request, and took the box-seat for me on the mail. In the evening I started, by that conveyance, down the road I had traversed under so many vicissitudes.

"Don't you think that," I asked the coachman, in the first

stage out of London, "a very remarkable sky? I don't remember to have seen one like it."

"Nor I—not equal to it," he replied. "That's wind, sir. There'll be mischief done at sea, I expect, before long."

It was a murky confusion—here and there blotted with a colour like the colour of the smoke from damp fuel—of flying clouds tossed up into most remarkable heaps, suggesting greater heights in the clouds than there were depths below them to the bottom of the deepest hollows in the earth, through which the wild moon seemed to plunge headlong, as if, in a dread disturbance of the laws of nature, she had lost her way and were frightened. There had been a wind all day; and it was rising then, with an extraordinary great sound. In another hour it had much increased, and the sky was more overcast, and blew hard.

But as the night advanced, the clouds closing in and densely overspreading the whole sky, then very dark, it came on to blow, harder and harder. It still increased, until our horses could scarcely face the wind. Many times, in the dark part of the night (it was then late in September, when the nights were not short), the leaders turned about, or came to a dead stop; and we were often in serious apprehension that the coach would be blown over. Sweeping gusts of rain came up before this storm, like showers of steel; and, at those times, when there was any shelter of trees or lee walls to be got, we were fain to stop, in a sheer impossibility of continuing the struggle.

When the day broke, it blew harder and harder. I had been in Yarmouth when the seamen said it blew great guns, but I had never known the like of this, or anything approaching to it. We came to Ipswich—very late, having had to fight every inch of ground since we were ten miles out of London; and found a cluster of people in the market-place, who had risen from their beds in the night, fearful of falling chimneys. Some of these, congregating about the inn-yard while we changed horses, told us of great sheets of lead having been ripped off a high church-tower, and flung into a bye-street, which they then blocked up. Others had to tell of country people, coming in from neighbouring villages, who had seen great trees lying torn out of the earth, and whole ricks scattered about the roads and fields. Still, there was no abatement in the storm, but it blew harder.

As we struggled on, nearer and nearer to the sea, from which this mighty wind was blowing dead on shore, its force became more and more terrific. Long before we saw the sea, its spray was on our lips, and showered salt rain upon us. The water was out, over miles and miles of the flat country adjacent to Yarmouth; and every sheet and puddle lashed its banks, and had its stress of little breakers setting heavily towards us. When we came within sight of the sea, the waves on the horizon, caught at intervals above the rolling abyss, were like glimpses of another shore with towers and buildings. When at last we got into the town, the people came out to their doors, all aslant, and with streaming hair, making a wonder of the mail that had come through such a night.

I put up at the old inn, and went down to look at the sea; staggering along the street, which was strewn with sand and seaweed, and with flying blotches of sea-foam; afraid of falling slates and tiles; and holding by people I met, at angry corners. Coming near the beach, I saw, not only the boatmen, but half the people of the town, lurking behind buildings; some, now and then braving the fury of the storm to look away to sea, and blown sheer out of their course in trying to get zigzag back.

Joining these groups, I found bewailing women whose husbands were away in herring or oyster boats, which there was too much reason to think might have foundered before they could run in anywhere for safety. Grizzled old sailors were among the people, shaking their heads, as they looked from water to sky, and muttering to one another; ship-owners, excited and uneasy; children, huddling together, and peering into older faces; even stout mariners, disturbed and anxious, levelling their glasses at the sea from behind places of shelter, as if they were surveying an enemy.

The tremendous sea itself, when I could find sufficient pause to look at it, in the agitation of the blinding wind, the flying stones and sand, and the awful noise, confounded me. As the high watery walls came rolling in, and, at their highest, tumbled into surf, they looked as if the least would engulf the town. As the receding wave swept back with a hoarse roar, it seemed to scoop out deep caves in the beach, as if its purpose were to undermine the earth. When some white-headed billows thundered on, and dashed themselves to pieces before they reached the land, every fragment of the late whole seemed possessed by the full might of its wrath, rushing to be gathered to the composition of another monster. Undulating hills were changed to valleys, undulating valleys (with a solitary storm-bird sometimes skimming through them) were lifted up to hills ; masses of water shivered and shook the beach with a booming sound ; every shape tumultuously rolled on, as soon as made, to change its shape and place, and beat another shape and place away ; the ideal shore on the horizon, with its towers and buildings, rose and fell ; the clouds fell fast and thick ; I seemed to see a rending and upheaving of all nature.

Not finding Ham among the people whom this memorable wind—for it is still remembered down there, as the greatest ever known to blow upon that coast—had brought together, I made my way to his house. It was shut; and as no one answered to my knocking, I went, by back ways and bye-lanes, to the yard where he worked. I learned, there, that he had gone to Lowestoft, to meet some sudden exigency of ship-repairing in which his skill was required ; but that he would be back to-morrow morning, in good time.

I went back to the inn; and when I had washed and dressed, and tried to sleep, but in vain, it was five o'clock in the afternoon. I had not sat five minutes by the coffee-room fire, when the waiter coming to stir it, as an excuse for talking, told me that two colliers had gone down, with all hands, a few miles away; and that some other ships had been seen labouring hard in the Roads, and trying, in great distress, to keep off shore. Mercy on them, and on all poor sailors, said he, if we had another night like the last!

I was very much depressed in spirits; very solitary; and felt an uneasiness in Ham's not being there, disproportionate to the occasion. I was seriously affected, without knowing how much, by late events; and my long exposure to the fierce wind had confused me. There was that jumble in my thoughts and recollections, that I had lost the clear arrangement of time and distance. Thus, if I had gone out into the town, I should not have been surprised, I think, to encounter some one who I knew must be then in London. So to speak, there was in these respects a curious inattention in my mind. Yet it was busy, too, with all the remembrances the place naturally awakened; and they were particularly distinct and vivid.

In this state, the waiter's dismal intelligence about the ships immediately connected itself, without any effort of my volition, with my uneasiness about Ham. I was persuaded that I had an apprehension of his returning from Lowestoft by sea, and being lost. This grew so strong with me, that I resolved to go back to the yard before I took my dinner, and ask the boat-builder if he thought his attempting to return by sea at all likely? If he gave me the least reason to think so, I would go over to Lowestoft and prevent it by bringing him with me.

I hastily ordered my dinner, and went back to the yard. I was none too soon; for the boat-builder, with a lantern in his hand, was locking the yard-gate. He quite laughed when I asked him the question, and said there was no fear; no man in his senses, or out of them, would put off in such a gale of wind, least of all Ham Peggotty, who had been born to seafaring.

So sensible of this, beforehand, that I had really felt ashamed of doing what I was nevertheless impelled to do, I went back to the inn. If such a wind could rise, I think it was rising. The howl and roar, the rattling of the doors and windows, the rumbling in the chimneys, the apparent rocking of the very house that sheltered me, and the prodigious tumult of the sea, were more fearful than in the morning. But there was now a great darkness besides; and that invested the storm with new terrors, real and fanciful.

I could not eat, I could not sit still, I could not continue stedfast to anything. Something within me, faintly answering to the storm without, tossed up the depths of my memory and made a tumult in them. Yet, in all the hurry of my thoughts, wild running with the thundering sea,—the storm and my uneasiness regarding Ham, were always in the foreground.

My dinner went away almost untasted, and I tried to refresh myself with a glass or two of wine. In vain. I fell into a dull slumber before the fire, without losing my consciousness, either of the uproar out of doors, or of the place in which I was. Both became overshadowed by a new and indefinable horror; and when I awoke—or rather when I shook off the lethargy that bound me in my chair—my whole frame thrilled with objectless and unintelligible fear.

I walked to and fro, tried to read an old gazetteer, listened to the awful noises : looked at faces, scenes, and figures in the fire. At length, the steady ticking of the undisturbed clock on the wall, tormented me to that degree that I resolved to go to bed.

It was reassuring, on such a night, to be told that some of the inn-servants had agreed together to sit up until morning. I went to bed, exceedingly weary and heavy; but, on my lying down, all such sensations vanished, as if by magic, and I was broad awake, with every sense refined.

For hours I lay there, listening to the wind and water; imagining, now, that I heard shrieks out at sea; now, that I distinctly heard the firing of signal guns; and now, the fall of houses in the town. I got up, several times, and looked out; but could see nothing, except the reflection in the window-panes of the faint candle I had left burning, and of my own haggard face looking in at me from the black void.

At length, my restlessness attained to such a pitch, that I hurried on my clothes, and went down-stairs. In the large kitchen, where I dimly saw bacon and ropes of onions hanging from the beams, the watchers were clustered together, in various attitudes, about a table, purposely moved away from the great chimney, and brought near the door. A pretty girl, who had her ears stopped with her apron, and her eyes upon the door, screamed when I appeared, supposing me to be a spirit; but the others had more presence of mind, and were glad of an addition to their company. One man, referring to the topic they had been discussing, asked me whether I thought the souls of the collier-crews who had gone down, were out in the storm?

I remained there, I dare say, two hours. Once, I opened the yard-gate, and looked into the empty street. The sand, the seaweed, and the flakes of foam, were driving by; and I was obliged to call for assistance before I could shut the gate again, and make it fast against the wind.

There was a dark gloom in my solitary chamber, when I at length returned to it; but I was tired now, and, getting into bed again, fell—off a tower and down a precipice—into the depths of sleep. I have an impression that for a long time, though I dreamed of being elsewhere and in a variety of scenes, it was always blowing in my dream. At length, I lost that feeble hold upon reality, and was engaged with two dear friends, but who they were I don't know, at the siege of some town in a roar of cannonading.

The thunder of the cannon was so loud and incessant, that I could not hear something I much desired to hear, until I made a great exertion and awoke. It was broad day—eight or nine o'clock; the storm raging, in lieu of the batteries; and some one knocking and calling at my door.

" What is the matter ? " I cried.

" A wreck ! Close by ! "

I sprung out of bed, and asked, what wreck ?

" A schooner, from Spain or Portugal, laden with fruit and wine. Make haste, sir, if you want to see her ! It's thought, down on the beach, she'll go to pieces every moment."

The excited voice went clamouring along the staircase; and I wrapped myself in my clothes as quickly as I could, and ran into the street.

Numbers of people were there before me, all running in one direction, to the beach. I ran the same way, outstripping a good many, and soon came facing the wild sea.

The wind might by this time have lulled a little, though not more sensibly than if the cannonading I had dreamed of, had been diminished by the silencing of half-a-dozen guns out of hundreds. But, the sea, having upon it the additional agitation of the whole night, was infinitely more terrific than when I had seen it last. Every appearance it had then presented, bore the expression of being *swelled* ; and the height to which the breakers rose, and, looking over one another, bore one another down, and rolled in, in interminable hosts, was most appalling.

In the difficulty of hearing anything but wind and waves, and in the crowd, and the unspeakable confusion, and my first breathless efforts to stand against the weather, I was so confused that I looked out to sea for the wreck, and saw nothing but the foaming heads of the great waves. A half-dressed boatman, standing next me, pointed with his bare arm (a tattoo'd arrow on it, pointing in the same direction) to the left. Then, O great Heaven, I saw it, close in upon us !

One mast was broken short off, six or eight feet from the deck, and lay over the side, entangled in a maze of sail and rigging ; and all that ruin, as the ship rolled and beat—which she did without a moment's pause, and with a violence quite inconceivable—beat the side as if it would stave it in. Some efforts were even then being made, to cut this portion of the wreck away; for, as the ship, which was broadside on, turned towards us in her rolling, I plainly descried her people at work with axes, especially one active figure with long curling hair, conspicuous among the rest. But, a great cry, which was audible even above the wind and water, rose from the shore at this moment; the sea, sweeping over the rolling wreck, made a clean breach, and carried men, spars, casks, planks, bulwarks, heaps of such toys, into the boiling surge.

The second mast was yet standing, with the rags of a rent sail, and a wild confusion of broken cordage flapping to and fro. The ship had struck once, the same boatman hoarsely said in my ear, and then lifted in and struck again. I understood him to add that she was parting amidships, and I could readily suppose so, for the rolling and beating were too tremendous for any human work to suffer long. As he spoke, there was another great cry of pity from the beach; four men arose with the wreck out of the deep, clinging to the rigging of the remaining mast; uppermost, the active figure with the curling hair.

There was a bell on board; and as the ship rolled and dashed, like a desperate creature driven mad, now showing us the whole sweep of her deck, as she turned on her beam-ends towards the shore, now nothing but her keel, as she sprung wildly over and turned towards the sea, the bell rang; and its sound, the knell of those unhappy men, was borne towards us on the wind. Again we lost her, and again she rose. Two men were gone. The agony on shore increased. Men groaned, and clasped their hands; women shrieked, and turned away their faces. Some ran wildly up and down along the beach, crying for help where no help could be. I found myself one of these, frantically imploring a knot of sailors whom I knew, not to let those two lost creatures perish before our eyes.

They were making out to me, in an agitated way—I don't know how, for the little I could hear I was scarcely composed enough to understand—that the lifeboat had been bravely manned an hour ago, and could do nothing; and that as no man would be so desperate as to attempt to wade off with a rope, and establish a communication with the shore, there was nothing left to try; when I noticed that some new sensation moved the people on the beach, and saw them part, and Ham come breaking through them to the front.

I ran to him—as well as I know, to repeat my appeal for help. But, distracted though I was, by a sight so new to me and terrible, the determination in his face, and his look, out to sea—exactly the same look as I remembered in connexion with the morning after Emily's flight—awoke me to a knowledge of his danger. I held him back with both arms; and implored the men with whom I had been speaking, not to listen to him, not to do murder, not to let him stir from off that sand!

Another cry arose on shore; and looking to the wreck, we saw the cruel sail, with blow on blow, beat off the lower of the two men, and fly up in triumph round the active figure left alone upon the mast.

Against such a sight, and against such determination as that of the calmly desperate man who was already accustomed to lead half the people present, I might as hopefully have entreated the wind. "Mas'r Davy," he said, cheerily grasping me by both hands, "if my time is come, 'tis come. If 'tan't, I'll bide it. Lord above bless you, and bless all! Mates, make me ready! I'm a going off!"

I was swept away, but not unkindly, to some distance, where the people around me made me stay; urging, as I confusedly perceived, that he was bent on going, with help or without, and that I should endanger the precautions for his safety by troubling those with whom they rested. I don't know what I answered, or what they rejoined; but, I saw hurry on the beach, and men running with ropes from a capstan that was there, and penetrating into a circle of figures that hid him from me. Then, I saw him standing alone, in a seaman's frock and trowsers: a rope in his hand, or slung to his wrist: another round his body: and several of the best men holding, at a little distance, to the latter, which he laid out himself, slack upon the shore, at his feet.

The wreck, even to my unpractised eye, was breaking up. I saw that she was parting in the middle, and that the life of the solitary man upon the mast hung by a thread. Still, he clung to it. He had a singular red cap on,—not like a sailor's cap, but of a finer colour; and as the few yielding planks between him and destruction rolled and bulged, and his anticipative death-knell rung, he was seen by all of us to wave it. I saw him do it now, and thought I was going distracted, when his action brought an old remembrance to my mind of a once dear friend.

Ham watched the sea, standing alone, with the silence of suspended breath behind him, and the storm before, until there was a great retiring wave, when, with a backward glance at those who held the rope which was made fast round his body, he dashed in after it, and in a moment was buffetting with the water; rising with the hills, falling with the valleys, lost beneath the foam; then drawn again to land. They hauled in hastily.

He was hurt. I saw blood on his face, from where I stood; but he took no thought of that. He seemed hurriedly to give them some directions for leaving him more free—or so I judged from the motion of his arm—and was gone as before.

And now he made for the wreck,· rising with the hills, falling with the valleys, lost beneath the rugged foam, borne in towards the shore, borne on towards the ship, striving hard and valiantly. The distance was nothing, but the power of the sea and wind made the strife deadly. At length he neared the wreck. He was so near, that with one more of his vigorous strokes he would be clinging to it,—when, a high, green, vast hill-side of water, moving on shoreward, from beyond the ship, he seemed to leap up into it with a mighty bound, and the ship was gone !

Some eddying fragments I saw in the sea, as if a mere cask had been broken, in running to the spot where they were hauling in. Consternation was in every face. They drew him to my very feet—insensible—dead. He was carried to the nearest house; and, no one preventing me now, I remained near him, busy, while every means of restoration were tried; but he had been beaten to death by the great wave, and his generous heart was stilled for ever.

As I sat beside the bed, when hope was abandoned and all was done, a fisherman, who had known me when Emily and I were children, and ever since, whispered my name at the door.

"Sir," said he, with tears starting to his weather-beaten face, which, with his trembling lips, was ashy pale, "will you come over yonder?"

The old remembrance that had been recalled to me, was in his look. I asked him, terror-stricken, leaning on the arm he held out to support me:

"Has a body come ashore?"

He said, "Yes."

"Do I know it?" I asked then.

He answered nothing.

But, he led me to the shore. And on that part of it where she and I had looked for shells, two children—on that part of it where some lighter fragments of the old boat, blown down last night, had been scattered by the wind— among the ruins of the home he had wronged—I saw him lying with his head upon his arm, as I had often seen him lie at school.

CHAPTER LVI.

THE NEW WOUND, AND THE OLD.

No need, O Steerforth, to have said, when we last spoke together, in that hour which I so little deemed to be our parting-hour—no need to have said, "Think of me at my best!" I had done that ever; and could I change now, looking on this sight!

They brought a hand-bier, and laid him on it, and covered him with a flag, and took him up and bore him on towards the houses. All the men who carried him had known him, and gone sailing with him, and seen him merry and bold. They carried him through the wild roar, a hush in the midst of all the tumult; and took him to the cottage where Death was already.

But, when they set the bier down on the threshold, they looked at one another, and at me, and whispered. I knew why. They felt as if it were not right to lay him down in the same quiet room.

We went into the town, and took our burden to the inn. So soon as I could at all collect my thoughts, I sent for Joram, and begged him to provide me a conveyance in which it could be got to London in the night. I knew that the care of it, and the hard duty of preparing his mother to receive it, could only rest with me; and I was anxious to discharge that duty as faithfully as I could.

I chose the night for the journey, that there might be less curiosity when I left the town. But, although it was nearly midnight when I came out of the yard in a chaise, followed by what I had in charge, there were many people waiting. At intervals, along the town, and even a little way out upon the road, I saw more; but at length only the bleak night and the open country were around me, and the ashes of my youthful friendship.

Upon a mellow autumn day, about noon, when the ground was perfumed by fallen leaves, and many more, in beautiful tints of yellow, red, and brown, yet hung upon the trees, through which the sun was shining, I arrived at Highgate. I walked the last mile, thinking as I went along of what I had to do; and left the carriage that had followed me all through the night, awaiting orders to advance.

The house, when I came up to it, looked just the same. Not a blind was raised; no sign of life was in the dull paved court, with its covered way leading to the disused door. The wind had quite gone down, and nothing moved.

I had not, at first, the courage to ring at the gate; and when I did ring, my errand seemed to me to be expressed in the very sound of the bell. The little parlour-maid came out, with the key in her hand; and looking earnestly at me as she unlocked the gate, said:

"I beg your pardon, sir. Are you ill?"

"I have been much agitated, and am fatigued."

"Is anything the matter, sir?—Mr. James?——"

"Hush!" said I. "Yes, something has happened, that I have to break to Mrs. Steerforth. She is at home?"

The girl anxiously replied that her mistress was very seldom out now, even in a carriage; that she kept her room; that she saw no company, but would see me. Her mistress was up, she said, and Miss Dartle was with her. What message should she take up-stairs?

Giving her a strict charge to be careful of her manner, and only to carry in my card and say I waited, I sat down in the drawing-room (which we had now reached) until she should come back. Its former pleasant air of occupation was

I am the Bearer of Evil Tidings

gone, and the shutters were half closed. The harp had not been used for many and many a day. His picture, as a boy, was there. The cabinet in which his mother had kept his letters was there. I wondered if she ever read them now ; if she would ever read them more !

The house was so still that I heard the girl's light step up-stairs. On her return, she brought a message, to the effect that Mrs. Steerforth was an invalid and could not come down ; but, that if I would excuse her being in her chamber, she would be glad to see me. In a few moments I stood before her.

She was in his room ; not in her own. I felt, of course, that she had taken to occupy it, in remembrance of him ; and that the many tokens of his old sports and accomplishments, by which she was surrounded, remained there, just as he had left them, for the same reason. She murmured, however, even in her reception of me, that she was out of her own chamber because its aspect was unsuited to her infirmity ; and with her stately look repelled the least suspicion of the truth.

At her chair, as usual, was Rosa Dartle. From the first moment of her dark eyes resting on me, I saw she knew I was the bearer of evil tidings. The scar sprung into view that instant. She withdrew herself a step behind the chair, to keep her own face out of Mrs. Steerforth's observation ; and scrutinised me with a piercing gaze that never faltered, never shrunk.

" I am sorry to observe you are in mourning, sir," said Mrs. Steerforth.

" I am unhappily a widower," said I.

" You are very young to know so great a loss," she returned. " I am grieved to hear it. I am grieved to hear it. I hope Time will be good to you."

" I hope Time," said I, looking at her, " will be good to all of us. Dear Mrs. Steerforth, we must all trust to that, in our heaviest misfortunes."

The earnestness of my manner, and the tears in my eyes, alarmed her. The whole course of her thoughts appeared to stop, and change.

I tried to command my voice in gently saying his name, but it trembled. She repeated it to herself, two or three times, in a low tone. Then, addressing me, she said, with enforced calmness :

" My son is ill."

" Very ill."

" You have seen him ? "

" I have."

" Are you reconciled ? "

I could not say Yes, I could not say No. She slightly turned her head towards the spot where Rosa Dartle had been standing at her elbow, and in that moment I said, by the motion of my lips, to Rosa, " Dead ! "

That Mrs. Steerforth might not be induced to look behind her, and read, plainly written, what she was not yet prepared to know, I met her look quickly; but I had seen Rosa Dartle throw her hands up in the air with vehemence of despair and horror, and then clasp them on her face.

The handsome lady—so like, Oh so like !—regarded me with a fixed look, and put her hand to her forehead. I besought her to be calm, and prepare herself to bear what I had to tell ; but I should rather have entreated her to weep, for she sat like a stone figure.

" When I was last here," I faltered, " Miss Dartle told me he was sailing here and there. The night before last was a dreadful one at sea. If he were at sea that night, and near a dangerous coast, as it is said he was ; and if the vessel that was seen should really be the ship which—— "

" Rosa ! " said Mrs. Steerforth, " come to me ! "

She came, but with no sympathy or gentleness. Her eyes gleamed like fire as she confronted his mother, and broke into a frightful laugh.

" Now," she said, " is your pride appeased, you madwoman ?

Now has he made atonement to you——with his life! Do you hear?—His life!"

Mrs. Steerforth, fallen back stiffly in her chair, and making no sound but a moan, cast her eyes upon her with a wide stare.

"Aye!" cried Rosa, smiting herself passionately on the breast, "look at me! Moan, and groan, and look at me! Look here!" striking the scar, "at your dead child's handiwork!"

The moan the mother uttered, from time to time, went to my heart. Always the same. Always inarticulate and stifled. Always accompanied with an incapable motion of the head, but with no change of face. Always proceeding from a rigid mouth and closed teeth, as if the jaw were locked and the face frozen up in pain.

"Do you remember when he did this?" she proceeded. "Do you remember when, in his inheritance of your nature, and in your pampering of his pride and passion, he did this, and disfigured me for life? Look at me, marked until I die with his high displeasure; and moan and groan for what you made him!"

"Miss Dartle," I entreated her. "For Heaven's sake——"

"I *will* speak!" she said, turning on me with her lightning eyes. "Be silent, you! Look at me, I say, proud mother of a proud false son! Moan for your nurture of him, moan for your corruption of him, moan for your loss of him, moan for mine!"

She clenched her hand, and trembled through her spare worn figure, as if her passion were killing her by inches.

"You, resent his self-will!" she exclaimed. "You, injured by his haughty temper! You, who opposed to both, when your hair was grey, the qualities which made both when you gave him birth! You, who from his cradle reared him to be what he was, and stunted what he should have been! Are you rewarded, *now*, for your years of trouble?"

"Oh Miss Dartle, shame! Oh cruel!"

439

"I tell you," she returned, "I *will* speak to her. No power on earth should stop me, while I was standing here! Have I been silent all these years, and shall I not speak now? I loved him better than you ever loved him!" turning on her fiercely. "I could have loved him, and asked no return. If I had been his wife, I could have been the slave of his caprices for a word of love a-year. I should have been. Who knows it better than I? You were exacting, proud, punctilious, selfish. My love would have been devoted—would have trod your paltry whimpering under foot!"

With flashing eyes, she stamped upon the ground as if she actually did it.

"Look here!" she said, striking the scar again, with a relentless hand. "When he grew into the better understanding of what he had done, he saw it, and repented of it! I could sing to him, and talk to him, and show the ardour that I felt in all he did, and attain with labour to such knowledge as most interested him; and I attracted him. When he was freshest and truest, he loved *me*. Yes, he did! Many a time, when you were put off with a slight word, he has taken Me to his heart!"

She said it with a taunting pride in the midst of her frenzy—for it was little less—yet with an eager remembrance of it, in which the smouldering embers of a gentler feeling kindled for the moment.

"I descended—as I might have known I should, but that he fascinated me with his boyish courtship—into a doll, a trifle for the occupation of an idle hour, to be dropped, and taken up, and trifled with, as the inconstant humour took him. When he grew weary, I grew weary. As his fancy died out, I would no more have tried to strengthen any power I had, than I would have married him on his being forced to take me for his wife. We fell away from one another without a word. Perhaps you saw it, and were not sorry. Since then, I have been a mere disfigured piece of furniture between you both; having no eyes, no ears, no feelings, no remembrances. Moan? Moan for what you made him; not for your love. I tell you that the time was, when I loved him better than you ever did!"

She stood with her bright angry eyes confronting the wide stare, and the set face; and softened no more, when the moaning was repeated, than if the face had been a picture.

"Miss Dartle," said I, "if you can be so obdurate as not to feel for this afflicted mother—— "

"Who feels for me?' she sharply retorted. "She has sown this. Let her moan for the harvest that she reaps to-day!"

" And if his faults—— " I began.

"Faults!" she cried, bursting into passionate tears. "Who dares malign him? He had a soul worth millions of the friends to whom he stooped!"

"No one can have loved him better, no one can hold him in dearer remembrance than I," I replied. "I meant to say, if you have no compassion for his mother; or if his faults— you have been bitter on them—— "

"It's false," she cried, tearing her black hair; "I loved him!"

"—if his faults cannot," I went on, "be banished from your remembrance, in such an hour; look at that figure, even as one you have never seen before, and render it some help!"

All this time, the figure was unchanged, and looked unchangeable. Motionless, rigid, staring; moaning in the same dumb way from time to time, with the same helpless motion of the head; but giving no other sign of life. Miss Dartle suddenly kneeled down before it, and began to loosen the dress.

" A curse upon you!" she said, looking round at me, with a mingled expression of rage and grief. "It was in an evil hour that you ever came here! A curse upon you! Go!"

After passing out of the room, I hurried back to ring the bell, the sooner to alarm the servants. She had then taken the impassive figure in her arms, and, still upon her knees,

441

was weeping over it, kissing it, calling to it, rocking it to and fro upon her bosom like a child, and trying every tender means to rouse the dormant senses. No longer afraid of leaving her, I noiselessly turned back again; and alarmed the house as I went out.

Later in the day, I returned, and we laid him in his mother's room. She was just the same, they told me; Miss Dartle never left her; doctors were in attendance, many things had been tried; but she lay like a statue, except for the low sound now and then.

I went through the dreary house, and darkened the windows. The windows of the chamber where he lay, I darkened last. I lifted up the leaden hand, and held it to my heart; and all the world seemed death and silence, broken only by his mother's moaning.

CHAPTER LVII.

ONE thing more, I had to do, before yielding myself to the shock of these emotions. It was, to conceal what had occurred, from those who were going away; and to dismiss them on their voyage in happy ignorance. In this, no time was to be lost.

I took Mr. Micawber aside that same night, and confided to him the task of standing between Mr. Peggotty and intelligence of the late catastrophe. He zealously undertook to do so, and to intercept any newspaper through which it might, without such precautions, reach him.

"If it penetrates to him, sir," said Mr. Micawber, striking himself on the breast, "it shall first pass through this body!"

Mr. Micawber, I must observe, in his adaptation of himself to a new state of society, had acquired a bold buccaneering air, not absolutely lawless, but defensive and prompt. One might have supposed him a child of the wilderness, long accustomed to live out of the confines of civilisation, and about to return to his native wilds.

He had provided himself, among other things, with a complete suit of oil-skin, and a straw hat with a very low crown, pitched or caulked on the outside. In this rough clothing, with a common mariner's telescope under his arm, and a shrewd trick of casting up his eye at the sky as looking out for dirty weather, he was far more nautical, after his manner, than Mr. Peggotty. His whole family, if I may so express it, were cleared for action. I found Mrs. Micawber in the closest and most uncompromising of bonnets, made fast under the chin; and in a shawl which tied her up (as I had been tied up, when my aunt first received me) like a bundle, and was secured behind at the waist, in a strong knot. Miss Micawber I found made snug for stormy weather, in the same manner; with nothing superfluous about her. Master Micawber was hardly visible in a Guernsey shirt, and the shaggiest suit of slops I ever saw; and the children were done up, like preserved meats, in impervious cases. Both Mr. Micawber and his eldest son wore their sleeves loosely turned back at the wrists, as being ready to lend a hand in any direction, and to "tumble up," or sing out, "Yeo—Heave—Yeo!" on the shortest notice.

Thus Traddles and I found them at nightfall, assembled on the wooden steps, at that time known as Hungerford Stairs, watching the departure of a boat with some of their property on board. I had told Traddles of the terrible event, and it had greatly shocked him; but there could be no doubt of the kindness of keeping it a secret, and he had come to help me in this last service. It was here that I took Mr. Micawber aside, and received his promise.

The Micawber family were lodged in a little, dirty, tumble-down public-house, which in those days was close to the stairs, and whose protruding wooden rooms overhung the river. The family, as emigrants, being objects of some interest in and about Hungerford, attracted so many beholders, that we were glad to take refuge in their room. It was one of the wooden chambers up-stairs, with the tide flowing underneath. My aunt and Agnes were there, busily making some little extra comforts, in the way of dress, for the children. Peggotty was quietly assisting, with the old insensible work-box, yard measure, and bit of wax candle before her, that had now outlived so much.

It was not easy to answer her inquiries; still less to whisper Mr. Peggotty, when Mr. Micawber brought him in, that I had given the letter, and all was well. But I did both, and

444

made them happy. If I showed any trace of what I felt, my own sorrows were sufficient to account for it.

"And when does the ship sail, Mr. Micawber?" asked my aunt.

Mr. Micawber considered it necessary to prepare either my aunt or his wife, by degrees, and said, sooner than he had expected yesterday.

"The boat brought you word, I suppose?" said my aunt.

"It did, ma'am," he returned.

"Well?" said my aunt. "And she sails—"

"Madam," he replied, "I am informed that we must positively be on board before seven to-morrow morning."

"Heyday!" said my aunt, "that's soon. Is it a sea-going fact, Mr. Peggotty?"

"'Tis so, ma'am. She'll drop down the river with that theer tide. If Mas'r Davy and my sister comes aboard at Gravesen', arternoon o' next day, they'll see the last on us."

"And that we shall do," said I, "be sure!"

"Until then, and until we are at sea," observed Mr. Micawber, with a glance of intelligence at me, "Mr. Peggotty and myself will constantly keep a double look-out together, on our goods and chattels. Emma, my love," said Mr. Micawber, clearing his throat in his magnificent way, "my friend Mr. Thomas Traddles is so obliging as to solicit, in my ear, that he should have the privilege of ordering the ingredients necessary to the composition of a moderate portion of that Beverage which is peculiarly associated, in our minds, with the Roast Beef of Old England. I allude to—in short, Punch. Under ordinary circumstances, I should scruple to entreat the indulgence of Miss Trotwood and Miss Wickfield, but—"

"I can only say for myself," said my aunt, "that I will drink all happiness and success to you, Mr. Micawber, with the utmost pleasure."

"And I too!" said Agnes, with a smile.

Mr. Micawber immediately descended to the bar, where he

appeared to be quite at home; and in due time returned with a steaming jug. I could not but observe that he had been peeling the lemons with his own clasp-knife, which, as became the knife of a practical settler, was about a foot long; and which he wiped, not wholly without ostentation, on the sleeve of his coat. Mrs. Micawber and the two elder members of the family I now found to be provided with similar formidable instruments, while every child had its own wooden spoon attached to its body by a strong line. In a similar anticipation of life afloat, and in the Bush, Mr. Micawber, instead of helping Mrs. Micawber and his eldest son and daughter to punch, in wine-glasses, which he might easily have done, for there was a shelf-full in the room, served it out to them in a series of villainous little tin pots; and I never saw him enjoy anything so much as drinking out of his own particular pint pot, and putting it in his pocket at the close of the evening.

"The luxuries of the old country," said Mr. Micawber, with an intense satisfaction in their renouncement, "we abandon. The denizens of the forest cannot, of course, expect to participate in the refinements of the land of the Free."

Here, a boy came in to say that Mr. Micawber was wanted down-stairs.

"I have a presentiment," said Mrs. Micawber, setting down her tin pot, "that it is a member of my family!"

"If so, my dear," observed Mr. Micawber, with his usual suddenness of warmth on that subject, "as the member of your family—whoever he, she, or it, may be—has kept *us* waiting for a considerable period, perhaps the Member may now wait *my* convenience."

"Micawber," said his wife, in a low tone, "at such a time as this—"

"'It is not meet,'" said Mr. Micawber, rising, "'that every nice offence should bear its comment!' Emma, I stand reproved."

446

"The loss, Micawber," observed his wife, "has been my family's, not yours. If my family are at length sensible of the deprivation to which their own conduct has, in the past, exposed them, and now desire to extend the hand of fellowship, let it not be repulsed."

"My dear," he returned, " so be it ! "

"If not for their sakes ; for mine, Micawber," said his wife.

"Emma," he returned, " that view of the question is, at such a moment, irresistible. I cannot, even now, distinctly pledge myself to fall upon your family's neck ; but the member of your family, who is now in attendance, shall have no genial warmth frozen by me."

Mr. Micawber withdrew, and was absent some little time ; in the course of which Mrs. Micawber was not wholly free from an apprehension that words might have arisen between him and the Member. At length the same boy re-appeared, and presented me with a note written in pencil, and headed, in a legal manner, " Heep v. Micawber." From this document, I learned that Mr. Micawber being again arrested, was in a final paroxysm of despair ; and that he begged me to send him his knife and pint pot, by bearer, as they might prove serviceable during the brief remainder of his existence in jail. He also requested, as a last act of friendship, that I would see his family to the Parish Workhouse, and forget that such a Being ever lived.

Of course I answered this note by going down with the boy to pay the money, where I found Mr. Micawber sitting in a corner, looking darkly at the Sheriff's Officer who had effected the capture. On his release, he embraced me with the utmost fervour ; and made an entry of the transaction in his pocket-book—being very particular, I recollect, about a halfpenny I inadvertently omitted from my statement of the total.

This momentous pocket-book was a timely reminder to him of another transaction. On our return to the room upstairs (where he accounted for his absence by saying that it had been occasioned by circumstances over which he had no

447

control), he took out of it a large sheet of paper, folded small, and quite covered with long sums, carefully worked. From the glimpse I had of them, I should say that I never saw such sums out of a school ciphering-book. These, it seemed, were calculations of compound interest on what he called "the principal amount of forty-one, ten, eleven and a half," for various periods. After a careful consideration of these, and an elaborate estimate of his resources, he had come to the conclusion to select that sum which represented the amount with compound interest to two years, fifteen calendar months, and fourteen days, from that date. For this he had drawn a note-of-hand with great neatness, which he handed over to Traddles on the spot, a discharge of his debt in full (as between man and man), with many acknowledgments.

"I have still a presentiment," said Mrs. Micawber, pensively shaking her head, "that my family will appear on board, before we finally depart."

Mr. Micawber evidently had his presentiment on the subject too, but he put it in his tin pot and swallowed it.

"If you have any opportunity of sending letters home, on your passage, Mrs. Micawber," said my aunt, "you must let us hear from you, you know."

"My dear Miss Trotwood," she replied, "I shall only be too happy to think that any one expects to hear from us. I shall not fail to correspond. Mr. Copperfield, I trust, as an old and familiar friend, will not object to receive occasional intelligence, himself, from one who knew him when the twins were yet unconscious?"

I said that I should hope to hear, whenever she had an opportunity of writing.

"Please Heaven, there will be many such opportunities," said Mr. Micawber. "The ocean, in these times, is a perfect fleet of ships; and we can hardly fail to encounter many, in running over. It is merely crossing," said Mr. Micawber, trifling with his eye-glass, "merely crossing. The distance is quite imaginary."

A MERE QUESTION OF CROSSING.

I think, now, how odd it was, but how wonderfully like Mr. Micawber, that, when he went from London to Canterbury, he should have talked as if he were going to the farthest limits of the earth; and, when he went from England to Australia, as if he were going for a little trip across the channel.

"On the voyage, I shall endeavour," said Mr. Micawber, "occasionally to spin them a yarn; and the melody of my son Wilkins will, I trust, be acceptable at the galley-fire. When Mrs. Micawber has her sea-legs on—an expression in which I hope there is no conventional impropriety—she will give them, I dare say, Little Tafflin. Porpoises and dolphins, I believe, will be frequently observed athwart our Bows, and, either on the Starboard or the Larboard Quarter, objects of interest will be continually descried. In short," said Mr. Micawber, with the old genteel air, "the probability is, all will be found so exciting, alow and aloft, that when the look-out, stationed in the main-top, cries Land-oh! we shall be very considerably astonished!"

With that he flourished off the contents of his little tin pot, as if he had made the voyage, and had passed a first-class examination before the highest naval authorities.

"What *I* chiefly hope, my dear Mr. Copperfield," said Mrs. Micawber, "is, that in some branches of our family we may live again in the old country. Do not frown, Micawber! I do not now refer to my own family, but to our children's children. However vigorous the sapling," said Mrs. Micawber, shaking her head, "I cannot forget the parent-tree; and when our race attains to eminence and fortune, I own I should wish that fortune to flow into the coffers of Britannia."

"My dear," said Mr. Micawber, "Britannia must take her chance. I am bound to say that she has never done much for me, and that I have no particular wish upon the subject."

"Micawber," returned Mrs. Micawber, "there you are wrong. You are going out, Micawber, to this distant clime.

to strengthen, not to weaken, the connexion between yourself and Albion."

"The connexion in question, my love," rejoined Mr. Micawber, "has not laid me, I repeat, under that load of personal obligation, that I am at all sensitive as to the formation of another connexion."

"Micawber," returned Mrs. Micawber, "there, I again say, you are wrong. You do not know your power, Micawber. It is that which will strengthen, even in this step you are about to take, the connexion between yourself and Albion."

Mr. Micawber sat in his elbow-chair, with his eyebrows raised; half receiving and half repudiating Mrs. Micawber's views as they were stated, but very sensible of their foresight.

"My dear Mr. Copperfield," said Mrs. Micawber, "I wish Mr. Micawber to feel his position. It appears to me highly important that Mr. Micawber should, from the hour of his embarkation, feel his position. Your old knowledge of me, my dear Mr. Copperfield, will have told you that I have not the sanguine disposition of Mr. Micawber. My disposition is, if I may say so, eminently practical. I know that this is a long voyage. I know that it will involve many privations and inconveniences. I cannot shut my eyes to those facts. But, I also know what Mr. Micawber is. I know the latent power of Mr. Micawber. And therefore I consider it vitally important that Mr. Micawber should feel his position."

"My love," he observed, "perhaps you will allow me to remark that it is barely possible that I *do* feel my position at the present moment."

"I think not, Micawber," she rejoined. "Not fully. My dear Mr. Copperfield, Mr. Micawber's is not a common case. Mr. Micawber is going to a distant country expressly in order that he may be fully understood and appreciated for the first time. I wish Mr. Micawber to take his stand upon that vessel's prow, and firmly say, 'This country I am come to conquer! Have you honours? Have you riches? Have

you posts of profitable pecuniary emolument? Let them be
brought forward. They are mine!'"

Mr. Micawber, glancing at us all, seemed to think there
was a good deal in this idea.

"I wish Mr. Micawber, if I make myself understood," said
Mrs. Micawber, in her argumentative tone, "to be the Cæsar
of his own fortunes. That, my dear Mr. Copperfield, appears
to me to be his true position. From the first moment of
this voyage, I wish Mr. Micawber to stand upon that vessel's
prow and say, 'Enough of delay: enough of disappointment: enough of limited means. That was in the old
country. This is the new. Produce your reparation. Bring
it forward!'"

Mr. Micawber folded his arms in a resolute manner, as if
he were then stationed on the figure-head.

"And doing that," said Mrs. Micawber, " —feeling his
position—am I not right in saying that Mr. Micawber will
strengthen, and not weaken, his connexion with Britain?
An important public character arising in that hemisphere,
shall I be told that its influence will not be felt at home?
Can I be so weak as to imagine that Mr. Micawber, wielding
the rod of talent and of power in Australia, will be nothing
in England? I am but a woman; but I should be unworthy
of myself, and of my papa, if I were guilty of such absurd
weakness."

Mrs. Micawber's conviction that her arguments were un-
answerable, gave a moral elevation to her tone which I think
I had never heard in it before.

"And therefore it is," said Mrs. Micawber, "that I the
more wish, that, at a future period, we may live again on
the parent soil. Mr. Micawber may be—I cannot disguise
from myself that the probability is, Mr. Micawber will be
—a page of History; and he ought then to be represented
in the country which gave him birth, and did *not* give him
employment!"

"My love," observed Mr. Micawber, "it is impossible for

me not to be touched by your affection. I am always willing to defer to your good sense. What will be—will be. Heaven forbid that I should grudge my native country any portion of the wealth that may be accumulated by our descendants!"

"That's well," said my aunt, nodding towards Mr. Peggotty, "and I drink my love to you all, and every blessing and success attend you!"

Mr. Peggotty put down the two children he had been nursing, one on each knee, to join Mr. and Mrs. Micawber in drinking to all of us in return; and when he and the Micawbers cordially shook hands as comrades, and his brown face brightened with a smile, I felt that he would make his way, establish a good name, and be beloved, go where he would.

Even the children were instructed, each to dip a wooden spoon into Mr. Micawber's pot, and pledge us in its contents. When this was done, my aunt and Agnes rose, and parted from the emigrants. It was a sorrowful farewell. They were all crying; the children hung about Agnes to the last; and we left poor Mrs. Micawber in a very distressed condition, sobbing and weeping by a dim candle, that must have made the room look, from the river, like a miserable lighthouse.

I went down again next morning to see that they were away. They had departed, in a boat, as early as five o'clock. It was a wonderful instance to me of the gap such partings make, that although my association of them with the tumble-down public-house and the wooden stairs dated only from last night, both seemed dreary and deserted, now that they were gone.

In the afternoon of the next day, my old nurse and I went down to Gravesend. We found the ship in the river, surrounded by a crowd of boats; a favourable wind blowing; the signal for sailing at her mast head. I hired a boat directly, and we put off to her; and getting through the little vortex of confusion of which she was the centre, went on board.

Mr. Peggotty was waiting for us on deck. He told me that Mr. Micawber had just now been arrested again (and for the last time) at the suit of Heep, and that, in compliance with a request I had made to him, he had paid the money: which I repaid him. He then took us down between decks; and there, any lingering fears I had of his having heard any rumours of what had happened, were dispelled by Mr. Micawber's coming out of the gloom, taking his arm with an air of friendship and protection, and telling me that they had scarcely been asunder for a moment, since the night before last.

It was such a strange scene to me, and so confined and dark, that, at first, I could make out hardly anything; but, by degrees, it cleared, as my eyes became more accustomed to the gloom, and I seemed to stand in a picture by Ostade. Among the great beams, bulks, and ringbolts of the ship, and the emigrant-berths, and chests, and bundles, and barrels, and heaps of miscellaneous baggage—lighted up, here and there, by dangling lanterns; and elsewhere by the yellow daylight straying down a windsail or a hatchway—were crowded groups of people, making new friendships, taking leave of one another, talking, laughing, crying, eating and drinking; some, already settled down into the possession of their few feet of space, with their little households arranged, and tiny children established on stools, or in dwarf elbow-chairs; others, despairing of a resting-place, and wandering disconsolately. From babies who had but a week or two of life behind them, to crooked old men and women who seemed to have but a week or two of life before them; and from ploughmen bodily carrying out soil of England on their boots, to smiths taking away samples of its soot and smoke upon their skins; every age and occupation appeared to be crammed into the narrow compass of the 'tween decks.

As my eye glanced round this place, I thought I saw

sitting, by an open port, with one of the Micawber children near her, a figure like Emily's; it first attracted my attention, by another figure parting from it with a kiss; and as it glided calmly away through the disorder, reminding me of—Agnes! But in the rapid motion and confusion, and in the unsettlement of my own thoughts, I lost it again; and only knew that the time was come when all visitors were being warned to leave the ship; that my nurse was crying on a chest beside me; and that Mrs. Gummidge, assisted by some younger stooping woman in black, was busily arranging Mr. Peggotty's goods.

"Is there any last wured, Mas'r Davy?" said he. "Is there any one forgotten thing afore we parts?"

"One thing!" said I. "Martha!"

He touched the younger woman I have mentioned on the shoulder, and Martha stood before me.

"Heaven bless you, you good man!" cried I. "You take her with you!"

She answered for him, with a burst of tears. I could speak no more, at that time, but I wrung his hand; and if ever I have loved and honoured any man, I loved and honoured that man in my soul.

The ship was clearing fast of strangers. The greatest trial that I had, remained. I told him what the noble spirit that was gone, had given me in charge to say at parting. It moved him deeply. But when he charged me, in return, with many messages of affection and regret for those deaf ears, he moved me more.

The time was come. I embraced him, took my weeping nurse upon my arm, and hurried away. On deck, I took leave of poor Mrs. Micawber. She was looking distractedly about for her family, even then; and her last words to me were, that she never would desert Mr. Micawber.

We went over the side into our boat, and lay at a little distance to see the ship wafted on her course. It was then calm, radiant sunset. She lay between us, and the red light;

The Emigrants

and every taper line and spar was visible against the glow. A sight at once so beautiful, so mournful, and so hopeful, as the glorious ship, lying, still, on the flushed water, with all the life on board her crowded at the bulwarks, and there clustering, for a moment, bare-headed and silent, I never saw.

Silent, only for a moment. As the sails rose to the wind, and the ship began to move, there broke from all the boats three resounding cheers, which those on board took up, and echoed back, and which were echoed and re-echoed. My heart burst out when I heard the sound, and beheld the waving of the hats and handkerchiefs—and then I saw her!

Then I saw her, at her uncle's side, and trembling on his shoulder. He pointed to us with an eager hand; and she saw us, and waved her last good-bye to me. Aye, Emily, beautiful and drooping, cling to him with the utmost trust of thy bruised heart; for he has clung to thee, with all the might of his great love!

Surrounded by the rosy light, and standing high upon the deck, apart together, she clinging to him, and he holding her, they solemnly passed away. The night had fallen on the Kentish hills when we were rowed ashore—and fallen darkly upon me.

CHAPTER LVIII.

IT was a long and gloomy night that gathered on me, haunted by the ghosts of many hopes, of many dear remembrances, many errors, many unavailing sorrows and regrets.

I went away from England; not knowing, even then, how great the shock was that I had to bear. I left all who were dear to me, and went away ; and believed that I had borne it, and it was past. As a man upon a field of battle will receive a mortal hurt, and scarcely know that he is struck, so I, when I was left alone with my undisciplined heart, had no conception of the wound with which it had to strive.

The knowledge came upon me, not quickly, but little by little, and grain by grain. The desolate feeling with which I went abroad, deepened and widened hourly. At first it was a heavy sense of loss and sorrow, wherein I could distinguish little else. By imperceptible degrees, it became a hopeless consciousness of all that I had lost—love, friendship, interest; of all that had been shattered—my first trust, my first affection, the whole airy castle of my life ; of all that remained—a ruined blank and waste, lying wide around me, unbroken, to the dark horizon.

If my grief were selfish, I did not know it to be so. I mourned for my child-wife, taken from her blooming world, so young. I mourned for him who might have won the love and admiration of thousands, as he had won mine long ago. I mourned for the broken heart that had found rest in the

456

stormy sea; and for the wandering remnants of the simple home, where I had heard the night-wind blowing, when I was a child.

From the accumulated sadness into which I fell, I had at length no hope of ever issuing again. I roamed from place to place, carrying my burden with me everywhere. I felt its whole weight now; and I drooped beneath it, and I said in my heart that it could never be lightened.

When this despondency was at its worst, I believed that I should die. Sometimes, I thought that I would like to die at home; and actually turned back on my road, that I might get there soon. At other times, I passed on farther away, from city to city, seeking I know not what, and trying to leave I know not what behind.

It is not in my power to retrace, one by one, all the weary phases of distress of mind through which I passed. There are some dreams that can only be imperfectly and vaguely described; and when I oblige myself to look back on this time of my life, I seem to be recalling such a dream. I see myself passing on among the novelties of foreign towns, palaces, cathedrals, temples, pictures, castles, tombs, fantastic streets—the old abiding places of History and Fancy—as a dreamer might; bearing my painful load through all, and hardly conscious of the objects as they fade before me. Listlessness to everything, but brooding sorrow, was the night that fell on my undisciplined heart. Let me look up from it—as at last I did, thank Heaven!—and from its long, sad, wretched dream, to dawn.

For many months I travelled with this ever-darkening cloud upon my mind. Some blind reasons that I had for not returning home—reasons then struggling within me, vainly, for more distinct expression—kept me on my pilgrimage. Sometimes, I had proceeded restlessly from place to place, stopping nowhere; sometimes, I had lingered long in one spot. I had had no purpose, no sustaining soul within me, anywhere.

DAVID COPPERFIELD.

I was in Switzerland. I had come out of Italy, over one of the great passes of the Alps, and had since wandered with a guide among the by-ways of the mountains. If those awful solitudes had spoken to my heart, I did not know it. I had found sublimity and wonder in the dread heights and precipices, in the roaring torrents, and the wastes of ice and snow; but as yet, they had taught me nothing else.

I came, one evening before sunset, down into a valley, where I was to rest. In the course of my descent to it, by the winding track along the mountain-side, from which I saw it shining far below, I think some long-unwonted sense of beauty and tranquillity, some softening influence awakened by its peace, moved faintly in my breast. I remember pausing once, with a kind of sorrow that was not all oppressive, not quite despairing. I remember almost hoping that some better change was possible within me.

I came into the valley, as the evening sun was shining on the remote heights of snow, that closed it in, like eternal clouds. The bases of the mountains forming the gorge in which the little village lay, were richly green; and high above this gentler vegetation, grew forests of dark fir, cleaving the wintry snow-drift, wedge-like, and stemming the avalanche. Above these, were range upon range of craggy steeps, grey rock, bright ice, and smooth verdure-specks of pasture, all gradually blending with the crowning snow. Dotted here and there on the mountain's side, each tiny dot a home, were lonely wooden cottages, so dwarfed by the towering heights that they appeared too small for toys. So did even the clustered village in the valley, with its wooden bridge across the stream, where the stream tumbled over broken rocks, and roared away among the trees. In the quiet air, there was a sound of distant singing—shepherd voices; but, as one bright evening cloud floated midway along the mountain's side, I could almost have believed it came from there, and was not earthly music. All at once, in this serenity, great Nature spoke to me; and soothed me to lay down my weary head upon the grass, and weep as I had not wept yet, since Dora died!

I had found a packet of letters awaiting me but a few minutes before, and had strolled out of the village to read them while my supper was making ready. Other packets had missed me, and I had received none for a long time. Beyond a line or two, to say that I was well, and had arrived at such a place, I had not had fortitude or constancy to write a letter since I left home.

The packet was in my hand. I opened it, and read the writing of Agnes.

She was happy and useful, was prospering as she had hoped. That was all she told me of herself. The rest referred to me.

She gave me no advice; she urged no duty on me; she only told me, in her own fervent manner, what her trust in me was. She knew (she said) how such a nature as mine would turn affliction to good. She knew how trial and emotion would exalt and strengthen it. She was sure that in my every purpose I should gain a firmer and a higher tendency, through the grief I had undergone. She, who so gloried in my fame, and so looked forward to its augmentation, well knew that I would labour on. She knew that in me, sorrow could not be weakness, but must be strength. As the endurance of my childish days had done its part to make me what I was, so greater calamities would nerve me on, to be yet better than I was; and so, as they had taught me, would I teach others. She commended me to God, who had taken my innocent darling to His rest; and in her sisterly affection cherished me always, and was always at my side go where I would; proud of what I had done, but infinitely prouder yet of what I was reserved to do.

I put the letter in my breast, and thought what had I been an hour ago! When I heard the voices die away, and saw the quiet evening cloud grow dim, and all the colours in the valley fade, and the golden snow upon the mountain

459

tops become a remote part of the pale night sky, yet felt that the night was passing from my mind, and all its shadows clearing, there was no name for the love I bore her, dearer to me, henceforward, than ever until then.

I read her letter, many times. I wrote to her before I slept. I told her that I had been in sore need of her help; that without her I was not, and I never had been, what she thought me; but, that she inspired me to be that, and I would try.

I did try. In three months more, a year would have passed since the beginning of my sorrow. I determined to make no resolutions until the expiration of those three months, but to try. I lived in that valley, and its neighbourhood, all the time.

The three months gone, I resolved to remain away from home for some time longer; to settle myself for the present in Switzerland, which was growing dear to me in the remembrance of that evening; to resume my pen; to work.

I resorted humbly whither Agnes had commended me; I sought out Nature, never sought in vain; and I admitted to my breast the human interest I had lately shrunk from. It was not long, before I had almost as many friends in the valley as in Yarmouth: and when I left it, before the winter set in, for Geneva, and came back in the spring, their cordial greetings had a homely sound to me, although they were not conveyed in English words.

I worked early and late, patiently and hard. I wrote a Story, with a purpose growing, not remotely, out of my experience, and sent it to Traddles, and he arranged for its publication very advantageously for me; and the tidings of my growing reputation began to reach me from travellers whom I encountered by chance. After some rest and change, I fell to work, in my old ardent way, on a new fancy, which took strong possession of me. As I advanced in the execution of this task, I felt it more and more, and roused my utmost energies to do it well. This was my third work of fiction.

THE CLOUD BEGINS TO RISE.

It was not half written, when, in an interval of rest, I thought of returning home.

For a long time, though studying and working patiently, I had accustomed myself to robust exercise. My health, severely impaired when I left England, was quite restored. I had seen much. I had been in many countries, and I hope I had improved my store of knowledge.

I have now recalled all that I think it needful to recall here, of this term of absence—with one reservation. I have made it, thus far, with no purpose of suppressing any of my thoughts; for, as I have elsewhere said, this narrative is my written memory. I have desired to keep the most secret current of my mind apart, and to the last. I enter on it now.

I cannot so completely penetrate the mystery of my own heart, as to know when I began to think that I might have set its earliest and brightest hopes on Agnes. I cannot say at what stage of my grief it first became associated with the reflection, that, in my wayward boyhood, I had thrown away the treasure of her love. I believe I may have heard some whisper of that distant thought, in the old unhappy loss or want of something never to be realised, of which I had been sensible. But the thought came into my mind as a new reproach and new regret, when I was left so sad and lonely in the world.

If, at that time, I had been much with her, I should, in the weakness of my desolation, have betrayed this. It was what I remotely dreaded when I was first impelled to stay away from England. I could not have borne to lose the smallest portion of her sisterly affection; yet, in that betrayal, I should have set a constraint between us hitherto unknown.

I could not forget that the feeling with which she now regarded me had grown up in my own free choice and course. That if she had ever loved me with another love—and I sometimes thought the time was when she might have done so—I had cast it away. It was nothing, now, that I had

461

accustomed myself to think of her, when we were both mere children, as one who was far removed from my wild fancies. I had bestowed my passionate tenderness upon another object; and what I might have done, I had not done; and what Agnes was to me, I and her own noble heart had made her.

In the beginning of the change that gradually worked in me, when I tried to get a better understanding of myself and be a better man, I did glance, through some indefinite probation, to a period when I might possibly hope to cancel the mistaken past, and to be so blessed as to marry her. But, as time wore on, this shadowy prospect faded, and departed from me. If she had ever loved me, then, I should hold her the more sacred, remembering the confidences I had reposed in her, her knowledge of my errant heart, the sacrifice she must have made to be my friend and sister, and the victory she had won. If she had never loved me, could I believe that she would love me now?

I had always felt my weakness, in comparison with her constancy and fortitude; and now I felt it more and more. Whatever I might have been to her, or she to me, if I had been more worthy of her long ago, I was not now, and she was not. The time was past. I had let it go by, and had deservedly lost her.

That I suffered much in these contentions, that they filled me with unhappiness and remorse, and yet that I had a sustaining sense that it was required of me, in right and honour, to keep away from myself, with shame, the thought of turning to the dear girl in the withering of my hopes, from whom I had frivolously turned when they were bright and fresh—which consideration was at the root of every thought I had concerning her—is all equally true. I made no effort to conceal from myself, now, that I loved her, that I was devoted to her; but I brought the assurance home to myself, that it was now too late, and that our long-subsisting relation must be undisturbed.

I had thought, much and often, of my Dora's shadowing

out to me what might have happened, in those years that were destined not to try us. I had considered how the things that never happen, are often as much realities to us, in their effects, as those that are accomplished. The very years she spoke of, were realities now, for my correction; and would have been, one day, a little later perhaps, though we had parted in our earliest folly. I endeavoured to convert what might have been between myself and Agnes, into a means of making me more self-denying, more resolved, more conscious of myself, and my defects and errors. Thus, through the reflection that it might have been, I arrived at the conviction that it could never be.

These, with their perplexities and inconsistencies, were the shifting quicksands of my mind, from the time of my departure to the time of my return home, three years afterwards. Three years had elapsed since the sailing of the emigrant ship; when, at that same hour of sunset, and in the same place, I stood on the deck of the packet vessel that brought me home, looking on the rosy water where I had seen the image of that ship reflected.

Three years. Long in the aggregate, though short as they went by. And home was very dear to me, and Agnes too—but she was not mine—she was never to be mine. She might have been, but that was past!

CHAPTER LIX.

RETURN.

I LANDED in London on a wintry autumn evening. It was dark and raining, and I saw more fog and mud in a minute than I had seen in a year. I walked from the Custom House to the Monument before I found a coach; and although the very house-fronts, looking on the swollen gutters, were like old friends to me, I could not but admit that they were very dingy friends.

I have often remarked—I suppose everybody has—that one's going away from a familiar place, would seem to be the signal for change in it. As I looked out of the coach-window, and observed that an old house on Fish-street Hill, which had stood untouched by painter, carpenter, or brick-layer, for a century, had been pulled down in my absence; and that a neighbouring street, of time-honoured insalubrity and inconvenience, was being drained and widened; I half expected to find St. Paul's Cathedral looking older.

For some changes in the fortunes of my friends, I was prepared. My aunt had long been re-established at Dover, and Traddles had begun to get into some little practice at the Bar, in the very first term after my departure. He had chambers in Gray's Inn, now; and had told me, in his last letters, that he was not without hopes of being soon united to the dearest girl in the world.

They expected me home before Christmas; but had no idea of my returning so soon. I had purposely misled them, that

464

I might have the pleasure of taking them by surprise. And yet, I was perverse enough to feel a chill and disappointment in receiving no welcome, and rattling, alone and silent, through the misty streets.

The well-known shops, however, with their cheerful lights, did something for me; and when I alighted at the door of the Gray's Inn Coffee-house, I had recovered my spirits. It recalled, at first, that so-different time when I had put up at the Golden Cross, and reminded me of the changes that had come to pass since then; but that was natural.

"Do you know where Mr. Traddles lives in the Inn?" I asked the waiter, as I warmed myself by the coffee-room fire.

"Holborn Court, sir. Number two."

"Mr. Traddles has a rising reputation among the lawyers, I believe?" said I.

"Well, sir," returned the waiter, "probably he has, sir; but I am not aware of it myself."

This waiter, who was middle-aged and spare, looked for help to a waiter of more authority—a stout, potential old man, with a double-chin, in black breeches and stockings, who came out of a place like a churchwarden's pew, at the end of the coffee-room, where he kept company with a cash-box, a Directory, a Law-list, and other books and papers.

"Mr. Traddles," said the spare waiter. "Number two in the Court."

The potential waiter waved him away, and turned, gravely, to me.

"I was inquiring," said I, "whether Mr. Traddles, at number two in the Court, has not a rising reputation among the lawyers?"

"Never heard his name," said the waiter, in a rich husky voice.

I felt quite apologetic for Traddles.

"He's a young man, sure?" said the portentous waiter, fixing his eyes severely on me. "How long has he been in the Inn?"

465

"Not above three years," said I.

The waiter, who I supposed had lived in his churchwarden's pew for forty years, could not pursue such an insignificant subject. He asked me what I would have for dinner?

I felt I was in England again, and really was quite cast down on Traddles's account. There seemed to be no hope for him. I meekly ordered a bit of fish and a steak, and stood before the fire musing on his obscurity.

As I followed the chief waiter with my eyes, I could not help thinking that the garden in which he had gradually blown to be the flower he was, was an arduous place to rise in. It had such a prescriptive, stiff-necked, long-established, solemn, elderly air. I glanced about the room, which had had its sanded floor sanded, no doubt, in exactly the same manner when the chief waiter was a boy—if he ever was a boy, which appeared improbable; and at the shining tables, where I saw myself reflected, in unruffled depths of old mahogany; and at the lamps, without a flaw in their trimming or cleaning; and at the comfortable green curtains, with their pure brass rods, snugly enclosing the boxes; and at the two large coal fires, brightly burning; and at the rows of decanters, burly as if with the consciousness of pipes of expensive old port wine below; and both England, and the law, appeared to me to be very difficult indeed to be taken by storm. I went up to my bedroom to change my wet clothes; and the vast extent of that old wainscotted apartment (which was over the archway leading to the Inn, I remember), and the sedate immensity of the four-post bedstead, and the indomitable gravity of the chests of drawers, all seemed to unite in sternly frowning on the fortunes of Traddles, or on any such daring youth. I came down again to my dinner; and even the slow comfort of the meal, and the orderly silence of the place—which was bare of guests, the Long Vacation not yet being over—were eloquent on the audacity of Traddles, and his small hopes of a livelihood for twenty years to come.

I had seen nothing like this since I went away, and it quite dashed my hopes for my friend. The chief waiter had had enough of me. He came near me no more; but devoted himself to an old gentleman in long gaiters, to meet whom a pint of special port seemed to come out of the cellar of its own accord, for he gave no order. The second waiter informed me, in a whisper, that this old gentleman was a retired conveyancer living in the Square, and worth a mint of money, which it was expected he would leave to his laundress's daughter; likewise that it was rumoured that he had a service of plate in a bureau, all tarnished with lying by, though more than one spoon and a fork had never yet been beheld in his chambers by mortal vision. By this time, I quite gave Traddles up for lost; and settled in my own mind that there was no hope for him.

Being very anxious to see the dear old fellow, nevertheless, I despatched my dinner, in a manner not at all calculated to raise me in the opinion of the chief waiter, and hurried out by the back way. Number two in the Court was soon reached; and an inscription on the door-post informing me that Mr. Traddles occupied a set of chambers on the top story, I ascended the staircase. A crazy old staircase I found it to be, feebly lighted on each landing by a club-headed little oil wick, dying away in a little dungeon of dirty glass.

In the course of my stumbling up-stairs, I fancied I heard a pleasant sound of laughter; and not the laughter of an attorney or barrister, or attorney's clerk or barrister's clerk, but of two or three merry girls. Happening, however, as I stopped to listen, to put my foot in a hole where the Honourable Society of Gray's Inn had left a plank deficient, I fell down with some noise, and when I recovered my footing all was silent.

Groping my way more carefully, for the rest of the journey, my heart beat high when I found the outer door, which had MR. TRADDLES painted on it, open. I knocked.

467

A considerable scuffling within ensued, but nothing else. I therefore knocked again.

A small sharp-looking lad, half-footboy and half-clerk, who was very much out of breath, but who looked at me as if he defied me to prove it legally, presented himself.

"Is Mr. Traddles within?" I said.

"Yes, sir, but he's engaged."

"I want to see him."

After a moment's survey of me, the sharp-looking lad decided to let me in; and opening the door wider for that purpose, admitted me, first, into a little closet of a hall, and next into a little sitting-room; where I came into the presence of my old friend (also out of breath), seated at a table, and bending over papers.

"Good God!" cried Traddles, looking up. "It's Copperfield!" and rushed into my arms, where I held him tight.

"All well, my dear Traddles?"

"All well, my dear, dear Copperfield, and nothing but good news!"

We cried with pleasure, both of us.

"My dear fellow," said Traddles, rumpling his hair in his excitement, which was a most unnecessary operation, "my dearest Copperfield, my long-lost and most welcome friend, how glad I am to see you! How brown you are! How glad I am! Upon my life and honour, I never was so rejoiced, my beloved Copperfield, never!"

I was equally at a loss to express my emotions. I was quite unable to speak, at first.

"My dear fellow!" said Traddles. "And grown so famous! My glorious Copperfield! Good gracious me, *when* did you come, *where* have you come from, *what* have you been doing?"

Never pausing for an answer to anything he said, Traddles, who had clapped me into an easy chair by the fire, all this time impetuously stirred the fire with one hand, and pulled at my neck-kerchief with the other, under some wild delusion that it was a great coat. Without putting down the poker, he now hugged me again; and I hugged him; and, both laughing, and both wiping our eyes, we both sat down, and shook hands across the hearth.

"To think," said Traddles, "that you should have been so nearly coming home as you must have been, my dear old boy, and not at the ceremony!"

"What ceremony, my dear Traddles?"

"Good gracious me!" cried Traddles, opening his eyes in his old way. "Didn't you get my last letter?"

"Certainly not, if it referred to any ceremony."

"Why, my dear Copperfield," said Traddles, sticking his hair upright with both hands, and then putting his hands on my knees, "I am married!"

"Married!" I cried joyfully.

"Lord bless me, yes!" said Traddles—"by the Rev. Horace—to Sophy—down in Devonshire. Why, my dear boy, she's behind the window curtain! Look here!"

To my amazement, the dearest girl in the world came at that same instant, laughing and blushing, from her place of concealment. And a more cheerful, amiable, honest, happy, bright-looking bride, I believe (as I could not help saying on the spot) the world never saw. I kissed her as an old acquaintance should, and wished them joy with all my might of heart.

"Dear me," said Traddles, "what a delightful re-union this is! You are so extremely brown, my dear Copperfield! God bless my soul, how happy I am!"

"And so am I," said I.

"And I am sure I am!" said the blushing and laughing Sophy.

"We are all as happy as possible!" said Traddles. "Even the girls are happy. Dear me, I declare I forgot them!"

"Forgot?" said I.

"The girls," said Traddles. "Sophy's sisters. They are staying with us. They have come to have a peep at

London. The fact is, when—was it you that tumbled up-stairs, Copperfield?"

"It was," said I, laughing.

"Well then, when you tumbled up-stairs," said Traddles, "I was romping with the girls. In point of fact, we were playing at Puss in the Corner. But as that wouldn't do in Westminster Hall, and as it wouldn't look quite professional if they were seen by a client, they decamped. And they are now—listening, I have no doubt," said Traddles, glancing at the door of another room.

"I am sorry," said I, laughing afresh, "to have occasioned such a dispersion."

"Upon my word," rejoined Traddles, greatly delighted, "if you had seen them running away, and running back again, after you had knocked, to pick up the combs they had dropped out of their hair, and going on in the maddest manner, you wouldn't have said so. My love, will you fetch the girls?"

Sophy tripped away, and we heard her received in the adjoining room with a peal of laughter.

"Really musical, isn't it, my dear Copperfield?" said Traddles. "It's very agreeable to hear. It quite lights up these old rooms. To an unfortunate bachelor of a fellow who has lived alone all his life, you know, it's positively delicious. It's charming. Poor things, they have had a great loss in Sophy—who, I do assure you, Copperfield, is, and ever was, the dearest girl!—and it gratifies me beyond expression to find them in such good spirits. The society of girls is a very delightful thing, Copperfield. It's not professional, but it's very delightful."

Observing that he slightly faltered, and comprehending that in the goodness of his heart he was fearful of giving me some pain by what he had said, I expressed my concurrence with a heartiness that evidently relieved and pleased him greatly.

"But then," said Traddles, "our domestic arrangements

are, to say the truth, quite unprofessional altogether, my dear Copperfield. Even Sophy's being here, is unprofessional. And we have no other place of abode. We have put to sea in a cockboat, but we are quite prepared to rough it. And Sophy's an extraordinary manager! You'll be surprised how those girls are stowed away. I am sure I hardly know how it's done."

"Are many of the young ladies with you?" I inquired.

"The eldest, the Beauty is here," said Traddles, in a low confidential voice, "Caroline. And Sarah's here—the one I mentioned to you as having something the matter with her spine, you know. Immensely better! And the two youngest that Sophy educated are with us. And Louisa's here."

"Indeed!" cried I.

"Yes," said Traddles. "Now the whole set—I mean the chambers—is only three rooms; but Sophy arranges for the girls in the most wonderful way, and they sleep as comfortably as possible. Three in that room," said Traddles, pointing. "Two in that."

I could not help glancing round, in search of the accommodation remaining for Mr. and Mrs. Traddles. Traddles understood me.

"Well!" said Traddles, "we are prepared to rough it, as I said just now, and we *did* improvise a bed last week, upon the floor here. But there's a little room in the roof—a very nice room, when you're up there—which Sophy papered herself, to surprise me; and that's our room at present. It's a capital little gipsy sort of place. There's quite a view from it."

"And you are happily married at last, my dear Traddles!" said I. "How rejoiced I am!"

"Thank you, my dear Copperfield," said Traddles, as we shook hands once more. "Yes, I am as happy as it's possible to be. There's your old friend, you see," said Traddles, nodding triumphantly at the flower-pot and stand; "and there's the table with the marble top! All the other furniture is plain and serviceable, you perceive. And as to plate, Lord bless you, we haven't so much as a teaspoon."

"All to be earned?" said I, cheerfully.

"Exactly so," replied Traddles, "all to be earned. Of course we have something in the shape of tea-spoons, because we stir our tea. But they're Britannia metal."

"The silver will be the brighter when it comes," said I.

"The very thing we say!" cried Traddles. "You see, my dear Copperfield," falling again into the low confidential tone, "after I had delivered my argument in Doe *dem.* Jipes *versus* Wigzell, which did me great service with the profession, I went down into Devonshire, and had some serious conversation in private with the Reverend Horace. I dwelt upon the fact that Sophy—who I do assure you, Copperfield, is the dearest girl!——"

"I am certain she is!" said I.

"She is, indeed!" rejoined Traddles. "But I am afraid I am wandering from the subject. Did I mention the Reverend Horace?"

"You said that you dwelt upon the fact——"

"True! Upon the fact that Sophy and I had been engaged for a long period, and that Sophy, with the permission of her parents, was more than content to take me—in short," said Traddles, with his old frank smile, "on our present Britannia-metal footing. Very well. I then proposed to the Reverend Horace—who is a most excellent clergyman, Copperfield, and ought to be a Bishop; or at least ought to have enough to live upon, without pinching himself—that if I could turn the corner, say of two hundred and fifty pounds, in one year; and could see my way pretty clearly to that, or something better, next year; and could plainly furnish a little place like this, besides; then, and in that case, Sophy and I should be united. I took the liberty of representing that we had been patient for a good many years; and that the circumstance of Sophy's being extraordinarily useful at

472

home, ought not to operate with her affectionate parents, against her establishment in life—don't you see?"

"Certainly it ought not," said I.

"I am glad you think so, Copperfield," rejoined Traddles, "because, without any imputation on the Reverend Horace, I do think parents, and brothers, and so forth, are sometimes rather selfish in such cases. Well! I also pointed out, that my most earnest desire was, to be useful to the family; and that if I got on in the world, and anything should happen to him—I refer to the Reverend Horace—"

"I understand," said I.

"—Or to Mrs. Crewler—it would be the utmost gratification of my wishes, to be a parent to the girls. He replied in a most admirable manner, exceedingly flattering to my feelings, and undertook to obtain the consent of Mrs. Crewler to this arrangement. They had a dreadful time of it with her. It mounted from her legs into her chest, and then into her head—"

"What mounted?" I asked.

"Her grief," replied Traddles, with a serious look. "Her feelings generally. As I mentioned on a former occasion, she is a very superior woman, but has lost the use of her limbs. Whatever occurs to harass her, usually settles in her legs; but on this occasion it mounted to the chest, and then to the head, and, in short, pervaded the whole system in a most alarming manner. However, they brought her through it by unremitting and affectionate attention; and we were married yesterday six weeks. You have no idea what a Monster I felt, Copperfield, when I saw the whole family crying and fainting away in every direction! Mrs. Crewler couldn't see me before we left—couldn't forgive me, then, for depriving her of her child—but she is a good creature, and has done so since. I had a delightful letter from her, only this morning."

"And in short, my dear friend," said I, "you feel as blest as you deserve to feel!"

"Oh! That's your partiality!" laughed Traddles. "But, indeed, I am in a most enviable state. I work hard, and read Law insatiably. I get up at five every morning, and don't mind it at all. I hide the girls in the day-time, and make merry with them in the evening. And I assure you I am quite sorry that they are going home on Tuesday, which is the day before the first day of Michaelmas Term. But here," said Traddles, breaking off in his confidence, and speaking aloud, "*are* the girls! Mr. Copperfield, Miss Crewler—Miss Sarah—Miss Louisa—Margaret and Lucy!"

They were a perfect nest of roses; they looked so wholesome and fresh. They were all pretty, and Miss Caroline was very handsome; but there was a loving, cheerful, fireside quality in Sophy's bright looks, which was better than that, and which assured me that my friend had chosen well. We all sat round the fire; while the sharp boy, who I now divined had lost his breath in putting the papers out, cleared them away again, and produced the tea-things. After that, he retired for the night, shutting the outer door upon us with a bang. Mrs. Traddles, with perfect pleasure and composure beaming from her household eyes, having made the tea, then quietly made the toast as she sat in a corner by the fire.

She had seen Agnes, she told me, while she was toasting. "Tom" had taken her down into Kent for a wedding trip, and there she had seen my aunt, too; and both my aunt and Agnes were well, and they had all talked of nothing but me. "Tom" had never had me out of his thoughts, she really believed, all the time I had been away. "Tom" was the authority for everything. "Tom" was evidently the idol of her life; never to be shaken on his pedestal by any commotion; always to be believed in, and done homage to with the whole faith of her heart, come what might.

The deference which both she and Traddles showed towards the Beauty, pleased me very much. I don't know that I thought it very reasonable; but I thought it very delightful, and essentially a part of their character. If Traddles ever for an instant missed the tea-spoons that were still to be won, I have no doubt it was when he handed the Beauty her tea. If his sweet-tempered wife could have got up any self-assertion against any one, I am satisfied it could only have been because she was the Beauty's sister. A few slight indications of a rather petted and capricious manner, which I observed in the Beauty, were manifestly considered, by Traddles and his wife, as her birthright and natural endowment. If she had been born a Queen Bee, and they labouring Bees, they could not have been more satisfied of that.

But their self-forgetfulness charmed me. Their pride in these girls, and their submission of themselves to all their whims, was the pleasantest little testimony to their own worth I could have desired to see. If Traddles were addressed as "a darling," once in the course of that evening; and besought to bring something here, or carry something there, or take something up, or put something down, or find something, or fetch something, he was so addressed, by one or other of his sisters-in-law, at least twelve times in an hour. Neither could they do anything without Sophy. Somebody's hair fell down, and nobody but Sophy could put it up. Somebody forgot how a particular tune went, and nobody but Sophy could hum that tune right. Somebody wanted to recall the name of a place in Devonshire, and only Sophy knew it. Something was wanted to be written home, and Sophy alone could be trusted to write before breakfast in the morning. Somebody broke down in a piece of knitting, and no one but Sophy was able to put the defaulter in the right direction. They were entire mistresses of the place, and Sophy and Traddles waited on them. How many children Sophy could have taken care of in her time, I can't imagine; but she seemed to be famous for knowing every sort of song that ever was addressed to a child in the English tongue; and she sang dozens to order with the clearest little voice in the world, one after another (every sister issuing directions for a different tune, and the Beauty generally striking in last), so that I was quite fascinated. The best of all was, that, in the midst of their exactions, all the sisters had a great tenderness and respect both for Sophy and Traddles. I am sure, when I took my leave, and Traddles was coming out to walk with me to the coffee-house, I thought I had never seen an obstinate head of hair, or any other head of hair, rolling about in such a shower of kisses.

Altogether, it was a scene I could not help dwelling on with pleasure, for a long time after I got back and had wished Traddles good night. If I had beheld a thousand roses blowing in a top set of chambers, in that withered Gray's Inn, they could not have brightened it half so much. The idea of those Devonshire girls, among the dry law-stationers and the attorneys' offices; and of the tea and toast, and children's songs, in that grim atmosphere of pounce and parchment, red-tape, dusty wafers, ink-jars, brief and draft paper, law reports, writs, declarations, and bills of costs, seemed almost as pleasantly fanciful as if I had dreamed that the Sultan's famous family had been admitted on the roll of attorneys, and had brought the talking bird, the singing tree, and the golden water into Gray's Inn Hall. Somehow, I found that I had taken leave of Traddles for the night, and come back to the coffee-house, with a great change in my despondency about him. I began to think he would get on, in spite of all the many orders of chief waiters in England.

Drawing a chair before one of the coffee-room fires to think about him at my leisure, I gradually fell from the consideration of his happiness to tracing prospects in the live-coals, and to thinking, as they broke and changed, of the principal vicissitudes and separations that had marked my life. I had not seen a coal fire, since I had left England three years ago: though many a wood fire had I watched, as it crumbled into hoary ashes, and mingled with the feathery heap upon the hearth, which not inaptly figured to me, in my despondency, my own dead hopes.

I could think of the past now, gravely, but not bitterly; and could contemplate the future in a brave spirit. Home, in its best sense, was for me no more. She in whom I might have inspired a dearer love, I had taught to be my sister. She would marry, and would have new claimants on her tenderness: and in doing it, would never know the love for her that had grown up in my heart. It was right that I should pay the forfeit of my headlong passion. What I reaped, I had sown.

I was thinking, And had I truly disciplined my heart to this, and could I resolutely bear it, and calmly hold the place in her home which she had calmly held in mine,—when I found my eyes resting on a countenance that might have arisen out of the fire, in its association with my early remembrances.

Little Mr. Chillip the Doctor, to whose good offices I was indebted in the very first chapter of this history, sat reading a newspaper in the shadow of an opposite corner. He was tolerably stricken in years by this time; but, being a mild, meek, calm little man, had worn so easily, that I thought he looked at that moment just as he might have looked when he sat in our parlour, waiting for me to be born.

Mr. Chillip had left Blunderstone six or seven years ago, and I had never seen him since. He sat placidly perusing the newspaper, with his little head on one side, and a glass of warm sherry negus at his elbow. He was so extremely conciliatory in his manner that he seemed to apologise to the very newspaper for taking the liberty of reading it.

I walked up to where he was sitting, and said, " How do you do, Mr. Chillip?"

He was greatly fluttered by this unexpected address from a stranger, and replied, in his slow way, " I thank you, sir, you are very good. Thank you, sir. I hope *you* are well."

" You don't remember me?" said I.

" Well, sir," returned Mr. Chillip, smiling very meekly,

and shaking his head as he surveyed me, "I have a kind of an impression that something in your countenance is familiar to me, sir; but I couldn't lay my hand upon your name, really."

"And yet you knew it, long before I knew it myself," I returned.

"Did I indeed, sir?" said Mr. Chillip. "Is it possible that I had the honour, sir, of officiating when—— ?"

"Yes," said I.

"Dear me!" cried Mr. Chillip. "But no doubt you are a good deal changed since then, sir?"

"Probably," said I.

"Well, sir," observed Mr. Chillip, "I hope you'll excuse me, if I am compelled to ask the favour of your name?"

On my telling him my name, he was really moved. He quite shook hands with me—which was a violent proceeding for him, his usual course being to slide a tepid little fish-slice, an inch or two in advance of his hip, and evince the greatest discomposure when anybody grappled with it. Even now, he put his hand in his coat pocket as soon as he could disengage it, and seemed relieved when he had got it safe back.

"Dear me, sir!" said Mr. Chillip, surveying me with his head on one side. "And it's Mr. Copperfield, is it? Well, sir, I think I should have known you, if I had taken the liberty of looking more closely at you. There's a strong resemblance between you and your poor father, sir."

"I never had the happiness of seeing my father," I observed.

"Very true, sir," said Mr. Chillip, in a soothing tone. "And very much to be deplored it was, on all accounts! We are not ignorant, sir," said Mr. Chillip, slowly shaking his little head again, "down in our part of the country, of your fame. There must be great excitement here, sir," said Mr. Chillip, tapping himself on the forehead with his forefinger. "You must find it a trying occupation, sir!"

"What is your part of the country now?" I asked, seating myself near him.

" I am established within a few miles of Bury St. Edmund's, sir," said Mr. Chillip. "Mrs. Chillip coming into a little property in that neighbourhood, under her father's will, I bought a practice down there, in which you will be glad to hear I am doing well. My daughter is growing quite a tall lass now, sir," said Mr. Chillip, giving his little head another little shake. "Her mother let down two tucks in her frocks only last week. Such is time, you see, sir!"

As the little man put his now empty glass to his lips, when he made this reflection, I proposed to him to have it refilled, and I would keep him company with another. "Well, sir," he returned, in his slow way, "it's more than I am accustomed to; but I can't deny myself the pleasure of your conversation. It seems but yesterday that I had the honour of attending you in the measles. You came through them charmingly, sir!"

I acknowledged this compliment, and ordered the negus, which was soon produced. "Quite an uncommon dissipation!" said Mr. Chillip, stirring it, "but I can't resist so extraordinary an occasion. You have no family, sir?"

I shook my head.

"I was aware that you sustained a bereavement, sir, some time ago," said Mr. Chillip. "I heard it from your father-in-law's sister. Very decided character there, sir?"

"Why, yes," said I, "decided enough. Where did you see her, Mr. Chillip?"

"Are you not aware, sir," returned Mr. Chillip, with his placidest smile, "that your father-in-law is again a neighbour of mine?"

"No," said I.

"He is indeed, sir!" said Mr. Chillip. "Married a young lady of that part, with a very good little property, poor thing.—And this action of the brain now, sir? Don't you find it fatigue you?" said Mr. Chillip, looking at me like an admiring Robin.

I waived that question, and returned to the Murdstones.

"I was aware of his being married again. Do you attend the family?" I asked.

"Not regularly. I have been called in," he replied. "Strong phrenological development of the organ of firmness, in Mr. Murdstone and his sister, sir."

I replied with such an expressive look, that Mr. Chillip was emboldened by that, and the negus together, to give his head several short shakes, and thoughtfully exclaim, "Ah, dear me! We remember old times, Mr. Copperfield!"

"And the brother and sister are pursuing their old course, are they?" said I.

"Well, sir," replied Mr. Chillip, "a medical man, being so much in families, ought to have neither eyes nor ears for anything but his profession. Still, I must say, they are very severe, sir: both as to this life and the next."

"The next will be regulated without much reference to them, I dare say," I returned: "what are they doing as to this?"

Mr. Chillip shook his head, stirred his negus, and sipped it.

"She was a charming woman, sir!" he observed in a plaintive manner.

"The present Mrs. Murdstone?"

"A charming woman indeed, sir," said Mr. Chillip; "as amiable, I am sure, as it was possible to be! Mrs. Chillip's opinion is, that her spirit has been entirely broken since her marriage, and that she is all but melancholy mad. And the ladies," observed Mr. Chillip, timorously, "are great observers, sir."

"I suppose she was to be subdued and broken to their detestable mould, Heaven help her!" said I. "And she has been."

"Well, sir, there were violent quarrels at first, I assure you," said Mr. Chillip; "but she is quite a shadow now. Would it be considered forward if I was to say to you, sir, in confidence, that since the sister came to help, the brother and sister between them have nearly reduced her to a state of imbecility?"

I told him I could easily believe it.

" I have no hesitation in saying," said Mr. Chillip, fortifying himself with another sip of negus, " between you and me, sir, that her mother died of it—or that tyranny, gloom, and worry have made Mrs. Murdstone nearly imbecile. She was a lively young woman, sir, before marriage, and their gloom and austerity destroyed her. They go about with her, now, more like her keepers than her husband and sister-in-law. That was Mrs. Chillip's remark to me, only last week. And I assure you, sir, the ladies are great observers. Mrs. Chillip herself is a *great* observer ! "

" Does he gloomily profess to be (I am ashamed to use the word in such association) religious still ? " I inquired.

" You anticipate, sir," said Mr. Chillip, his eyelids getting quite red with the unwonted stimulus in which he was indulging. " One of Mrs. Chillip's most impressive remarks. Mrs. Chillip," he proceeded, in the calmest and slowest manner, " quite electrified me, by pointing out that Mr. Murdstone sets up an image of himself, and calls it the Divine Nature. You might have knocked me down on the flat of my back, sir, with the feather of a pen, I assure you, when Mrs. Chillip said so. The ladies are great observers, sir ? "

" Intuitively," said I, to his extreme delight.

" I am very happy to receive such support in my opinion, sir," he rejoined. " It is not often that I venture to give a non-medical opinion, I assure you. Mr. Murdstone delivers public addresses sometimes, and it is said,—in short, sir, it is said by Mrs. Chillip,—that the darker tyrant he has lately been, the more ferocious is his doctrine."

" I believe Mrs. Chillip to be perfectly right," said I.

" Mrs. Chillip does go so far as to say," pursued the meekest of little men, much encouraged, " that what such people miscall their religion, is a vent for their bad humours and arrogance. And do you know I must say, sir," he continued, mildly laying his head on one side, " that I *don't*

481

find authority for Mr. and Miss Murdstone in the New Testament?"

"I never found it either!" said I.

"In the meantime, sir," said Mr. Chillip, "they are much disliked; and as they are very free in consigning everybody who dislikes them to perdition, we really have a good deal of perdition going on in our neighbourhood! However, as Mrs. Chillip says, sir, they undergo a continual punishment; for they are turned inward, to feed upon their own hearts, and their own hearts are very bad feeding. Now, sir, about that brain of yours, if you'll excuse my returning to it. Don't you expose it to a good deal of excitement, sir?"

I found it not difficult, in the excitement of Mr. Chillip's own brain, under his potations of negus, to divert his attention from this topic to his own affairs, on which, for the next half-hour, he was quite loquacious; giving me to understand, among other pieces of information, that he was then at the Gray's Inn Coffee-house to lay his professional evidence before a Commission of Lunacy, touching the state of mind of a patient who had become deranged from excessive drinking.

"And I assure you, sir," he said, "I am extremely nervous on such occasions. I could not support being what is called Bullied, sir. It would quite unman me. Do you know it was some time before I recovered the conduct of that alarming lady, on the night of your birth, Mr. Copperfield?"

I told him that I was going down to my aunt, the Dragon of that night, early in the morning; and that she was one of the most tender-hearted and excellent of women, as he would know full well if he knew her better. The mere notion of the possibility of his ever seeing her again, appeared to terrify him. He replied with a small pale smile, "Is she so, indeed, sir? Really?" and almost immediately called for a candle, and went to bed, as if he were not quite safe anywhere else. He did not actually stagger under the negus; but I should think his placid little pulse must have made two or three more beats in a minute, than it had done since the great night of my aunt's disappointment, when she struck at him with her bonnet.

Thoroughly tired, I went to bed too, at midnight; passed the next day on the Dover coach; burst safe and sound into my aunt's old parlour while she was at tea (she wore spectacles now); and was received by her, and Mr. Dick, and dear old Peggotty, who acted as housekeeper, with open arms and tears of joy. My aunt was mightily amused, when we began to talk composedly, by my account of my meeting with Mr. Chillip, and of his holding her in such dread remembrance; and both she and Peggotty had a great deal to say about my poor mother's second husband, and "that murdering woman of a sister,"—on whom I think no pain or penalty would have induced my aunt to bestow any Christian or Proper Name, or any other designation.

CHAPTER LX.

My aunt and I, when we were left alone, talked far into the night. How the emigrants never wrote home, otherwise than cheerfully and hopefully; how Mr. Micawber had actually remitted divers small sums of money, on account of those "pecuniary liabilities," in reference to which he had been so business-like as between man and man; how Janet, returning into my aunt's service when she came back to Dover, had finally carried out her renunciation of mankind by entering into wedlock with a thriving tavern-keeper; and how my aunt had finally set *her* seal on the same great principle, by aiding and abetting the bride, and crowning the marriage-ceremony with her presence; were among our topics—already more or less familiar to me through the letters I had had. Mr. Dick, as usual, was not forgotten. My aunt informed me how he incessantly occupied himself in copying everything he could lay his hands on, and kept King Charles the First at a respectful distance by that semblance of employment; how it was one of the main joys and rewards of her life that he was free and happy, instead of pining in monotonous restraint; and how (as a novel general conclusion) nobody but she could ever fully know what he was.

"And when, Trot," said my aunt, patting the back of my hand, as we sat in our old way before the fire, "when are you going over to Canterbury?"

"I shall get a horse, and ride over to-morrow morning, aunt, unless you will go with me?"

"No!" said my aunt, in her short abrupt way. "I mean to stay where I am."

Then, I should ride, I said. I could not have come through Canterbury to-day without stopping, if I had been coming to any one but her.

She was pleased, but answered, "Tut, Trot; *my* old bones would have kept till to-morrow!" and softly patted my hand again, as I sat looking thoughtfully at the fire.

Thoughtfully, for I could not be here once more, and so near Agnes, without the revival of those regrets with which I had so long been occupied. Softened regrets they might be, teaching me what I had failed to learn when my younger life was all before me, but not the less regrets. "Oh, Trot," I seemed to hear my aunt say once more; and I understood her better now—"Blind, blind, blind!"

We both kept silence for some minutes. When I raised my eyes, I found that she was steadily observant of me. Perhaps she had followed the current of my mind; for it seemed to me an easy one to track now, wilful as it had been once.

"You will find her father a white-haired old man," said my aunt, "though a better man in all other respects—a reclaimed man. Neither will you find him measuring all human interests, and joys, and sorrows, with his one poor little inch-rule now. Trust me, child, such things must shrink very much, before they can be measured off in *that* way."

"Indeed they must," said I.

"You will find her," pursued my aunt, "as good, as beautiful, as earnest, as disinterested, as she has always been. If I knew higher praise, Trot, I would bestow it on her."

There was no higher praise for her; no higher reproach for me. Oh, how had I strayed so far away!

"If she trains the young girls whom she has about her, to

485

be like herself," said my aunt, earnest even to the filling of her eyes with tears, "Heaven knows, her life will be well employed! Useful and happy, as she said that day! How could she be otherwise than useful and happy!"

"Has Agnes any—" I was thinking aloud, rather than speaking.

"Well? Hey? Any what?" said my aunt, sharply.

"Any lover," said I.

"A score," cried my aunt, with a kind of indignant pride. "She might have married twenty times, my dear, since you have been gone!"

"No doubt," said I. "No doubt. But has she any lover who is worthy of her? Agnes could care for no other."

My aunt sat musing for a little while, with her chin upon her hand. Slowly raising her eyes to mine, she said:

"I suspect she has an attachment, Trot."

"A prosperous one?" said I.

"Trot," returned my aunt gravely, "I can't say. I have no right to tell you even so much. She has never confided it to me, but I suspect it."

She looked so attentively and anxiously at me (I even saw her tremble), that I felt now, more than ever, that she had followed my late thoughts. I summoned all the resolutions I had made, in all those many days and nights, and all those many conflicts of my heart.

"If it should be so," I began, "and I hope it is—"

"I don't know that it is," said my aunt curtly. "You must not be ruled by my suspicions. You must keep them secret. They are very slight, perhaps. I have no right to speak."

"If it should be so," I repeated, "Agnes will tell me at her own good time. A sister to whom I have confided so much, aunt, will not be reluctant to confide in me."

My aunt withdrew her eyes from mine, as slowly as she had turned them upon me; and covered them thoughtfully with her hand. By and by she put her other hand on my shoulder; and so we both sat, looking into the past, without saying another word, until we parted for the night.

I rode away, early in the morning, for the scene of my old school days. I cannot say that I was yet quite happy, in the hope that I was gaining a victory over myself; even in the prospect of so soon looking on her face again.

The well-remembered ground was soon traversed, and I came into the quiet streets, where every stone was a boy's book to me. I went on foot to the old house, and went away with a heart too full to enter. I returned; and looking, as I passed, through the low window of the turret-room where first Uriah Heep, and afterwards Mr. Micawber, had been wont to sit, saw that it was a little parlour now, and that there was no office. Otherwise the staid old house was, as to its cleanliness and order, still just as it had been when I first saw it. I requested the new maid who admitted me, to tell Miss Wickfield that a gentleman who waited on her from a friend abroad, was there; and I was shown up the grave old staircase (cautioned of the steps I knew so well), into the unchanged drawing-room. The books that Agnes and I had read together, were on their shelves; and the desk where I had laboured at my lessons, many a night, stood yet at the same old corner of the table. All the little changes that had crept in when the Heeps were there, were changed again. Everything was as it used to be, in the happy time.

I stood in a window, and looked across the ancient street at the opposite houses, recalling how I had watched them on wet afternoons, when I first came there; and how I had used to speculate about the people who appeared at any of the windows, and had followed them with my eyes up and down stairs, while women went clicking along the pavement in pattens, and the dull rain fell in slanting lines, and poured out of the waterspout yonder, and flowed into the road. The feeling with which I used to watch the tramps, as they came into the town on those wet evenings, at dusk, and limped past, with their bundles drooping over their shoulders at the ends of sticks, came freshly back to me; fraught, as then, with the smell of damp earth, and wet leaves and briar, and the sensation of the very airs that blew upon me in my own toilsome journey.

The opening of the little door in the panelled wall made me start and turn. Her beautiful serene eyes met mine as she came towards me. She stopped and laid her hand upon her bosom, and I caught her in my arms.

"Agnes! my dear girl! I have come too suddenly upon you."

"No, no! I am so rejoiced to see you, Trotwood!"

"Dear Agnes, the happiness it is to me, to see you once again!"

I folded her to my heart, and for a little while, we were both silent. Presently we sat down, side by side; and her angel-face was turned upon me with the welcome I had dreamed of, waking and sleeping, for whole years.

She was so true, she was so beautiful, she was so good,— I owed her so much gratitude, she was so dear to me, that I could find no utterance for what I felt. I tried to bless her, tried to thank her, tried to tell her (as I had often done in letters) what an influence she had upon me; but all my efforts were in vain. My love and joy were dumb.

With her own sweet tranquillity, she calmed my agitation; led me back to the time of our parting; spoke to me of Emily, whom she had visited, in secret, many times; spoke to me tenderly of Dora's grave. With the unerring instinct of her noble heart, she touched the chords of my memory so softly and harmoniously, that not one jarred within me; I could listen to the sorrowful, distant music, and desire to shrink from nothing it awoke. How could I, when, blended with it all, was her dear self, the better angel of my life?

"And you, Agnes," I said, by and by. "Tell me of yourself. You have hardly ever told me of your own life, in all this lapse of time!"

"What should I tell?" she answered, with her radiant

smile. "Papa is well. You see us here, quiet in our own home; our anxieties set at rest, our home restored to us: and knowing that, dear Trotwood, you know all."

"All, Agnes?" said I.

She looked at me, with some fluttering wonder in her face.

"Is there nothing else, Sister?" I said.

Her colour, which had just now faded, returned, and faded again. She smiled; with a quiet sadness, I thought; and shook her head.

I had sought to lead her to what my aunt had hinted at; for, sharply painful to me as it must be to receive that confidence, I was to discipline my heart, and do my duty to her. I saw, however, that she was uneasy, and I let it pass.

"You have much to do, dear Agnes?"

"With my school?" said she, looking up again, in all her bright composure.

"Yes. It is laborious, is it not?"

"The labour is so pleasant," she returned, "that it is scarcely grateful in me to call it by that name."

"Nothing good is difficult to you," said I.

Her colour came and went once more; and once more, as she bent her head, I saw the same sad smile.

"You will wait and see papa," said Agnes, cheerfully, "and pass the day with us? Perhaps you will sleep in your own room? We always call it yours."

I could not do that, having promised to ride back to my aunt's, at night; but I would pass the day there, joyfully.

"I must be a prisoner for a little while," said Agnes, "but here are the old books, Trotwood, and the old music."

"Even the old flowers are here," said I, looking round; "or the old kinds."

"I have found a pleasure," returned Agnes, smiling, "while you have been absent, in keeping everything as it used to be when we were children. For we were very happy then, I think."

"Heaven knows we were!" said I.

"And every little thing that has reminded me of my brother," said Agnes, with her cordial eyes turned cheerfully upon me, "has been a welcome companion. Even this," showing me the basket-trifle, full of keys, still hanging at her side, "seems to jingle a kind of old tune!"

She smiled again, and went out at the door by which she had come.

It was for me to guard this sisterly affection with religious care. It was all that I had left myself, and it was a treasure. If I once shook the foundations of the sacred confidence and usage, in virtue of which it was given to me, it was lost, and could never be recovered. I set this steadily before myself. The better I loved her, the more it behoved me never to forget it.

I walked through the streets; and, once more seeing my old adversary the butcher—now a constable, with his staff hanging up in the shop—went down to look at the place where I had fought him; and there meditated on Miss Shepherd and the eldest Miss Larkins, and all the idle loves and likings, and dislikings, of that time. Nothing seemed to have survived that time but Agnes; and she, ever a star above me, was brighter and higher.

When I returned, Mr. Wickfield had come home, from a garden he had, a couple of miles or so out of town, where he now employed himself almost every day. I found him as my aunt had described him. We sat down to dinner, with some half-dozen little girls; and he seemed but the shadow of his handsome picture on the wall.

The tranquillity and peace belonging, of old, to that quiet ground in my memory, pervaded it again. When dinner was done, Mr. Wickfield taking no wine, and I desiring none, we went up-stairs; where Agnes and her little charges sang and played, and worked. After tea the children left us; and we three sat together, talking of the bygone days.

"My part in them," said Mr. Wickfield, shaking his white head, "has much matter for regret—for deep regret, and deep contrition, Trotwood, you well know. But I would not cancel it, if it were in my power."

I could readily believe that, looking at the face beside him.

"I should cancel with it," he pursued, "such patience and devotion, such fidelity, such a child's love, as I must not forget, no! even to forget myself."

"I understand you, sir," I softly said. "I hold it—I have always held it—in veneration."

"But no one knows, not even you," he returned, "how much she has done, how much she has undergone, how hard she has striven. Dear Agnes!"

She had put her hand entreatingly on his arm, to stop him; and was very, very pale.

"Well, well!" he said with a sigh, dismissing, as I then saw, some trial she had borne, or was yet to bear, in connexion with what my aunt had told me. "Well! I have never told you, Trotwood, of her mother. Has any one?"

"Never, sir."

"It's not much—though it was much to suffer. She married me in opposition to her father's wish, and he renounced her. She prayed him to forgive her, before my Agnes came into this world. He was a very hard man, and her mother had long been dead. He repulsed her. He broke her heart."

Agnes leaned upon his shoulder, and stole her arm about his neck.

"She had an affectionate and gentle heart," he said; "and it was broken. I knew its tender nature very well. No one could, if I did not. She loved me dearly, but was never happy. She was always labouring, in secret, under this distress; and being delicate and downcast at the time of his last repulse—for it was not the first, by many—pined away and died. She left me Agnes, two weeks old; and the grey hair that you recollect me with, when you first came."

He kissed Agnes on her cheek.

"My love for my dear child was a diseased love, but my

491

mind was all unhealthy then. I say no more of that. I am not speaking of myself, Trotwood, but of her mother, and of her. If I give you any clue to what I am, or to what I have been, you will unravel it, I know. What Agnes is, I need not say. I have always read something of her poor mother's story, in her character; and so I tell it you to-night, when we three are again together, after such great changes. I have told it all."

His bowed head, and her angel-face and filial duty, derived a more pathetic meaning from it than they had had before. If I had wanted anything by which to mark this night of our re-union, I should have found it in this.

Agnes rose up from her father's side, before long; and going softly to her piano, played some of the old airs to which we had often listened in that place.

"Have you any intention of going away again?" Agnes asked me, as I was standing by.

"What does my sister say to that?"

"I hope not."

"Then I have no such intention, Agnes."

"I think you ought not, Trotwood, since you ask me," she said, mildly. "Your growing reputation and success enlarge your power of doing good; and if *I* could spare my brother," with her eyes upon me, "perhaps the time could not."

"What I am, you have made me, Agnes. You should know best."

"*I* made you, Trotwood?"

"Yes! Agnes, my dear girl!" I said, bending over her. "I tried to tell you, when we met to-day, something that has been in my thoughts since Dora died. You remember, when you came down to me in our little room—pointing upward, Agnes?"

"Oh, Trotwood!" she returned, her eyes filled with tears. "So loving, so confiding, and so young! Can I ever forget?"

"As you were then, my sister, I have often thought since,

you have ever been to me. Ever pointing upward, Agnes; ever leading me to something better; ever directing me to higher things!"

She only shook her head; through her tears I saw the same sad quiet smile.

"And I am so grateful to you for it, Agnes, so bound to you, that there is no name for the affection of my heart. I want you to know, yet don't know how to tell you, that all my life long I shall look up to you, and be guided by you, as I have been through the darkness that is past. Whatever betides, whatever new ties you may form, whatever changes may come between us, I shall always look to you, and love you, as I do now, and have always done. You will always be my solace and resource as you have always been. Until I die, my dearest sister, I shall see you always before me, pointing upward!"

She put her hand in mine, and told me she was proud of me, and of what I said; although I praised her very far beyond her worth. Then she went on softly playing, but without removing her eyes from me.

"Do you know, what I have heard to-night, Agnes," said I, "strangely seems to be a part of the feeling with which I regarded you when I saw you first—with which I sat beside you in my rough school days?"

"You knew I had no mother," she replied with a smile, "and felt kindly towards me."

"More than that, Agnes, I knew, almost as if I had known this story, that there was something inexplicably gentle and softened, surrounding you; something that might have been sorrowful in some one else (as I can now understand it was), but was not so in you."

She softly played on, looking at me still.

"Will you laugh at my cherishing such fancies, Agnes?"

"No!"

"Or at my saying that I really believe I felt, even then, that you could be faithfully affectionate against all

493

discouragement, and never cease to be so, until you ceased to live?—Will you laugh at such a dream?"

"Oh, no! Oh, no!"

For an instant, a distressful shadow crossed her face; but, even in the start it gave me, it was gone; and she was playing on, and looking at me with her own calm smile.

As I rode back in the lonely night, the wind going by me like a restless memory, I thought of this, and feared she was not happy. *I* was not happy; but, thus far, I had faithfully set the seal upon the Past, and, thinking of her, pointing upward, thought of her as pointing to that sky above me, where, in the mystery to come, I might yet love her with a love unknown on earth, and tell her what the strife had been within me when I loved her here.

CHAPTER LXI.

For a time—at all events until my book should be completed, which would be the work of several months—I took up my abode in my aunt's house at Dover; and there, sitting in the window from which I had looked out at the moon upon the sea, when that roof first gave me shelter, I quietly pursued my task.

In pursuance of my intention of referring to my own fictions only when their course should incidentally connect itself with the progress of my story, I do not enter on the aspirations, the delights, anxieties, and triumphs of my art. That I truly devoted myself to it with my strongest earnestness, and bestowed upon it every energy of my soul, I have already said. If the books I have written be of any worth, they will supply the rest. I shall otherwise have written to poor purpose, and the rest will be of interest to no one.

Occasionally I went to London; to lose myself in the swarm of life there, or to consult with Traddles on some business point. He had managed for me, in my absence, with the soundest judgment; and my worldly affairs were prospering. As my notoriety began to bring upon me an enormous quantity of letters from people of whom I had no knowledge—chiefly about nothing, and extremely difficult to answer—I agreed with Traddles to have my name painted up on his door. There, the devoted postman on that beat

495

delivered bushels of letters for me; and there, at intervals, I laboured through them, like a Home Secretary of State without the salary.

Among this correspondence, there dropped in, every now and then, an obliging proposal from one of the numerous outsiders always lurking about the Commons, to practise under cover of my name (if I would take the necessary steps remaining to make a proctor of myself), and pay me a percentage on the profits. But I declined these offers; being already aware that there were plenty of such covert practitioners in existence, and considering the Commons quite bad enough, without my doing anything to make it worse.

The girls had gone home, when my name burst into bloom on Traddles's door; and the sharp boy looked, all day, as if he had never heard of Sophy, shut up in a back room, glancing down from her work into a sooty little strip of garden with a pump in it. But, there I always found her, the same bright housewife; often humming her Devonshire ballads when no strange foot was coming up the stairs, and blunting the sharp boy in his official closet with melody.

I wondered, at first, why I so often found Sophy writing in a copy-book; and why she always shut it up when I appeared, and hurried it into the table-drawer. But the secret soon came out. One day, Traddles (who had just come home through the drizzling sleet from Court) took a paper out of his desk, and asked me what I thought of that handwriting?

"Oh, *don't*, Tom!" cried Sophy, who was warming his slippers before the fire.

"My dear," returned Tom, in a delighted state, "why not? What do you say to that writing, Copperfield?"

"It's extraordinarily legal and formal," said I. "I don't think I ever saw such a stiff hand."

"Not like a lady's hand, is it?" said Traddles.

"A lady's!" I repeated. "Bricks and mortar are more like a lady's hand!"

Traddles broke into a rapturous laugh, and informed me that it was Sophy's writing; that Sophy had vowed and declared he would need a copying-clerk soon, and she would be that clerk; that she had acquired this hand from a pattern; and that she could throw off—I forget how many folios an hour. Sophy was very much confused by my being told all this, and said that when "Tom" was made a judge he wouldn't be so ready to proclaim it. Which "Tom" denied; averring that he should always be equally proud of it, under all circumstances.

"What a thoroughly good and charming wife she is, my dear Traddles!" said I, when she had gone away, laughing.

"My dear Copperfield," returned Traddles, "she is, without any exception, the dearest girl! The way she manages this place; her punctuality, domestic knowledge, economy, and order; her cheerfulness, Copperfield!"

"Indeed, you have reason to commend her!" I returned. "You are a happy fellow. I believe you make yourselves, and each other, two of the happiest people in the world."

"I am sure we *are* two of the happiest people," returned Traddles. "I admit that, at all events. Bless my soul, when I see her getting up by candle-light on these dark mornings, busying herself in the day's arrangements, going out to market before the clerks come into the Inn, caring for no weather, devising the most capital little dinners out of the plainest materials, making puddings and pies, keeping everything in its right place, always so neat and ornamental herself, sitting up at night with me if it's ever so late, sweet-tempered and encouraging always, and all for me, I positively sometimes can't believe it, Copperfield!"

He was tender of the very slippers she had been warming, as he put them on, and stretched his feet enjoyingly upon the fender.

"I positively sometimes can't believe it," said Traddles. "Then, our pleasures! Dear me, they are inexpensive, but they are quite wonderful! When we are at home here of an evening, and shut the outer door, and draw those curtains —which she made—where could we be more snug? When it's fine, and we go out for a walk in the evening, the streets abound in enjoyment for us. We look into the glittering windows of the jewellers' shops; and I show Sophy which of the diamond-eyed serpents, coiled up on white satin rising grounds, I would give her if I could afford it; and Sophy shows me which of the gold watches that are capped and jewelled and engine-turned, and possessed of the horizontal lever-escape-movement, and all sorts of things, she would buy for me if *she* could afford it; and we pick out the spoons and forks, fish-slices, butter-knives, and sugar-tongs, we should both prefer if we could both afford it; and really we go away as if we had got them! Then, when we stroll into the squares, and great streets, and see a house to let, sometimes we look up at it, and say, how would *that* do, if I was made a judge? And we parcel it out—such a room for us, such rooms for the girls, and so forth; until we settle to our satisfaction that it would do, or it wouldn't do, as the case may be. Sometimes, we go at half-price to the pit of the theatre—the very smell of which is cheap, in my opinion, at the money—and there we thoroughly enjoy the play: which Sophy believes every word of, and so do I. In walking home, perhaps we buy a little bit of something at a cook's-shop, or a little lobster at the fishmonger's, and bring it here, and make a splendid supper, chatting about what we have seen. Now, you know, Copperfield, if I was Lord Chancellor, we couldn't do this!"

"You would do something, whatever you were, my dear Traddles," thought I, "that would be pleasant and amiable. And by the way," I said aloud, "I suppose you never draw any skeletons now?"

"Really," replied Traddles, laughing, and reddening, "I can't wholly deny that I do, my dear Copperfield. For, being in one of the back rows of the King's Bench the other day, with a pen in my hand, the fancy came into my head to try how I had preserved that accomplishment. And I am afraid there's a skeleton—in a wig—on the ledge of the desk."

After we had both laughed heartily, Traddles wound up by looking with a smile at the fire, and saying, in his forgiving way, "Old Creakle!"

"I have a letter from that old—Rascal here," said I. For I never was less disposed to forgive him the way he used to batter Traddles, than when I saw Traddles so ready to forgive him himself.

"From Creakle the schoolmaster?" exclaimed Traddles. "No!"

"Among the persons who are attracted to me in my rising fame and fortune," said I, looking over my letters, "and who discover that they were always much attached to me, is the self-same Creakle. He is not a schoolmaster now, Traddles. He is retired. He is a Middlesex Magistrate."

I thought Traddles might be surprised to hear it, but he was not so at all.

"How do you suppose he comes to be a Middlesex Magistrate?" said I.

"Oh dear me!" replied Traddles, "it would be very difficult to answer that question. Perhaps he voted for somebody, or lent money to somebody, or bought something of somebody, or otherwise obliged somebody, or jobbed for somebody, who knew somebody who got the lieutenant of the county to nominate him for the commission."

"On the commission he is, at any rate," said I. "And he writes to me here, that he will be glad to show me, in operation, the only true system of prison discipline; the only unchallengeable way of making sincere and lasting converts and penitents—which, you know, is by solitary confinement. What do you say?"

"To the system?" inquired Traddles, looking grave.

"No. To my accepting the offer, and your going with me?"

"I don't object," said Traddles.

499

"Then I'll write to say so. You remember (to say nothing of our treatment) this same Creakle turning his son out of doors, I suppose, and the life he used to lead his wife and daughter?"

"Perfectly," said Traddles.

"Yet, if you'll read his letter, you'll find he is the tenderest of men to prisoners convicted of the whole calendar of felonies," said I; "though I can't find that his tenderness extends to any other class of created beings."

Traddles shrugged his shoulders, and was not at all surprised. I had not expected him to be, and was not surprised myself; or my observation of similar practical satires would have been but scanty. We arranged the time of our visit, and I wrote accordingly to Mr. Creakle that evening.

On the appointed day—I think it was the next day, but no matter—Traddles and I repaired to the prison where Mr. Creakle was powerful. It was an immense and solid building, erected at a vast expense. I could not help thinking, as we approached the gate, what an uproar would have been made in the country, if any deluded man had proposed to spend one half the money it had cost, on the erection of an industrial school for the young, or a house of refuge for the deserving old.

In an office that might have been on the ground-floor of the Tower of Babel, it was so massively constructed, we were presented to our old schoolmaster; who was one of a group, composed of two or three of the busier sort of magistrates, and some visitors they had brought. He received me, like a man who had formed my mind in bygone years, and had always loved me tenderly. On my introducing Traddles, Mr. Creakle expressed, in like manner, but in an inferior degree, that he had always been Traddles's guide, philosopher, and friend. Our venerable instructor was a great deal older, and not improved in appearance. His face was as fiery as ever; his eyes were as small, and rather deeper set. The scanty, wet-looking grey hair, by which I remembered him,

500

was almost gone; and the thick veins in his bald head were none the more agreeable to look at.

After some conversation among these gentlemen, from which I might have supposed that there was nothing in the world to be legitimately taken into account but the supreme comfort of prisoners, at any expense, and nothing on the wide earth to be done outside prison-doors, we began our inspection. It being then just dinner-time, we went, first into the great kitchen, where every prisoner's dinner was in course of being set out separately (to be handed to him in his cell), with the regularity and precision of clock-work. I said aside, to Traddles, that I wondered whether it occurred to anybody, that there was a striking contrast between these plentiful repasts of choice quality, and the dinners, not to say of paupers, but of soldiers, sailors, labourers, the great bulk of the honest, working community; of whom not one man in five hundred ever dined half so well. But I learned that the "system" required high living; and, in short, to dispose of the system, once for all, I found that on that head and on all others, "the system" put an end to all doubts, and disposed of all anomalies. Nobody appeared to have the least idea that there was any other system, but *the* system, to be considered.

As we were going through some of the magnificent passages, I inquired of Mr. Creakle and his friends what were supposed to be the main advantages of this all-governing and universally over-riding system? I found them to be the perfect isolation of prisoners—so that no one man in confinement there, knew anything about another; and the reduction of prisoners to a wholesome state of mind, leading to sincere contrition and repentance.

Now, it struck me, when we began to visit individuals in their cells, and to traverse the passages in which those cells were, and to have the manner of the going to chapel and so forth, explained to us, that there was a strong probability of the prisoners knowing a good deal about each other, and of

501

their carrying on a pretty complete system of intercourse. This, at the time I write, has been proved, I believe, to be the case; but, as it would have been flat blasphemy against the system to have hinted such a doubt then, I looked out for the penitence as diligently as I could.

And here again, I had great misgivings. I found as prevalent a fashion in the form of the penitence, as I had left outside in the forms of the coats and waistcoats in the windows of the tailors' shops. I found a vast amount of profession, varying very little in character: varying very little (which I thought exceedingly suspicious) even in words. I found a great many foxes, disparaging whole vineyards of inaccessible grapes; but I found very few foxes whom I would have trusted within reach of a bunch. Above all, I found that the most professing men were the greatest objects of interest: and that their conceit, their vanity, their want of excitement, and their love of deception (which many of them possessed to an almost incredible extent, as their histories showed), all prompted to these professions, and were all gratified by them.

However, I heard so repeatedly, in the course of our goings to and fro, of a certain Number Twenty Seven, who was the favourite, and who really appeared to be a Model Prisoner, that I resolved to suspend my judgment until I should see Twenty Seven. Twenty Eight, I understood, was also a bright particular star; but it was his misfortune to have his glory a little dimmed by the extraordinary lustre of Twenty Seven. I heard so much of Twenty Seven, of his pious admonitions to everybody around him, and of the beautiful letters he constantly wrote to his mother (whom he seemed to consider in a very bad way), that I became quite impatient to see him.

I had to restrain my impatience for some time, on account of Twenty Seven being reserved for a concluding effect. But, at last, we came to the door of his cell; and Mr. Creakle, looking through a little hole in it, reported to us, in a state of the greatest admiration, that he was reading a Hymn Book.

There was such a rush of heads immediately, to see Number Twenty Seven reading his Hymn Book, that the little hole was blocked up, six or seven heads deep. To remedy this inconvenience, and give us an opportunity of conversing with Twenty Seven in all his purity, Mr. Creakle directed the door of the cell to be unlocked, and Twenty Seven to be invited out into the passage. This was done; and whom should Traddles and I then behold, to our amazement, in this converted Number Twenty Seven, but Uriah Heep!

He knew us directly; and said, as he came out—with the old writhe,—

"How do you do, Mr. Copperfield? How do you do, Mr. Traddles?"

This recognition caused a general admiration in the party. I rather thought that every one was struck by his not being proud, and taking notice of us.

"Well, Twenty Seven," said Mr. Creakle, mournfully admiring him. "How do you find yourself to-day?"

"I am very umble, sir!" replied Uriah Heep.

"You are always so, Twenty Seven," said Mr. Creakle.

Here, another gentleman asked, with extreme anxiety: "Are you quite comfortable?"

"Yes, I thank you, sir!" said Uriah Heep, looking in that direction. "Far more comfortable here, than ever I was outside. I see my follies now, sir. That's what makes me comfortable."

Several gentlemen were much affected; and a third questioner, forcing himself to the front, inquired with extreme feeling: "How do you find the beef?"

"Thank you, sir," replied Uriah, glancing in the new direction of this voice, "it was tougher yesterday than I could wish; but it's my duty to bear. I have committed follies, gentlemen," said Uriah, looking round with a meek smile, "and I ought to bear the consequences without repining."

DAVID COPPERFIELD.

A murmur, partly of gratification at Twenty Seven's celestial state of mind, and partly of indignation against the Contractor who had given him any cause of complaint (a note of which was immediately made by Mr. Creakle), having subsided, Twenty Seven stood in the midst of us, as if he felt himself the principal object of merit in a highly meritorious museum. That we, the neophytes, might have an excess of light shining upon us all at once, orders were given to let out Twenty Eight.

I had been so much astonished already, that I only felt a kind of resigned wonder when Mr. Littimer walked forth, reading a good book!

"Twenty Eight," said a gentleman in spectacles, who had not yet spoken, "you complained last week, my good fellow, of the cocoa. How has it been since?"

"I thank you, sir," said Mr. Littimer, "it has been better made. If I might take the liberty of saying so, sir, I don't think the milk which is boiled with it is quite genuine; but I am aware, sir, that there is great adulteration of milk, in London, and that the article in a pure state is difficult to be obtained."

It appeared to me that the gentleman in spectacles backed his Twenty Eight against Mr. Creakle's Twenty Seven, for each of them took his own man in hand.

"What is your state of mind, Twenty Eight?" said the questioner in spectacles.

"I thank you, sir," returned Mr. Littimer; "I see my follies now, sir. I am a good deal troubled when I think of the sins of my former companions, sir; but I trust they may find forgiveness."

"You are quite happy yourself?" said the questioner, nodding encouragement.

"I am much obliged to you, sir," returned Mr. Littimer. "Perfectly so."

"Is there anything at all on your mind, now?" said the questioner. "If so, mention it, Twenty Eight."

I am shown Two Interesting Penitents

"Sir," said Mr. Littimer, without looking up, "if my eyes have not deceived me, there is a gentleman present who was acquainted with me in my former life. It may be profitable to that gentleman to know, sir, that I attribute my past follies, entirely to having lived a thoughtless life in the service of young men; and to having allowed myself to be led by them into weaknesses, which I had not the strength to resist. I hope that gentleman will take warning, sir, and will not be offended at my freedom. It is for his good. I am conscious of my own past follies. I hope he may repent of all the wickedness and sin, to which he has been a party."

I observed that several gentlemen were shading their eyes, each, with one hand, as if they had just come into church.

"This does you credit, Twenty Eight," returned the questioner. "I should have expected it of you. Is there anything else?"

"Sir," returned Mr. Littimer, slightly lifting up his eyebrows, but not his eyes, "there was a young woman who fell into dissolute courses, that I endeavoured to save, sir, but could not rescue. I beg that gentleman, if he has it in his power, to inform that young woman from me that I forgive her her bad conduct towards myself; and that I call her to repentance—if he will be so good."

"I have no doubt, Twenty Eight," returned the questioner, "that the gentleman you refer to feels very strongly—as we all must—what you have so properly said. We will not detain you."

"I thank you, sir," said Mr. Littimer. "Gentlemen, I wish you a good day, and hoping you and your families will also see your wickedness, and amend!"

With this, Number Twenty Eight retired, after a glance between him and Uriah; as if they were not altogether unknown to each other, through some medium of communication; and a murmur went round the group, as his door shut upon him, that he was a most respectable man, and a beautiful case.

505

"Now, Twenty Seven," said Mr. Creakle, entering on a clear stage with *his* man, "is there anything that any one can do for you? If so, mention it."

"I would umbly ask, sir," returned Uriah, with a jerk of his malevolent head, "for leave to write again to mother."

"It shall certainly be granted," said Mr. Creakle.

"Thank you, sir! I am anxious about mother. I am afraid she ain't safe."

Somebody incautiously asked, what from? But there was a scandalised whisper of "Hush!"

"Immortally safe, sir," returned Uriah, writhing in the direction of the voice. "I should wish mother to be got into my state. I never should have been got into my present state if I hadn't come here. I wish mother had come here. It would be better for everybody, if they got took up, and was brought here."

This sentiment gave unbounded satisfaction—greater satisfaction, I think, than anything that had passed yet.

"Before I come here," said Uriah, stealing a look at us, as if he would have blighted the outer world to which we belonged, if he could, "I was given to follies; but now I am sensible of my follies. There's a deal of sin outside. There's a deal of sin in mother. There's nothing but sin everywhere—except here."

"You are quite changed?" said Mr. Creakle.

"Oh dear, yes, sir!" cried this hopeful penitent.

"You wouldn't relapse, if you were going out?" asked somebody else.

"Oh de-ar no, sir!"

"Well!" said Mr. Creakle, "this is very gratifying. You have addressed Mr. Copperfield, Twenty Seven. Do you wish to say anything further to him?"

"You knew me a long time before I came here and was changed, Mr. Copperfield," said Uriah, looking at me; and a more villainous look I never saw, even on his visage. "You knew me when, in spite of my follies, I was umble among them

that was proud, and meek among them that was violent—
you was violent to me yourself, Mr. Copperfield. Once, you
struck me a blow in the face, you know."

General commiseration. Several indignant glances directed
at me.

"But I forgive you, Mr. Copperfield," said Uriah, making
his forgiving nature the subject of a most impious and awful
parallel, which I shall not record. "I forgive everybody.
It would ill become me to bear malice. I freely forgive you,
and I hope you'll curb your passions in future. I hope Mr.
W. will repent, and Miss W., and all of that sinful lot.
You've been visited with affliction, and I hope it may do
you good; but you'd better have come here. Mr. W. had
better have come here, and Miss W. too. The best wish I
could give you, Mr. Copperfield, and give all of you gentlemen,
is, that you could be took up and brought here. When I
think of my past follies, and my present state, I am sure
it would be best for you. I pity all who ain't brought
here!"

He sneaked back into his cell, amidst a little chorus of
approbation; and both Traddles and I experienced a great
relief when he was locked in.

It was a characteristic feature in this repentance, that I
was fain to ask what these two men had done, to be there
at all. That appeared to be the last thing about which
they had anything to say. I addressed myself to one of the
two warders, who, I suspected, from certain latent indications
in their faces, knew pretty well what all this stir was worth.

"Do you know," said I, as we walked along the passage,
"what felony was Number Twenty Seven's last 'folly?'"

The answer was that it was a Bank case.

"A fraud on the Bank of England?" I asked.

"Yes, sir. Fraud, forgery, and conspiracy. He and some
others. He set the others on. It was a deep plot for a
large sum. Sentence, transportation for life. Twenty Seven
was the knowingest bird of the lot, and had very nearly kept

507

himself safe ; but not quite. The Bank was just able to put salt upon his tail—and only just."

" Do you know Twenty Eight's offence ? "

"Twenty Eight," returned my informant, speaking throughout in a low tone, and looking over his shoulder as we walked along the passage, to guard himself from being overheard, in such an unlawful reference to these Immaculates, by Creakle and the rest; "Twenty Eight (also transportation) got a place, and robbed a young master of a matter of two hundred and fifty pounds in money and valuables, the night before they were going abroad. I particularly recollect his case, from his being took by a dwarf."

" A what ? "

" A little woman. I have forgot her name."

" Not Mowcher ? "

"That's it! He had eluded pursuit, and was going to America in a flaxen wig and whiskers, and such a complete disguise as never you see in all your born days; when the little woman, being in Southampton, met him walking along the street—picked him out with her sharp eye in a moment —ran betwixt his legs to upset him—and held on to him like grim Death."

" Excellent Miss Mowcher ! " cried I.

" You'd have said so, if you had seen her, standing on a chair in the witness-box at the trial, as I did," said my friend. "He cut her face right open, and pounded her in the most brutal manner, when she took him ; but she never loosed her hold till he was locked up. She held so tight to him, in fact, that the officers were obliged to take 'em both together. She gave her evidence in the gamest way, and was highly complimented by the Bench, and cheered right home to her lodgings. She said in Court that she'd have took him single-handed (on account of what she knew concerning him), if he had been Samson. And it's my belief she would !

It was mine too, and I highly respected Miss Mowcher for it.

REFLECTIONS ON THE MODEL SYSTEM.

We had now seen all there was to see. It would have been in vain to represent to such a man as the worshipful Mr. Creakle, that Twenty Seven and Twenty Eight were perfectly consistent and unchanged; that exactly what they were then, they had always been; that the hypocritical knaves were just the subjects to make that sort of profession in such a place; that they knew its market-value at least as well as we did, in the immediate service it would do them when they were expatriated; in a word, that it was a rotten, hollow, painfully suggestive piece of business altogether. We left them to their system and themselves, and went home wondering.

"Perhaps it's a good thing, Traddles," said I, "to have an unsound Hobby ridden hard; for it's the sooner ridden to death."

I hope so," replied Traddles.

CHAPTER LXII.

THE year came round to Christmas-time, and I had been at home above two months. I had seen Agnes frequently. However loud the general voice might be in giving me encouragement, and however fervent the emotions and endeavours to which it roused me, I heard her lightest word of praise as I heard nothing else.

At least once a week, and sometimes oftener, I rode over there, and passed the evening. I usually rode back at night; for the old unhappy sense was always hovering about me now —most sorrowfully when I left her—and I was glad to be up and out, rather than wandering over the past in weary wakefulness or miserable dreams. I wore away the longest part of many wild sad nights, in those rides; reviving, as I went, the thoughts that had occupied me in my long absence.

Or, if I were to say rather that I listened to the echoes of those thoughts, I should better express the truth. They spoke to me from afar off. I had put them at a distance, and accepted my inevitable place. When I read to Agnes what I wrote; when I saw her listening face; moved her to smiles or tears; and heard her cordial voice so earnest on the shadowy events of that imaginative world in which I lived; I thought what a fate mine might have been—but only thought so, as I had thought after I was married to Dora, what I could have wished my wife to be.

510

MY LOVE AND MY DUTY.

My duty to Agnes, who loved me with a love, which, if I disquieted, I wronged most selfishly and poorly, and could never restore; my matured assurance that I, who had worked out my own destiny, and won what I had impetuously set my heart on, had no right to murmur and must bear; comprised what I felt and what I had learned. But I loved her: and now it even became some consolation to me, vaguely to conceive a distant day when I might blamelessly avow it; when all this should be over; when I could say "Agnes, so it was when I came home; and now I am old, and I never have loved since!"

She did not once show me any change in herself. What she always had been to me, she still was; wholly unaltered.

Between my aunt and me there had been something, in this connexion, since the night of my return, which I cannot call a restraint, or an avoidance of the subject, so much as an implied understanding that we thought of it together, but did not shape our thoughts into words. When, according to our old custom, we sat before the fire at night, we often fell into this train; as naturally, and as consciously to each other, as if we had unreservedly said so. But we preserved an unbroken silence. I believed that she had read, or partly read, my thoughts that night; and that she fully comprehended why I gave mine no more distinct expression.

This Christmas-time being come, and Agnes having reposed no new confidence in me, a doubt that had several times arisen in my mind—whether she could have that perception of the true state of my breast, which restrained her with the apprehension of giving me pain—began to oppress me heavily. If that were so, my sacrifice was nothing; my plainest obligation to her unfulfilled; and every poor action I had shrunk from, I was hourly doing. I resolved to set this right beyond all doubt;—if such a barrier were between us, to break it down at once with a determined hand.

It was—what lasting reason have I to remember it!—a cold, harsh, winter day. There had been snow some hours

511

before; and it lay, not deep, but hard-frozen on the ground. Out at sea, beyond my window, the wind blew ruggedly from the north. I had been thinking of it, sweeping over those mountain wastes of snow in Switzerland, then inaccessible to any human foot; and had been speculating which was the lonelier, those solitary regions, or a deserted ocean.

"Riding to-day, Trot?" said my aunt, putting her head in at the door.

"Yes," said I, "I am going over to Canterbury. It's a good day for a ride."

"I hope your horse may think so, too," said my aunt; "but at present he is holding down his head and his ears, standing before the door there, as if he thought his stable preferable."

My aunt, I may observe, allowed my horse on the forbidden ground, but had not at all relented toward the donkeys.

"He will be fresh enough, presently!" said I.

"The ride will do his master good, at all events," observed my aunt, glancing at the papers on my table. "Ah, child, you pass a good many hours here! I never thought, when I used to read books, what work it was to write them."

"It's work enough to read them, sometimes," I returned. "As to the writing, it has its own charms, aunt."

"Ah! I see!" said my aunt. "Ambition, love of approbation, sympathy, and much more, I suppose? Well: go along with you!"

"Do you know anything more," said I, standing composedly before her—she had patted me on the shoulder, and sat down in my chair—"of that attachment of Agnes?"

She looked up in my face a little while, before replying:

"I think I do, Trot."

"Are you confirmed in your impression?" I inquired.

"I think I am, Trot."

She looked so steadfastly at me: with a kind of doubt, or pity, or suspense in her affection: that I summoned the stronger determination to show her a perfectly cheerful face.

I MAKE A FIRM RESOLVE.

"And what is more, Trot—" said my aunt.

"Yes!"

"I think Agnes is going to be married."

"God bless her!" said I, cheerfully.

"God bless her!" said my aunt, "and her husband too!"

I echoed it, parted from my aunt, went lightly down-stairs, mounted, and rode away. There was greater reason than before to do what I had resolved to do.

How well I recollect the wintry ride! The frozen particles of ice, brushed from the blades of grass by the wind, and borne across my face; the hard clatter of the horse's hoofs, beating a tune upon the ground; the stiff-tilled soil; the snow-drift, lightly eddying in the chalk-pit as the breeze ruffled it; the smoking team with the waggon of old hay, stopping to breathe on the hill-top, and shaking their bells musically; the whitened slopes and sweeps of Down-land lying against the dark sky, as if they were drawn on a huge slate!

I found Agnes alone. The little girls had gone to their own homes now, and she was alone by the fire, reading. She put down her book on seeing me come in; and having welcomed me as usual, took her work-basket and sat in one of the old-fashioned windows.

I sat beside her on the window-seat, and we talked of what I was doing, and when it would be done, and of the progress I had made since my last visit. Agnes was very cheerful; and laughingly predicted that I should soon become too famous to be talked to, on such subjects.

"So I make the most of the present time, you see," said Agnes, "and talk to you while I may."

As I looked at her beautiful face, observant of her work, she raised her mild clear eyes, and saw that I was looking at her.

"You are thoughtful to-day, Trotwood!"

"Agnes, shall I tell you what about? I came to tell you."

She put aside her work, as she was used to do when we were seriously discussing anything; and gave me her whole attention.

"My dear Agnes, do you doubt my being true to you?"

"No!" she answered, with a look of astonishment.

"Do you doubt my being what I always have been to you?"

"No!" she answered, as before.

"Do you remember that I tried to tell you, when I came home, what a debt of gratitude I owed you, dearest Agnes, and how fervently I felt towards you?"

"I remember it," she said, gently, "very well."

"You have a secret," said I. "Let me share it, Agnes."

She cast down her eyes, and trembled.

"I could hardly fail to know, even if I had not heard—but from other lips than yours, Agnes, which seems strange—that there is some one upon whom you have bestowed the treasure of your love. Do not shut me out of what concerns your happiness so nearly! If you can trust me as you say you can, and as I know you may, let me be your friend, your brother, in this matter, of all others!"

With an appealing, almost a reproachful, glance, she rose from the window; and hurrying across the room as if without knowing where, put her hands before her face, and burst into such tears as smote me to the heart.

And yet they awakened something in me, bringing promise to my heart. Without my knowing why, these tears allied themselves with the quietly sad smile which was so fixed in my remembrance, and shook me more with hope than fear or sorrow.

"Agnes! Sister! Dearest! What have I done?"

"Let me go away, Trotwood. I am not well. I am not myself. I will speak to you by and by—another time. I will write to you. Don't speak to me now. Don't! don't!"

I sought to recollect what she had said, when I had spoken to her on that former night, of her affection needing no return. It seemed a very world that I must search through in a moment.

"Agnes, I cannot bear to see you so, and think that I have been the cause. My dearest girl, dearer to me than anything in life, if you are unhappy, let me share your unhappiness. If you are in need of help or counsel, let me try to give it to you. If you have indeed a burden on your heart, let me try to lighten it. For whom do I live now, Agnes, if it is not for you?"

"Oh, spare me! I am not myself! Another time!" was all I could distinguish.

Was it a selfish error that was leading me away? Or, having once a clue to hope, was there something opening to me that I had not dared to think of?

"I must say more. I cannot let you leave me so! For Heaven's sake, Agnes, let us not mistake each other after all these years, and all that has come and gone with them! I must speak plainly. If you have any lingering thought that I could envy the happiness you will confer; that I could not resign you to a dearer protector, of your own choosing; that I could not, from my removed place, be a contented witness of your joy; dismiss it, for I don't deserve it! I have not suffered quite in vain. You have not taught me quite in vain. There is no alloy of self in what I feel for you."

She was quiet now. In a little time, she turned her pale face towards me, and said in a low voice, broken here and there, but very clear,

"I owe it to your pure friendship for me, Trotwood—which, indeed, I do not doubt—to tell you, you are mistaken. I can do no more. If I have sometimes, in the course of years, wanted help and counsel, they have come to me. If I have sometimes been unhappy, the feeling has passed away. If I have ever had a burden on my heart, it has been lightened for me. If I have any secret, it is—no new one; and is—not what you suppose. I cannot reveal it, or divide it. It has long been mine, and must remain mine."

"Agnes! Stay! A moment!"

She was going away, but I detained her. I clasped my arm about her waist. "In the course of years!" "It is not a new one!" New thoughts and hopes were whirling through my mind, and all the colours of my life were changing.

"Dearest Agnes! Whom I so respect and honour—whom I so devotedly love! When I came here to-day, I thought that nothing could have wrested this confession from me. I thought I could have kept it in my bosom all our lives, till we were old. But, Agnes, if I have indeed any new-born hope that I may ever call you something more than Sister, widely different from Sister!——"

Her tears fell fast; but they were not like those she had lately shed, and I saw my hope brighten in them.

"Agnes! Ever my guide, and best support! If you had been more mindful of yourself, and less of me, when we grew up here together, I think my heedless fancy never would have wandered from you. But you were so much better than I, so necessary to me in every boyish hope and disappointment, that to have you to confide in, and rely upon in everything, became a second nature, supplanting for the time the first and greater one of loving you as I do!"

Still weeping, but not sadly—joyfully! And clasped in my arms as she had never been, as I had thought she never was to be!

"When I loved Dora—fondly, Agnes, as you know——"

"Yes!" she cried, earnestly. "I am glad to know it!"

"When I loved her—even then, my love would have been incomplete, without your sympathy. I had it, and it was perfected. And when I lost her, Agnes, what should I have been without you, still!"

Closer in my arms, nearer to my heart, her trembling hand upon my shoulder, her sweet eyes shining through her tears, on mine!

"I went away, dear Agnes, loving you. I stayed away, loving you. I returned home, loving you!"

AGNES TELLS ME HER SECRET.

And now, I tried to tell her of the struggle I had had, and the conclusion I had come to. I tried to lay my mind before her, truly, and entirely. I tried to show her how I had hoped I had come into the better knowledge of myself and of her; how I had resigned myself to what that better knowledge brought; and how I had come there, even that day, in my fidelity to this. If she did so love me (I said) that she could take me for her husband, she could do so, on no deserving of mine, except upon the truth of my love for her, and the trouble in which it had ripened to be what it was; and hence it was that I revealed it. And O, Agnes, even out of thy true eyes, in that same time, the spirit of my child-wife looked upon me, saying it was well; and winning me, through thee, to tenderest recollections of the Blossom that had withered in its bloom!

" I am so blest, Trotwood—my heart is so overcharged— but there is one thing I must say."

" Dearest, what ? "

She laid her gentle hands upon my shoulders, and looked calmly in my face.

" Do you know, yet, what it is ? "

" I am afraid to speculate on what it is. Tell me, my dear."

" I have loved you all my life ! "

Oh, we were happy, we were happy ! Our tears were not for the trials (hers so much the greater) through which we had come to be thus, but for the rapture of being thus, never to be divided more !

We walked, that winter evening, in the fields together; and the blessed calm within us seemed to be partaken by the frosty air. The early stars began to shine while we were lingering on, and looking up to them, we thanked our GOD for having guided us to this tranquillity.

We stood together in the same old-fashioned window at

night, when the moon was shining; Agnes with her quiet eyes raised up to it; I following her glance. Long miles of road then opened out before my mind; and, toiling on, I saw a ragged way-worn boy forsaken and neglected, who should come to call even the heart now beating against mine, his own.

It was nearly dinner-time next day when we appeared before my aunt. She was up in my study, Peggotty said: which it was her pride to keep in readiness and order for me. We found her, in her spectacles, sitting by the fire.

"Goodness me!" said my aunt, peering through the dusk, "who's this you're bringing home?"

"Agnes," said I.

As we had arranged to say nothing at first, my aunt was not a little discomfited. She darted a hopeful glance at me, when I said "Agnes;" but seeing that I looked as usual, she took off her spectacles in despair, and rubbed her nose with them.

She greeted Agnes heartily, nevertheless; and we were soon in the lighted parlour down-stairs, at dinner. My aunt put on her spectacles twice or thrice, to take another look at me, but as often took them off again, disappointed, and rubbed her nose with them. Much to the discomfiture of Mr. Dick, who knew this to be a bad symptom.

"By the bye, aunt," said I, after dinner; "I have been speaking to Agnes about what you told me."

"Then, Trot," said my aunt, turning scarlet, "you did wrong, and broke your promise."

"You are not angry, aunt, I trust? I am sure you won't be, when you learn that Agnes is not unhappy in any attachment."

"Stuff and nonsense!" said my aunt.

As my aunt appeared to be annoyed, I thought the best way was to cut her annoyance short. I took Agnes in my arm to the back of her chair, and we both leaned over her. My aunt with one clap of her hands, and one look through her spectacles, immediately went into hysterics, for the first and only time in all my knowledge of her.

The hysterics called up Peggotty. The moment my aunt was restored, she flew at Peggotty, and calling her a silly old creature, hugged her with all her might. After that, she hugged Mr. Dick (who was highly honoured, but a good deal surprised); and after that, told them why. Then we were all happy together.

I could not discover whether my aunt, in her last short conversation with me, had fallen on a pious fraud, or had really mistaken the state of my mind. It was quite enough, she said, that she had told me Agnes was going to be married; and that I now knew better than any one how true it was.

We were married within a fortnight. Traddles and Sophy, and Doctor and Mrs. Strong, were the only guests at our quiet wedding. We left them full of joy; and drove away together. Clasped in my embrace, I held the source of every worthy aspiration I had ever had; the centre of myself, the circle of my life, my own, my wife; my love of whom was founded on a rock!

"Dearest husband!" said Agnes. "Now that I may call you by that name, I have one thing more to tell you."

"Let me hear it, love."

"It grows out of the night when Dora died. She sent you for me."

"She did."

"She told me that she left me something. Can you think what it was?"

I believed I could. I drew the wife who had so long loved me, closer to my side.

"She told me that she made a last request to me, and left me a last charge."

"And it was—— "

"That only I would occupy this vacant place."

And Agnes laid her head upon my breast, and wept; and I wept with her, though we were so happy.

CHAPTER LXIII.

A VISITOR.

WHAT I have purposed to record is nearly finished; but there is yet an incident conspicuous in my memory, on which it often rests with delight, and without which one thread in the web I have spun, would have a ravelled end.

I had advanced in fame and fortune, my domestic joy was perfect, I had been married ten happy years. Agnes and I were sitting by the fire, in our house in London, one night in spring, and three of our children were playing in the room, when I was told that a stranger wished to see me.

He had been asked if he came on business, and had answered No; he had come for the pleasure of seeing me, and had come a long way. He was an old man, my servant said, and looked like a farmer.

As this sounded mysterious to the children, and moreover was like the beginning of a favourite story Agnes used to tell them, introductory to the arrival of a wicked old Fairy in a cloak who hated everybody, it produced some commotion. One of our boys laid his head in his mother's lap to be out of harm's way, and little Agnes (our eldest child) left her doll in a chair to represent her, and thrust out her little heap of golden curls from between the window-curtains, to see what happened next.

"Let him come in here!" said I.

There soon appeared, pausing in the dark doorway as he

entered, a hale, grey-haired old man. Little Agnes, attracted by his looks, had run to bring him in, and I had not yet clearly seen his face, when my wife, starting up, cried out to me, in a pleased and agitated voice, that it was Mr. Peggotty!

It *was* Mr. Peggotty. An old man now, but in a ruddy, hearty, strong old age. When our first emotion was over, and he sat before the fire with the children on his knees, and the blaze shining on his face, he looked, to me, as vigorous and robust, withal as handsome, an old man, as ever I had seen.

"Mas'r Davy," said he. And the old name in the old tone fell so naturally on my ear! "Mas'r Davy, 'tis a joyful hour as I see you, once more, 'long with your own trew wife!"

"A joyful hour indeed, old friend!" cried I.

"And these heer pretty ones," said Mr. Peggotty. "To look at these heer flowers! Why, Mas'r Davy, you was but the heighth of the littlest of these, when I first see you! When Em'ly warn't no bigger, and our poor lad were *but* a lad!"

"Time has changed me more than it has changed you since then," said I. "But let these dear rogues go to bed; and as no house in England but this must hold you, tell me where to send for your luggage (is the old black bag among it, that went so far, I wonder!), and then, over a glass of Yarmouth grog, we will have the tidings of ten years!"

"Are you alone?" asked Agnes.

"Yes, ma'am," he said, kissing her hand, "quite alone."

We sat him between us, not knowing how to give him welcome enough; and as I began to listen to his old familiar voice, I could have fancied he was still pursuing his long journey in search of his darling niece.

"It's a mort of water," said Mr. Peggotty, "fur to come across, and on'y stay a matter of fower weeks. But water ('specially when 'tis salt) comes nat'ral to me; and friends is dear, and I am heer.—Which is verse," said Mr. Peggotty, surprised to find it out, "though I hadn't such intentions."

"Are you going back those many thousand miles, so soon?" asked Agnes.

"Yes, ma'am," he returned. "I giv the promise to Em'ly, afore I come away. You see, I doen't grow younger as the years comes round, and if I hadn't sailed as 'twas, most like I shouldn't never have done 't. And it's allus been on my mind, as I *must* come and see Mas'r Davy and your own sweet blooming self, in your wedded happiness, afore I got to be too old."

He looked at us, as if he could never feast his eyes on us sufficiently. Agnes laughingly put back some scattered locks of his grey hair, that he might see us better.

"And now tell us," said I, "everything relating to your fortunes."

"Our fortuns, Mas'r Davy," he rejoined, "is soon told. We haven't fared nohows, but fared to thrive. We've allus thrived. We've worked as we ought to 't, and maybe we lived a leetle hard at first or so, but we have allus thrived. What with sheep-farming, and what with stock-farming, and what with one thing and what with t'other, we are as well to do, as well could be. Theer's been kiender a blessing fell upon us," said Mr. Peggotty, reverentially inclining his head, "and we've done nowt but prosper. That is, in the long run. If not yesterday, why then to-day. If not to-day, why then to-morrow."

"And Emily?" said Agnes and I, both together.

"Em'ly," said he, "arter you left her, ma'am—and I never heerd her saying of her prayers at night, t'other side the canvas screen, when we was settled in the Bush, but what I heerd your name—and arter she and me lost sight of Mas'r Davy, that theer shining sundown—was that low, at first, that, if she had know'd then what Mas'r Davy kep from us so kind and thowtful, 'tis my opinion she'd have drooped away. But theer was some poor folks aboard as had illness among 'em, and she took care of *them*; and theer was the children in our company, and she took care of *them*; and so she got to be busy, and to be doing good, and that helped her."

"When did she first hear of it?" I asked.

"I kep it from her arter I heerd on 't," said Mr. Peggotty, "going on nigh a year. We was living then in a solitary place, but among the beautifullest trees, and with the roses a covering our Bein' to the roof. Theer come along one day, when I was out a working on the land, a traveller from our own Norfolk or Suffolk in England (I doen't rightly mind which), and of course we took him in, and giv him to eat and drink, and made him welcome. We all do that, all the colony over. He'd got an old newspaper with him, and some other account in print of the storm. That's how she know'd it. When I come home at night, I found she know'd it."

He dropped his voice as he said these words, and the gravity I so well remembered overspread his face.

"Did it change her much?" we asked.

"Aye, for a good long time," he said, shaking his head; "if not to this present hour. But I think the solitoode done her good. And she had a deal to mind in the way of poultry and the like, and minded of it, and come through. I wonder," he said thoughtfully, "if you could see my Em'ly now, Mas'r Davy, whether you'd know her!"

"Is she so altered?" I inquired.

"I doen't know. I see her ev'ry day, and doen't know; but, odd-times, I have thowt so. A slight figure," said Mr. Peggotty, looking at the fire, "kiender worn; soft, sorrowful, blue eyes; a delicate face; a pritty head, leaning a little down; a quiet voice and way—timid a'most. That's Em'ly!"

We silently observed him as he sat, still looking at the fire.

"Some thinks," he said, "as her affection was ill-bestowed; some, as her marriage was broke off by death. No one knows

523

how 'tis. She might have married well a mort of times, 'but, uncle,' she says to me, 'that's gone for ever.' Cheerful along with me; retired when others is by; fond of going any distance fur to teach a child, or fur to tend a sick person, or fur to do some kindness tow'rds a young girl's wedding (and she's done a many, but has never seen one); fondly loving of her uncle; patient; liked by young and old; sowt out by all that has any trouble. That's Em'ly!"

He drew his hand across his face, and with a half-suppressed sigh looked up from the fire.

"Is Martha with you yet?" I asked.

"Martha," he replied, "got married, Mas'r Davy, in the second year. A young man, a farm-labourer, as come by us on his way to market with his mas'r's drays—a journey of over five hundred mile, theer and back—made offers fur to take her fur his wife (wives is very scarce theer), and then to set up fur their two selves in the Bush. She spoke to me fur to tell him her trew story. I did. They was married, and they live fower hundred mile away from any voices but their own and the singing birds."

"Mrs. Gummidge?" I suggested.

It was a pleasant key to touch, for Mr. Peggotty suddenly burst into a roar of laughter, and rubbed his hands up and down his legs, as he had been accustomed to do when he enjoyed himself in the long-shipwrecked boat.

"Would you believe it!" he said. "Why, someun even made offers fur to marry *her!* If a ship's cook that was turning settler, Mas'r Davy, didn't make offers fur to marry Missis Gummidge, I'm Gormed—and I can't say no fairer than that!"

I never saw Agnes laugh so. This sudden ecstasy on the part of Mr. Peggotty was so delightful to her, that she could not leave off laughing; and the more she laughed the more she made me laugh, and the greater Mr. Peggotty's ecstasy became, and the more he rubbed his legs.

"And what did Mrs. Gummidge say?" I asked, when I was grave enough.

LATEST NEWS OF MR. MICAWBER.

"If you'll believe me," returned Mr. Peggotty, "Missis Gummidge, 'stead of saying 'thank you, I'm much obleeged to you, I ain't a going fur to change my condition at my time of life,' up'd with a bucket as was standing by, and laid it over that theer ship's cook's head 'till he sung out fur help, and I went in and reskied of him."

Mr. Peggotty burst into a great roar of laughter, and Agnes and I both kept him company.

"But I must say this for the good creetur," he resumed, wiping his face when we were quite exhausted; "she has been all she said she'd be to us, and more. She's the willingest, the trewest, the honestest-helping woman, Mas'r Davy, as ever draw'd the breath of life. I have never know'd her to be lone and lorn, for a single minute, not even when the colony was all afore us, and we was new to it. And thinking of the old 'un is a thing she never done, I do assure you, since she left England!"

"Now, last, not least, Mr. Micawber," said I. "He has paid off every obligation he incurred here—even to Traddles's bill, you remember, my dear Agnes—and therefore we may take it for granted that he is doing well. But what is the latest news of him?"

Mr. Peggotty, with a smile, put his hand in his breast-pocket, and produced a flat-folded, paper parcel, from which he took out, with much care, a little odd-looking newspaper.

"You are to understan', Mas'r Davy," said he, "as we have left the Bush now, being so well to do; and have gone right away round to Port Middlebay Harbour, wheer theer's what *we* call a town."

"Mr. Micawber was in the Bush near you?" said I.

"Bless you, yes," said Mr. Peggotty, "and turned to with a will. I never wish to meet a better gen'l'man for turning to, with a will. I've seen that theer bald head of his, a perspiring in the sun, Mas'r Davy, 'till I a'most thowt it would have melted away. And now he's a Magistrate."

"A Magistrate, eh?" said I.

Mr. Peggotty pointed to a certain paragraph in the newspaper, where I read aloud as follows, from the "Port Middlebay Times:"

" ☞ The public dinner to our distinguished fellow-colonist and townsman, WILKINS MICAWBER, ESQUIRE, Port Middlebay District Magistrate, came off yesterday in the large room of the Hotel, which was crowded to suffocation. It is estimated that not fewer than forty-seven persons must have been accommodated with dinner at one time, exclusive of the company in the passage and on the stairs. The beauty, fashion, and exclusiveness of Port Middlebay, flocked to do honour to one so deservedly esteemed, so highly talented, and so widely popular. Doctor Mell (of Colonial Salem-House Grammar School, Port Middlebay) presided, and on his right sat the distinguished guest. After the removal of the cloth, and the singing of Non Nobis (beautifully executed, and in which we were at no loss to distinguish the bell-like notes of that gifted amateur, WILKINS MICAWBER, ESQUIRE, JUNIOR), the usual loyal and patriotic toasts were severally given and rapturously received. Dr. Mell, in a speech replete with feeling, then proposed 'Our distinguished Guest, the ornament of our town. May he never leave us but to better himself, and may his success among us be such as to render his bettering himself impossible!' The cheering with which the toast was received defies description. Again and again it rose and fell, like the waves of ocean. At length all was hushed, and WILKINS MICAWBER, ESQUIRE, presented himself to return thanks. Far be it from us, in the present comparatively imperfect state of the resources of our establishment, to endeavour to follow our distinguished townsman through the smoothly-flowing periods of his polished and highly-ornate address! Suffice it to observe, that it was a masterpiece of eloquence; and that those passages in which he more particularly traced his own successful career to its source, and warned the younger portion of his auditory from the shoals of ever incurring pecuniary liabilities which they were unable to liquidate, brought a tear into the manliest eye present. The remaining toasts were DOCTOR MELL; MRS. MICAWBER (who gracefully bowed her acknowledgments from the side-door, where a galaxy of beauty was elevated on chairs, at once to witness and adorn the gratifying scene); MRS. RIDGER BEGS (late Miss Micawber); MRS. MELL; WILKINS MICAWBER, ESQUIRE, JUNIOR (who convulsed the assembly by humorously remarking that he found himself unable to return thanks in a speech, but would do so, with their permission, in a song); MRS. MICAWBER'S FAMILY (well known, it is needless to remark, in the mother-country), &c. &c. &c. At the conclusion of the proceedings the tables were cleared as if by art-magic for dancing. Among the votaries of TERPSICHORE, who disported themselves until Sol gave warning for departure, Wilkins Micawber, Esquire, Junior, and the lovely and accomplished Miss Helena, fourth daughter of Doctor Mell, were particularly remarkable."

I was looking back to the name of Doctor Mell, pleased to have discovered, in these happier circumstances, Mr. Mell, formerly poor pinched usher to my Middlesex magistrate, when Mr. Peggotty pointing to another part of the paper, my eyes rested on my own name, and I read thus:

"TO DAVID COPPERFIELD, ESQUIRE.
THE EMINENT AUTHOR.

"MY DEAR SIR,

"Years have elapsed, since I had an opportunity of ocularly perusing the lineaments, now familiar to the imaginations of a considerable portion of the civilised world.

"But, my dear sir, though estranged (by the force of circumstances over which I have had no control) from the personal society of the friend and companion of my youth, I have not been unmindful of his soaring flight. Nor have I been debarred,

Though seas between us braid ha' roared,

527

(BURNS) from participating in the intellectual feasts he has spread before us.

"I cannot, therefore, allow of the departure from this place of an individual whom we mutually respect and esteem, without, my dear sir, taking this public opportunity of thanking you, on my own behalf, and, I may undertake to add, on that of the whole of the Inhabitants of Port Middlebay, for the gratification of which you are the ministering agent.

"Go on, my dear sir! You are not unknown here, you are not unappreciated. Though 'remote,' we are neither 'unfriended,' 'melancholy,' nor (I may add) 'slow.' Go on, my dear sir, in your Eagle course! The inhabitants of Port Middlebay may at least aspire to watch it, with delight, with entertainment, with instruction!

"Among the eyes elevated towards you from this portion of the globe, will ever be found, while it has light and life,

"The
"Eye
"Appertaining to
"WILKINS MICAWBER.
"Magistrate."

I found, on glancing at the remaining contents of the newspaper, that Mr. Micawber was a diligent and esteemed correspondent of that Journal. There was another letter from him in the same paper, touching a bridge; there was an advertisement of a collection of similar letters by him, to be shortly republished, in a neat volume, "with considerable additions;" and, unless I am very much mistaken, the Leading Article was his also.

We talked much of Mr. Micawber, on many other evenings while Mr. Peggotty remained with us. He lived with us during the whole term of his stay,—which, I think, was something less than a month,—and his sister and my aunt came to London to see him. Agnes and I parted from him aboard-ship, when he sailed ; and we shall never part from him more, on earth.

But before he left, he went with me to Yarmouth, to see a little tablet I had put up in the churchyard to the memory of Ham. While I was copying the plain inscription for him at his request, I saw him stoop, and gather a tuft of grass from the grave, and a little earth.

"For Em'ly," he said, as he put it in his breast. "I promised, Mas'r Davy."

CHAPTER LXIV.

AND now my written story ends. I look back, once more—for the last time—before I close these leaves.

I see myself, with Agnes at my side, journeying along the road of life. I see our children and our friends around us; and I hear the roar of many voices, not indifferent to me as I travel on.

What faces are the most distinct to me in the fleeting crowd? Lo, these; all turning to me as I ask my thoughts the question!

Here is my aunt, in stronger spectacles, an old woman of fourscore years and more, but upright yet, and a steady walker of six miles at a stretch in winter weather.

Always with her, here comes Peggotty, my good old nurse, likewise in spectacles, accustomed to do needlework at night very close to the lamp, but never sitting down to it without a bit of wax candle, a yard measure in a little house, and a work-box with a picture of St. Paul's upon the lid.

The cheeks and arms of Peggotty, so hard and red in my childish days, when I wondered why the birds didn't peck her in preference to apples, are shrivelled now; and her eyes, that used to darken their whole neighbourhood in her face, are fainter (though they glitter still); but her rough forefinger, which I once associated with a pocket nutmeg grater, is just the same, and when I see my least child catching at it as it

530

totters from my aunt to her, I think of our little parlour at home, when I could scarcely walk. My aunt's old disappointment is set right, now. She is godmother to a real living Betsey Trotwood; and Dora (the next in order) says she spoils her.

There is something bulky in Peggotty's pocket. It is nothing smaller than the Crocodile-Book, which is in rather a dilapidated condition by this time, with divers of the leaves torn and stitched across, but which Peggotty exhibits to the children as a precious relic. I find it very curious to see my own infant face, looking up at me from the Crocodile stories; and to be reminded by it of my old acquaintance Brooks of Sheffield.

Among my boys, this summer holiday time, I see an old man making giant kites, and gazing at them in the air, with a delight for which there are no words. He greets me rapturously, and whispers, with many nods and winks, "Trotwood, you will be glad to hear that I shall finish the Memorial when I have nothing else to do, and that your aunt's the most extraordinary woman in the world, sir!"

Who is this bent lady, supporting herself by a stick, and showing me a countenance in which there are some traces of old pride and beauty, feebly contending with a querulous, imbecile, fretful wandering of the mind? She is in a garden; and near her stands a sharp, dark, withered woman, with a white scar on her lip. Let me hear what they say.

"Rosa, I have forgotten this gentleman's name."

Rosa bends over her, and calls to her, "Mr. Copperfield."

"I am glad to see you, sir. I am sorry to observe you are in mourning. I hope Time will be good to you."

Her impatient attendant scolds her, tells her I am not in mourning, bids her look again, tries to rouse her.

"You have seen my son, sir," says the elder lady. "Are you reconciled?"

Looking fixedly at me, she puts her hand to her forehead, and moans. Suddenly, she cries, in a terrible voice, "Rosa,

531

come to me. He is dead!" Rosa kneeling at her feet, by turns caresses her, and quarrels with her; now fiercely telling her, "I loved him better than you ever did!"—now soothing her to sleep on her breast, like a sick child. Thus I leave them; thus I always find them; thus they wear their time away, from year to year.

What ship comes sailing home from India, and what English lady is this, married to a growling old Scotch Crœsus with great flaps of ears? Can this be Julia Mills?

Indeed it is Julia Mills, peevish and fine, with a black man to carry cards and letters to her on a golden salver, and a copper-coloured woman in linen, with a bright handkerchief round her head, to serve her Tiffin in her dressing-room. But Julia keeps no diary in these days; never sings Affection's Dirge; eternally quarrels with the old Scotch Crœsus, who is a sort of yellow bear with a tanned hide. Julia is steeped in money to the throat, and talks and thinks of nothing else. I liked her better in the Desert of Sahara.

Or perhaps this *is* the Desert of Sahara! For, though Julia has a stately house, and mighty company, and sumptuous dinners every day, I see no green growth near her; nothing that can ever come to fruit or flower. What Julia calls "society," I see; among it Mr. Jack Maldon, from his Patent Place, sneering at the hand that gave it him, and speaking to me, of the Doctor, as "so charmingly antique." But when society is the name for such hollow gentlemen and ladies, Julia, and when its breeding is professed indifference to everything that can advance or can retard mankind, I think we must have lost ourselves in that same Desert of Sahara, and had better find the way out.

And lo, the Doctor, always our good friend, labouring at his Dictionary (somewhere about the letter D), and happy in his home and wife. Also the Old Soldier, on a considerably reduced footing, and by no means so influential as in days of yore!

Working at his chambers in the Temple, with a busy

aspect, and his hair (where he is not bald) made more rebellious than ever by the constant friction of his lawyer's wig, I come, in a later time, upon my dear old Traddles. His table is covered with thick piles of papers; and I say, as I look around me:

"If Sophy were your clerk, now, Traddles, she would have enough to do!"

"You may say that, my dear Copperfield! But those were capital days, too, in Holborn Court! Were they not?"

'When she told you you would be a Judge? But it was not the town talk *then!*"

"At all events," says Traddles, "if I ever am one—"

"Why, you know you will be."

"Well, my dear Copperfield, *when* I am one, I shall tell the story, as I said I would."

We walk away, arm in arm. I am going to have a family dinner with Traddles. It is Sophy's birthday; and, on our road, Traddles discourses to me of the good fortune he has enjoyed.

"I really have been able, my dear Copperfield, to do all that I had most at heart. There's the Reverend Horace promoted to that living at four hundred and fifty pounds a year; there are our two boys receiving the very best education, and distinguishing themselves as steady scholars and good fellows; there are three of the girls married very comfortably; there are three more living with us; there are three more keeping house for the Reverend Horace since Mrs. Crewler's decease; and all of them happy."

"Except—" I suggest.

"Except the Beauty," says Traddles. "Yes. It was very unfortunate that she should marry such a vagabond. But there was a certain dash and glare about him that caught her. However, now we have got her safe at our house, and got rid of him, we must cheer her up again."

Traddles's house is one of the very houses—or it easily may have been—which he and Sophy used to parcel out, in

533

their evening walks. It is a large house; but Traddles keeps his papers in his dressing-room, and his boots with his papers; and he and Sophy squeeze themselves into upper rooms, reserving the best bedrooms for the Beauty and the girls. There is no room to spare in the house; for more of "the girls" are here, and always are here, by some accident or other, than I know how to count. Here, when we go in, is a crowd of them, running down to the door, and handing Traddles about to be kissed, until he is out of breath. Here, established in perpetuity, is the poor Beauty, a widow with a little girl; here, at dinner on Sophy's birthday, are the three married girls with their three husbands, and one of the husband's brothers, and another husband's cousin, and another husband's sister, who appears to me to be engaged to the cousin. Traddles, exactly the same simple, unaffected fellow as he ever was, sits at the foot of the large table like a Patriarch; and Sophy beams upon him, from the head, across a cheerful space that is certainly not glittering with Britannia metal.

And now, as I close my task, subduing my desire to linger yet, these faces fade away. But, one face, shining on me like a Heavenly light by which I see all other objects, is above them and beyond them all. And that remains.

I turn my head, and see it, in its beautiful serenity, beside me. My lamp burns low, and I have written far into the night; but the dear presence, without which I were nothing, bears me company.

Oh Agnes, Oh my soul, so may thy face be by me when I close my life indeed; so may I, when realities are melting from me like the shadows which I now dismiss, still find thee near me, pointing upward!

This book, designed by
William B. Taylor,
is a production of
Heron Books, London.

Printed in Switzerland